God, Girls,

Golf & the Gridiron

(Not Always in
That Order)

...A Love Story

by Nathan Birr

Beacon Books LLC

Published by BEACON BOOKS, LLC

Cover & Interior Images Copyright ©
KavalenkavaVolha/iStock/Thinkstock
Koya79/iStock/Thinkstock
Kreatiw/iStock/Thinkstock

Holy Bible, New International Version ®, NIV®
Copyright © 1973, 1978, 1984 by Biblica, Inc.®
Used by permission. All rights reserved worldwide.

"Scripture quotations taken from the Amplified® Bible,
Copyright © 2015 by The Lockman Foundation
Used by permission." (www.Lockman.org)

The Holy Bible, King James Version. Cambridge Edition: 1769; *King James Bible Online*, 2016.
www.kingjamesbibleonline.org.

Library of Congress Control Number: 2016930043

ISBN: 978-0-9967691-3-6 (hc)
ISBN: 978-0-9967691-4-3 (sc)
ISBN: 978-0-9967691-5-0 (e)

This novel is a work of fiction. Names, characters, businesses, places, events, and incidents are either the products of the author's imagination or used in a fictitious manner. Any resemblance to actual persons, living or dead, or actual events is purely coincidental.

www.nathanbirr.com

Also by Nathan Birr

Overnight Delivery
The Douglas Files: Book One

Three's a Crowd
The Douglas Files: Book Two

All an Illusion
The Douglas Files: Book Three

Black Male
A Douglas Files Short

WinterKill
A Douglas Files Short

To the girl of my dreams —
Thank you for allowing me to win your heart,
and for winning mine again and again.

Author's Note

"This is how I write." II Thessalonians 3:17

This is a work of fiction.

I mention this because it is also, at times, something of a satire—a commentary on the Church and on Christians. Mostly it's just a story, and much of what you will read is merely me telling a fictional tale. It exists solely to further the plot and drive the story or to make you laugh. The thoughts, attitudes, and actions of my characters are just that—the thoughts, attitudes, and actions of my characters. Writing in first person puts me and you in the head of my protagonist, but it doesn't mean that he always reflects the mindset of his creator.

Some of what you will read, however, is me using my characters to shine a candid light on what I consider to be very real issues. Sometimes I *am* expressing my opinions and beliefs through them. Like those of my characters, my views are subject to personal preference and selfishness, and my motives aren't always altruistic. Like that of my characters, my voice is sometimes the voice of reason, needing to be heard amidst the fray. And like my characters, I'm not always certain which case is which. Like them, I'm still thinking through a lot of things.

As a writer, I want to entertain you with a good story, but I also want to compel you to think, examine, and ask questions. Maybe you'll read something in this novel that will offend you. Please don't put the book down. Keep reading. You may ultimately find that my character was in the wrong and changes his or her mind. You may find that he or she doesn't but that you do. Or you may find your viewpoint stands the test of criticism—mine or my character's. Whatever the case, I suggest thinking through the issue will be a healthy exercise.

i

To that end, I've written some discussion questions at the back of the book. They're not meant to be an authoritative rod of instruction. I don't have all the answers (even though I sometimes act like I do) and my opinions, although strongly felt at times, aren't infallible. But I hope these questions will inspire you to think deeply on some important issues, as I have. I hope they will help you contemplate your view and mine. I hope, ultimately, they will drive you to share the only opinion that truly matters — God's.

Throughout the book, I take some jabs and poke a little fun. Humor can be a powerful medium for exposing folly and driving home a point. Humor can also be a powerful method of keeping a reader turning pages. Whatever the reason, the humor (or attempts at humor) in this book is never meant to be harsh or insulting.

Lastly, some of you will see yourselves in these pages. Some of that is on purpose. I have a vivid imagination, but not this vivid. Most of the events and experiences in this story were inspired, in some way or another, by real life. While I used some of them to make a point, I also attempted to depict them lightheartedly, and I changed the names and details to protect the — ahem — innocent. I also named a few characters after real people and pulled certain quirks and characteristics from folks I've met along the way. Any strong resemblances are either purely coincidental or were fashioned with respect.

All that said, I truly hope you will enjoy *God, Girls, Golf & the Gridiron (Not Always in That Order) . . . A Love Story*. I hope the novel is compelling and humorous while also thought-provoking. I hope, after reading it, you're better for the experience, as I believe I am for writing it.

Like I said, this is a work of fiction.

But it's not just about entertainment.

Prologue

"Because of the present crisis . . ." I Corinthians 7:26

This is a love story, and it's all about me.

Me and my midlife crisis.

My name is Joshua Roosevelt—Josh to everybody but my mom when she's angry—and I'm only twenty years old. Which is why having a midlife crisis is somewhat disconcerting. In theory, you're supposed to be forty with a wife and three kids, a house in the suburbs, and a nine-to-five job when you have your midlife crisis. But life is not lived in theory.

In addition to only being half the requisite age for a midlife crisis, I do not have a wife or even a girlfriend (part, as you'll see, of the problem). In fact, I've only been on three dates in my entire life, all with different girls. Being an evangelical Christian, that pretty much rules out the three kids. And as for work, I've never had a nine-to-five, or even an eight-to-four. It's been part-time and odd jobs all my life. Suffice to say, I'm not exactly loaded, which isn't helping matters either.

But let me back up. This crisis has its roots in high school when I started to realize my career and life path wasn't going to be a freeway. Like so many of the roads out here in rural Nebraska, it wasn't even paved yet. With no other viable plan after graduating from Morgan High, I went off to a nice Christian college outside Omaha. I assumed it (the college, not Omaha) was the place to figure out what to do with the rest of my life. I also hoped that going off to college and having to live on my own and grow up and be a man and all that would help me find my purpose in life. I envisioned graduating in four years, finding my place in the world, and looking back to see that my maturation into an upstanding Christian man was complete. But after taking three and a half semesters of general math courses, general history courses, general communications courses, general science courses, and general Bible courses, I was generally confused.

1

And going broke.

I've been a Christian almost since before I can remember, since I was five. And while I've always been a pretty good person—never rebelled against my parents, never experimented with drugs or alcohol, never tattooed myself or gotten anything pierced without permission (and been a gentleman on the aforementioned three dates)—I just felt like something was missing. I was a little ho-hum in my walk with God and not really sure why or what to do about it.

Like I said, midlife crisis.

So with no direction to speak of, I decided to leave college and return home to my family. I didn't register for fall classes and came home during spring break to deliver the surprising news to my parents in person. But the folks had a surprise they'd been waiting to share in person too: After pastoring the Morgan Bible Church for twenty-plus years, my father was being let go. (He was canned, but because it's church, they called it "letting him go.") If that wasn't enough of a jolt, my parents also informed me that Dad had already candidated and been accepted to pastor a new church in Oklahoma, and they were moving to Norman the Monday after Easter. While it was a great new challenge for them, it left me all alone in Morgan.

Well, not all alone. I still had my best friend Scotty Austin, who I've known since I was six. He's also twenty, and still lives in Morgan with his dad, Dirk. I also had Cassie Larson, my other best friend, who I've known even longer than Scotty. Cassie's nineteen and, like Scotty, had remained in Morgan after high school.

And I had Erica. Or at least, I had dreams of Erica. Remember how I said the lack of a girlfriend was part of my midlife crisis? Well, I also thought going off to college would afford me the perfect opportunity to meet the future Mrs. Roosevelt. It hadn't. Or rather, I hadn't taken advantage of the opportunity. At age twenty, I wasn't exactly desperate, but I was starting to wonder what God's plan was for me in the marriage category.

All these boiling waters came to a head one weekend in April, just after my parents completed a whirlwind house sale and move to Oklahoma, and less than a month before my college days came to a close.

That's when I met Erica. I'd had my share of junior and senior high crushes, and had gone on those three dates. But no girl had ever struck me the way she did. I was head-over-paws in puppy love at first sight, as stupid as I've always found that concept to be.

But what can I say? Erica Nicole Chamberlain was a ray of sunshine, an undeniable proof that God was smiling down on me, that my midlife crisis was a thing of the past.

Ha!

Act 1

Chapter 1

"Some time later, he fell in love with a woman . . ." Judges 16:4

Nebraskans pride themselves on a great many things: Their Midwestern values. A blue-collar work ethic. Good old-fashioned friendliness and hospitality. A state with more geographic charm than people give it credit for.

And their football team.

The bond between the University of Nebraska Cornhuskers and the residents of Nebraska is an unusual one to be sure. It's based in part on the fact that so many Cornhusker stars have come from within the state. It also has something to do with the lack of other major university or professional sports teams to cheer for. And then there's Nebraska's long tradition of winning—forty-three conference and five national titles, to be exact.

So while it may seem odd to outsiders, Nebraskans think nothing of filling Memorial Stadium for the annual Red-White Spring Game. Little more than a glorified scrimmage, it's a chance for folks from Lincoln to Chadron, McCook to O'Neill; for businessmen and farmers, collegians and kindergarteners; football junkies and football flunkies to congregate in the venerable "old lady" on T Street and Stadium Drive to catch a first glimpse at the new team. It's also why, a week after returning to Morgan for Easter break—and after a tearful goodbye with my parents—I was back again, crashing in Scotty's basement (my temporary residence until I found my own apartment). A group of "young people" from Morgan Bible had made plans to attend the spring game, and like any good friend, Scotty had made sure I was invited.

Saturday morning, we arrived at the Morgan Bible Church parking lot early, realized we had forgotten Dirk's grill, and backtracked to get it. By the time we returned, the first car had already departed for Lincoln. The remaining nine of us quickly made sure we had everything—and weren't waiting for any other forgetful folks—and loaded into two vehicles. Scotty and I rode with Mike Baxter in his pickup, which also carried two charcoal grills, two sacks of charcoal, and three coolers full of meats, drinks, and extra ice.

Mike drove fast to make up for lost time, and we arrived in the Hawks Field parking lot first. We unloaded the truck, and I was helping Mike light the grill—difficult on a breezy morning—when the other two cars in our convoy arrived. So far, all the faces had been familiar. But then a new girl got out of the passenger seat of Rena Schroers' Toyota Camry, and the world around me slowed. I think the edges of my vision even blurred.

"Hey, Josh, works better if you toss the match into the grill."

I looked up at Mike, then down at the tiny flame that was about to singe my thumb and forefinger. "Sorry," I said, flicking the match at the wad of paper underneath a pile of coals. It flamed out, and I quickly lit another. As soon as I saw paper burning, I redirected my eyes to her.

So it was finished. The Great Artist had completed His masterpiece. His *magnum opus*. His *pièce de résistance*.

She was about my height, tall for a girl, and magnificently shaped. Even a red "Husker Power" T-shirt and distressed blue jeans couldn't hide that. Her face was positively cherubic—smooth cheeks, small ears, and curvaceous lips that framed perfect teeth. I knew that because she was smiling, beatifically, the smile of a person full of life and vigor and happiness.

My heart threatened to stop as she walked our way, her shoulder-length hair bouncing with each step. It was brown, the color of decadent dark chocolate, with a hint of natural wave. The ends were wisps blowing in the breeze, alighting on her shoulders or in front of her neck. Her hair was rich and full, almost alive, a perfect complement to tanned, silky skin.

She stopped just feet from us, and my entire body began to tingle at the proximity. She wore sandals, allowing her toes to peek out from under her jeans. The nails were painted—red, of course—as were those on her fingers, which I noticed when she reached into the cooler to inspect our choice of meats.

"Is this all from Bernice's?" she asked. Bernice's being the meat market in Morgan. Their cuts are legendary in the southeastern corner of Lancaster County, and throughout the county, for that matter.

"Yep," Mike answered.

"Looks good," she said. Her voice was pure and velvety, as would be expected for an angel. Helping Mike, I was already on one knee, and would have proposed except I thought it proper to wait until I knew her name.

"We need another match," Mike said, and I realized he was talking to me. I stood as Scotty announced that what we needed was some lighter fluid.

"Lighter fluid ruins the taste."

"So does eating them raw, Emeril."

"Hand me the matches," Mike said.

I tossed the pack to him and wiped my hands on my jeans. Then I looked at her. She hadn't gone anywhere, and smiled in my direction.

"I don't think we've met," she said.

"I'm Josh," I replied, offering my hand, remarkably pleased that I had remembered my name. And that my voice hadn't cracked.

"Erica," she said, and we touched for the first time. So this is how Ben Franklin felt when he went kite flying.

"Nice to meet you," I said.

Before she could reply, I was forced to step back as Scotty unleashed a stream of lighter fluid into the grill from the bed of Mike's truck. Flames shot into the air and Mike jumped away from the grill.

"Hey!"

"Kickoff's in ninety minutes," Scotty said. "I don't have time to wait for Rosie to get the hang of matches."

I unsuccessfully tried to fight off the blush that was engulfing my face.

"Rosie?" Erica asked.

Thanks, dude.

Scotty had always called me Rosie. Initially, as a six-year-old brat, he had done it to tease me about my last name. After one short wrestling match in the church foyer, we'd become fast friends. Unfortunately, the nickname had stuck. Everybody else got a new one each time Scotty addressed them. I was always Rosie. I guess it was a term of endearment. Just not one I wanted Erica to hear right off the bat.

Hiding a sigh and trying to play it cool, I smiled pathetically and reached into the cooler for some pre-shaped hamburger patties.

Memorial Stadium stands like a beacon in the Heartland, towering over the Nebraska campus. I let the appropriate awe fill me as we crossed the railroad tracks via a footbridge and approached the colossal stadium. As I thought of the great teams that had called Memorial Stadium home, my chest swelled with pride, matching my stomach that was bloated from several burgers.

We were late, thanks to grill-lighting problems and slow eaters, and were relegated to seats high in the southeast corner. I tried as casually as possible to end up next to Erica. It didn't work, and I found myself between Scotty and Mike—who were still debating the appropriate way to grill meat—one row behind her and a few seats over.

So far, it had been a mostly cloudy morning, one of those days where the pale blue sky keeps trying to peek out through low, puffy clouds. It hadn't been cool, but it hadn't been warm either. Now, just before kickoff, while the Cornhusker Marching Band was warming up, the skies parted and the sun shone down on Memorial Stadium with full force. It was downright allegorical. And a little hot.

For the first few minutes, everyone was into the game, as if the outcome really mattered. The Red Team drove for a field goal, we applauded politely, and everyone released their balloons—a Nebraska tradition after the first score. As the band played, I surveyed the three-quarter-full stadium, its patrons decked exclusively in red. The balloons trailed off into a pure blue sky, and I felt like that guy in *Field of Dreams*, wondering if this was heaven.

And yet, as the game wore on, I found that it couldn't hold my interest, largely because of the girl just ahead of me to my left. I couldn't take my eyes or my mind off her. I wanted to know everything there was to know about Erica. Starting with her last name.

I nudged Scotty with my elbow.

"What's the deal with Erica?" I asked quietly.

"What do you mean?"

"I mean, where's she from?"

"She goes to Morgan Bible."

"Since when?"

He shrugged and removed his LSU ball cap. It was the same cap he wore almost every day, often backwards, like now. It had originally been purple, but had faded so much from wear and sweat stains that it was now lavender. He shook out his shaggy blond hair and replaced the cap. "A few months ago, I think. I think her family —"

The rest of Scotty's words were cut off as the stadium erupted after an interception. When the enthusiasm died down, I leaned back in.

"Why, you got the hots for her or something?" he asked.

"Is it that obvious?"

"Unless you're fascinated by the goalpost and are really staring past her at it."

"Right."

A smattering of applause rewarded an off-tackle run.

"I don't know much about her," Scotty said. "Just that she's been around lately."

I nodded and tried my hardest to concentrate on football. It wasn't easy when Erica tucked her hair behind her ear. It was the cutest ear I had ever seen, and I suddenly wanted to whisper secrets into it, maybe in a way that tickled a little. I was losing it, but losing never felt so good.

The game was actually kind of boring, which isn't that unusual for spring football scrimmages. At halftime, a handful of our group joined the throngs headed for the restrooms and concessions. I thought about moving in to chat with Erica, but couldn't think of an excuse. So I sat there and waited for Scotty to return with my Pepsi and a slice of Valentino's pizza.

The action picked up in the third quarter, encouraging some 65,000 fans that Nebraska might have an offense to go with the Blackshirt[1] defense, as it's called. For a few minutes, I actually forgot about Erica as dreams of a Big Ten championship began to fill my mind.

At the quarter break, that all changed. A trio in front of me got up to use the restrooms, and Erica turned and stretched her legs on the bleacher bench, tanning her bare feet in the sun. She looked up at me.

"So, Rosie. Where does that come from?"

Had my nickname been on her mind for three quarters? Was that a good thing or a bad thing? She probably expected an answer.

"My last name's Roosevelt," I said. "And Scotty nicknames everybody."

She wrinkled her nose. "My last name's Chamberlain. Not sure what you can make with that."

Wedding invitations?

"So are you new in Morgan?" I asked.

"About to ask you the same thing."

I gave her the I-asked-first look.

"We moved from Lincoln in January," she said. "My dad transferred to the bank here in town and didn't feel like commuting."

I nodded.

"You can say what you want about a twenty-year-old who moves with her parents," she said, flexing her toes, "but I'm in the in-between stage in life right now."

It was kismet.

"Me too," I said.

"You live with your parents too?" There was a trace of flirtatious challenge in her question.

"At present, I live in a dorm," I said.

"Here?"

---

[1] The Nebraska defense is nicknamed the "Blackshirts," reflecting a long tradition of starters wearing black practice jerseys.

"No. Vernon-Bedford."

She wrinkled her nose again. I liked it.

"It's a small Bible college in Omaha," I said.

"I think I might have heard of it."

"But in twenty-seven days, I will be a Morganite again."

Erica narrowed one eye. "You don't look old enough to be a college graduate."

"I'm not. That in-between stage thing."

"Ah."

The trio returned, and Erica slid her legs off the bench. Just that quickly, our bonding was over.

"Morganite," Scotty said quietly. "Smooth."

I cracked him in the ribs.

Chapter 2

"...he went down and talked with the woman, and he liked her." Judges 14:7

Red beat White 24-21. It really didn't matter. The team looked good. Then again, it was April, and how much can you tell about your team when they're playing themselves?

We took our time getting out of the stadium, mingling with our fellow Husker fanatics and simultaneously analyzing the game we had just seen while forecasting the twelve we couldn't wait to see come fall. Back in the parking lot, the argument started.

We had reservations for the entire group at Lazlo's in the Historic Haymarket District. But Lazlo's was technically a "Brewery and Grill" and it was debated whether or not we should go to a brewery.

"Why shouldn't we go to a brewery?"

"Christians shouldn't drink alcohol."

"Who says?"

"Does it matter since every place serves alcohol?"

"Wait, whose point are you making?"

"Isn't a pub or brewery different from a regular restaurant?"

"I think the deciding factor is if it has a bar."

"So it's okay to drink beer at a table, just not a bar?"

"No one's going to be drinking beer."

"Says who?"

"Why don't we go to Misty's instead?"

"They serve alcohol at Misty's."

"We'd never get in without a reservation."

"Do we have reservations for Lazlo's?"

And on and on it went. Scotty whispered to me that this had all been decided a week ago, and everyone had agreed to Lazlo's. But for various reasons, that everyone was different than this everyone, and like in all small town church groups, there were a few sticklers to tradition and rules.

And of course, there were a few "freedom in Christ" sorts who had no problem doing anything short of devil worship. Us poor folk in the happy medium always got dragged into the fight and possibly had to forfeit our reservations at Lazlo's, where we really wanted to eat because the only dinner restaurant in Morgan is the Morgan Family Restaurant, and while the food isn't bad, it isn't big city Lazlo's.

I looked to Erica during the debate. Was she a legalist or a freedom fighter? She appeared bored, and I sidled over to her. Casually of course.

"Are you like me, thinking we're going to end up eating at McDonald's if we don't decide soon?" I asked.

"Hmm? No, I'm just thinking about our defense. We looked a little weak against the power sets."

This girl was incredible.

"Maybe our O-line is just that good," I said.

"Remember the bowl game?"

I did remember the bowl game. We had played miserable for three quarters, getting blown off the ball, getting stuffed on short yardage runs, getting sacked time and time again. Then somebody had flipped a switch and we'd gone on a still inexplicable rampage and scored twenty-eight unanswered points to shock Auburn 35-27. Talk about a Happy New Year.

"Our O-line isn't that good," she said. "Wisconsin will exploit us. Iowa too. And . . . ugh, Ohio State."

"Maybe we've improved."

"Maybe."

Somebody suggested we split and go to two different restaurants.

"That's silly, we came as a group."

"So what, drinkers and non-drinkers?"

"Nobody's going to drink."

"What if I want to drink?"

"Drinking isn't the point."

"Then what is the point?"

"Are you even twenty-one?"

15

Scotty nodded at Mike. "Hey, Bobby Flay, there any charcoal left in that sack?"

"Doesn't matter, dude. We're out of meat."

"We ate it all?"

"You had three burgers, man."

Erica leaned over my shoulder. I smelled her perfume. It was citrusy. It was heavenly.

"I'm eating at Lazlo's if I have to walk home," she said quietly.

"Me too," I replied, as if it was the food motivating me. If she was eating at Village Inn, so was I.

The group finally decided to split, with nine of us going to Lazlo's and the remaining four teetotalers striking out on their own in search of a place that didn't serve beer, or if they did, didn't serve it at a bar. That took some time, sorting out who really believed what, and who believed it but wasn't convicted, and who would have to drive where. Finally, we got it all figured out.

I again rode with Scotty and Mike, who had no problem dining amongst boozers and who wasn't letting anyone else drive his pickup. Erica went in the other car, an old Buick that seated six. At the restaurant, after a brief round of musical chairs, I found myself across the table and one spot down from her. Not bad.

Dinner was great, both the food and the atmosphere, along with some not-so-Christian picking at the foursome in search of prohibition. The truth is, legalism and traditionalism are a sore spot in Morgan. Twenty years ago, when Dad took over the pastorate, there was just one church in town. Dad preached the Word, and to my examination (and that of the elders of that day) made sure Morgan Bible Church accurately adhered to it. But that meant straying from some of the traditions. It meant speaking out on things that some of the blue bloods didn't like having spoken out against. It meant allowing the playing of cards and going to movies and a handful of other things that the legalists opposed. (It did not mean accepting or tolerating homosexuality, promiscuity, divorce, or sin of any kind—or for that matter, drinking beer after the spring game—which is how it sort of got played by the "separatists.") They split, forming their own church. The

True Way Church. It sounded like a cult. And a dig at my dad and everyone else at Morgan Bible. And it caused a rift that still has repercussions to this day because a lot of the folks at Morgan Bible had some of the leanings of the folks at True Way, and vice versa. And so occasionally, we pick on them. And, I'm sure, they on us.

We took our time eating, savoring the food and a festive moment. Lazlo's was filled with Husker fans who lived up to their reputation by being warm and friendly. It didn't matter that none of us knew each other; we were all united by a common bond. If only Christians could be that way.

I did not get a chance to talk with Erica much because there was too much noise for us to converse across the table. But the noise didn't prohibit me from stealing glances at her vivacious brown eyes or admiring her brilliant smile. And she smiled a lot, like it was her default setting. She also had an absolutely adorable laugh—but not when Joey Travis told a dirty joke about Iowa fans. (Not all Nebraskans are classy all the time.)

After dinner, a group of us decided to take a stroll. The Haymarket District is only a few blocks wide and long, a former industrial region between downtown and the freight yard. But in recent years, it has been regenerated and rejuvenated, its distinctive brick buildings turned into commercial and residential spaces. Now the Haymarket is home to an abundance of eateries, distinctive shops, and art galleries that give the area a charming, cozy feel. It's also where the new basketball arena was constructed just a few years back, providing a huge economic boom to the district.

"I love this place," Erica said, as if breathing in an aroma as we walked.

"The Haymarket?" I asked.

"Yeah. I've only been gone three and a half months and I still miss it. Especially in the fall, right before sunset, when the sun hits the buildings like this," she said, turning her head left and right.

"Cool and crisp, a big football game the next day?"

"Mm, yeah."

We were simpatico.

After ducking in and out of a few shops and galleries, our group stopped and gawked at the new basketball arena. It sort of resembled a spaceship. Or a bedpan, Brad Ostrander said. Blasphemer. At any rate, I was glad to be back outside—Scotty was dangerous in small spaces with expensive knickknacks. Besides, the setting sun cast a resplendent orange glow on Erica's face that made me wish I'd brought my camera. Instead I just burned the image into my mind. I needed something to get me through finals.

The six of us who had set out on the stroll returned to P Street where we had parked our vehicles. And found that only Mike's truck was remaining.

"Where'd they go?" Mike asked.

"Who can't count?" Brad said.

"Maybe they're just punking you," Scotty said.

"They're gone," Brad said. "It was Joey."

"Maybe it wasn't on purpose," Cora de Vries said.

"Nothing's on purpose with him," Brad replied.

"Maybe the prohibitionists are still in town," Mike said.

"They already had a full car."

"They can squeeze one more."

"I'm not riding with them."

"That's not very Christian."

"Your mom's not very Christian."

I looked at Erica and rolled my eyes.

"Forget it," Brad said. "We can just ride in the back of the truck."

"Not with two grills and a cooler we can't," I said. I was enjoying the dilemma, because the longer we stood on the sidewalk by Lazlo's, the longer I had with Erica.

"Besides, this ain't Morgan," Mike said. "Cops will pull us over if we've got people in the back."

"So we'll squeeze," Cora said.

"There're six of us."

"We can sit on laps."

Bless that Joey Travis.

Mike sighed. "We can squeeze."

"Six people? I'll ride in back."

"No you won't, because I'd have to pay the ticket. We can squeeze."

And so we squeezed into the vehicle, five-sixths of our group madder than hornets at one Joseph J. Travis. It turned out that no one had to sit on anyone else's lap. Cora squeezed in front between Mike and Brad, leaving Scotty, me, and Erica in the very squished backseat. I sat in the middle, and being a dude, made sure to give fellow dude Scotty plenty of room.

We talked football as we headed out of Lincoln. The defense looked good (except against power sets) and the offense showed promise. We detoured to Dairy Queen and joined the throng on a warm spring evening. While I licked a cone (I was too poor to spring for a Blizzard, especially after springing for the game, my contribution toward lunch, and dinner at Lazlo's) and waited for everyone else to go through the line, Erica approached. She had a cone too, only hers was dipped in chocolate.

"So how long have you been a Morganite?" she asked, maybe teasing just a little.

I winced. And licked my ice cream. "All my life."

"Really?"

"My dad was the pastor at MBC since before I was born," I said, opening both a painful can of worms and the door at the same time. I held it for her and we stepped out into the balmy night. The sun had set, but the sky was still light in the west. It was perfect.

"Your dad is Gary Roosevelt?"

I nodded.

She took a lick of exposed chocolate ice cream. "I'm sorry."

"It kind of came as a surprise," I said. "Especially to me."

"We just started going a few weeks before it happened," Erica said. "It was definitely out of the blue."

My turn to lick.

"So what happened?" she asked. "Or is that too personal?"

"No," I said, glancing over my shoulder. You never knew who was listening, or who had allegiance to whom. Mom and Dad both said that the "firing" was handled peaceably and with no hard feelings. But these things were bound to have their share of bad blood. You don't just can a pastor after two decades unless something happened. And I knew the something wasn't on my parents' end.

"They said it was 'just time to move on,'" I said. "It wasn't doctrinal, wasn't anything he or Mom had done. I don't really know. I don't think they even do for sure."

"That kind of stinks."

"Kind of."

We strolled toward Mike's truck. There was some sort of hold-up inside.

"So do they still live in town?"

"Moved to Oklahoma," I answered.

"Oklahoma?"

"Dad's pastoring a church in Norman."

"Norman?"

Norman, Oklahoma. Home of the Sooners, Nebraska's oldest football rival (regardless of what conference affiliation had dictated for most of my life).

"Heart of enemy territory," I said. "Believe me, I know."

"And I thought going to be a missionary nurse in darkest Africa was a sacrifice."

My heart sunk. She was a missionary-to-be. That was it. Our destiny was ruined because she was off to save souls and I . . . wasn't.

I kept it cool. "Is that where you're headed?"

Erica shrugged. "The idea occurred to me once. I really don't know. I took a few pre-nursing courses at UNL, but it just wasn't right."

I breathed a few sighs of relief. God should really send orphans and widowers to Africa to save the lost, not attractive young girls from the Heartland.

"I'm in a holding pattern, I guess," she said. "Hold this?" She handed me her cone, and then placed her left hand on my shoulder. With her right, she reached for her sandal. She slid it off her foot, shook out a rock, and replaced it, nearly losing her balance in the process. Then she took her cone back. "Thanks."

"Sure." Anytime.

"That's why I moved in with my parents," she said. "I could have gotten an apartment in the city, but we've been close . . . We're close, so I decided to join them, until I get clearance from the Tower."

"Makes sense," I said. It had been my plan until the church axed Pops.

Erica turned back toward the restaurant. "What is taking so long?" She shook her hair out of her eyes as she turned back to me. "So will you still go to MBC?"

"I guess so. The only other church in town is True Way, and —"

"I know about them," she said. "We tried going there one Sunday." Now she looked over her shoulder before leaning in close. "I think they might be a cult."

"Rumor has it," I replied. We both smiled. And leaned against Mike's truck. I hoped they had to send to Omaha for more ice cream mix.

"Tell me about college," she said.

"What do you want to know?"

"I went to UNL, lived in a dorm for a semester. What's it like in a sanctified institution?"

"Not as sanctified as you might think."

"Oh?"

My cone was in need of some attention, and I took a moment to get things under control. "No," I said at last. "You'd be surprised at the number of Christian people who don't live like Christians."

Erica grunted — in a way that was not unattractive. "Unfortunately, I doubt I would."

"It wasn't all bad. I had some fun, but you can only take so many general courses without a field of study."

"Did you have a plan going in?"

"To hopefully figure out a major."

"I see."

Scotty arrived with a banana split, followed by the rest of the group, and we piled back into the truck. I again had the pleasure of sitting snuggly close to Erica. But our time for private conversation was over, and I had to enjoy her general nearness for the rest of the ride home. Mike cut through the back country, driving much faster than was necessary, and soon we were back in Morgan.

We all said our goodbyes, all very casual, and Scotty and I started for his place, a three-block walk from the church.

"You're quiet," he said.

"I am?"

"Uh-huh." He switched his hat around forward. "You in love?"

"Yeah, I think I might be."

"Well, that should make for a fun summer."

Chapter 3

"Great fear seized the whole church and all who heard about these events." Acts 5:11

The final three weeks of classes could not go fast enough. I was a lame duck, done with college for the time being, and so advanced algebra and biology suddenly had little bearing on my life. Plus I was anxious to get back to Morgan, back to my friends, and back to Erica. Before somebody else wooed her.

Finals were a pain, not because they were hard, but because they were dragged out over four days. I pretty much mailed in my sociology final, figuring a low C was as good as a low B in a class I didn't care about anyhow. It was the last one, Thursday afternoon, and when I was done, I busied myself packing.

On Friday Scotty came up in his Chevy Blazer and we brought everything home. There was plenty of room in his basement, next to the ping-pong table and the old couch that would serve as my bed, and we stacked my college belongings next to the boxes of stuff I'd moved over a month earlier, when Mom and Dad had packed up our house.

Saturday we went apartment hunting to no avail. There weren't that many apartments in Morgan, and the available ones were either dives or out of my somewhat limited price range. It was cool, Scotty said. He and his dad didn't mind having me around. Right, but after a few weeks . . .

Sunday I had butterflies as we walked to church. We were three bachelors, in a manner of speaking, strolling down the street in our varied Sunday garb: Dirk wore a dress shirt and jeans, with boots. Very Texan. Scotty wore a polo and shorts. He always wears shorts, every day, even in winter. I think he'll wear shorts to his wedding. I had a plaid button-down, sleeves rolled up, tucked into a loose pair of khakis. Not the pleated kind old men wear. These were actually stylish, and I looked good. At least all right. I hadn't seen Erica in twenty-nine days, and I was anxious. But ready.

It felt weird walking through the doors of Morgan Bible and knowing that Dad was not going to be behind the pulpit, smiling at me and Mom as he started his sermon. For that matter, Mom wasn't going to be playing the piano for the congregational singing, or making people say "Amen" with her rousing offertories. I didn't even know the new pastor, who had only been on the job for a few weeks, so I really had no idea what to expect.

The church looked the same. It was a simple building, peaked roof, a small cross on top. (True Way, after meeting at the high school for five years, erected a building that looked as if it should have been on the cover of a puzzle . . . all white, little bell tower and steeple, stained glass windows.) Inside, MBC still smelled the same—a little bit like old people— still had the same faded carpet from a different era, and still had the weekly attendance total (for both the worship service and Sunday school) displayed in the foyer.

The sanctuary was straight ahead from the foyer, and we entered through a pair of old wooden doors that creaked a little. They always had. Morgan Bible was slightly deficient in the janitorial department.

I stopped in my tracks.

There were drums on the stage.

We had never had drums before.

Geoff de Boer had played his guitar once or twice, and Mom eventually bought an electric piano that could emulate a variety of other instruments. But we'd never had drums. I shrugged. I was not in the crowd that thought syncopation was evil.

Scotty and I split off from Dirk. As a little kid, with Dad preaching and leading the singing and Mom at the piano, I had been deemed incapable of sitting and behaving decently by myself. So I was seated by Cassie and her family. As I grew older, since I would be sitting alone for half of the service anyhow, I continued to sit with her. Scotty eventually joined us. When we matured into cool teenagers, we concluded that we should sit by ourselves, not by her parents. Sitting together had stuck until I left for college. And I saw, by following a half pace behind Scotty, that it still stuck.

"Hey, Cass," he said, sliding into the row.

Cassie practically ignored him, reaching around him to give me a big hug. Aside from third grade, when I thought she had cooties, Cassie and I had always been friends. When I was five, we pledged ourselves to get married when we grew up. We settled on ten as a good age. The marriage dissolved before it was formed, but our friendship stuck through thick and thin. Medical and financial complications kept my parents from having another child, and Cassie became the kid sister I never had.

"How were finals?" she asked, worry filling her bright blue eyes. A good student, Cassie had always fretted over tests.

"Good," I answered. "And better than good, they're done."

"Scoot over," she said to Scotty. He rolled his eyes and made room for me between them. As I sat down, I noticed that the drums were not alone on stage. There were stands holding several guitars too. Yikes, a revolution.

"You get everything settled at Scotty's?" Cassie asked.

I nodded.

"Sorry I couldn't help."

"Scotty said you were working."

"Yeah, but still . . ."

"How is work?"

Cassie shook her wrist and the bead bracelet she always wore around it, and sighed. "I'm zonked."

"Zonked . . . is that a good thing?"

She smiled, displaying dimples in her round cheeks. "No." The smile faded. "I figure I worked about eighty hours this week."

"Eighty?"

"Schedules are messed up with people coming and going."

"You're not going to work eighty hours all summer, are you?"

"Not if I can help it."

She made a face and reached up to undo her hair. It was blond and bright, and hung to the middle of her back when she let it. Nine times out of ten, she had it in a ponytail or bunched up in the back of her head. Today it was bunched, and as she redid it, I watched carefully. I had never understood how girls managed to wad up all that hair, keep it in place, and actually make it look decent. After watching Cassie effortlessly put her hair back, I still had no idea.

Scotty kicked my foot. "Watch this, dude."

I turned to him, and followed his nod toward the stage. Three guys and two girls had ascended, all dressed for a work project, it appeared. T-shirts and polos with faded colors and ragged hems, torn jeans. Were we commissioning them to do some landscaping? Nope, I realized as they took their places; they were the music team.

"Good morning!" one of them shouted into the microphone wrapped around his head. He was by far the oldest of the group—I guessed early forties—and had the only jeans without holes in them. (To be fair, the girl on his right was wearing a skirt, albeit one cut a little high for leading a worship service, but now I sounded like the True Way crowd.)

"Please stand with me and clap!"

"What the heck for?" I whispered to Cassie. She shrugged.

We slowly stood, and I looked around. Everybody else was standing. And nobody was walking out. Dad always wore a suit, or at least a tie, when he preached. And Mom played piano in dresses and skirts (appropriately cut and slit). I expected to see a mass exodus to True Way when I saw the worship team's garb. But the congregation remained, stood, and offered a very light round of applause.

"Why are we clapping?" I asked Scotty, nonchalantly slapping my palms together.

"We do this now," he said. "We clap for God."

"I see."

"It's kind of pathetic. It sounds like He saved par or something."

The guy with the microphone clapped louder than anybody, and then encouraged us to greet someone. I looked to see if Erica might happen to be in greeting distance, but didn't spot her. Oh well. I shook hands with a couple of old-timers I recognized in the row in front of us. Old-timers make up a fair amount of the population at Morgan Bible. Then again, old-timers make up a pretty fair amount of the population in Morgan in general. That's okay. I like old-timers.

And then my eardrums were shattered. Microphone guy had picked up a guitar, and seemed bound and determined to snap the strings. The drummer was going to town, and one of the ladies had strapped into a bass guitar and was getting her grunge on. Mom shook the rafters now and again on "Wonderful Grace of Jesus," but never like this.

I had never heard the song they sang. I'm not sure the worship team had either. It did not have any sort of rhythm or flow to it, but that didn't stop them. The lady in the questionable skirt danced in place, her knees and elbows going everywhere. She sang too, but a different part than the guy with the mic. Possibly a different song.

I watched. The words were projected on the screen behind them, a new installation a few years ago, but I couldn't have caught the tune with a fishing net. The quintet on stage was into it. So were a handful here and there in the congregation. But the majority seemed like me, unsure of what or when to sing. Follow the guy? Follow the girl? Pick a part somewhere in the middle? Just stare at the guy on the electric guitar and try to determine if he's actually playing?

When the song finally finished—it took a while—the girl clapped her hands over her head to some sort of drum roll. Then she began singing a new song. Her voice was pretty. The music, at least until the grunge joined in halfway through the first verse, wasn't bad. But the lyrics were missing something. It hit me after the chorus. Substance.

We praise You, Lord.
We love You, Lord.
We are here for You and You alone.
You are God.
You love us.
You are here for us, Lord.

It wasn't false, but it also wasn't exactly groundbreaking theology.

I stuck my hands in my pockets and scanned the sanctuary for Erica. My vision was limited to the one hundred eighty degrees from right to left in front of me—and a few peeks over the shoulder—but I didn't see her. Attendance at Morgan Bible had averaged about a hundred and fifty for my last few years in high school, and the board in the foyer said 141 had attended last week. She could conceivably blend into such a crowd.

I recognized the third song, a hymn I'd known since childhood. Only I didn't know the tune they sang it to, or the pace. It was close to what I'd known, but different enough that I found myself singing when I shouldn't, and vice versa. My singing voice isn't exactly melodious, so I prefer not to sing a solo, especially when a solo isn't called for. So I gave up and waited for the sermon.

After the offering was collected while the worship team serenaded us, the guy adjusted his guitar strap. "You know," he said, "we've been singing these great praise songs to God, but we're not limited to singing. For example, we can make music by whistling too. So let's do it. Let's whistle to God."

They started playing the music again, a tune that was vaguely familiar. But instead of singing, they whistled the lyrics. A guy goes off to college for a few years, and what happens?

I turned, eyebrows raised, to Scotty. He returned the look.

"I can't whistle," Cassie whispered.

"Try humming."

"Or clapping," Scotty said.

One of the old guys in front of me started fiddling with his hearing aid. His neighbor leaned over to whisper something.

"What?" the first guy asked, louder than necessary.

The second guy leaned a little farther. "They're whistling," he said in a loud whisper.

"Yours too? I can't get them to stop," Guy One said, digging deeper into his ear.

Cassie grabbed my knee, and I turned to see that her face was beet red as she tried to keep in her laughter. A squeak slipped out, but it was masked by the whistling from on stage and in random places throughout the sanctuary. It sounded like the aviary at the zoo. The guy in front of me was about ready to chuck his hearing aid on the ground and stomp on it.

Fortunately, the leader's lips were getting chapped, and he broke into actual singing to finish the song. Cassie maintained her composure, although I could tell a fit was just below the surface. It wouldn't have been the first time she disrupted the morning service with hysterical laughter. Mary Tyler Moore at a funeral laughter.

"Whooh," the leader said after they had finished, as he, the girl next to him, and a couple of other folks clapped a little more. Then he slipped the guitar off his shoulder and while the rest of the team descended from the stage, he pulled over a music stand. Not the fine hand-crafted pulpit Dad had always preached from, but a cheap music stand. He adjusted the height and wiped some sweat from his brow.

"Wasn't that fabulous?" he asked. "Join me in prayer."

I bowed my head, but I didn't join him in prayer. It had just hit me. This was Curtis Teasdale. Reverend Curtis Teasdale, to be precise. The guy who had replaced my dad.

He preached for thirty minutes, I'm not sure what on. We jumped from verse to verse, Testament to Testament, and while he was clearly speaking from Scripture, I couldn't quite figure out his point. I gave him a pass. He was probably lightheaded from whistling.

"Instead of a closing song today," Teasdale said when he was done, "we'd like to honor mothers, on this, Mother's Day. So I'd like to ask all moms out there in the audience to stand."

Those of us who hadn't given birth craned our necks to see those who had. And then we clapped for them. Eleven times louder than we had clapped for God. Apparently moms had made an across-the-green eagle putt.

Teasdale read a verse from Proverbs, incited more clapping (this was getting to be worse than *Wheel of Fortune*), and had us all rise.

He held up his hands. "Friends," he said with a goofy grin, "you are dismissed."

"You know," Scotty said, turning to face Cassie and me, "that may have been the most sterling benediction I've ever heard."

Cassie gave him a playful frown.

"I don't know," the old guy in front of me said to a woman on his left, likely his wife. "It happened during the last song."

"I'm surprised you could hear it over the music," she replied. "My head is still shaking from those drums."

Cassie's smile covered her face, and I knew she was in danger of splitting a gut.

"You sure you don't want to come with us?" Scotty asked.

"No, go ahead," I said. "It's your thing."

"Okay, dude. Later. Later, Cass."

I said goodbye. She waved. Then asked me, "What's his thing?"

"He and Dirk go golfing on Mother's Day," I answered.

"Don't they go golfing every day?"

I shrugged.

"So you're stuck all by yourself?"

"I'll call Mom, ask about life in Oklahoma."

Cassie bit her lip. "I feel terrible about that."

I shrugged again. "What's a guy to do?"

"That's very mature."

"You sound surprised."

Now she shrugged. We do a lot of shrugging in Morgan.

"So tell me something," I said, gesturing at the stage. "Is this standard? Was this a typical Sunday morning service?"

"Pretty much. But we've never whistled before."

"That was weird."

"Kinda."

I sighed. "They still have donuts and coffee in the foyer?"

"Yep."

"They still not let you bring them in here?"

"Nope."

It had always been the case. In the fifteen minutes between church and Sunday school, bitter coffee and stale donuts were served. There were never enough to go around, which was fine, because they weren't allowed in the sanctuary where the adult class always met. So if you were over eighteen and wanted a donut or coffee, you had to consume it in a hurry in the foyer. Hate to spill anything on forty-year-old green carpet.

Cassie followed me out into the foyer, and I kept an eye scanned for Erica. I didn't see her. I tried not to panic. There were plenty of reasons she might not be there, other than her family had left the church or moved to Virginia or something like that. It was, after all, Mother's Day.

There were two cake donuts left in a box, and I reached for the one with chocolate frosting. "Want half?" I asked Cassie.

"Yes, but I can't."

I took a bite. "Why not?"

"I'm on a diet."

"You sure?"

"Yeah," she said forlornly. Cassie was not overweight, but she wasn't model thin either. It drove her nuts because she ate healthily and got plenty of exercise, but always felt a pound or two heavy. I had told her many times that she looked great and had nothing to worry about, but she wasn't convinced. I had stopped belaboring the point for fear that it would look like I was doing just that.

I inhaled the donut, easy on top of cereal that morning, and Cassie and I headed back into the sanctuary. Morgan Bible wasn't a huge facility, so the adult class didn't have its own room. In the past, we'd even had to split the sanctuary between classes.

Cassie and I took seats in the middle right, and I wondered who was teaching the adult class. Cassie didn't know. They had just finished a study on I Samuel, so it was likely to change. Unless they went into II Samuel.

"Your class is meeting in Room 104," a female voice announced. I looked up to see a tall woman with long, dark hair. Pointed nose. Pointed at Cassie and me.

"Our class?" Cassie asked.

"The Young Adults Fellowship."

"I didn't know there was a young adults class."

"It's just starting," the woman said. "Today."

Cassie turned to me. "They never announced it," she said, as if she owed me an explanation.

I shrugged.

The woman stood over us. "It was in the worship folder."

"The what?" I asked.

This was apparently the stupidest question anyone had ever asked.

"The bulletin," Cassie whispered.

"Ah. I didn't get a bulletin this morning." Too busy looking at the drums.

"Me either," Cassie said quietly. We were bad little parishioners.

The woman didn't move.

"Are we required to attend?" Cassie asked.

"Are you young adults?"

Cassie and I looked at each other. Whatever. We got up and trekked out of the sanctuary. "She's friendly," I said.

"She's Sandra Teasdale," Cassie answered through a closed mouth.

Room 104 had been used for miscellaneous storage most of my years, but it had been converted into a makeshift Sunday school—er, Young Adults Fellowship—room. There was a small traffic jam in the doorway, and it gave me a chance to look over the class. There were a dozen people gathered, none of whom were knockout brunettes who recognized porous run defense when they saw it.

The jam cleared and Cassie and I took seats in the middle. Our teacher was clearly identifiable, the only guy wearing a tie. And jacket. And carrying a Trapper Keeper. He was probably thirty, and looked vaguely familiar.

I nudged Cassie. "Who's that?"

"Derek Peterson."

"That's Petey?"

"Shhh."

"He looks different."

"He grew about a foot."

Little Petey had always been ten years older than me, but had never been taller than me. He was still gangly thin, and still had hair that was too long, flopped over his head in the Keanu Reeves style. Petey did not look like Keanu Reeves. Not even close.

"Where is Scotty?"

I knew the voice before looking up.

Angelia Engracia Torres. Gia. The antagonist of my life. And Scotty's. And probably of everybody else she knew. She was Cuban, which meant she probably sympathized with the Communists and cheated at Little League. But her biggest flaw was her feisty disposition. Or her feminism. Or her brash, argumentative style. Or the chip on her shoulder. It was a four-way tie.

"Golfing," I said. "I'll be sure to let him know you asked."

Gia turned with a flick of her curly brown hair.

"She still goes here," I said to Cassie.

"Shush."

"Maybe we could trade her to True Way for a baby baptizer to be named later."

Cassie elbowed me in the ribs.

Petey called the class to start, citing the fact that it was already a minute past starting time. He apologized for this. He turned to the chalkboard and broke his chalk halfway through the word Revelation. We snickered appropriately.

"Never mind," Petey said, leaving "Revela" on the board. He looked up. "Welcome. The purpose of this class is to give us a well-rounded, biblically-based understanding of the end times."

"Didn't Tim LaHaye already do that?" somebody behind me asked.

"No."

"It was Jerry B. Jenkins," another voice piped up.

"The *Left Behind* series was a work of fiction," Petey said, his voice an octave higher and loud enough to take over the conversation. "And while I do believe the authors made every effort to preserve Scriptural accuracy, they were writing novels. Their writings, and any other fictional interpretations of the end times, are just that—fictional. In this class, we are going to study the Bible exclusively, and in particular, the book of Revelation. We will not be shading Scripture with our beliefs and ideas, but rather deducing from God's Word the truth about the end of the age."

"How do we know the truth?" It was one of the two voices from before.

"I beg your pardon."

"Revelation's hard, dude."

Petey bristled at being called dude.

"How do we know what it means?"

"Through rather exhaustive and analytical study."

"I don't want to do exhaustive and analytical study."

"That's the purpose of this class," Petey said. "That difficult work has already been undertaken. My job will be to relate the results of that work to you, in a condensed form."

"So we just listen to you talk all the time?"

Petey cleared his throat. "There will be ample time for discussion, but a majority of the class will be in lecture format. With frequent consultation of Scripture, of course. Today will be a contextual overview."

I turned to Cassie. She made a face.

I wished I had taken Dirk and Scotty up on their golf offer.

It had to beat Petey's lecture on "Revela."

Chapter 4

"I long to see you, so that I may be filled with joy." II Timothy 1:4

The week passed. I spent it filling out applications and working part-time at the Prairie View Golf Club outside of town. Dirk owned and ran the place, and although I don't think he really needed the help since Scotty already worked there part-time and did the odds and ends the regular greenskeeper Tommy didn't, he was kind enough to give me a few hours a day until something steady turned up. If it did. After applying just about everywhere in town—and a few places not in town—the prospects weren't great. I had one interview scheduled for next Monday. That was it. Otherwise, I was left to apply to places in Lincoln, in which case gas to get me to work and back would pretty much eat my profits.

Friday afternoon we played nine holes, one of the perks of working at the course. And being tight with the boss. Dirk had some meeting of local businessmen that night, so after showering and changing, Scotty and I made dinner ourselves. Or tried to. We realized the fridge was kind of bare, so we headed for the store.

Morgan has one grocery store, a mom and pop place called Don & Flo's. Don and Flo now live in Tampa and play shuffleboard while their kids run the place and maintain the old-fashioned charm. And high prices. But what do you expect from the only grocery store in a small town?

It was another beautiful evening, and since just about every place in Morgan is in walking distance, Scotty and I went on foot. "We're not getting pizzas," Scotty said as we crossed Main Street. We'd already had two frozen pizzas that week.

"Okay."

"And we're not getting some cheap TV dinners."

"You want a four course meal from scratch tonight?"

"I just want something a little different. We've been eating frozen dinners and grilled meats for fourteen years, and I could use a change now and again."

Scotty had double-bogeyed the ninth hole, and he'd been a little out of sorts ever since.

"I will eat anything," I said.

"How about spaghetti?"

"It's kind of hot for spaghetti."

"Spaghetti isn't any hotter than any other food. Unless you want ice cream for dinner."

"I'm just picturing steaming bowls of noodles and sauce, steam everywhere."

"Fine, what do you want?"

"And it's kind of a heavy meal."

"Fine," Scotty said.

"How about stir fry?" I asked.

"You think stir fry is cool?"

"Cooler than spaghetti."

"Boiling rice and a wok full of sizzling meat and veggies?"

"You guys have a wok?"

He raised his eyebrows.

"Okay, no spaghetti and no stir fry," I said. "What do you want?"

"How about subs?"

"You want to make subs?"

"No, we'll get them from Wieskamps'."

I shrugged. Scotty shrugged. And instead of entering Don & Flo's, we kept on walking.

Wieskamps' Phillips 66 station is on the western edge of town, at the corner of 1st and Main. It had been renovated a few years back and gone from just a tiny two-pump station to a four-stall, pay-at-the-pump, full-service facility. The added on mini-mart sold a little bit of everything, including pretty good hot and cold sub sandwiches. They beat frozen pizzas and TV dinners.

We walked through Morgan's historic downtown. Historic in that it was old. Nothing of even the remotest significance had ever happened there. It did contain a handful of shops and stores and some residences, and was pretty well kept up. A lot of the buildings were attractive red brick, and the town had completely repaved all of the sidewalks, planted a few trees, and incorporated old-fashioned lampposts and signage to add to the antique feel. So while insignificant, downtown was at least inviting.

"So you come up with a plan for this girl of yours?" Scotty asked as we walked.

"I thought I'd start by hopefully seeing her again."

"You could go over to her house."

"You know where she lives?"

"I'm guessing there's a way to find out."

I shook my head. "That's a little forward."

"You want to go backwards?"

"There's an art to this sort of thing, Scotty. You don't want to rush falling in love. You want to take it nice and slow, enjoy every minute of it."

"Are you enjoying it?"

"It's miserable."

He smiled.

My misery was short-lived. We entered Wieskamps' and Scotty turned toward the food. I headed for the snack aisle where a gorgeous brunette was deliberating over candy. She wore a Kelly green tank top, white cotton shorts, and flip-flops. Her hair was in a bouncy ponytail, with several strands left loose at the side of her face. She was adorable.

I slipped beside her. "Definitely the Lemonheads."

Erica jerked her head my way. "Hey, Josh."

She remembered my name. I found that incredibly promising.

"How you been?" I asked.

"Great," she answered with a smile. It made the last thirty-four days worthwhile. "You?"

"Not bad," I answered. "Looking for work. And a place to live. And supper. Other than that I'm good."

"How was the last month of school?"

37

"Bearable," I answered. "But I'm glad to be back."

"Grab me a couple Kit Kat's please," she said.

They were right in front of me, and I handed them to her. "You stocking up for movie night?"

"Vacation," she answered.

"Vacation?"

"Mm-hmm. We're leaving tomorrow morning, through Memorial Day."

I did the math. Nine days, spanning two Sundays. That meant I wouldn't likely see her again for at least two weeks. I wanted to make the moment count, even if a peek to my left indicated Scotty was getting antsy. He could work on his putting stroke.

"Where are you headed?" I asked.

"Estes Park, Colorado."

"Nice."

"I know," she said, grinning ear to ear. "I can't wait."

She plucked a box of Hot Tamales off the shelf. Then reconsidered and made it two. "You ever been?"

"Estes Park? Once. I was like five or something."

"You should go again."

"I'd love to. Even at five, I still remember it. The mountains, the blue skies . . ."

"Flowery meadows . . ."

"Quaking aspens . . ."

"Bugling bull elk . . ."

"A trip to the dentist." I nodded at all her candy.

Stopping midway to a box of Gobstoppers, her hand instead swung over and whacked me in the shoulder. "It's for the whole family," she said.

I nodded, trying to enjoy the memory of her touch.

"Besides, Mom and Dad have a weakness for sweets."

"Our secret," I said.

She winked. Then, "I'd better get going. I still have to pack."

"Have fun."

"Thanks, we will." She stacked her candy in her arm, almost like a football. As she passed, she turned over her shoulder. "Maybe I'll send you a postcard."

"Make sure it has mountains on it."

"Of course."

I watched her go until doing so any longer would have been awkward. Then I found Scotty.

"I haven't eaten since noon, but you go on flirting."

"She hit me," I said.

"What'd you say to her?"

"No, a good hit," I said, backhanding him in the shoulder. "Like that."

"Well, let me go rent my tux."

"Hitting's a good thing, isn't it?"

He shrugged. "I suppose."

"You're just sore because you four-putted."

"And because my stomach sounds like Aslan. Can we get going?"

We picked out our subs, grabbed some Cheetos, paid, and started back to Scotty's house. Throughout the process, I kept an eye out for Erica, but she had split right away. Oh well, I'd made it almost five weeks; I could make it two more.

"So what'd you two lovebirds talk about?" Scotty asked.

"She's going on vacation. To Colorado."

He nodded.

"She said she might send me a postcard."

"I'm sure it was just a conversation closer."

"Sending mail's a good sign too, isn't it?"

"Only if she knows your address."

I stopped. I didn't have an address.

The best-laid plans of mice, men, and beautiful women.

Chapter 5

"I gave him the wasteland as his home . . ." Job 39:6

Saturday Scotty had to work, helping Dirk with some best-ball scramble tournament or something. I slept in, filled out a few more job apps, and early in the afternoon, after her shift at the Morgan Family Restaurant, I met Cassie to go apartment hunting. I'd scoured the local paper, a weekly that came out on Thursday and did nothing but run horseshoe and darts scores, print photos of 4-H clubs and Girl Scout troops, and list a very small selection of apartments, jobs, and other sundry items in the classified section. I'd found a couple possibilities.

Cassie wore khaki pants that were too long, and had thus been stepped on and torn to tatters — the story of all her pants — and a Creighton Blue Jay tee. Her sister Candace had spent a year at Creighton on a full music scholarship before wandering from the path of righteousness, still a sore subject to the Larson family. Creighton, apparently, was not. Cassie's hair was stuck behind her head with chopsticks, and she fiddled with the trademark bead bracelet around her wrist as we walked from Scotty's to the first apartment, a few blocks over on Ash Street.

"So Scotty tells me you've got yourself a girlfriend," she said, grinning.

"Did he now?"

"Uh-huh."

"Not a girlfriend," I said.

"But a girl?"

"Hopefully."

"Anybody I know?"

"Erica Chamberlain."

"She's pretty."

"She is."

"Does she like you?"

"She hit me last night." I lightly backhanded Cassie's shoulder, as I had Scotty's, as Erica had mine.

"That's a good sign."

"I thought so. And she's sending me a postcard from Estes Park."

"Does she know you're living with Scotty?"

Why did everyone have to rain on my parade?

"I've always wanted to go to Estes Park," Cassie said.

"You should go to school in Colorado."

"If I can go anywhere."

"Remind me again, why ASU?"

"They've got one of the best art history programs in the country," she said.

I nodded. Cassie had always been artistic and creative. Unfortunately, her parents did not have nearly enough money to send her to a university, let alone one across the country. For years, she had been scrimping and saving, working two or three jobs, and taking the odd college level course when and where she could, trying to earn cheap credits. But Arizona State was still something of a fantasy.

"Besides, I've always had a fascination with Arizona," she said. "And Candace is in Las Vegas."

"Las Vegas isn't in Arizona."

"No, but it's very close."

After leaving Creighton, Candace's wandering had taken her to Sin City. The details were sketchy, but I gathered that she was making a living by less than biblical methods. Like I said, a sore subject.

Two little old ladies met us out front of the two-story apartment building. Both were dressed for much cooler weather, possibly snow. The one on the left had reddish hair that was clearly dyed. It was almost purple where it wasn't fading back to gray. Her eyes were hidden behind huge wraparound sunglasses lifted from an astronaut's helmet. The one on the right had frizzy gray hair and had apparently applied her makeup with a paintbrush. They smelled like mothballs and peppermint candy, and seemed surprised that there were two of us.

I introduced myself to Fran—Purple Hair—and Eloise—Frizzy Hair. Then I introduced Cassie.

"Is this your wife?" Eloise asked.

"No."

"Girlfriend?"

"We don't approve of young people shacking up together," Fran said sternly.

"We're just friends," I said.

"That doesn't make it any better in the Lord's sight."

"I won't be living here," Cassie said with a nervous glance in my direction. "I'm just here for moral support."

"Call it whatever you want," Fran said. "We don't approve."

"We live in apartment 1A," Eloise said. "We keep tabs on all of the tenants . . . and their visitors."

"Overnight guests need to be approved," Fran stated, sternly. She closed her mouth suddenly, and appeared to be fighting to keep her teeth from sliding around.

"Well, would you like to see the place?" Eloise asked.

I was having second thoughts, what with the Granny Gestapo living beneath me, but I'd come this far. I nodded, and raised my eyebrows at Cassie as we followed the women inside.

A central corridor that smelled like cat pee (or human pee, for that matter) led to all eight apartments—four on the bottom and four up a flight of stairs. The flight took Eloise quite a while. When we made it, she hobbled to the far end of the hallway and apartment 2D. As she fiddled with the key, Fran reached into her purse.

"Here . . ." she sucked her teeth back in. "Put these on." She passed out little plastic shoe covers to Cassie and me.

"We have everyone wear them," Eloise said. "You can't be too careful." She finally got the door unlocked, and after Cassie and I put on our booties, we followed her into the apartment.

The 1970s had not been kind, leaving behind green shag carpet and a wood-paneled wall, which was actually an improvement from the other three that were wallpapered in a hideous paisley pattern. The adjoined kitchen had yellow Formica countertops and a refrigerator that would more accurately be described as an icebox. A maroon stain covered the peeling linoleum in the corner.

"You can do what you want with the walls," Eloise said as she started shambling toward the hallway. "Personally, I think they go pretty well with the carpet."

Couldn't argue with that.

She showed us the bedroom and bathroom, which were similarly old and in need of some repairs. Cassie checked the water, which came out brown at first, and then intermittently after that. I realized there was no closet in the bedroom, or anywhere for that matter. I missed dormitories.

"Five hundred twenty-five a month," Eloise said when we were back in the living room. "Includes water and heat. You pay electric."

I did some math. Dirk paid me ten dollars per hour, fifteen to twenty hours per week, and had already said he could probably keep me on all summer if I didn't find anything else. After taxes, that would just about pay the rent. It would not pay the electric company or Don & Flo's for my food. Or buy furniture.

"We're speaking with contractors about replacing the linoleum in the kitchen," Fran said. "We'll pay for that when the time comes."

I nodded.

"No loud music, no roughhousing, and no parties."

I nodded again, and looked at Cassie. She looked at me. So did Eloise and Fran.

"Okay," I said. "We've got a few other places to check too."

"Don't take too much time," Eloise said. "We've got another couple —"

"They're married," Fran interjected.

" — looking this afternoon. It's first come, first served."

"I understand."

Fran asked that we return the booties on our way out. She stuffed them back into her purse. Cassie and I made it out onto the sidewalk and around the corner before we made faces at each other.

"Do you think everybody wears those same booties?" she asked.

"They were adjustable. One size fits all."

"Maybe the next place will be nicer."

"We can hope."

The next place was not nicer. It was an upstairs apartment in one of the older buildings in town, on Main Street. The landlord was late arriving, and even later dressing. His considerable and exposed upper body was covered in crumbs of drywall and he explained that he was helping his brother remodel. He also apologized for the delay. He then put on a shirt, a size too small, with a hole under the left arm and another in the middle of the belly.

Cassie grabbed my arm as we followed him inside. The current residents were moving out at the end of the month, the landlord explained. The current residents apparently did not know this. The place was trashed, as if they had unpacked by just tossing things out of the box, and then lived in the place ever since. Toys, dirty dishes, beer bottles, clothes — including underwear — and stacks of bills cluttered the living room. A vacuum cleaner sat in the middle of the room, either as a reminder or an accent piece. The kitchen was just as bad, but without any underwear. We didn't check the drawers.

The apartment wasn't without features. It did have a back door — that opened directly into space. No porch or balcony or even a roof to step out onto. And the kitchen floor could double as a skateboard halfpipe. The bedroom did have a closet, and the bathroom water came out clear as crystal. I was the one to try it. Cassie refused to touch anything, what with the toothbrushes, razors, and bottles of ointment on the vanity.

It was also stifling hot, because the window air conditioner was "on the fritz." Contractors were apparently not being spoken to.

The price was only $375 per month, and that included heat but not water. I told the landlord we'd think about it, which was as close to a lie as this preacher's kid has ever told. We left in a hurry.

"Well, this is going well," I said.

"Patience," Cassie said.

"There aren't many more apartments in town."

"So there are more?"

I nodded. "Yes, there are more."

"Then patience."

We headed a block east, and then turned north toward the final place on my list. They were asking $550 a month, and I was not encouraged.

"I should talk," Cassie muttered, snapping her bracelet.

"Why's that?"

"All I can think about is ASU, ASU, ASU."

"It's understandable," I said. "You've had a lifelong dream."

"But that's just it. Is it my dream, or God's dream?"

"I don't think God dreams."

She backhanded me. "You know what I mean."

"You just hit me."

"So?"

"So maybe when Erica hit me she hit me the same way you hit me, not because she has a thing for me."

"Girls have lots of reasons for hitting boys," Cassie said. "Now can I be selfish for just one more minute?"

"Of course."

"I've been praying every day that God would show me if this is His will or not, so I know if I should keep pushing for it or just give up."

"I don't think God wants you to give up."

"We're supposed to surrender," she said.

"That's giving in," I answered. "Giving in and giving up are different."

Cassie cocked her head and squinted at me—and into the sun. "I'm not sure if that's incredibly insightful or just hogwash."

I shook my head. "I'm not either."

"Maybe He has told me His will. I'm still short on cash, still haven't been accepted. Maybe that's a no."

"Maybe."

"Or maybe it's a not yet."

"Maybe Petey should be teaching a young adults class on discerning God's will instead of on the end times."

Cassie sighed. "I guess I keep praying."

"And I keep looking at crummy apartments."

"So what's on the top of your list so far?"

"Scotty's basement."

"Seriously?"

I kicked at a rock. "No. It's bad form to overstay your welcome." I sighed. "Truthfully, the booties win right now. I could at least stare out the window at the park and dream that I wasn't living there."

"It could be worse . . ." Cassie said.

"I could be Paul," I said, finishing her trademark complaint about the oft-persecuted apostle.

The landlord for the third place was a middle-aged woman with a smart skirt-and-blouse combo and a pleasant smile. She shook our hands, did not assume we were going to be shacking up together, and showed us to the second floor apartment at "The Cove." It was small, with a living room, kitchenette, and dining room all combined in one. The bedroom was small too, although it did have a closet, and the bathroom was simple but modern.

The walls were white instead of paisley, there was no underwear on the floor, and the sliding doors in the living room opened to an actual deck, not just empty space. Aside from its small size, the place was nice. And it faced west, so I could watch the sun set over downtown and the grain elevator. It was almost as good as the park.

Five hundred fifty dollars per month rented the apartment, paid for heat but not air conditioning, and covered water. Hot water, since it was controlled by an electric water heater, would cost me extra.

I debated internally.

"What's holding you up, if I may ask?" the landlord questioned.

"The money," I replied.

"Five-fifty's pretty good for the condition of the apartment."

"Oh, I know. But right now, I'm only working part-time, and my salary would just cover the rent."

"You have anything in savings?" Cassie asked.

"A little."

"Where do you work?" the landlord asked. I told her, and that I was looking. She pursed her lips. "Do you have a car?"

"In a manner of speaking." It was a 1992 Escort that, for the moment, ran.

"My cousin works at the First State Bank in Firth. She says they're looking for a part-time teller. If your schedule at the golf course is flexible, you may want to apply there."

Dirk's weeds could be whacked any old time. I said I might just do that, and the very kind landlord expressed no qualms about a guy of questionable income renting her apartment. I looked to Cassie, who nodded as she smiled with lips closed, and asked where I signed.

Fifteen minutes later, Cassie and I were happily strolling back south toward Scotty's. As of June 1, the apartment would be mine. I called, and the First State Bank of Firth was not open on Saturdays, so my application would have to wait. But I had a positive feeling. Something would turn up.

"So tell me more about Erica," Cassie said as we walked.

"Like what?"

"What is it about her that has you making that goofy smile every time I mention her name?"

I smiled goofily. "I don't know."

"Come on, don't weasel out."

"No, I really don't know. I don't even know her that well."

"Is she just 'smoking hot'?"

"You've picked up Candace language," I said.

"Is that it?"

"She's not exactly hard on the eyes."

"It takes more than looks, Josh."

"I know that. And it's more than looks. When I'm around her . . . I can't explain it, Cass. And I've really only been around her twice. I just want to be around her more."

"Well you want some advice?"

"Does it matter?"

She gave me an evil eye combined with a smile. "Take it slow, Josh."

I nodded.

"I'm sure Scotty's telling you to drive over to her house and ask her out . . ."

Had she been eavesdropping?

"But if it's God's will, and if there's something there besides a physical infatuation, it will happen. And His timing is better than ours."

I nodded again.

She stopped walking. "I should try that speech out on myself, huh?"

I put my arm on her shoulder. "That's the trouble with you, Cassie. You're so focused on the plank in my eye that—"

"Shut your face," she said, stomping on my foot.

I dropped my arm. "I've got an idea."

"Mmm, what's that?"

"Let's surprise Scotty when he comes home by having spaghetti ready for him."

"Spaghetti?" she asked.

"Um-hmm."

"Why spaghetti?"

"No reason," I said with a shrug.

She thought about it for a second. "I suppose. I don't think Mom and Dad will mind."

"Good."

"Although it is kind of hot for spaghetti."

Chapter 6

"But avoid foolish controversies . . . and arguments and quarrels . . ." Titus 3:9

There was no whistling and no clapping in church on Sunday. There was also no apparent rhyme or reason to the songs we sang. They had nothing to do with the sermon, which was from James and was on the power of faith in healing. I know from experience that Dad used to spend hours flipping through the hymnal and chorus book, looking for just the right songs to accompany his sermon.

Then again, the songs of Dad's day had a little more weight and matter to them. We went from extolling the virtue of praise (in other words, singing about singing) to a song that had more I's and me's in it than any reference to God, to a song that—I kid you not—repeated the phrase "The Lord is God," six times before following up with a chorus of "la-la-la-la-la, la-la-la-la-la, la-la-la-la-hey." Repeated four times.

Maybe I'm just a fuddy-duddy. Or maybe I'm a traditionalist who should join the other rebels at True Way. I'm not saying we have to sing all hymns all the time (trust me, more experience speaking, there are some really weird hymns). But couldn't we at least mix in a few songs with a tune everybody can carry and with words that have a little substance to them?

I was getting jaded fast. It was only two weeks, but I had a feeling I was witnessing the rule and not the exception. I also found the worship team dress code a little appalling. I am well aware that people can worship God equally well in jackets and ties, blue jeans and T-shirts, or pajamas. But my mother raised me to dress respectfully when I entered the House of the Lord, and although I occasionally wear denim, I at least try to look like I'm not getting ready to clean out the garage. And I'm not on stage, either.

Sunday school (I wasn't going to stop calling it that) was something of a pick-me-up. Petey got five minutes into his Revelation 1 lecture, covering greetings and John's vision. He took a break for a drink of water (food and beverage are allowed in Room 104) and some wisenheimer in the back row asked if Petey was pre-trib, mid-trib, or post-trib.

"We'll get to the rapture and the tribulation a little later on in our study," Petey said.

"How can it be post-trib?" a female asked. "Then wouldn't the rapture and the millennial reign be at the same time?"

"What's wrong with that?" a different man's voice asked.

"So we just get beamed up to heaven and then beamed right back down?"

"I don't think the rapture should be compared to *Star Wars*," Petey said.

"That's *Star Trek*."

"I don't think it should be compared to any intergalactic television program."

"*Star Wars* was a movie."

"So was *Star Trek*."

"Uh-uh, *Star Trek* was on TV."

"You're thinking of *Star Trek: Deep Space Nine*."

"Is that the one with LeVar Burton?"

"It's the one with William Shatner."

"Shatner was *Star Wars*."

"LeVar Burton from *Roots*?"

"I thought Harrison Ford was *Star Wars*."

"Harrison Ford and William Shatner were both *Star Wars*."

"Shatner was only *Star Trek*," came the insistent reply.

"People!" Petey said for about the fourth time, finally able to raise his voice enough to get everyone's attention. Cassie, beside me, had almost fallen off her chair in laughter, and if not for my shoulder and forearm bracing her, would have.

"Who starred in which space program or movie is not relevant to the book of Revelation. Kindly conduct your debate outside of class."

"Shatner was not *Star Wars*," the insistent guy muttered.

Petey cleared his throat. "Now, as I was saying, if you look at verse three—"

"So I still don't get why it can't be post-trib," the second male voice asked. I had long since glanced over my shoulder to see it belonged to Brad Ostrander. Should have known. His voice and his argumentative nature were hard to miss.

"Because then you'd know when it was coming, and the Bible says nobody will know when the rapture occurs," another female voice said. Rena Schroers. "Isn't that right, Petey?"

"It's partially correct, Rena," he answered. "The Bible does say we won't know the hour or the date, but that doesn't necessarily mean it's going to occur pre-trib. We'll get into that—"

"Why not?" Rena asked. "If the tribulation is seven years long, and marked by specific events, if the rapture doesn't come at the beginning, we'll know it either has to come three and a half years into the tribulation, or at the end of it."

"Unless mid-trib doesn't mean the exact middle," Brad said.

"I thought you were post-trib," Rena said.

"I'm just asking."

"It can't come at the end," the first female said. I turned around. I just had to identify the parties. It was Cora de Vries. "It makes no sense."

"Who says Revelation makes sense?" Brad asked.

"Petey, apparently," Scotty said just loudly enough for Cassie and me to hear.

"Is the idea of pre-, mid-, or post-trib even supported in Scripture?" the original wisenheimer asked. Brett Baker.

"When else would it come?" Rena asked.

"I'm not sure the Bible even mentions the rapture, in those words," somebody in front of us chimed in.

"It does," Mike Baxter said from the front left.

"Where?"

"Timothy."

"Thessalonians," Petey corrected. "Now can we please get back on topic? We will discuss the rapture in a later class."

"Not if it comes first," Rena said in a tone similar to a harrumph.

"She's got him there," I whispered to Cassie. She, I realized, was lost in internal laughter. That was good—it was the quiet kind.

Speaking of lost, the class kind of derailed after that. Petey steered us away from any more rapture talk, but his lecture paled in comparison to knowing when we would get beamed up to heaven, and if it was going to be like an elevator that didn't open because we had to come right back down for the millennial reign. Two weeks back at church, four hours total between church and Sunday school, and I hadn't learned a blamed thing. I wondered how the First Community Church of Norman, Oklahoma, was faring.

Monday at eleven a.m. I had an interview with Wendy Ferrara, the manager of Nebraska Novelties in downtown Morgan. Nebraska Novelties is an ice cream/candy/coffee shop that, for as long as I had known, had been run by a kindly old couple. Where they had gone, and who Wendy was in relation to them, I had no idea. But I was not the one doing the interviewing.

We shook hands, and she led me through an old-fashioned soda shop straight out of a Norman Rockwell painting. An L-shaped counter was on the right, containing a cash register, a few stools for spinning and sundae spooning, and slanted glass panels that provided a look at all the flavors of the day. In the old days, they had changed daily and weekly and you never knew what flavor would be available—aside from vanilla and chocolate, which were always present.

To the left were a few small tables and an entire wall of candy, cookies, and other snacks that were terrible for your teeth, as well as coffee and tea in various flavors and quantities and a few other odds and ends. The combination was a smell that was intoxicating, one sniff short of being sickeningly sweet.

At the back of the store was a unisex bathroom and a small, cramped, cluttered office. Wendy closed the door behind us (in the office) and cleared some papers off her desk while apologizing for the mess. Then she offered me a seat. I took it.

"Why do you want to work here?" she asked when we were seated, her with her legs crossed, me with my hands sweating in my lap. Apparently she didn't pull punches.

Neither would I.

"I need a job," I answered. "Frankly, I'm willing to work anywhere."

Wendy made some notes. "You're honest at least."

"I try to be."

"I'll rephrase," she said. "Why should I hire you to work here?"

I hated tooting my own horn, but I'd been through the drill a few times, and knew that was how it was done. Brag without bragging. Wasn't there something in Proverbs about that?

"Well," I said, "I'm generally a quick study. I only need to be told or shown something once. I am honest, and I work hard and do the job—whatever it is—well. And while it's true that I'm filling out applications all over town, I loved coming here as a little kid, and it would be kind of cool to work here."

Wendy nodded and wrote some more. I couldn't tell from her expression if mine had been a good answer or not.

"What's your favorite flavor?"

"Ice cream?"

She nodded.

"Always been partial to rocky road."

"Do you drink coffee?"

"Socially."

Wendy frowned. "Tea?"

"Iced," I answered.

"What about candy?"

"I eat candy."

Was I being interviewed for a job or as a prospective patron?

53

Wendy switched directions. "Have you ever worked in customer service before?"

"I sacked groceries at Don & Flo's one summer. Back when Don and Flo still ran it."

"Ever taken or processed money?"

"A few times. My friend's dad owns Prairie View Golf Club, and I've helped out at the register."

"How are you under stress?"

"You mean like when there are eight people in the store, all wanting to order, crying kids, somebody complaining his flavor isn't in stock, and teenage girls messing around with all the candy jars?"

"Have you worked here before?"

I smiled.

So did Wendy. "Yeah, that's what I mean."

I took a deep breath. "I get panicky," I answered. "But only for a few seconds, sort of like a relief valve, and then I get busy. It's like at school, when I got my syllabus and it was so daunting and it seemed like I would never get everything done. But once I started working, I got all my papers in early and was always ahead of schedule."

"It's different working with people," Wendy said.

"True. Back when the Weslinks ran this place, they always had a smile, always were friendly and chatted with you. They kind of made you feel at ease. I guess I'd try to be like that, while shoveling ice cream as fast as possible."

Wendy nodded again. I was having trouble with her nods, knowing just what she meant by them. I was pretty sure I was either acing the interview or completely failing it, but I didn't know which.

Wendy picked my application off a stack on her desk, and we went over it for fifteen minutes. She asked me about my references, and what I thought they'd say about me. She asked about college, what I'd learned and why I'd left. And if I'd be returning in the fall. I said no. And she asked about my flexibility. The position was dayside, mornings and afternoons, about thirty hours per week. Could I work the occasional weekend or evening if need be? I said, sure, why not?

The entire interview lasted only thirty minutes, and when it was finished, I still didn't have a take on where I stood. Wendy said she was considering three people for the job, and hoped to decide shortly. She'd expect me to start on the day after Memorial Day. That was fine by me. I'd be moving into an apartment soon and would need the money.

Chapter 7

"We work hard with our own hands . . ." I Corinthians 4:12

Tuesday afternoon I drove out to the farm of Dave Clifford. Dave had long been an elder at Morgan Bible (he wasn't anymore) and a good family friend. From junior high up, I spent summers helping him bale and unload hay or with random other tasks on the farm. It was terrible, back-breaking work, especially on hot, humid days. But when he came to church the following Sunday with a check in my name, it was all worth it.

Dave's wife had died when I was just a little kid. He hadn't remarried, and they didn't have any kids of their own, so he still relied on whatever help he could get come haying season. On the third Tuesday of May, he got me.

In addition to being an elder, Dave had taught Sunday school to one age level or another most of his life. He'd been my teacher for much of my formative years, and after my parents, had probably been the most influential person in my life, spiritually speaking. So I was anxious to hear his thoughts on the transformation of Morgan Bible. I knew for a fact he had been sad to see Mom and Dad go.

But first there was work to be done. Six wagons full of bales. I say full, not stacked, because Dave had switched to a kick baler which, instead of "sliding" the bale back to a guy riding on the wagon who would then stack the bale neatly, expelled the bale into a cage on wheels. It made it possible for one guy to bale the hay in his field, but it made it nearly impossible to untangle and unload the bales onto the elevator.

After greeting one another and chatting for a few minutes, Dave and I got to work. I started on the wagon, with him in the mow of the barn. I loaded the bales, and when they fell off the elevator with a thud, he stacked them. We'd done the operation with two people on the wagon before, and as many as three in the mow. One to one was a little slower.

After the first two loads, we took a break to chug lemonade. It was a hot, sticky day, with only the occasional whisper of a breeze. And it was just May. Wait until third crop in August.

"So what's new in Josh's life?" Dave asked, resting the arm holding his cup on his knee. We were both seated on stray bales. "You meet any girls at college?"

"Funny you should mention that."

"You did?"

"Not at college."

"Where?"

"Hawks Field parking lot." I briefly recounted meeting Erica at the spring game and falling for her instantly.

Dave grinned. "I don't know Erica—met her once—but her folks seem like good people."

Great. I'd have swell in-laws.

"You asked her out yet?"

"Unh-uh. Not even sure she likes me yet."

"One way to find out."

"You think I should go for it?"

"I think you should play it by ear," Dave answered. "And pray about it. There's no request too small, you know."

I nodded and slugged some lemonade.

"Heard from your parents lately?" Dave asked.

"Just yesterday," I answered. "Things are going well for them."

"That's good."

"Except it was 104 Saturday."

"Oklahoma's a furnace."

Says the guy with the hay mow that could consume Shadrach, Meshach, and Abednego. I took a swig of lemonade, hay particles and all.

"How are you handling the switch?" he asked.

Just like Dave, cutting to the heart of the matter.

"Not terribly well. Not to air dirty laundry, but I'm still a little miffed that Dad got fired."

"Church politics are a volatile business," he said. "More so than regular politics, sometimes."

"I don't even know why they fired him, Dave. It's like somebody got an idea in their head and that quick he's gone and the new guy's here, like he was waiting in the wings."

"It was an awfully quick transition."

I sighed. "I just can't believe it. Twenty years of service didn't mean anything."

"That's not true, Josh. They mean something to the King, and to the people they've ministered to over that time. They certainly mean something to me."

"So you don't agree with the decision?"

He nodded his head, I gathered not in answer, but as he composed his answer. "I know your Mom and Dad, and I'm sure they didn't commit any so-called 'fireable offense.' Sometimes there doesn't need to be one. In this case, we were just told that this was 'the direction the church was taking.' Without any more facts, I can't say whether I agree with their decision or not. But knowing your parents the way I do, I'd have to say probably not."

He stood and tapped my shoulder. "You want the mow this time?"

It was an even trade-off. In the mow you missed what little breeze there was. But you also missed the sun. So I nodded.

We unloaded two more wagons, and the hay in the mow rose so that bales were hardly dropping off the elevator. It made things a little safer. Mike Baxter had nearly been decapitated one July afternoon when he got careless.

We took another break after the fourth load and downed some more lemonade. It was lukewarm at best by now, but it was still wet. Besides, Dave had once told me drinking an ice-cold beverage when you were really hot would give you a sore throat. I took his word for it. (I also concluded Erica better not drink ice-cold beverages, if you catch my drift.)

"Can I ask you something?" I said as I refilled my plastic cup.

"Sure."

"What do you make of this new 'direction' of the church?"

"How do you mean?"

"You haven't noticed any differences?"

"I've noticed, but I want to know how *you* mean."

"Clapping and whistling, for one thing. The casual approach. The songs we sing."

Dave nodded. "That's a tricky subject."

"I mean, I get that I'm at the far end of the spectrum," I said. "I like meaty hymns and melodic tunes, and this whole whistling thing was just too strange. But I also get that singing modern songs and clapping for God isn't opposed to Scripture."

"But . . . ?"

"But . . . it just feels wrong."

"Wrong or different?"

"Both. It just feels too casual, too modern. I don't know. I just wondered what your take was."

"My take," Dave said, pausing to drain his cup, "is that there are different strokes for different folks and there are doctrinal issues. And the things you mentioned sound more like different strokes."

I nodded.

"That being said, ideally you want to keep a balance, unless you've got a church where everybody wants all hymns or where the entire congregation prefers to whistle instead of sing."

"You think we're balanced?" I asked.

"I think we used to lean more toward the traditional, which is how most of the people in the congregation preferred it. Now, we lean more contemporary. Quite a bit, in fact."

"It's mostly the same people, isn't it?"

"Largely, and I'm not sure they prefer the changes. Time will tell."

We went back to unloading, me wondering where the line was between catering to the congregation and straying from the truth. Or between keeping balance at the expense of accuracy. Maybe the whole world was wondering.

We started to falter late in the fifth load and took another break before the last one. It took twice as long as it should have, and we were both beat by the time we finally finished. I was too exhausted to think about church anymore. Dave wasn't.

"How's the new Sunday school class?"

"The Young Adults Fellowship? Interesting."

"Good?"

"Not so much. It's not the subject matter that's interesting so much as the teacher-pupil interaction." I explained about our discussion from the day before, about when the rapture would come and who had been in *Star Trek* and who had been in *Star Wars* and what LeVar Burton and *Roots* had to do with anything.

He chuckled. "Let me know if you figure it out."

"You got a leaning one way or the other?" I asked.

"Pre-trib," he answered. "But every reason I give you, the mid-trib folks could give you just as many."

"What about post-trib?"

"They're just plain off the wall."

"That's what I say."

I waited while Dave wrote me a check, and then I headed back to Scotty's to shower and crawl in the freezer. Scotty and Dirk were out back, grilling burgers. They told me to hurry, and I did. I emerged from the shower clean but still sweating and joined them on the deck.

"You got a message by the way," Scotty said.

"Huh?"

"On the answering machine."

I nodded and, since Dirk was still tending the burgers, retreated inside to listen.

"Hi, this message is for Josh. Josh, this is Wendy from Nebraska Novelties. I've made a decision and I'm calling to offer you a job. I'll be in between nine and five tomorrow, so please give me a call. Thanks."

"Hmm," I said to myself. Then I went out and ate three hamburgers.

Chapter 8

"Write this on a scroll as something to be remembered . . ." Exodus 17:14

"Start it just layft of the hole and sneeze," Scotty said with an Irish accent, his best David Feherty[2] impersonation. I took his advice as he stepped out from behind my line, and aimed my putt a hair to the left of the hole ten feet in front of me. And at least a foot below me in elevation. As softly as possible, I tapped the ball.

It burned the left edge and rolled five feet by.

"That's still not deceased," Scotty said as he dropped down behind his ball, four feet away from par. I was now looking at double-bogey.

"It's a lousy pin placement for a Memorial Day," Dirk declared from my left as I circled the hole and placed a coin behind my ball. I picked it up and scanned its dimpled surface for dirt or any other impediment that could have affected its path. Nope, it was my sneezing.

"Tommy thinks he's setting the course for the U.S. Open sometimes," Dirk continued, without the Texan accent a guy born in Dallas should have. He had worked hard on it, he'd told me.

"Speaking of," I asked. "You ready for Sectionals?"

Dirk nodded. "Ready as I'll ever be. If I can keep from getting the yips."

"And don't lose your ball," Scotty said. "His old eyes struggle sometimes."

"That's what my caddy is supposed to be for," Dirk said as Scotty tapped in his par putt. I moved around to my ball.

"Where at again?" I asked.

"Auburn Hills, outside Detroit."

---

2 David Feherty is a well-known golf analyst famous for his Irish accent and colorful phrases.

I nodded. Dirk was a scratch golfer — meaning he generally shot par or better. That was at championship courses. At Prairie View, which was a mid-length municipal course, he considered par a bad score. He'd once shot a 26, he told me — ten under par. At forty-two, Dirk could play. Several times he'd attempted to qualify for the U.S. Open, one of the most prestigious golf tournaments in the world. He'd never yet made it. He had qualified for both the Texas Open and the Canadian Open, but failed to make the cut each time. Making a cut in a PGA Tour Event was still his lifelong goal. That and playing in the U.S. Open.

I figured my putt back up the hill had to follow the same path as the one down it, which was pretty straight. I aimed for the dead center of the cup and hit it firmly, knocking the ball in off the "backboard."

"That's the way to hit 'em," Dirk said. "Firm up the hill. Don't give 'em the chance to miss."

"Six?" Scotty asked.

I nodded and we all marked our scorecards.

"You're playing solid," Dirk said.

"I'm eleven over through six holes."

"It's hot," Dirk said. "You're grinding." He removed his cap and wiped the sweat from his brow. He was right, about the heat at least. It was early afternoon, and already approaching ninety degrees. We didn't mind. The previous week had been mostly rainy and cool, which killed my hours working at the course. Scotty and I had spent the time putting balls toward a glass on the carpet of Prairie View's small "clubhouse."

I had also spent the week reflecting, mostly on my conversation with Dave. He was right, of course. As long as the gospel was being preached and the doctrines of the church adhered to Scripture, the different strokes of singing (or whistling and clapping) or ripped jeans by worship leaders didn't really matter.

And yet, maybe they did. What was the purpose of congregational singing? Wasn't it to express worship to God? Didn't it then make sense that the way we corporately expressed that worship be a way that was most accessible to the most people — easy to sing tunes and words that were the most meaningful to the most number of people — assuming all was even and all the songs were equally truthful and biblically accurate? And what about that passage in Corinthians about outsiders seeing your behavior and thinking you were all crazy loons (rough translation)? I didn't know. So I asked Scotty and Dirk for their opinion as we trudged to the seventh hole, a par-five that doglegged around the only pond on the course.

"It's like the Masters," Dirk said. "In 2007, Zach Johnson laid up at every single par five. Never made an eagle that way, but he also didn't hit it in the water. Won the tournament. A few years later, Phil[3] hits a six iron off the pine straw, over the creek, within ten feet. Makes bird, wins the green jacket."

I frowned. "To each his own?"

"Not sure there is a right way," he answered. "One that's better than the other."

"Yeah, but Billy and Hootie[4] don't force you to lay up or go for it," Scotty said. "At church, they sort of tell you which club to hit."

"Okay, so they tell you six iron," Dirk said. "Maybe it's how you swing it. Draw, fade, punch. Maybe it's how much time you spend in the gym that determines how far you can hit it."

"But even Tiger in his heyday couldn't hit a six iron two-fifty over water," Scotty countered.

I was getting lost in the metaphor. "So what's the answer?"

"Maybe the club is the wrong analogy," Dirk said as we reached the tee. "Maybe it's more like when you show up at The Open Championship[5] — it could be a beautiful sunny day, or it could be cold and rainy, wind blowing forty miles an hour."

"And you've still got to find your way around the course," I said.

Dirk nodded. "Believe I have the honor?"

"You have the honor," Scotty muttered. Their competitions got a little fierce. "There's a problem with your wind and rain metaphor, though," he said as Dirk took a practice swing.

---

[3] Phil Mickelson is a professional golfer and three-times Masters champion.

[4] William "Billie" Payne (2006-present) and William "Hootie" Johnson (1998-2006) are chairmen of the Augusta National Golf Club.

[5] The Open Championship, also known as "The Open" or "The British Open," is the oldest of the four major championships in men's professional golf.

"Yeah, what's that?"

"European golfers get to play in wind and rain all the time, so they're more used to it."

"Meaning?"

"Meaning the weather isn't an equalizer in golf. It gives certain people an advantage and puts others at a disadvantage."

"May not be fair," Dirk said, stepping up to his ball. "But you still have to tee it up." He swung and launched a drive that started toward the water but then faded back toward the center of the fairway. Perfect.

"You're saying suck it up and whistle?" I asked.

Dirk shook his head. "No, the whistling's ridiculous."

I was thoroughly confused and instead of setting myself up for another golf metaphor, I grabbed my driver and waited for Scotty to hit. His drive split the fairway as well, and I swapped my driver for a six iron. I decided to table the discussion on corporate worship and focus on making a good golf score. And to that end, maybe Dirk's metaphor could help after all. I was slicing drives terribly, and figured three six irons might equal a drive and two "rescue" shots.

It didn't. I bogeyed the hole while Scotty and Dirk both birdied it. The two-shot differential was pretty standard.

We finished the last two holes and tallied our scores. Dirk had edged Scotty by three strokes, and this called for a rematch. I had lost by twenty-one, but agreed to another nine holes.

I made a rather impressive — and shocking — birdie on the first hole to take an early lead. I then shanked my drive on the second hole into the weeds, got stuck in a greenside bunker, and three-putted. It had been great while it lasted.

After four holes, by which time I was three strokes behind both Dirk and Scotty, I posed another question. "What'd you think about what Teasdale said yesterday?"

"You'd have to be a little more specific," Dirk said.

"About a new way of reaching a new generation?"

Dirk frowned, perhaps trying to remember. Scotty shrugged. The sermon, which had been a little disjointed, had been about recognizing that just as people had different love languages and different ways of learning, they also had different ways of receiving God's love. Thus, our methods of witnessing to non-believers and of ministering to everyone needed to vary, depending on how they would best receive it. Specifically, in the twenty-first century, that meant adapting our methods to reach the current generation.

I wasn't sure about it. I mean, in principle, I understood where he was coming from. But why did I also hear alarm bells, albeit very quietly, in the background? I said as much to Dirk and Scotty as we played the fourth hole.

"Didn't Paul write about being like the Jews to win the Jews and like the Gentiles to win the Gentiles and so forth?" Dirk asked.

"Yeah, but when does adapting to the culture cross the line and become changing the truth?"

"Right around the puckering phase," Scotty said.

"There's nothing wrong with whistling," Dirk said.

"I thought you said it was ridiculous."

"I did. And it is. But it's not heretical."

"But doesn't all this tie together? Singing all 'contemporary' songs, casual dress, a message on doing things differently?"

The conversation lulled while Dirk sized up a chip and Scotty tended the flagstick. Dirk's chip rolled an inch wide of the hole and stopped a foot beyond it.

"Maybe it's like when they Tigerized Augusta," Dirk said as he walked to mark his ball. He thought better of it and just tapped it into the hole. "A lot of people didn't like the changes."

I squinted, trying to figure this one out.

"It's still the greatest course in the world," Dirk said. "Still par 72, still a fair but hard test of golf. You still have the dogwoods and azaleas, McKenzie Bunker, Amen Corner, Magnolia Drive."

"So you're saying that maybe my negativity is just because it's different than it used to be, not because it's wrong?" I asked, then whacked my ball. I had made an eight on the last hole and didn't really care about score anymore.

"I'm saying," Dirk said, "if I may play Bones[6] and call off a driver off the deck, that maybe your problem with church isn't so much because it violates what you believe, but because it's different than it used to be . . . when your parents were here."

Scotty looked up just before striking his putt. He glanced from me to Dirk, then back, apparently expecting that Dirk's comment had struck a nerve. Truth be told, it had, but maybe a nerve that needed to be struck.

"Hmm."

"Not saying it's the case," Dirk said. "Just that it might be."

"Yeah," I said. I had a lot more to think about.

"So answer this," Scotty said after holing out. "When's the rapture come? Pre-trib, mid-trib, post-trib, or is the tribulation all symbolic?"

I smiled as I finished making a mess of the fourth hole. Sunday school had been more of the same. Petey had started by chastising the class for getting off base the week before. Then he had launched into a lecture on the first four churches admonished in Revelation 2 and 3. He'd gotten to the church in Smyrna before the rapture discussion started again. Petey's class had done homework and showed up with ammunition, and it had gotten a little heated.

"It's like a great golfer who's been struggling," Dirk said. "Take Tiger."

"He's comparing the rapture to Tiger?" Scotty asked me as he placed the flag back in the hole. I shrugged.

"Hear me out," Dirk said. "Tiger's still got game, and if he can figure out his swing, stay healthy, he can still be a force on the tour. And at his level as a championship golfer, it could be the slightest little tweak one day on the range. Same for Phil or any of the guys who are struggling."

"So it could be anytime?"

Dirk nodded.

"Sounds pre-trib to me," I said.

"At the same time, however, you could see signs that it's coming. He starts hitting more good shots, playing more consistently. You know it's

---

[6] Jim "Bones" Mackay is professional golfer Phil Mickelson's long-time caddy.

just a matter of time, but you still don't know which session with his coach or which adjustment is going to be the one."

Scotty shook his head. "I think I see why they've never asked you to teach Sunday school."

I played the final five holes in just two over par, which was one of my better stretches of golf. I spent much of the time walking to my ball thinking about what Dirk had said, weighing whether my frustrations with Morgan Bible were a result of the new "direction" the church had taken or of their having taken a different direction at all. And if those were actually two different things. Sometimes, I still insisted to myself, there was only one way to do the right thing, and any other way was less than right. But was this one of those times or not?

As my golfing heated up, my thoughts on spiritual matters cooled off. I hit a great shot from behind the final green and drained a ten-foot putt to save par, congratulated Scotty for the birdie that had given him a one-stroke victory over Dirk on the second nine (Dirk quickly reminded him that he had won the overall day by two) and joined them both for a post-game drink at the bar. Two Pepsis and a coffee. Dirk drank coffee all the time, no matter the temperature.

Then we headed back to their place — and still mine for a few more days — for a Memorial Day barbecue. Angus steaks, corn on the cob, and baked beans. I showered downstairs and joined Dirk on the deck while he primed the grill. The sun was still hot, but soon would be sinking behind the giant pin oak near the corner of the property. Not a moment too soon.

Dirk and I chatted for a few minutes about our golf games and U.S. Open qualifying, and then he headed inside to get some seasoning for the steaks. I leaned against the deck and pulled Erica's postcard from my pocket.

That's right, it had come. Addressed as follows:

Josh Roosevelt
c/o Scotty Austin
Address unknown in . . .
Morgan, Nebraska 68301

A credit to the mailman, it had found its mark. That was nothing, Dirk said. His cousin delivered mail in Texas and got all sorts of crazy addresses. "Family of five on Richland Street with twin girls" was the best. "Brown and white house with red truck in front" was a close second.

Anyhow, the postcard. You may think it's lame to carry around in my pocket a postcard from a girl I'd met twice. But cool guys on TV always have folded up pictures of girlfriends and daughters and the one that got away in their wallets. I figured this was close. And besides, even though I'd read it dozens of times, it still caused my heart to race.

The image on the front of the postcard was of a row of snow-covered mountains, with the town of Estes Park in the foreground. I admired it for a full two seconds before flipping it over to read Erica's note:

Josh,

We are having a blast. I wish you could have been here this morning to see the elk behind our cabin. He couldn't have been more than twenty feet from the deck, and he was HUGE. Twelve-pointer, if you care. You probably don't, but it goes to hugeness. We've been hitting all the souvenir shops, buying junk we don't really need and tomorrow . . . You don't care about that. We went to a Big Red shop yesterday. They still don't like us much out here. I saw it as a bastion of light in a citadel of evil, but that's just me. But I am running out of space. I'm taking a million pictures. I'll have to show you when I get back, especially the bighorns in the canyon. Incredible. Now to find a post office. And a stamp. –Erica

I sighed as I read it again. My mind locked onto phrases like "I wish you could have been here" and "I'll have to show you when I get back." Plus there was something about the "E" in Erica, a little bit of a swoosh to it, a flair, perhaps. And the entire nature of the note, mostly about nothing, was so casual and comfortable, as if we were the best of friends already.

I sighed again as I put the postcard back into my pocket. Maybe that was it. Maybe she saw me as just as a friend. But unless she was making the effort to send postcards to all of her friends and was planning a little vacation picture soirée, I rated pretty high on the list. And good friend was a step closer to betrothed than friend was, right?

"You okay?" Dirk asked.

"Hmm? Yeah."

"He's dreaming about Erica again," Scotty said, following his dad onto the deck. He pulled a T-shirt over his wet hair, which he then tousled with his hand and covered with his LSU baseball cap. Backwards, of course.

"You want my advice?" Dirk asked.

I shrugged. "Why not?"

"Relationships are like a golf tournament, Josh," Dirk said, brushing his own spice mix onto the steaks. "You can't win the Masters on Thursday, but you can lose it if you pump four balls into Rae's Creek."

"You know, Dad, these golf metaphors would work a lot better if there was any way to relate them to real life."

Dirk just looked at his son as he continued brushing.

"What's the relational equivalent to hitting four balls into the creek?" I asked.

"You've seen this girl, what, twice?"

I nodded.

"Okay, so maybe you're at even par through the front nine," Dirk said. "First time at the Masters. You're feeling your oats, think this isn't so hard, and decide to go at the pin on twelve. Just as you swing, the wind picks up, and slams your ball into the water."

I shook my head.

"Smart play," Dirk continued, "is to play to the center of the green, take your two-putt par, and get out of there."

"Meaning?"

"Don't try to force the relationship. Let it come to you."

"Yeah, but what if while I'm biding my time she falls for some other guy?"

"Don't look at the leaderboard yet. It's still Thursday. Nobody wins the tournament on Thursday."

Scotty shook his head and Dirk turned to flip the steaks. I had to move out soon, I realized, or my entire philosophy of life—from God to girls—would be based on the game of golf.

The steaks were delicious. The corn and beans weren't bad either. The sun was behind the pin oak and a gentle breeze made the evening quite pleasant.

"So tell me about this girl," Dirk said after refilling all of our drinks. "Erica . . . I can't picture her."

"Rosie doesn't have that problem."

"What's she look like?"

I tried to describe her. I failed miserably. A toddler with finger paint trying to replicate the *Mona Lisa*.

Dirk shook his head. "Still doesn't ring a bell. She sounds cute."

"That's an understatement," I said.

"Scale of one to ten?"

"Ten."

He looked to Scotty, who stuck a bite of steak in his mouth. "Eight-five." He swallowed. "Maybe nine. She's cute."

"Eight-five?" I asked.

Scotty nodded.

"Come on, she's the best-looking girl I've ever seen."

"No. She's the best-looking girl you've ever seen in person. Remember that teenage chick on the Brookline three-story?"

"Oh yeah, with the huge winding staircase?"

"And that fireplace you liked."

"Oh yeah. Yeah, she was pretty cute."

Dirk set down his second cob of corn. "What are you two talking about?"

"*This Old House*," Scotty answered, reaching for his glass.

"You have the houses and homeowners memorized?"

We nodded.

"She was the homeowner's daughter," Scotty said, "and the cutest girl, we're pretty sure, in the world."

"I don't know," I said. "I think it's a tie."

"That girl was perfect," Scotty said.

"So's Erica."

"Her ears are a little small."

"I think they're cute."

"She's got a small nose too."

"It's called a button nose, widely acknowledged as an attractive feature on a female."

"How are her teeth?"

"You haven't seen them?"

"Seen, sure. Looked, no."

"They're like Regis Philbin's."

"What about her ankles?"

"What?" Dirk asked.

"I haven't seen her ankles. Not really."

Scotty smirked.

I shook my head. "You haven't seen . . . what's her name?"

"Alexis, and yes I have."

"When?"

"The hardwood floors."

"Oh. And they were perfect too, weren't they?"

Scotty nodded.

"You two are something else, you know that?" Dirk said. He sawed off a bite of his steak, chewed and swallowed, and washed it down with some iced tea. "So this one's special, huh?"

"I hope so," I said. "Morgan's not a real big town; I don't have a lot of other prospects."

"That what this is, you afraid you're running out of holes to make a Sunday charge?"

I shrugged. "Not running out of time," I said. "There just aren't that many birdie holes on this course."

Scotty shook his head and sat back. "You're getting as bad as him now."

I shrugged again.

"So Morgan going to be it for you?" Dirk asked.

"I don't know. I don't know much of anything right now."

"Welcome to adulthood," Dirk said.

"Go ahead, Dad. Tell him how figuring out your career plan is like Sunday in a major."

Dirk furrowed his brow. And his chin. "I was going to say more like reading the tenth green at Augusta, which is to say, impossible. Especially in the shadows. But that's not very encouraging."

"That's okay. It's only Thursday in that department too."

Dirk nodded, pointing at me with his knife before turning it back to his steak.

"Besides, Morgan's not a bad town," Scotty said. "There're quite a few cute girls. Even at church."

I tilted my head back and forth. It depended on the day. But then again, Scotty had it easy. He's better looking than me—I'm not bad, mind you, especially on the days when my hair decides not to be stupid—but Scotty's got the ruggedly handsome look all girls seem to crave, and he's got natural charisma and charm. I mean, Scotty's never been so nervous that he called up a date and said, "Hi, Josh, it's Tammy," or suddenly swatted at a fly in front of Lisa Browning and knocked his baseball cap off his head and across the floor in the process. Scotty's throat doesn't tighten up around cute girls and his brain doesn't suddenly forget to insert vowels, spaces, and punctuation in his sentences. Scotty is, by nature, cool. I'm not exactly those guys on *The Big Bang Theory*, but I'm not George Clooney either.

Dirk sat back. "If that's true, that there's so many girls in Morgan, how come you haven't had a date since you were sixteen?"

Scotty shrugged. "Not interested."

"Should I be worried, Son?"

"Girls are too high maintenance. I don't need the aggravation."

"So at twenty you've decided to stay single for life?"

"Not necessarily. But I'm not going to waste my time until I'm serious about it. I've got better things to do."

"Right," I said. "Like watching *Independence Day*."

"Yeah," Scotty said. "Like that."

It was a Memorial Day tradition, one that had started five years ago when, as idiots, we'd confused Independence Day for Memorial Day—something about the Fourth of July being its own holiday and thus Independence Day must be the one in May. It was really quite pathetic and embarrassing. The haze only lasted until the shadow crept over the moon, and then we realized our mistake. Oh well, we were already watching the movie. And why not every Memorial Day for the next five years?

So we finished dinner, helped Dirk clean up, and settled down in the living room to watch Will Smith and Jeff Goldblum save the planet.

And of course, they both got the girl.

Chapter 9

"How long will you lie there, you sluggard? When will you get up from your sleep?" Proverbs 6:9

Much to my chagrin, Erica did not come into Nebraska Novelties to order a scoop of rocky road ice cream, show me pictures of elk mid-bugle, and flirt.

Otherwise, my new career was a success. By Friday afternoon, four days in, I felt like a pro. I had messed up a couple of drinks and weighed candy I should have just scanned. And the waffle cone maker was still a mystery to me. But those were minor snags in an otherwise smooth learning curve.

I got off at four on Friday, which didn't please my new coworker Sydney. She was tall, thin, and very white, which she made up for with an abundance of tattoos and wild, almost orange hair. Her tats and tresses matched her personality, which was to say, dark and a little unusual. She'd spent the better part of the day lamenting a recent breakup, and I was glad to be free of her complaints as I hurried home—to my home. I was meeting the landlord to get my key and do the walkthrough of the property, after which it would be mine.

I had already contacted the necessary utilities—the power company, the phone company, and Morgan's only DSL provider. I had debated whether or not to have Internet, but decided in this day and age, it really wasn't an option. I would be making do with broadcast TV, which supposedly got pretty good reception in the apartment. Me and my rabbit ears would see, but I had a feeling I'd be spending a lot of time at Scotty's come Saturdays and Sundays in the fall.

I took my time during the inspection, making sure I didn't get nickel-and-dimed later for scratches and dents and tears that weren't my fault. By five o'clock, I had the key to my first apartment.

Dirk took Scotty and me out to dinner to celebrate. We dined at the Morgan Family Restaurant, our waitress one Cassandra May Larson. Since it was a special occasion and since our waitress sort of talked us into it, we had pie for dessert. Every small town restaurant claims to have the world's best pie, but only the Morgan Family Restaurant is accurate in that claim.

"You know, home-owning is a wonderful thing," Dirk said. "But if you can find the right place, renting is the way to go." He stabbed down on a bite of peach pie and lifted it into the air. "And don't let all those equity and investment people tell you otherwise," he said before eating.

I looked to Scotty, who shrugged. We both ate our pie too.

Dirk continued. "They tell you about how you're just throwing your money away when you rent, whereas with a home you're building equity. But those people forget that tiny little thing called interest. You end up paying three times as much money as the house cost, which isn't very frugal either. Not to mention the costs of repairs and upkeep, all the utilities that are now on you, landscaping, and so on."

"Were you scorned by a mortgage once?" I asked.

"No, he's from Texas," Scotty said. "By nature he's just one step from secession all the time."

Dirk cut off another bite of pie, this time topped with ice cream. "But seriously, Josh. Your first home is a big deal, rented or bought. Congrats."

"Thanks."

"And just remember, you've always got a place if you need one."

I looked down at my pie because I was getting a touch emotional. Dirk had always sort of been like an uncle to me. Now, with the folks two states away, he and his crazy golf advice were almost like a second father. Perhaps, I realized, that had been the case all along.

Like a man, I pulled it together in a hurry. "I appreciate that, Dirk. And thank you." I glanced at Scotty and back. "I'd have been sunk without you guys. Living in my Escort or something."

"Or the Larson's stable," Scotty said.

Dirk huffed. "If they hadn't ridden your dad out of town on a rail, you wouldn't have been in this mess to begin with."

"Please," Scotty said. "Let's not get into this again. I can't take any more religious golf metaphors."

"Amen," I said.

"Fine. Fire Stevie Williams[7]. See where it gets you."

We finished our pie, left our waitress a huge tip, and headed back to our joint house one last time.

Saturday morning we were up early. Between my hatchback Escort and Scotty's Blazer, we managed to get all of my stuff over to the apartment in one trip. We finished unloading by ten and headed to Lincoln for furniture. I'd bought a bed over Memorial Day weekend, and had scheduled to have it delivered later that afternoon. I'd also bought a small glider at a garage sale and had a few end tables and plastic drawer organizers from my days at Vernon-Bedford. Everything else still needed to be purchased.

We hit several furniture stores in Lincoln before deciding to just run to Walmart instead. I got a kitchen table and chairs on sale and a futon instead of a couch. I also bought a cheap computer desk and a small rolling cart that would serve as my entertainment center. My TV was a twenty-year-old beast of a box, not one of those slick flat screens that I continually broke the Tenth Commandment over. It didn't need much space width-wise, but it did need a sturdy base. The cart would provide that and room for my meager collection of DVDs.

We took the scenic route home, Scotty's Blazer weighted down with boxes of furniture. We hit a few garage sales in and around Hickman, Panama, and Adams before returning to my apartment. I scored a coffee table and a small dresser for the bedroom. The dresser would never fit into Scotty's Blazer with everything else, so after unloading everything, Scotty and I waited around for the folks from Sears while Dirk returned to get the dresser.

"It's quaint," Scotty said, messing with the rabbit ears on my TV.

---

[7] Steve Williams caddied for professional golfer Tiger Woods from 1999 until he was fired in 2011.

"It's small," I said, noting all the boxes and furniture that still had to be unpacked and arranged.

"I can get you Channel 7 but not Channel 8," Scotty said.

I frowned.

"They're both ABC."

"Channel 8 is local."

"Omaha isn't exactly in the panhandle."

"Still."

"Well, I can get you Channel 8 but then you lose CBS."

"Which CBS?"

"All CBS's. Grand Island, Lincoln, Omaha."

"I need CBS."

"I know."

"*NCIS* is on CBS."

"I know."

"And SEC football."

He nodded.

"I guess I can do without the local news."

"I thought you might."

Scotty stepped away from the rabbit ears, and immediately the TV fuzzed. Super.

The doorbell rang, and I admitted the Sears delivery guys. My door opens into a little square entryway. Straight ahead is a small alcove with the washer, dryer, furnace, and hot water heater. To get to the kitchen, you have to make a sharp right through a doorway. This is difficult carrying a queen-sized box spring and mattress. We let the delivery guys handle it, which would have been funny if the guy who couldn't keep his pants up wouldn't have kept cussing.

"Dude, why'd you need a queen?" Scotty asked.

"Someday," I said, "the missus and I will probably prefer to sleep in the same bed. Since I'm buying now . . ."

"Does Erica know you're already buying a bed for her? That's very *Apple Dumpling Gang*."

"I'm just being practical."

"Well did you remember sheets and comforters, Mr. Practical?"

Gulp.

So once the Sears guys finally got my bed set up and Dirk returned with the dresser, we set out for Lincoln to buy bedding. First we stopped to see if Dirk had any extra sheets and blankets, but men from Texas aren't known to keep a spare set of queen sheets on hand.

Dirk and Scotty had both offered to go, but I didn't trust either of them to buy my bedding, or to unpack while I went. So we were a threesome again.

It was dinnertime by the time we found everything I needed. Then Scotty reminded me that I had been complaining about my pillow the last several nights and wanted a new one. I spent five minutes making my selection, and then we spent another ten looking for a pillowcase before Scotty noticed that pillowcases were included with the rest of the bedding.

"We need a woman," Dirk mumbled as we strode to the checkouts.

"Rosie's working on it."

I nodded.

Sure that we had purchased anything and everything required for a good night's sleep, we decided to get something to eat. We had been working through the day, snacking on junk instead of eating lunch, and were starved. I insisted on paying, as a thank you. They said I was spending all my money already, and they were right, but what was a little more? We debated long and hard between Arby's and Runza, settled on Runza, and ate while thunderstorms that had been building all day finally unleashed.

Runzas are another Nebraska thing. Essentially, they're rectangular bread pockets filled with beef and cabbage. I learned in middle school that you couldn't really taste the cabbage, and went from hating the things to loving them. And don't tell Mom, but the real thing from Runza are just a little better than the homemade variety.

Before heading home, we stopped at Walmart yet again. I didn't own a fan and determined that without air conditioning in my apartment, it might be a good investment. Finally we returned home to unpack. Dirk wanted to get in a couple practice rounds in the morning before his and

Scotty's flight to Detroit, so they cut out fairly early. That was okay; I'd rather put stuff away myself than have to tell them where to put everything. I thanked them profusely for everything, wished Dirk the best of luck at Sectionals, and got busy.

It was midnight before I knew it. Not feeling tired, I made instant coffee in the microwave and then, because it was so hot, drank it in front of my new fan. It gave me the energy to keep going, and by one-thirty, just after another batch of storms rolled through, I had enough put away that the end was in sight. And at least all of the decisions on where things went had been made.

I went to bed, my window open, fan blowing directly on me. It was still hot and muggy, and I ended up kicking all of my newly purchased linens onto the floor and sleeping on top of the bare mattress.

I realized soon after waking that I had not yet unpacked my alarm clock. But I could tell from the bright light streaming in through my window that Sunday was well underway. I got up, staggered around like I had a hangover — not that I know firsthand what a hangover is like — until I found my wall clock. It was 9:22.

If I hurried and skipped breakfast, I could make it for Sunday school. I pictured Petey and his paisley tie, lecturing us on the final three churches, and decided to skip. At Vernon-Bedford, we got a certain number of chapel skips per semester before being assigned extra homework — spiritual detention. Over-skippers were also considered to have backslidden.

But this was not Vernon-Bedford, and one week of not standing with my hands in my pockets pining for hymns or just a few familiar notes would not kill me. To make up, I decided to whistle a few bars in the shower. It was the *Andy Griffith* theme, but still.

My lone regret in not making it to church was not seeing Erica. It had been sixteen days since our short little interlude in the candy aisle at Wieskamps'. I still read her postcard every day, and would have pinned it to my refrigerator (well, magneted technically) except I knew it would just lead to ceaseless mocking.

But I thought about the advice I had been given, to take it slow and pray and not hit balls into Rae's Creek on Thursday. (I also thought about how I'd hate to have to look over her boyfriend to see those elk pictures.) Besides, I had a plan. Next Saturday, MBC was putting on a pizza party for high school and college students. I hoped that it would also appeal to brunettes currently in the in-between stage.

Bolstered by the thought of seeing Erica there — and possibly spending some quality time with her — I resolved not to worry about missing church. I prayed as I showered and dressed, and for good measure, I sang a quiet, apartment appropriate version of "Victory in Jesus" while I prepared to scramble some eggs for my brunch. My mother didn't raise a complete good-for-nothing. I knew how to make eggs and pancakes and French toast, cook rice and noodles, and brown hamburger or sear chicken or steak. I could fend for myself.

In theory.

But I had neglected to buy groceries for my new pad. So I set out for Wieskamps', as Don & Flo's wasn't open Sunday mornings. Few places in Morgan were. A lot of establishments didn't open at all on Sundays. But fortunately for me, Wieskamps' sold milk, eggs, bread, and a few other necessities. I bought enough to get me through the day, and returned home to a breakfast that had become lunch.

Finished, I got to work putting more stuff away. I had just started when my doorbell rang. It was Cassie.

"Hey," I said. "You come to check out my new digs?"

"I did." She entered and stood in the kitchen, looking around. She turned to me. "You weren't in church today."

"I was not."

"You didn't transfer to True Way, did you?"

"I attended Bedside Baptist. Alarm clock failure."

"Um-hmm."

"Honest. You guys were almost done with your whistling and stamping by the time I woke up."

Cassie nodded, perhaps not yet convinced. "You and Scotty left me all alone with the wrath of Petey."

"Was it bad?"

"A ten-minute lecture on staying on topic and maintaining proper decorum in class," she answered. "He insists we raise our hands before we speak now."

"Power went right to his head," I said. "You think Snotty Sandra will have her husband excommunicate us if we stop going?"

"And what, try to enter the adult class without a signed permission slip? No way."

I showed Cassie the apartment. That took all of twenty seconds. We ended up on the balcony, surveying the town. It was hot again, and getting hotter. And summer hadn't even officially started.

"I miss anything in church?" I asked. "Any humming or yodeling or anything?"

"We sang 'The Old Rugged Cross,'" Cassie said. "During communion."

"Of course." It was one of my favorite hymns.

She winced. "They did add some funny little bridge to it. Didn't quite fit."

I shook my head. It was a shame.

"And we had some special music," she said.

"Mm, what's that? Mrs. Roberts' class?" They were notorious. Mrs. Roberts was a dear old woman who had taught the preschool Sunday school class forever. But she insisted on having her class sing in church, and like all kids, they either got stage fright and stood there like stones, or got stage fright and sang at the top of their lungs and off key. Usually a lot more stones. Which meant we really got a solo from Mrs. Roberts, who didn't have the most angelic voice to begin with.

"Nope," Cassie answered while I envisioned the last time they had treated us. "A solo artist."

"Not that traveling gypsy guy?"

"Erica Chamberlain."

I turned to read Cassie's face. She never lied, but occasionally teased, and didn't hide it well when she did. She wasn't hiding anything.

"Erica sang special music?"

"Yeah, and she was good. We applauded when she was done. Even the old people who don't like to clap in church applauded."

Stupid hiding alarm clock.

"Then she asked about you."

"What?"

"In Sunday school."

"You mean the Young Adults Fellowship?"

"Before it, actually, as we're not allowed to have personal discussions during class."

"Erica asked about me?"

"She did."

"You're jerking my chain."

"I'm not."

"What'd she say?"

"She asked where you were. Said she had a bunch of photos from her vacation she wanted to show you, and she wanted to know if you got her postcard."

My deck was only one story off the ground, not high enough to do any real damage in a fall, or I would have jumped.

"I have a theory," Cassie said.

I was lost in a painful reverie, and she had to repeat herself.

"What's that?" I asked.

"Had you really been intent on coming to church, you would have remembered to find and set your alarm clock last night."

"Since when are you a psychiatrist?"

She shrugged.

"I didn't mean to skip, Cass."

"If you say so."

"I do."

"Okay."

This was the same girl who, at the age of seven, tattled to my mother because I didn't have my eyes closed during the benediction. Never mind how she knew that, unless her judgmental eyes were also open. It was okay, though. With my folks gone, somebody needed to look after me.

"So you need some help unpacking?" Cassie asked, turning back to look into the living room. Slash dining room. Slash kitchen. "I'm sorry I couldn't make it yesterday."

"We could have used you picking out bedding."

"Oh?"

"Did you know pillowcases are included with bed sheets?"

"Everyone knows that."

"Like I said, we could have used you."

"Well, I'm here now. Put me to work."

"Are you sure? I mean, I can handle it if you have something else to do."

"Would I be here if I did?"

"I'm too tired to banter," I said. "Sure."

"Hm, funny. I'd think you'd be wide awake after all the sleep you got last night."

"Cute."

Cassie smirked. "The truth is, my folks are having dinner with the de Vries, so I don't have anywhere to go."

"So I'm your backup plan?"

"Well, with Scotty on his way to Michigan . . ."

"You're just full of funnies today."

She grinned, ear to ear, dimples in her round cheeks. "Where do we start?"

"I can't believe she sang this morning," I said.

"Like a jaybird."

We started with my alarm clock.

Chapter 10

"Similarly, if anyone competes as an athlete . . ." II Timothy 2:5

The week went by quickly. By Tuesday, Wendy trusted me to open the store by myself. Taking heed lest I fall, I still was confident that I had it down. Except for that pesky waffle cone maker. Sydney, who proved to be a better dresser than at first, was also much friendlier and more helpful when she wasn't moping about boyfriends lost. By the end of my second week at Nebraska Novelties, I had come to consider her a friend. A strange, tattooed, once-scorned-by-a-guy-named-Keegan friend, but a friend nonetheless.

Dirk failed to qualify for the U.S. Open. It was close, but out of thousands, he just missed the final cut. There was always next year.

I didn't see Cassie, as she was working days at D&N (a small company that made benches and had for some reason chosen Morgan as its home) and most nights and Saturday morning at the restaurant. She claimed it was just a bad week, but I was afraid she was killing herself for the sake of her dream.

I also didn't see Erica. I went grocery shopping, banked in person, bought gas for my Escort, and went for two evening walks downtown. I did everything short of hanging out by the curb in front of her house. As Saturday approached, I just hoped she'd show up at church with all the other young adults for some pizza.

Saturday was the nicest day in weeks—pure blue sky, no haze or humidity, no rain, no oppressive heat. A number of years back, the good people of MBC had had the good sense to erect a basketball hoop in the corner of the church parking lot. Scotty and I went a little early to shoot around. Mostly he shot. Good form dictates that when a guy makes a shot, you "give him his change" and let him shoot again. With Scotty, the other guy could quickly go broke.

After half a dozen makes in a row, I turned over my shoulder and saw Pastor Curtis Teasdale ambling our way from the parsonage. "This is the day the Lord has made," he said, taking a deep breath of summer air. "Isn't it great how we can glorify God with simple things like playing basketball?"

I didn't know what to say. There were certain people who spiritualized everything. They generally annoyed me. Sure what they said was usually true—although I wasn't sure how glorifying Scotty's draining jumpers and my change-making were—but it just felt unnatural. Almost like they were forcing spirituality down my throat. And it was annoying. Then again, Teasdale probably could have said "Go Big Red!" and I would have found it annoying.

Scotty looked at him for a moment, then shot. Swish.

Teasdale eyed me as Scotty actually missed his follow-up and I grabbed the rebound. I dribbled out to what I considered three-point range.

"I don't think we've met," Teasdale said.

I hoisted a shot that drew iron but missed, caroming right to Scotty.

"Pastor Curtis Teasdale," he said, extending his hand.

"Josh Roosevelt," I answered, shaking his hand and studying his eyes. I so wanted to add, "son of Reverend Gary Roosevelt," but I restrained myself.

To Teasdale's credit, if he recognized the name, he didn't say anything. "Well it's nice to meet you, Josh."

"Nice to meet you too." Like I said before, my mother raised me right.

Teasdale stood there for a few minutes, looking awkward. When Mike Baxter arrived, Teasdale went inside and the three of us started a game of 21. Mike had been an All-Conference pitcher for dear old Morgan High and an all-around decent athlete, so I was out of my league. I had no chance of scoring against both of them, so I focused on my defense when I teamed up with either Mike or Scotty to stop Scotty or Mike. I accomplished little more than working up a sweat.

People began to arrive, some of them heading inside and the rest joining us. Our game went from three to five, and when we had six, we broke up into teams for a game of three-on-three. Scotty and Damon Harris — one of only two known black residents of Morgan, along with his mother — were captains, and Scotty picked me first. Aside from Mike, I was probably the best remaining candidate. But Scotty would have picked me if LeBron and Steph Curry had been available.

We had an even game, and by the time it was finished, there was a small crowd of people watching or waiting to get into the next game. We had enough people for a full five-on-five, so we held a quick draft and started again. I was teamed up with Scotty, Brett Baker, some guy named Mark who I'd never met, and the obligatory girl, Cora de Vries. Having been playing for over half an hour, I was somewhat winded. And yet, I ended up guarding Damon, who could blow by me when I was full of wind. He made me look foolish several times, the last of which actually left me sprawled on the pavement.

"You all right, man?" Damon asked, his words blending into one.

"Just broke both my ankles is all," I said, taking his hand and getting back to my feet.

"You want to pick your lingerie off the deck?" Scotty said with a glare.

"You want to guard him?" I asked.

I turned back to Damon as Scotty bounced him the ball (we were playing "make it, take it") and saw a blip of pink over his shoulder. It was a cap-sleeved shirt, on top of denim shorts. Dark brown hair alighted gently on the shoulders.

Erica.

She was coming our way.

I nearly slapped the pavement[8] as I got in Damon's grill and forced him to pass the ball to Geoff de Boer. Geoff took a jumper, missed, and as a dozen hands reached for the rebound, Damon swooped in, grabbed it, and blew past me toward the hoop. I wasn't about to get schooled again, not

---

[8] Basketball players, most notably those from Duke University, sometimes slap the floor with both palms to inspire the defense and fire up the crowd.

with my woman watching. I took two steps, guessed, and jumped as high as my white body would take me. Damon's black body went a little higher, but I had inches in height and thus wingspan and reached the ball just after it rolled off his fingers.

My testosterone took over. I yelled and instead of just tipping the ball away, swatted it like the Lady Huskers do in the Devaney Center.

Our joint momentum took Damon and me both to the ground, tumbling over each other as the basketball rolled into the grass and down into a culvert.

"Nice block," Damon said as I helped him up this time. He was immediately back onto the court, ready for action. I slapped Scotty's fingers and casually looked to see if Erica had seen my impressive feat.

She was gone, headed back toward church, as was most of the group. Awesome.

Pastor Teasdale appeared on the fringe and told us it was time to begin. Five minutes later, he warned us again, and we decided the next team to score would win. After Scotty missed a contested shot, Damon went past me like I was standing still and floated a little runner off the backboard for the winning score. I could barely breathe as we trudged inside for pizza.

However, we were in for a video first, Teasdale announced as we filed in.

"All I can say is this had better not be on abstinence," Tim Harte said.

"You not abstaining?" Mark asked.

"It's all I ever hear — abstinence, purity, no sex till marriage."

"What do you expect, Don Juan?" Scotty asked. "You're nineteen."

"But I've been hearing it since I was twelve. The point's made. One more lecture isn't going to make me suddenly decide not to sleep with my girlfriend."

"Does your girlfriend know about this?" Mark asked.

"Hypothetically speaking."

"So there is no girlfriend," Cora said. "You're dismissed from the abstinence video."

The video was not on abstinence. I wish it had been. Instead it was a Christian comedian who wasn't very comedic. After five minutes — of what turned out to be twenty-three, Tim timed it—I gave up and scanned the room for Erica. The lighting was low but I saw her, sitting on the far side. Alone. She looked like she could use an arm around her shoulder. Then I looked at my sweaty arm, and determined that playing basketball for an hour maybe hadn't been such a great idea.

When the video was mercifully finished, Teasdale got up to talk. I nudged Damon, who was pretending to be asleep—or maybe was asleep—just before the lights came on.

"Huh? Oh, thanks, man."

I nodded.

"I want to thank all of you for coming," Teasdale said. "Even those who were late." He looked at the basketball group. I think he was just joking. I think.

"You know, when you think about it, the entire purpose of our life is to praise. And we don't have to be singing songs or reading our Bible to praise God. We can also praise him with our fellowship, by being together corporately. And that's what tonight is about. But we can't fellowship if we don't know one another, so before we eat and play, I'd like to take a few minutes and have everyone get to know each other. I see some faces I don't recognize, and I'm sure that's the case for you. So what I'd like you to do is get into groups of three or four—try to find someone you don't know and include them in your group. And what I want is for you to find out what's on each other's hearts and spend a few minutes praying together. What better way to get to know each other than by talking to the Father, right? Fellowshipping together, and with Him?"

Well, in theory. But asking people, some of whom didn't know each other all that well, to get together and bare their souls and pray out loud in front of each other, in my experience, didn't have great results. Especially when a third of them were sweating like hogs.

Scotty, Damon, and I determined that none of us knew Mark that well, so he could be included in our group and solve that problem. Now, for the soul-baring.

"You still working at D&N?" Scotty asked Damon. He ran his hand through his hair, wiped the sweat on his shorts, and placed the LSU cap back on his head, facing forward, a little lopsided.

"Naw, man. I'm working at The Piedmont."

"The Piedmont?" I asked.

"Shoot, man," Scotty said, "you scoop ice cream for little kiddies."

"At least I don't have to clean up their poop."

"I don't have to clean up poop, man. Well, there was once last month, but that was with a bucket and a mop."

Mark shook his head. "What's The Piedmont?"

"Retirement-slash-nursing home in town," Scotty answered.

"In town?"

"On 8th Street, just south of Main. You new to Morgan?"

"I'm not from Morgan," Mark answered. "I live outside Panama."

"What brings you to MBC?" Damon asked.

"I've hit half a dozen churches around the area," Mark answered. He shrugged. "I like the small rural churches better than the big city version. They're more quaint."

"Great," Scotty said. "I get stuck praying with a poop-scooper, an ice cream man, and a guy who thinks country churches are quaint."

I felt a hand on my shoulder, and looked to see Curtis Teasdale peeking into our circle. "How's it going, gentlemen?"

"It's going," Scotty muttered.

"I don't want to interrupt your fellowship, but I just wanted to let you know that seven means seven."

Okay, so he hadn't been joking before.

"Sorry, but it was a tie game," Damon said.

Teasdale nodded. "Seven." He clapped our shoulders again and moved on to hover over another group. Scotty sent a lazy two-fingered salute to his back as he left.

"Yes, sir," Damon mumbled.

"Okay, have you all met his wife?" Mark asked.

"Sandra?" Damon asked. "She's twice as scary as he is."

"Dude, I know. I think she goes around with a ruler just looking for knuckles to crack."

"We should probably pretend to pray," Scotty said. "Else he won't let us eat."

We bowed our heads.

"You work in the area?" Scotty asked Mark.

"Yeah, with a home security company in Lincoln. My smile gets me in the door with old ladies." He shrugged. "It's a living."

"So why do you live in Panama?"

"It's my folks' old house, and it's way cheaper than an apartment in the city."

I wondered what kind of miserable, wretched souls pretended to pray instead of actually praying during prayer time. I guess the kind who didn't like to have fellowship forced on them. I'd had plenty of that at college. Under the guise of "Brother/Sister" floor events. It was kind of like arranged dating. I had no problem praying with a group of guys — even in front of them. I just didn't like to be told I had to do it by a cranky, hymn-hating, pizza-withholding pastor.

A few minutes later, Teasdale called for attention before closing in prayer and also blessing the pizza. Then he told us to have at it. Everyone hurried across the basement and mobbed the nice church ladies who had given their Saturday night to bake pizzas and serve them to a bunch of teens and twenty-somethings. I realized Erica was caught in the crowd so I headed for the bathroom to clean up a little.

I pulled out a wad of paper towels from the dispenser and dabbed them under each arm to mop up the sweat. I used another handful to wipe off my forehead, cheeks, neck, and arms, and then chucked the whole business in the garbage can. I quickly splashed some water on my face before heading out to join the rest of the group.

I grabbed three slices of pepperoni pizza and a can of Mountain Dew and searched for the guys. I did not see Scotty, Damon, Mark, or a few of the others, who had probably taken their pizza outside and away from Curtis Teasdale. But as my eyes cut across the room, they fell on a pink-shirted young lady with a couple of empty seats next to her. I clapped myself on the back for "freshening" up and headed her way.

"Mind if I join you?" I asked.

"Hey," she said, looking up. "I missed you last Sunday."

My heart melted.

"I had pictures to show you."

"Sorry, I had a technical malfunction. How was the trip?"

"Great. Perfect weather. The scenery was incredible. We had elk grazing in our yard all week."

"Well I had prairie dogs running away from my weed whacker, so . . ."

She grinned, and it was breathtaking. She filled me in on all the details of the vacation, and I caught her up on my life in Morgan. A new job, the apartment . . . there wasn't that much to catch. So I focused more on not dribbling pizza sauce on my chin as I ate.

"How are your folks doing?" Erica asked.

"Good."

"They haven't converted, have they?"

"No," I said. "Never."

"Good."

"Wait, converted to what?"

She frowned. "Sooner fans."

"No, never."

"What'd you think I meant?"

"The old MBC-True Way rift. I thought maybe you'd meant converted in the religious sense."

"Equally horrible," she said.

"They're still Bible-believing Huskers."

"Good to know."

I watched her eat for a moment, and realized I was staring. So did she, lifting her eyes to me. Ever clever, I covered quickly.

"You don't blot your pizza," I said, nodding at the new piece she had just started.

"Should I?"

"No. Most girls do."

Erica very nearly huffed. "Can I tell you something?"

I nodded.

"I find girls kind of annoying."

"Annoying?"

"Yeah. They blot their pizza and count calories and just talk about boys all the time."

"Whereas you eat candy till your teeth fall out."

She gave me a very quick evil eye.

"And they never want to play football," she added.

"You play football?"

"I don't just play. I'm good."

"Is that so?"

"You doubt me?"

"I've just never seen a good girl football player before," I said. We were clearly flirting. Or doing our very best to, in my case.

Erica smiled. "Well, I'll have to show you sometime."

"I'll hold you to that."

We'd practically made a date, and I was internally giddy. We finished our pizza and wandered outside, where the basketball was back in full force. I had my wind back, and very much wanted to D-up Damon again to impress Erica. But not at the expense of leaving her.

So we watched for a few minutes. Then Erica nudged my elbow. "You missed my solo Sunday," she said, as if greatly affronted.

"So I heard."

"I laid it out, too."

"I'm sorry." She didn't know how sorry.

Erica smirked as the breeze played lightly with her hair. Lucky breeze. "Cassie told me to give you a hard time. I talked to her in Sunday school."

"She gave me a hard time too," I said, and immediately realized that I was straying into dangerous territory. I covered once again. "She thinks one skip of church means I'm in danger of wandering from the faith."

"No, you get one," Erica said. If she had caught my little slip, she didn't let on. Maybe it wasn't so much of a slip as I thought. But I resolved to be more careful in the future.

"And you want to know a secret?" Erica asked, leaning in.

"What's that?"

"We didn't go to church in Estes Park."

I gasped in mock horror.

"But that's vacation, so two skips only count as one."

"I must have missed that passage of Scripture."

"It's buried in the Old Testament," she said. "Leviticus, I think. Might be Numbers."

"I'll have to look into that."

Erica sighed as she looked at her watch. "I should get going."

"Already?"

"I'm meeting someone for coffee."

My heart skipped at least two beats. Maybe three. It threatened to stop all together.

"My roommate from my days at UNL. We've kept in touch."

I nodded, relieved, breathing again. "Have fun."

"You going to be in church tomorrow?" she asked with a slight dig.

"Yeah."

"Promise?"

"Yeah. You singing again?"

"I'm bringing pictures for you to see."

"I'll be there."

"Then I'll see you tomorrow."

She smiled and I nodded as she turned away, hair flicking over her shoulder. I smiled too, but only for a moment. I saw Gia approaching.

"Josh." She wore blue jeans and a brown tank top. Her hair was a tangled mess, which wasn't unusual. Also not unusual, she wore perfume that surrounded her like a cloud. I couldn't help but give a tiny little cough.

"Gia."

"You are not playing?"

"Letting my food settle."

She looked across the parking lot to where Erica was getting into her car. "Is that all?" Gia asked.

"All what?"

"You and her . . ."

"Gotta stand somewhere."

"Rosie, run some ball?"

I looked away from Gia to Scotty. "Yeah, let's go."

Chapter 11

"But everything should be done in a fitting and orderly way." I Corinthians 14:40

True to my word, I was in church Sunday morning.

Stupid word.

Scotty, Cassie, and I were seated middle right, as usual, when the worship team bounded up onto the stage, dressed in clothes I wouldn't wear to mow lawn. Curtis Teasdale's jeans had holes in the knees — the pastor!

"Great is the Lord God Almighty!" he hollered. He looked around the sanctuary. "Am I right? Great is the Lord God Almighty!"

The women next to him breathed an, "Amen."

"Let's all shout that exaltation?" Teasdale asked.

And so five times, he led the congregation in shouting "Great is the Lord God Almighty!"

"What are we now, Muslims?" Scotty asked.

"Your mom's a Muslim," a voice muttered from behind us. I turned to see Mike. His eyes rolled.

"Before you're seated," Teasdale said (he'd made us stand to shout), "greet one another. But don't just turn around and greet the people behind you and in front of you. Seek someone out across the sanctuary, someone you don't normally sit by. Come on."

I looked down at Cassie. She bit her lip.

"So if we all go over there to shake their hands," she said, looking to the left half of the church, "what happens when they come over here to shake our hands?"

"Maybe we meet in the middle," I answered. I turned over my shoulder. "Baxter, what do you think?"

"I think we should all sit in somebody else's seat when we get back and mess everyone up."

"That's not very spiritual," Cassie said.

"Your mom's not—"

A glare from Cassie cut him off.

"Come on, everybody," Teasdale called.

"Shouldn't he be teaching aerobics somewhere?" Scotty asked.

"Well, somebody has to stay here to greet all the folks coming this way," Cassie said.

"All I know is if I see Mrs. Teasdale, I'm making a beeline for the far wall," Mike said.

"Good morning."

I turned to see a dear old woman in the row in front of us. Her walker made crossing the sanctuary a little impractical, but she couldn't find anyone's hand to shake since we were playing fruit basket upset.

"Good morning," I said, taking her hand.

"This is such a commotion," she said.

"Good morning." It was her husband, more mobile, but pinned in by his wife. His handshake was firm, and he pulled me slightly closer. "Miss your father."

"Thank you. Me too."

"Ahh," Teasdale called as if he had just eaten Thanksgiving dinner. "Be seated."

We sat. The worship team, sans Teasdale, stepped back, and he stated that we had a special announcement this morning. He called Greg de Boer (Geoff's dad) up onto the stage. Greg was an average guy, a regular usher, a deacon once or twice . . . maybe even an elder for all I knew. I didn't know him all that well. He took the mic from Teasdale and cleared his throat.

"I have the privilege of co-leading a team of young people from Morgan Bible—as well as several nearby churches—to Haiti next week. We'll be there for about two and a half weeks, helping with repairs from earthquake damage, providing some basic medical services, and conducting some Bible clubs for the children. At this time, I'd like to ask those who are here this morning who will be going with me to come on up to the stage. I want you all to see the faces so they will be ingrained in your mind over the next few weeks, as I really hope you'll keep us all in your prayers."

"I didn't even know about this trip," I said.

"Try coming to church every week," Cassie replied out of the side of her mouth.

About a dozen people, most of them teenagers or college-age kids, slowly made their way onto stage. I watched with casual disinterest, wondering if this was still the same earthquake from years ago, or if they'd had another one. My disinterest suddenly became interest when I saw Erica stepping onto the stage.

She wore a blue floral sundress, capped sleeves, flared slightly at the knees. Her hair was down, floating around her shoulders. I couldn't believe how incredibly calm and fluid she looked, always looked, as if floating through life. Maybe it was just good posture, but I doubted it.

I recognized a few other faces: Geoff, Mark, Jimmy — or maybe it was Jamie — Hendricks, Kevin Sprague, and another guy I couldn't put a name to. There were some girls too — including, to my surprise, Gia — but I wasn't much concerned about the girls. I didn't like the idea of my Erica being on a missions trip with single men.

I also didn't like her being in Haiti. Wasn't it dangerous? Weren't corrupt cops and street gangs and highly-communicable diseases running rampant down there? Not to mention the apparent propensity for earthquakes.

Greg gave a few more details about the trip and plenty of prayer requests. Since I now had a personal interest in the trip, I mentally jotted them down. Greg said they were leaving next Sunday morning, bright and early, and I did some more math. It would be another month before I saw Erica. Summer would be gone and we'd still be at the not-so-clever banter phase.

Then Greg announced that they were having a fund-raising ice cream social the following Friday. It would be a chance for the team to earn some more money to ultimately put toward the cost of the trip, as well as provide us as a church body one more chance to fellowship with them and encourage them before they departed. I smiled. My Friday calendar was clear.

After Teasdale prayed for the group, he invited us all to stand. "We're going to be doing things a little differently today," he announced. "You know, we always talk about coming to church and what we get out of it. But we never talk about what we can give to God. So today we're going to spend the day giving—giving our praise offering to God."

With that he attacked his guitar and off we went. Singing and singing and singing. I counted nine songs, four of which lasted over five minutes. That is way too long for any song. Even "Sweet Home Alabama" gets old after five minutes.

There were three hymns and one chorus I recognized from the "old days." But two of the hymns had been remodeled, with new bridges added and verses restructured. The other was to an altogether new tune. The chorus was meshed with a new chorus that I'd never heard, to a tune that clashed drastically. Three more of the songs I recognized from college and the radio. The other two I'd never heard.

I realized something as we sang on and on—and whistled one verse again (I looked for the old guy with the squealing hearing aid, but didn't spot him). Modern Christian music artists are largely hacks. All they do is take a song somebody else wrote and pen their own verse or edit the chorus or add a bridge. They're obsessed with bridges. Whoever came up with bridges anyhow? Bridges to where? Stop building bridges!

You don't see authors doing that, taking John Grisham or Clive Cussler plots and renaming the characters, switching the ending, adding an extra scene or two, and publishing it as their own work. Even in the ever-repeating world of film and television, the new *Ocean's Eleven* and *Hawaii Five-O* reinvent the concept.

And when somebody does write an original song—which is rare— everybody else sings it. Covering a song now and again is one thing, but Christian artists share music like bongs in a hippie commune. If they really can't think of anything new to write, I say get a real job. Whack weeds for a while at a golf course or something.

Halfway through the service, the old couple in front of us sat down. I realized they were not alone. Soon it became like one of those dance-a-thons where they tried to see who could last the longest. There was a group to my right, close to the speakers, hands raised and hips swaying, and I ceded the championship to them.

I don't mind singing. Like I said, I'm not real good at it, so I don't belt it out. But I enjoy it. I just can't get into these new songs. They don't flow. They aren't meant to be congregational. And they don't seem to be saying much—they're so generic, so basic.

I know, I know, it's not supposed to be about me, like Teasdale said. I'm supposed to worship God. But I do that a lot better with music I can sing, with words that have meaning. Otherwise, I might as well sit in the back and pray by myself.

After nine songs, the music finally stopped. My ears were ringing. We were still not allowed to be seated. Old-timers were dropping like flies. I wish I had a cane or a walker to give me a good excuse to sit down. Or to help some of them remain standing.

"We're going to close with one more song in a moment," Teasdale said. "It's a dear old hymn that I'm sure you all love, 'Come Thou Fount of Every Blessing.' Before we sing, I want to take a minute to let us all focus on the words and what they really mean."

He stepped back, the lights dimmed, and two members of the worship team stepped forward, a man and a woman. The man wore a dress shirt and tie, slacks, and nasty strap sandals. So close. The woman wore tattered jeans and was barefoot. I felt like I was at the beach.

"'*Come Thou Fount of Every Blessing* . . .'" the man read, from a hymnal.

"God, who gives us all good things," the woman quoted from a slip of paper.

"'*Tune my heart to sing Thy grace,*'" read the man.

"Make our hearts to praise Your mercy," said the woman.

"'*Streams of mercy never ceasing* . . .'"

"Your forgiveness that never ends . . ."

"'*Call for songs of loudest praise.*'"

"Compels me to worship you with all my heart."

I leaned over to Scotty. "What is this?"

"Hymns for Dummies, I think."

"'*Teach me some melodious sonnet . . .*'" the man read.

"Help me to understand the sweet song . . ."

"'*Sung by flaming tongues above.*'"

"That the angels in heaven repeat."

"'*Praise the Mount, I'm fixed upon it . . .*'"

"Worship the Lord God and focus intently . . ."

"'*Mount of Thy redeeming love.*'"

"On His love and salvation!"

The music started and we sang one of my favorite hymns. And I couldn't focus. All I could think about were Scotty's words. "Hymns for Dummies." He was right. They even had to reword the hymns. Were people so stupid these days that they couldn't understand simple English? Were melodious sonnets too perplexing? Was "hither to" beyond comprehension?

We sang one verse, then the man-woman reading thing continued. They read verse two, the real version and the watered down version, and then we sang it. I was too miffed to join in. The same thing happened for the third verse, and when the dumbing down of church was complete, we were dismissed.

Amen to that.

Chapter 12

"Do not be quickly provoked in your spirit . . ." Ecclesiastes 7:9

"You going to Sunday school?" I asked Scotty, at the same time looking around for Erica. I didn't see her. Why did she keep camouflaging herself in with the other churchgoers?

He turned to Cassie. "What's on the agenda today?"

"Chapter four," she answered. "Whatever that is."

I opened my Bible—It was feeling left out after the morning service. "'*The Throne in Heaven*,'" I said. "Short chapter."

"Time for rapture discussion," Cassie said.

"If Petey doesn't crack the whip," Scotty said as we stepped into the aisle behind an elderly couple.

"Huh?" the old guy asked, leaning toward his wife.

"Do you want some coffee?" she practically shouted.

He shook his head. "I can't hear you, Mother."

"It's that raucous music," she mumbled and grabbed his hand. "Come on."

I smirked at Cassie and we followed them into the foyer and down the hall to Room 104. We found three seats in the back row, which was further from Petey and gave a better vantage point if another argument developed. We also shaded slightly to the right side of the classroom, which Cassie explained was because we were pre-trib.

"We are?" Scotty asked.

"You're not?" she asked.

He shrugged.

"We're pre-trib," she said. "Sit down."

We sat.

We were early, so I watched as everyone entered to see where they sat. Rena and Cora were on our side. So was Tim Harte. Brad and Geoff seated themselves on the left. Gia joined them, likely because we were on the right. Damon Harris came in, slapped my hand and Scotty's, and sat down in front of Scotty. I wasn't sure his choice of seat was based on when he thought the rapture would occur. Mike, Brett, and Amy Stevenson were the only other "regulars" and they sat in the middle. Not sure if that meant mid-trib, undecided, or "hey, there's an open seat."

At ten-fifteen on the button, Petey called the class to order. "Just a reminder, we've been having some trouble staying on topic in this class," Petey said. "I understand that Revelation is very complex and we all have a lot of questions we'd like answered, but please, if we could, raise your hand if you have something to say. I'll call on you, and we can maintain a sense of order that way."

Somebody on our side booed, Petey glared, but the guilty party avoided detection. This was going to be fun.

The door opened and Erica slipped into the room. She grinned timidly at Petey, who responded only by glancing at the clock. If he had made a crack, I might have thrown my sword of the Spirit at his head.

Erica's eyebrows rose slightly as she saw me, and I offered a weak head nod. She took a chair in front of Cassie as Petey instructed us to open to Revelation chapter four.

Erica turned over her shoulder. "I forgot the pictures," she whispered.

"Next time," I said, fully aware that "next time" might be in July.

Petey looked up, having heard our whispers, but we were back in studious mode before his eyes reached us. He cleared his throat, and as had become habit, had us read through the chapter before we began, each person from front to back taking one verse at a time. We made it to verse three before there was a pause.

I looked up and chuckled, as did several other students. Tim, whose turn it was to read, had his hand up.

Petey finally looked up and noticed Tim's hand. "You have a question, Tim?"

"No, you said to raise our hand if we had something to say."

The lighting was such that I couldn't tell if steam actually came out of Petey's ears or if it was just my imagination. "Is anyone actually here to learn?" he asked. "Or do you all just want to goof off?"

"Is that an option?" Brett asked.

"You didn't raise your hand," Scotty called.

"Mr. Harte, verse three please," Petey said through clenched teeth. We read all eleven verses without further incident. Petey took a moment to compose himself before offering a somewhat preachy prayer about focusing on and gleaning from the Word. He closed and started his lecture.

Verse three tripped us up again. This time it was Brad with his hand up.

"Yes, Brad."

"What's carnelian?"

"Carnelian is a brownish-red mineral that is considered a semi-precious gemstone," Petey answered.

"What color's jasper?" Brad asked, his hand still in the air.

"Jasper is green," Brett answered.

"Jasper isn't green," Gia said. "That's jade."

"Jasper can be green."

"Can be green?"

"It can be any color but blue."

"What does that have to do with Revelation?"

"It only says it had the appearance of jasper."

"So what did it look like if jasper can be any color?"

"Let's just say green."

Petey whistled.

The conversation stopped.

Beside me, Scotty had slipped a spiral notebook from a shelf beside him and torn out a dozen pages. He began folding them into triangles on his lap, shielded from Petey's view by Damon's back.

"The important thing is not the color of jasper or carnelian," Petey said. "We are talking about the throne of the Lord God Almighty, and you're getting caught up on the color of gemstones?"

"You're the one who said this was an in-depth study," Mike said. "Sorry." He raised his hand.

Petey's cheeks were beet red. "Do you people want this class or not? Hmm? Because I can surely find a better way to spend my Sunday mornings."

To their credit, nobody said anything. After giving us all the evil eye, including a stare in every direction, Petey returned to his Bible and his notes.

"Let's move past the throne and to verse four. *'Surrounding the throne were twenty-four other thrones,'*" he read, *"'and seated on them were twenty-four elders. They were dressed in white and had crowns of gold on their heads.'"*

Petey looked up. "Can anyone tell me who these twenty-four elders are?"

Not the same elders who fired my father, I hoped.

Nobody could, which allowed Petey to launch into his lecture. It quickly became boring (too much Greek and culture and customs) and I quickly became distracted. Scotty's paper triangles, I realized, were paper footballs.

(Paper Football is possibly the greatest game ever invented — after real football, of course. You take this hard little triangle of folded paper and slide it back and forth across a table. The idea is to score a touchdown by getting the wedge to hang, but not fall, off the edge of the table. The real fun comes when you stand the football on end, point facing away, and "kick" the extra point by snapping the football with your finger, aiming at a "goalpost" made by your opponent's thumbs and forefingers.)

Scotty did not have a table, but his knee made an excellent tee. He sent one sailing just past the side of Petey's head, and managed to have his head down in his Bible, a serious look on his face, by the time Petey looked up.

I felt a little guilty. I mean, he was just trying to teach us from the Word. But if he would have lightened up a little, been a dude, and signaled a miss, wide left, I could have respected him a lot more.

I also felt a little guilty because of the second distraction. Erica. She had slipped off her slides and crossed her legs at the ankle (for the record, her ankles were quite lovely). Her dress came to the knee, perfectly modest, but all I could see were her legs. If I looked at the teacher, I saw them out of the bottom of my eyes. If I looked down at my Bible, I saw them out of the top of my eyes. I suppose I could have turned and stared straight at Scotty the whole class, but that would have been ridiculous.

From somewhere in the Song of Solomon, a phrase about "not awakening love until it pleases" popped into my head. I'd never paid much attention to it in the past, which was true of the entire book. Now I knew what it was talking about. Maybe the guys in the Old Testament had had it right, where they sent a delegate on camels to find a wife for their son. They brought her back, they were married, and that was it.

Then again, the guys in the Old Testament were largely perverts. More wives and concubines and servant girls than a genealogy could list. By comparison, looking at Erica's legs and ankles and feet didn't seem so horrible. And yet, I felt like a perv too.

"'Day and night they never stop saying: "Holy, holy, holy is the Lord God Almighty, who was, and is, and is to come."'"

I looked up as Petey read.

"'Whenever the living creatures give glory, honor and thanks to him who sits on the throne and who lives for ever and ever, the twenty-four elders fall down before him who sits on the throne, and worship him who lives for ever and ever. They lay their crowns before the throne and say: "You are worthy, our Lord and God, to receive glory and honor and power, for you created all things, and by your will they were created and have their being."'

"Yes, Geoff?" Petey asked, stepping away from his music stand.

"Isn't that incredible?" Geoff said. "For ever and ever and ever. I was so thankful for the worship service this morning, reminding me of how it will be in heaven."

Scotty got his hand up before I did.

"Yes, Scotty?"

"Are we going to whistle in heaven?"

Petey shrugged. "I don't see why not."

"Well, Cassie here can't whistle."

"But she'll have a glorified body then."

"Is whistling a part of glorification?"

Petey appeared dumbfounded.

"I don't think we're just going to sing worship songs all the time," Scotty said. "Do you?"

"It says so in the text."

"No, it says the elders worship God for ever and ever. It doesn't say sing."

"Good, because frankly I get sick of singing after about an hour," Mike said.

"More like thirty minutes for me," Tim said.

"Don't you think an hour's too long just to sing?" Amy asked.

"Why shouldn't we sing for an hour?" Geoff asked.

"You're musical—you like it," she replied. "It's a long time for some people."

"One hour of praising God is too long?"

"For some people."

"Especially old people," Rena said. "They can't stand that long."

"They can sit down," Gia said. About time for her to get into an argument with somebody.

"Then they can't see the words," Amy said. "Which is another thing. Can we make the people who insist on sticking their arms and hands in the air sit in back? I about fell into my neighbor today trying to read around a Pentecostal."

"What about people who just stick their hands in their pockets?" Gia asked.

"What about them?"

"Shouldn't they sit in back too so those of us who want to worship aren't discouraged by a bunch of downers?"

"I don't think we should be labeling people," Petey said. "And we're getting off track again."

"You never answered the question," Scotty piped up. "Are we all going to sing twenty-four-seven in heaven?"

"You don't think we'll be worshiping God all the time?" Geoff asked across the room.

"Worshiping, yes. Singing, no. There are other ways to worship."

"Do you think we'll be playing football like that one song says?" Cora asked.

"You can't worship God playing football," Amy said.

"Sure you can. Tim Tebow did."

"That's not worship," Gia said.

"We're supposed to worship with our lives," Tim said. "That's his life."

"So if your life is video gaming and watching TV, is that worship?" Geoff asked.

"Pay attention," Cassie whispered, tapping my knee.

"Shush."

"These are all very good questions," Petey said, raising his hand. "But we're straying off topic again."

"So stray," Scotty said. "This isn't school; we don't need to cover X material by the end of the semester."

"I agree," Erica said, and I paid extra close attention. I also mentally perched, ready to attack any knucklehead who dared oppose her. Unless, of course, she was Scripturally unsound. "We've got a legitimate question here," she continued, "not only of what constitutes worship in heaven, but also here on earth. Can't we take time out and discuss it?"

Petey nodded. "Yes, that is a fair point. Unfortunately, we're out of time for the day. But that sounds like a good homework assignment for next week. Think about that. How can we worship God in our everyday living? And what does that mean about worship in heaven?"

He looked around for a moment. "Okay, let's close in prayer."

We all bowed our heads and closed our eyes, and I finally had a reason not to look at Erica's legs. Unfortunately, they were now burned into my mind's eye, and I had no idea what Petey said. I almost missed the "Amen."

As we stood to leave, Erica turned toward us. Before I could think of anything cute and clever to say, Scotty spoke. "Thanks for backing me up," he said.

"You were right."

I wanted to say something, to ask about Haiti and if she was sure it was safe, but surrounded by everybody, it wasn't the place. I guessed then that it also wasn't good timing to compliment her on her sundress. So I offered a close-lipped smile, as did she, and we began filing for the exit.

"I believe this is yours," Gia said, stopping us and handing Scotty a paper football. "Missed its mark."

I started to wonder if he hadn't been aiming for Petey. Maybe his close call was actually an overshot intended for the back of her head.

"So, Haiti," Scotty said. "How long will you be gone?"

Gia faked a smile. "Two and a half weeks."

"You flying through Miami?"

"Yes." Her eyes narrowed. "Why?"

"I thought maybe you could catch a raft back home."

"And just how many ways did you mean for that to be insulting and insensitive?"

"Not half as many as I'm sure you'll take it to be, Fidel."

And then she slapped him. Right there, still in Room 104. With witnesses. Fortunately, Erica was already into the hallway. I'd hate for her to think I consorted with these types of people.

"What's going on?" Geoff asked. Brett was right behind him.

"Daisy here was just showing me how she's going to reach the Haitians for Christ," Scotty said, his eyes not leaving Gia.

"At least I am going," she retorted.

"Very good. More brownie points for you. Oh wait . . . we don't do brownie points."

"*El stupido.*"

"You got something to say to me, say it in English, *comprende?*"

Gia's dark eyes flashed. She leaned forward, her tangled hair falling in front of her face. "You are an animal."

"Hey, guys, come on," Geoff said.

"He started it," Gia said.

"There's a mature response," Scotty said. "How surprising."

"Come on, dude, knock it off," Geoff said.

Scotty flicked his eyes in Geoff's direction, but didn't say anything. Instead he looked at me and Cassie. "Let's go."

Giving Gia a wide berth, we exited into the hallway.

"What was that about?" Mike asked.

"Five years of hate bubbling to the surface," Scotty said.

"You gotta keep your dukes up, man," Mike said. He raised his fists in front of his face, like a boxer.

Geoff and Gia emerged from the room and started down the hallway. Gia and Scotty exchanged glares again.

"Didn't the two of you get into it at youth group once too?" Mike asked.

Scotty nodded.

"They'll probably end up married," Mike said with a wink at Cassie and me.

"Come on, Joba[9], keep it clean," Scotty replied.

"You want some ice for that cheek?" Mike asked. "Maybe a slab of steak?"

"You'll be the one needing the ice next," Scotty warned.

Mike grinned, whacked Scotty on the shoulder with his Bible, and nodded. "I'll see you all later."

He left the three of us alone, Scotty still scowling, me smirking at Mike's remarks, and Cassie frowning.

"Missed you last night," I said, trying to change the subject.

"We had trouble," she replied. "Horses out of the barn."

"Is that spy code for something, like —"

"No, the horses got loose."

Cassie didn't usually interrupt, so I could tell she was still miffed. So could Scotty.

"She's the one who hit me, Cass."

"You sort of gave her a reason, and you were the one to start it."

"I made a few offhanded remarks."

"It's different to girls sometimes."

"I'm sorry, Cass."

She shook her head. "You don't have to apologize to me."

"Well I'm not apologizing to her," Scotty said.

---

[9] Joba Chamberlain is a Major League Baseball pitcher who played collegiately at the University of Nebraska.

"Fine. I'll see you guys."

Cassie turned and started down the hallway. I took a step after her, but Scotty pulled my arm. "She'll be all right, dude. You want to come over for lunch?"

I nodded. "Sure."

That was the thing about being guys. Just that quickly, the fight was behind us and stacked homemade sub sandwiches were in front of us.

Chapter 13

"I am with you for only a short time . . ." John 7:33

I had one of those weeks. They hit me every once in a while, where everything in my life sort of converged to give my brain a heart attack.

I was still torn about how to play things with Erica. On one hand, the idea of not rushing in, taking things slow, letting the relationship "happen" sounded great. But relationships didn't happen unless you had some interaction with the person, and so far we were interacting about once a month for six minutes at a time. First I was at college, then she and her family were in Colorado, now she was going to Haiti for the better part of three weeks. Letting things play out didn't seem to be generating a lot of play.

But unfortunately, the only way to spend more time with Erica would be to ask her out, which kind of put the kibosh on taking things slow. I suppose in theory I could have called her up and asked her to hang out — just as friends. But any girl worth her salt could see through that ploy and I would just end up looking lame. What was a guy to do?

The thing with Scotty and Gia had me flustered too. Gia was a pain in the butt, but Scotty didn't do anything to temper the heat between them. If anything, he sought to exacerbate it. Always had. But I couldn't get over to the side of blaming him either, because Gia was indeed a pain in the butt. Maybe Mike was right — maybe they would end up married someday. No, that was even more distressing.

Cassie concerned me too. Not so much because she was upset with Scotty. I was sure by now that she was over that. No, she worried me because she was killing herself, working sixty or seventy hours every week, trying desperately to make enough money to get into Arizona State.

110

I worried about her getting in and being too burned out to maximize her opportunity. I worried about her more if she didn't make it.

And I worried about my soul. As ridiculous as it may seem, I couldn't shake the picture my brain had snapped of Erica in Sunday school. Was it even considered lust if you were just thinking of someone from the knees down? Was ankle-lust a gateway sin? Did the fact that it took place in Sunday school impact the judgment?

These thoughts all played through my mind when I wasn't scooping ice cream and blending milkshakes and weighing candy. Worst of all, I didn't really have anyone to talk to. Sure, I had Scotty and Dirk. But part of the issue was Scotty and his fights with Gia, and I didn't really want to talk about the rest of it with them. I had my parents, but as a twenty-year-old man, I was trying not to run to my parents with everything. And Cassie was too busy. I didn't even see her until Friday.

I spent more time with Sydney than anybody else. I did not struggle with lusting after her ankle because it was tattooed, and well, Sydney wasn't my type.

When Friday finally rolled around, I was relieved. Distance proved to be a good stress reliever, as Scotty and Gia's spat faded into the background and the images of Erica's legs came around less frequently. I still didn't know what to do about her, and hoped the ice cream social would give me a clue. If I could get more than two minutes with her.

Cassie did not have to work, and I offered to pick her up. She lived a few miles out into the country, and so while it wasn't practical, it gave us a few minutes to chat. She was her typical happy self, and quickly explained why.

"I sent in the application to ASU yesterday," she said. "It's out of my hands now."

"So if they accept you, you're going?"

"Not necessarily. I applied for a couple of grants and scholarships, so it depends on that too. If I get them all, I should be able to make it."

"That's good."

She exhaled. "I've done what I can. I guess now I find out if this is what God wants or not."

"Hmm," I said. "I wonder what the equivalent of applying for grants and scholarships is in the world of romance."

Cassie turned sideways in her seat, sliding the shoulder belt around her. It wasn't terribly safe, but I was a good driver.

"So let me get this straight," she said. "At the spring game, the two of you have several positive conversations. At the gas station, she whacks you in the shoulder. Then she sends you a postcard from vacation and brings her pictures for you to see at church — admittedly the week you decide to attend Bedside Baptist. And when you don't come and miss her singing, she's bummed. And you're wondering if she's interested?"

"When you put it like that . . ."

"So . . . stop worrying about it. It sounds to me like you guys are on the path to romance. This isn't I-80. Take your time, enjoy the scenery."

"What if I'm looking at the scenery and she goes off to Haiti and falls in love with some other guy?"

"A Haitian?"

"No, one of the guys on the trips. People always bond on these things."

"Have you ever been on a missions trip?"

"No, but it's the same with all youth trips or projects. Close proximity, shared purpose. It drives people together. Plus, three weeks in a tropical climate . . ."

Cassie shrugged. "Then I guess that means your application is denied."

"Wonderful."

"Well don't sit around and expect it to happen."

"Maybe I should send in a down payment."

"Huh?"

"Make my move. If she's into me like you say, maybe I should officially throw my hat into the ring."

"It's up to you," Cassie said. "But I'm not sure now is the right time."

"Why?"

"She's got a lot on her mind with the trip, I'm sure. Besides, like Daddy says, just because you see a buck and he's in range, doesn't mean it's time to shoot."

I winced. "I don't know which is more disturbing, Dirk comparing Erica to a golf course or you comparing her to a deer."

"Sorry, I'm not as good with metaphors as you and Scotty."

"I'm not so sure about that."

We arrived at church without Cassie being thrown into the windshield. I did make my left turn a little sharper and faster than necessary, and she pitched back into the door with a scream. She slapped my shoulder, and I remembered what she had said before, about how girls had lots of reasons for hitting boys. It also made me wonder if Scotty would show, and if he and Gia would have round two.

The social was in the church basement, but since it was a beautiful though somewhat muggy evening, the doors were open to let the party spill outside. Greg de Boer acted as host and gave a few remarks once everyone was gathered. Then he invited the team members "up front" and let several of them speak. They covered the high points, highlighting their itinerary and goals and mentioning some prayer requests.

Erica was one of three who spoke, handling the prayer requests. She wore denim shorts and a yellow polo shirt, and looked as beautiful as ever. I could not, from my seat, see her ankles. I focused on the prayer requests, committing them to memory so I could be sure and support her — and the rest of the team, I supposed — every day of the trip.

When she was finished, Curtis Teasdale (who wore navy slacks and a polo shirt — better apparel than he wore to lead singing in church) stepped forward to offer a brief prayer that Tim clocked at four minutes and forty-eight seconds. At the "Amen," Teasdale "turned things back over" to Greg, who asked us to give him and the team opportunity to get the ice cream and toppings prepared. They were serving us, he explained, as a thank you for our financial support.

"Subtle," Scotty said, nodding at collection plates at both ends of the kitchen counter. I had brought along a fresh, crisp twenty-dollar bill, which was above and beyond my regular tithe, thank you. Maybe mine would be the twenty dollars that paid for Erica's cab ride back to the house where they were staying one dark and stormy night, saving her from wandering the streets of Port-au-Prince after dark. Or something.

We got in line and I received my bowl of chocolate ice cream from Mark. I also received a "Hey, dude." I "hey duded" him back and found the chocolate chips and strawberries.

"You all right, man?" Scotty asked as we stood to the side of the basement, eating. "You've been quiet this week."

"Yeah. Lot on my mind," I answered.

"Erica?"

I glanced around out of the corner of my eye. We were alone-ish.

"Among other things."

"Worried about the trip?"

"Worried about the five guys serving ice cream. I'm afraid they'll spark a Caribbean romance."

"Jimmy's in high school," Scotty said. "And I think that Mark dude has a girlfriend."

"Why do you say that?"

He shrugged. "Just a vibe."

"Your vibes are somewhat less than soothing."

"And *Guitar Hero* won't make a move," he said with a nod at Geoff. "You're in the clear."

"Great." I was not convinced.

Cassie joined us. We chatted about nothing. She told Scotty what she'd told me on the ride over. Scotty was convinced she would get accepted, receive her funding, and go on to be a world-renowned artist. I warned her that he was in a "vibe" mood and not to believe everything he said. I was called a fuddy-duddy, twice over.

Gia materialized from nowhere. She glanced at Cassie and me, as if upset at our presence, but focused her eyes on Scotty. "I am sorry I hit you," she said.

"Forget it," he said.

"No. I was out of line. And I am sorry."

He nodded. "Me too."

She nodded in return.

"Have a good trip," Scotty said.

Gia nodded again and turned to leave.

Amazing how things were falling into place, all my chaotic problems suddenly being solved. Sometimes that happened with my brain heart attacks.

"I'm going to go get some more ice cream," I said to Scotty and Cassie. "See if I can get a pretty brunette to serve me this time."

"Are you talking about Erica?"

I turned to see Gia, who apparently had not left, but lingered.

"I think he was talking about your mom," Scotty said.

"Because Erica's the only brunette going on the trip," Gia said. "Except for me."

"Well you're safe there, Guantánamo," Scotty said.

She ignored him. "Josh, do you have a thing for Erica?"

I don't believe in lying. It is, after all, a sin. But so is lusting after ankles, and since I was already in trouble . . .

"No."

"You do," she said.

"And you've got a thing for de Boer," Scotty said.

"What?"

"I saw you two, 'fighting' over the ice cream bucket, yukking it up earlier. Maybe you want to gossip over that," Scotty said.

"We're just friends."

"Likely story. Wonder what Greg would think about a blossoming romance on his missions trip."

"It's not his trip."

"No, but it's his kid," Scotty said.

"Nothing is happening, Scott."

Nobody called him Scott, and I wondered how far we were from another slap.

"Okay," he said. "Must have misunderstood."

Gia glared at him, but then slipped away. I made sure of it this time.

"Thanks, dude."

"Go get your ice cream, Rosie."

Erica was indeed still serving ice cream, while most others in the group had started milling. I took this as a servant's heart, a great quality in a wife and mother. What a couple we'd be.

Jimmy — not Jamie — the high schooler was the one to serve me my second bowl, and I lingered by the toppings, hoping for Erica to offer to spoon some chocolate chips into my bowl, until it became ridiculous. Then I took my ice cream back to Scotty and Cassie. Only they had disappeared.

I scanned the room for friendlies, but most of them were occupied. So I leaned against the wall, ate a little, and then went to investigate outside. Maybe Scotty and Cassie were enjoying the summer night.

They weren't, but I did. Nebraska is pretty far west in the Central Time Zone, so by the clock, it's late when the sun sets. Especially a week before the solstice. It was close to eight o'clock, and the sun was still shining brightly. I stood for a few minutes, savoring my ice cream, marveling at what the evening sunshine could do to the treetops and blades of grass. It was breathtaking.

"Breathtaking, isn't it?"

I turned to Erica. She had her own bowl of ice cream, and she spooned a bite to her mouth and leaned against the side of the church.

"Hey," I said.

"Hey yourself."

"So . . . you excited or nervous?" I asked after a spoonful of ice cream.

"Both."

"All packed and ready?"

"Haven't even started yet," she replied, stirring her toppings around in her bowl.

"Got your candy?"

She smirked. "No."

"You leave Sunday morning?" I asked, even though I knew the answer.

"Five a.m. Drive to Omaha, fly to Chicago, then Miami, then Port-au-Prince. Thirteen hours, plus the time change. Puts us there in time for a late dinner."

"And when do you come back?" I asked as casually as possible. I smoothly took a spoonful of ice cream and looked over my spoon at her as she answered. Just a curious question.

"Friday the sixth."

"You'll miss the Fourth of July."

"They use the same calendar in Haiti, Josh."

"That's cute," I said. And it was.

"What do they do in Morgan?" she asked. "I've only ever celebrated in Lincoln or Norfolk."

"Why Norfolk?"

"Grandparents," she answered.

(An aside on Norfolk. It's pronounced Norfork. No one knows why.)

I nodded. Then shrugged. "We have fireworks, a big party at the park with games and dangerous rides and tons of food."

"And beer?"

"And beer."

"Do you drink beer, Josh?"

"I'm not old enough."

"That's not what I asked."

"I do not."

She nodded.

I had some more ice cream. "So what are you going to be doing in Haiti?"

"Weren't you listening?" she asked with a mischievous smile.

"I was listening," I said, and recited back the prayer requests to prove it. "I meant are you going to be painting or roofing or teaching Bible studies to little kids or playing doctor or what?"

"A little bit of everything, I hope," she said. She wrinkled her nose. "I'm a little worried about showers," she said. "I've heard the bathrooms, even at the house we're staying at, are somewhat primitive."

"Nineteen days is a long time to go without a decent shower."

"Maybe I can take a dip in the ocean," she said.

"Are you going to have time to do any sightseeing?"

"Not a lot, I don't think. But if I do, I'll send you a postcard."

"That'd be great."

"And maybe I'll bring you back some little island trinket that you'll hate but feel obliged to keep on your dresser, like missionaries always hand out to kids when they come back on furlough."

117

"I have nothing but keys and my wallet on my dresser," I said. "I'll take what I can get."

"Okay then," she said. She had finished her ice cream, and she offered me the most beautiful, placid smile. "I should get back in there. We're supposed to kind of make the rounds, schmooze with everybody."

"Consider me schmoozed," I said, trying to hide my disappointment. I was part of her rounds.

"That's not what I meant," she said quickly. "I meant, now I have to go schmooze."

I smirked, as if I'd known it all along. "Have a good trip. I'll be praying for you."

"Thanks. I'll see you later . . . Rosie."

She winked when she said it, in case I missed that she was teasing. I didn't, and I smiled in response as she turned and walked back into the church.

I waited outside for several minutes, letting the memory of our conversation, of that mischievous wink—of her—soak into my head. It would have to tide me over for three weeks.

I spent another thirty minutes at the social, chatting Husker football with Mark and entries in the state fair with Mike and about if I ever played video games online with Tim. I didn't talk with Erica again, but I saw her from across the room several times—more images that I burned into my mind.

At eight-thirty, Cassie showed up suddenly and asked if we could leave. She had to open tomorrow, which meant getting up at five. I said sure.

"Where'd you and Scotty disappear to?" I asked as we drove.

"Nowhere."

"There something I should know?"

She shook her head. "No. Wait. What do you mean?"

"The two of you weren't sneaking off for some Scotty-Cassie time were you?"

"No."

I raised my eyebrows.

"No," she said and made a face. "We were giving you some privacy so Erica could make a move. Baiting the trap, so to speak."

"Well, she took the bait."

"Oh?"

I gave Cassie the details of our conversation. She agreed it was another promising sign.

"So," she said as I turned into her driveway, "you think you can wait three weeks?"

"I've got no choice."

"We can keep each other company as we wait," Cassie said. "And we'll see if I get into college or you get Erica first."

"Sounds like a deal."

I coasted to a stop and put the car in park. Because my parents raised a gentleman, I walked Cassie to the door.

"Thanks for the ride," she said.

"Thanks for the pep talk."

"I'll see you Sunday."

"Yeah. Don't work too hard tomorrow."

Cassie slipped inside, and I waved at Mrs. Larson through the kitchen window. It was still a beautiful night, now a little closer to sundown, and I decided to burn some gas by bumming around the back roads for a little while.

I thought about how a week's worth of worrying and unease had been resolved so quickly. Cassie was no longer worried about her future, so neither was I. Scotty and Gia had patched things up—or at least applied a Band-Aid. The signs looked good for Erica and me, assuming another earthquake or tropical love didn't strike her in Haiti. Even my images of her were purer now, of her in that yellow polo spooning ice cream and smiling at the golden tree tops.

I returned home and, as was my habit, emptied my pockets. I found a fresh, crisp twenty-dollar bill. In my excitement about potentially getting ice cream from Erica, I had completely forgotten about dropping it in the plate.

I prayed that she could still find a cab to get her safely home at night in dangerous Port-au-Prince.

Chapter 14

". . . they do not restrain their feet." Jeremiah 14:10

I awoke at 4:59 a.m., per specific instructions given to my alarm clock. Sitting up in bed so that I'd stay awake, I prayed for Erica's safety as she traveled. Not being exactly sure how prayer worked, I asked that if ever there was a moment when she needed prayer, God would bring her to my attention. Being a swell guy, I tacked on a request for the rest of the team, as well as for the people they would be ministering to. Then I reset the alarm and dozed back off.

I slept fitfully, tossing and turning until the alarm went off again at eight. As I went through my morning routine, I wondered if God had been trying to get my attention already. I'd heard stories about people who woke up in the middle of the night, burdened to pray for a missionary, only later to find out that at that exact moment, the missionary had been surrounded by spear-wielding natives or being tracked through the bush by a ferocious tiger. As of eight o'clock, Erica was probably just boarding a United flight to Chicago, so I chalked it up to general restlessness.

I made it to church five minutes early, in plenty of time to grab the middle-right row that had become ours. (At Morgan Bible, like I suspect at so many churches, pews — or chairs — had become quite territorial. Certain people occupy the same seat every Sunday and expect you to know it. Same holds for missions conferences or special programs or any other events. We stop just short of printing labels.) But I didn't even make it into the sanctuary. I was stopped by a mound of shoes in the foyer, blocking the doors into the sanctuary.

I racked my brain — had I forgotten some kicks-for-kids charity drive? I didn't think so, and these weren't donated shoes. They were wingtips and dress sandals and new sneakers and flip-flops and everything. I glanced over the pile briefly, in case this turned out to be a receiving instead of a giving thing.

"Good morning," an usher greeted me. He was wearing an old suit, the color of once-eaten food. He was also wearing black, gold-toed socks. He was not wearing shoes.

"Morning," I replied, not yet ready to grant the day "good" status.

He offered me a bulletin — er, that is, worship folder.

I had to ask. "What's with the shoes?"

The usher turned and directed my attention to a cheap-looking cloth banner hanging over the entrance to the sanctuary. It was brown, with gold lettering: "Take off your sandals, for the place where you are standing is holy ground." – Exodus 3:5

"Seriously?" I asked.

Before the usher could answer, Curtis Teasdale himself stepped out of the sanctuary and stopped underneath the sign. "Welcome!" he called to me and a handful of others straggling in. "This is indeed holy ground! Please, take off your shoes."

He was barefoot in ripped blue jeans, and I wondered what gimmick my father had come up with for his Father's Day sermon.

I looked at the other recent arrivals and saw an old couple mumbling to each other as they took seats against the wall and began the painstaking process of removing their shoes. A teenage girl kicked off her flip-flops in the general direction of the pile. I didn't see anyone still shod entering the sanctuary.

Why hadn't I skipped?

I was faced with the age-old debate. Conform and do something awkward to avoid looking dumb for not conforming, or take the ridicule to avoid the awkwardness of looking dumb by conforming to something dumb? I had always been taught not to give into peer pressure, but this wasn't smoking behind the school; this was not wearing shoes to church.

I was pretty sure my black socks didn't have holes in them, and they weren't the kind that were barely more than panty hose for men (you know, so thin you can see flesh through them) so I untied and removed my shoes. I hated conforming. But I couldn't very well trounce on holy ground, could I? Never mind that it apparently hadn't been holy seven days prior.

"Do I get a claim slip for these?" I asked no one in particular. Teasdale appeared to hear my remark, and didn't appear to appreciate it particularly. I shrugged, dropped my size tens on the pile, and padded into the sanctuary.

Scotty was wearing his sneakers.

"Conformer," he mumbled.

"I was ambushed by the clergy," I replied. I nodded at Cassie, then reached for her knee and tugged her khaki pants up an inch to reveal a bare foot.

"She conformed too," I said to Scotty.

"I have a feeling we're in for a doozy today."

Five minutes late, Teasdale and company bounded up onto the stage, not a shoe in the bunch. "Good morning!" he bellowed as if it was his greatest pleasure on earth to wake up. "This is holy ground!" he hollered. "We celebrate Father's Day today, and we honor our Heavenly Father by proclaiming that this place, His house, is holy ground. If you haven't done so already, please remove your shoes, your sandals, whatever the case may be."

"Might not want to be too vague when asking people to remove clothes in church," Scotty whispered.

With gusto, the worship team started into one of their new favorite songs, one I'd never heard until five weeks ago, but was getting quite familiar with now. After a rousing rendition that lasted far longer than necessary considering the song only had one verse, one chorus, and one bridge, we were seated.

The woman beside Teasdale read from Exodus, the account of Moses and the burning bush, culminating with his removing of his sandals. When she was finished, Teasdale prayed about how the church was holy ground, and how as such we shouldn't desecrate it by wearing shoes. I feared this was going to become a habit. We'd be laughed at across the state as the BBB — the Barefoot Bible Believers.

Teasdale finished and launched into a brief set of announcements. He mentioned the missions team, and I thought of Erica, now probably in O'Hare International eating a Cinnabon. Then I thought of her ankles and how this service would have suited her nicely. I chased that thought away.

After the announcements, we sang some more songs, two of which were all right and one of which was downright laughable. It said something about how we should seek to be undignified before God, which at the very least was a misinterpretation of II Samuel 6. In truth, I think the writer just had some bad chili one night, tossed and turned the way I had, but instead of just tossing and turning, got up and wrote whatever nonsense was on his mind and put it to guitar plucking. Wasn't that how all musicians worked?

"Amen?" Teasdale asked when the song mercifully concluded to a drum roll and what sounded like a xylophone. "Lord, we want to be undignified in Your presence . . ."

"They're certainly accomplishing that," Scotty whispered.

"We want to be crazy with passion, mad with love for You. Help us to be unbridled, unrestrained in our worship. In Your Name . . . Amen. Be seated."

"Great," Scotty said. "One step short of temple prostitutes."

I sat and listened to a sermon that tried to connect being undignified to not wearing shoes to fathers to . . . well, I lost it at that point. I stuck on the song. Be it a hymn, a chorus, a poem, or prose, I had a problem with inaccuracy. And while most of the songs we had sung over the last month weren't terribly meaty, they also weren't inaccurate.

But I had to draw the line with this undignified business. It's one thing to look undignified or foolish in the world's eyes because we're following God or worshiping Him. But it's another to seek to be undignified, to be crazy, to be mad, as the song suggested. I get the idea of having intense love for God; but don't crazy and mad suggest something a little different—a frame of mind that isn't appropriate for Christians? Aren't we supposed to be of sound mind, clear-thinkers, rational—and yet passionate?

Maybe it was more different strokes, potato and po-tah-to. But I didn't think so. That analogy only spread so far. Some things were just across the line.

Then again, maybe the guy had written it at five a.m. after bad chili. Maybe, like so many musicians, he wasn't the greatest lyricist and couldn't find the words to say what he really meant. I gave him a pass. The guy who selected the song for congregational consumption—one Curtis Teasdale—I did not.

I wrestled with the idea a little, prayed about it, flipped to a few passages of Scripture, and as Teasdale was concluding his sermon with a story about a family camping trip one summer, I still had the same general feeling in my gut about the song. And about the pastor wearing ripped jeans and about Hymns for Dummies and a host of other things.

I understood what Dave and Dirk had said, about how maybe a lot of the problem I was having was because the church had canned my dad and now everything was different than what I had grown up with. But just because I had a conflict of interest, it didn't mean that I was wrong.

As we stood for the last song, Scotty leaned over. "I wonder if Shoeless Joe ever thought about a hundred and fifty people leaving at once, all trying to find and put on their shoes."

It was then that I realized I should have at least tied my shoelaces together. I turned and nudged Cassie. "Let's go now."

"What?"

"Get our shoes before the rush."

Her eyes widened and she followed me as I slipped out of the pew. She had to do a little digging for one of her sandals, and I took my time tying my shoes so I wouldn't have to help. This pile was only slightly less disgusting than the one Laura Dern had dug through on *Jurassic Park* to find the sat phone (Or had it been Julianne Moore in *The Lost World*? Téa Leoni in *Jurassic Park III*?) and there was no need for both of us to get athlete's hand.

The crowd was largely diminished for Sunday school, thanks to the Haitian trip. Those that did show up all wore shoes, except for Tim.

"Hey, Frodo, you can put your shoes back on," Scotty said. "This isn't holy ground . . . just the sanctuary."

"I couldn't find them," Tim said.

"What?"

"I left them in the pile, but by the time I could get to it, they were all gone."

"You lost your shoes because of that nonsense today?" Amy Stevenson asked.

"I don't think you should call it nonsense," Petey said.

"Save your admonitions for class," she retorted. "Making everyone take off their shoes in church is ridiculous. Especially old people with support hose and Dr. Scholl's inserts and bunions. And hello, did anyone notice the smell?"

"You're making that up."

"No I'm not. Maybe not where you were sitting, but in my row, there was a definite odor." She turned to Tim. "You seriously lost your shoes?"

"Yeah. The foyer's empty and they aren't there."

"Did you look under chairs and behind the welcome center?"

"I looked everywhere."

Amy sighed. "I'll be back."

Tim looked back at us and I, for my part, shrugged. Amy Stevenson was hard to figure. She was in her mid-twenties, may or may not have been married once, and never lacked an opinion. She had dark hair that was usually pulled back and thin black glasses, a combination that somehow gave credence to her arguments. Worse yet, she was kind of cute, which made being out-argued by her insufferable.

Amy returned carrying an offering plate.

"What are you doing with that?"

"Taking an offering to buy Tim some new shoes."

"I don't need new shoes."

"All evidence to the contrary."

"Well, what are you going to do," Brad asked, "run to the store and buy some before class ends?"

Amy gave him a stare, and I wouldn't have put it past her. But she just passed the offering plate around, and I pitched in a few bucks. The plate returned to Amy and she counted the money.

"Eleven dollars and thirty-six cents? Who's the smart aleck who put thirty-six cents into the plate?"

"Maybe it was to cover tax," Scotty said.

Amy scooped out the money and gave it to Tim, who reluctantly accepted our contribution for his new footwear.

"Do you mind if we start now?" Petey asked.

"Just because I broke off an engagement with your cousin doesn't mean you have to be snippy."

So that was it, Amy had been engaged.

"That's out of line," Petey said.

"You're the one who's bent out of shape."

"I disagree with your categorization, but if I am a little upset it's because we have a lot of material to cover today and we are already late."

"We're late because we started church late because everyone had to take off their shoes, which means we ended late, and then we were delayed because everyone—everyone but Tim—had to find their shoes, and then we took a collection for Tim so he could buy new shoes, and isn't that really what God wants from us, more than just a bunch of pious book-learning?"

"That Book you're referring to is the Bible."

"I meant your little lecture notebook," Amy said.

"Can I have a word with you outside?" he asked. He turned to the class. "Excuse us."

"Another Sunday school fight," I said to Cassie.

"Dude, I wonder who's on the card next week," Mike said from the row in front of us.

"Who wants to bet he comes in with a shiner?" Brett asked.

"Who wants to bet she doesn't come in?" Brad asked.

"Who wants to bet our church gets blackballed from the next area pastors' meeting?"

"That's okay, our pastor wouldn't wear shoes to the meeting anyhow."

"I think I just heard a slap."

"Scotty's still here."

"It was Gia who slapped him."

"Maybe somebody should go out there."

"Petey has self-control."

"Petey's the one I'm worried about."

I turned to Cassie. "You doing anything for Father's Day?"

"Going to see both grandpas," she replied. "Dad's dad in Nebraska City, and Grandpa de Haan at The Piedmont. You?"

"Having dinner and watching golf with my surrogate family," I said, nodding at Scotty.

She made a sad face. She was right. Every kid should be able to be with his pops on Father's Day.

Petey returned to class. Amy didn't.

"Did you banish her?" Brett asked.

"Our conversation is private."

"Where's Amy?"

Scotty started humming. It took me a moment to recognize it as an old Switchfoot tune. "Amy's Song."

"I believe she's returning the offering plate," Petey replied.

"So is she coming back?"

"I don't know, but we are ten minutes past starting time, so let's begin. Please turn to Revelation chapter—"

"Weren't we going to discuss something else?" Brad asked.

Petey looked up, perturbed at being interrupted. "Like what?"

"Romans twelve," Scotty said.

"Why would we look at Romans twelve?"

"Something about playing video games with Tim Tebow," Brett said.

Petey took a deep breath. "Okay, but let's make it quick. Did anyone give any thought to how we can worship God with our daily—"

Amy flew through the door, holding up a pair of Oxford slip-ons. "Found 'em."

"My shoes," Tim said. "Where were they?"

"In the ladies' room."

"What were they doing in the ladies' room?"

"Hiding under the sink."

"How did they get there?"

"Do you want your shoes or not?"

"Of course."

"That'll be eleven thirty-six," Amy said. She smirked as Tim handed her the money. She slapped it down on a vacant chair. "Now, let's see which wisenheimer claims the thirty-six cents."

We collected our money and ultimately got around to a rushed class. Petey was flustered and angry and did little more than read to us. When class was over, Scotty, Cassie, and I were the last ones to leave the room.

I looked down at the thirty-six cents, still lying on the seat where Amy had put it. The rest of the money had been claimed and she had given up on finding the "weasel."

I scooped up the money and slapped it into Cassie's hand. "Your secret's safe with us."

"It was all I had on me," she said, returning the coins to her pocket. I did not think to ask why she had brought thirty-six cents to church.

"Besides," she said as she turned for the door, "how do you think his shoes got into the ladies' room in the first place?"

The final few pairings were just teeing off at the U.S. Open as Scotty, Dirk, and I settled in for an afternoon of golf. And barbecue pork sandwiches. To Dirk, Sunday at the U.S. Open was a national holiday, and he had stayed home from church to monitor the pork in his slow cooker, seasoning it just so, making from-scratch coleslaw, and watching pre-round coverage on ESPN.

So before the tournament heated up and while we ate, Scotty and I briefed him on the happenings at Morgan Bible.

"You're kidding?" he asked.

"We are not."

"What was the sermon about? There was a sermon this week, right?"

"Yeah," I answered. "I don't know exactly. Scotty?"

"Mmm," he said, stuffing another bite of bun, pork, and coleslaw into his mouth. "I don't know. Exodus, I think."

"It was hard to follow, and I had other things on my mind," I said.

"Your girlfriend?"

"Would toward that she were."

"Any progress?"

"I think we're to Friday at the Masters," I said, "and all I've done is make eighteen pars."

"Make eighteen more and you'll be in the discussion come the weekend," Dirk said. He got up to make another sandwich. I watched Phil Mickelson on the range. He was in the final pairing, tied for the lead, but known for coming up just short in the U.S. Open. We all hoped this would be the year for "Lefty."

"Problem is," I said when Dirk returned, "I'm in one of the last groups out Friday, and all day I've been sitting there watching guys attack easy flags, making birdies and eagles. Middle of the green and two-putt seems overly cautious. I'm afraid par through thirty-six holes will leave me too far back."

"Which is exactly what several of the players ahead of you thought," Dirk said. "They're the ones who hit it in the creek on thirteen, said I won't make the same mistake twice, and scalded the ball over fifteen green and into the pond in front of sixteen."

"Has that happened?"

"Once or twice."

I paused, barbecue sauce and coleslaw dripping onto my plate. "What's that mean in real life?"

"You said it's Friday," Dirk said. "Saturday is moving day. Let these young guns shoot their sixty-fives. You play smart, stay in the tournament, and come out firing on Saturday and Sunday, when the real roars are heard."

"How long'd you date Mom?" Scotty asked.

"Six weeks," Dirk said as he took a bite.

"So when would you say you made your move, Thursday morning?"

"I also ended up OB[10]," Dirk replied. "I'm a wiser player now."

I sighed. "It doesn't matter anyhow. We're in a rain delay."

Dirk frowned for a moment. "That's right. She's over in Haiti, isn't she?"

"Halfway to Miami now, but yeah."

"That's good," Dirk said.

"Good?"

"Yeah. Rain softens the greens. Makes your approach land softer."

"This is getting ridiculous," Scotty said.

"You got some advice for the boy?" Dirk asked.

"Yeah. Hang out a few times when she comes back, and then ask her out."

"You think it's time?" I asked.

He rolled his head from side to side. "I think it could be. According to your accounting of Friday night."

"What happened Friday night?" Dirk asked. I explained. He nodded. "See what the rain does," he advised.

"Does that mean hang out a few times?"

"It does."

I sighed and got up to get another sandwich. "Assuming she doesn't come back in love with some guy from the team or smitten with some Haitian sensation or something."

"Dad, will you tell him to quit worrying?"

"I can't help it," I said, scooping pork onto my bun. "It's what I'm good at."

"Good," Scotty said, "because girls love a guy who worries."

I sighed again as I returned to the couch. Mickelson teed off and we turned our attention to literal golf. For several hours, we sat enthralled as he took the lead, lost the lead, and spent a lot of time tied for the lead. Finally, he surged in front by several strokes, and we celebrated his good fortune with chocolate chip cookie ice cream sandwiches. Dirk had made them himself.

---

[10] OB is short for hitting the ball out of bounds, a one-stroke penalty in golf.

"How's the job of yours going?" Dirk asked during a commercial break. Six hours of golf coverage and even the commercials were about golf.

"It's going," I said. "Keeping about thirty hours a week. No nights and weekends so far."

"They paying you well?"

"Well enough to pay the rent and buy groceries."

"Good to hear."

Mickelson's drive landed in the deep U.S. Open rough and our attention was diverted back to golf. He bogeyed the hole at the same time as his playing partner birdied it, and his lead was down to one. For the next hour, we watched with rapt attention as Mickelson made a complete mess of the final three holes, yet managed to save par on each of them. When his final ten-foot putt dropped into the hole, Lefty was finally a U.S. Open champion.

Hoping it was a sign of more good fortune to come, I went home and called my dad to wish him a happy Father's Day.

Chapter 15

"You said, 'We will ride off on swift horses.'" Isaiah 30:16

The week was languid. Temperatures soared into the 90s and even hit triple digits Tuesday and Wednesday. Combined with high humidity and dew points in the 80s (Falls City in the southeast corner of the state reported a dew point of 84 Wednesday afternoon) they made doing anything almost unbearable. Including sleeping in a hot apartment with no air conditioning. I had the motor on my fan smoking.

We got it good. Wednesday afternoon, tornadoes steamrolled through eastern Colorado, Kansas, and western and central Nebraska. One hundred forty-seven of them, to be exact. Several small towns were wiped right off the map.

Work had become a drag. I'd thought with temperatures so high, ice cream consumption would have been similarly high. But it wasn't and time stood still. So when Wendy called Thursday night and asked if I could work Friday night because one of the usuals was sick, I was less than enthusiastic. But I agreed. Then I got roped into working Saturday too. But what did I care? My woman was gone and I had nothing to do.

I slept until 8:20 on Sunday and seriously thought about skipping church. Who knew what article of clothing I would have to leave in the foyer this time. Jesus and his disciples often removed their outer garments and things. What was next, church in our underwear?

But I went. Scotty didn't, skipping to play golf, I assumed. So Cassie and I sat together, alone. The music was ho-hum, nothing that caused me to be distracted during the sermon at least. It was on love, and Pastor Teasdale "stepped on a few toes" (albeit, shod ones) when he said we had more love for our family, our friends, our pets, and even perhaps our football team than we did for God. I couldn't argue that at times he was right. Times like the fall. Particularly Saturdays. Say from two-thirty until six?

Teasdale closed in prayer. "Father, we don't just want to love You. We want to be in love with You. Passionately. Not the way Hollywood distorts being in love; not the way we distort being in love; but the way You intended for love to be expressed. Help us to be in love with You in just such a way . . . Amen."

We sang a slow, sad, dirge of a closing song, a seven-eleven as Dirk liked to call them. Seven words repeated eleven times. He thought it was clever.

I went to Sunday school expecting fireworks, but found no spark. There were six of us total. Cassie was the only girl, and I was the only potential troublemaker (unless you count heaving Tim Harte's Oxford slip-ons into the ladies' room to be troublemaking). I behaved myself, and Petey lectured on the six seals from Revelation 6. It was mildly interesting, and a little scary.

Cassie kicked my calf after the closing prayer. "You doing anything today?"

"Killing some baddies, but that's about it."

Cassie frowned for a moment. "Ah, video games."

"Yeah."

"Want to come over for lunch?"

"Hmm, what's cooking?"

"Does it matter?"

It did. Cassie's mom was a great cook, but she had a tendency to use a lot of natural items in her meals. Veggie casseroles were not all that uncommon. But Cassie was too sweet to turn down, especially since I gathered she was just trying to occupy my mind while Erica was gone.

"Sure," I said.

She cleared it with her folks, and then we both walked the block and a half to my apartment. I quickly changed into shorts and a T-shirt before driving us to her parents' farm outside town.

Cassie's dad had raised dairy and beef cows, but now was strictly beef. They also had chickens, an off-and-on goat, and horses. The horses were Cassie's, and she loved them at what I gathered from the morning's sermon might be a sinfully high level.

The Larson's farmhouse was old but homey, which was a credit to Mrs. Larson. She had insisted I call her Ruth, but somehow I just couldn't bring myself to do so. So I avoided nouns of direct address in her presence.

Lunch consisted of baked chicken, a cheesy potato salad, fresh green beans (Cassie's mom was also a green thumb in the garden) and a fresh fruit compote. We ate in their dining room, talking about the summer heat, the tornadoes, melting ice cream at Nebraska Novelties, life without my parents, and — repeatedly — how delicious the food was. Mr. Larson (I couldn't call him Wayne either) was especially complimentary.

At the end of dinner, Cassie's parents got into a friendly argument over whose turn it was to do the dishes. The argument went back and forth, covering this chore and that chore, until we were almost back to May. They were joking throughout, and Cassie and I both sat back and exchanged smiles. I thought of how, after my parents, Cassie's folks were probably the perfect example of a biblical husband and wife, father and mother. And just a little quirky too.

Finally Cassie put an end to the dispute. "Josh and I will do the dishes," she said. I was disappointed; she had stolen my thunder. Another thing Mom had taught me — if someone invites you over for dinner, you offer to do the dishes. Or help out in some way. I never got the chance.

Mrs. Larson accepted our offer and headed off to make her Sunday afternoon phone calls. (I had long ago learned that there was a group of ladies at Morgan Bible who spoke every Sunday afternoon — the topics were secret, but I could only guess it had to do with the quality of the sermon and who wore what to church.) Mr. Larson went into the living room to fall asleep with the newspaper on his lap. Cassie had told me this was his habit every Sunday. As hard as he worked, I couldn't blame him.

Cassie washed; I dried. An old desktop fan sat on the counter and kept us cool while helping to dry the dishes a little more quickly.

"I think Mom's glad you came," she said. "She gets tired of just cooking for us."

"I get tired of cooking for myself," I said.

"Your digestive system probably gets sick of it too," Cassie said, nudging on the water to rinse a plate. "I've seen how you 'cook.'"

"Aren't you the girl who once baked eleven chocolate chip cookies because you ate the rest of the dough?"

Cassie bit her lip and paid very close attention to the plate she was washing. She rinsed it and handed it to me. "There was brownie batter once too."

"We all have our vices."

"Yours being killing baddies?"

I nodded.

"I've lost four pounds this summer."

"That's good."

"It's terrible. I haven't had dessert since April."

"You had ice cream Friday."

"I know. And pie later today. I'm falling off the wagon. I'll gain them right back."

"For the record, you looked fine with the four pounds."

"You're just saying that."

"I am not. Besides, what I think's not important."

"I know, it's what God thinks," she says. "But you know what kind of people have I Samuel 16:7[11] on an index card on their bathroom mirror? Fatties."

"Do you have I Samuel 16:7 on an index card on your bathroom mirror?"

She banged off the faucet. "Are you saying I'm a fatty?"

"No. I thought you said it. Or implied it. How did we get here?"

"You brought up cookie dough."

---

[11] I Samuel 16:7: But the LORD said to Samuel, "Do not consider his appearance or his height, for I have rejected him. The LORD does not look at the things man looks at. Man looks at the outward appearance, but the LORD looks at the heart.

"You insulted my cooking," I countered.

"Your cooking's terrible. And it's not cooking. It's heating."

I dried the final plate. Cassie moved on to the serving bowls.

"And I wasn't going to that it's what God thinks," I said. "I was going to say Tim Harte."

She dropped the bowl into the water, sending suds everywhere. She blew them off her cheek, getting some loose strands of hair in the process. "Why Tim Harte?"

"You did hide his shoes in the ladies' bathroom," I said.

"You did what?" Mrs. Larson asked. Apparently the lines were busy.

"She threw Tim Harte's shoes in the ladies' room last Sunday," I said, turning over my shoulder.

"Cassandra."

"The poor guy thought he was going to have to walk home without his shoes. We even took up a collection in Sunday school until Amy Stevenson found them."

Mrs. Larson shook her head and tisked as she headed for the living room.

"I do not like Tim Harte," Cassie said under her breath, blowing at more strands of hair.

"Your mouth says 'no' but your shoe-hiding says tells a different story."

"I was just adding some levity to the class."

"So why Tim's shoes?"

"Because I recognized them. He wears Oxford slip-ons, for Pete's sake! I do not have a thing for Tim," she said, quite serious.

"Okay. I'll drop it."

"I don't."

"Okay."

"Now his brother, back when I was in junior high, that's another matter."

"Tyler?"

"But that does not leave this kitchen."

"He's married and living in Missouri or somewhere."

"Arkansas," Cassie said.

"How do you know that?"

"It does not leave this kitchen." Her eyes were intense.

I sealed my lips.

"I haven't gone blabbing to any of my girl friends who you like."

"Who do you like, Josh?" Mrs. Larson asked, crossing back through the kitchen.

"Yikes, Mom, cough when you enter a room or something."

"Sorry, sweetie."

I was off the hook, and we finished the dishes. Cassie dried her hands on a dishtowel and tucked her hair behind her ears. "Come with me. I want to show you something."

"Okay."

I followed her up the creaky old stairs to her bedroom. It was spacious, twice the size of a standard bedroom, with plenty of natural lighting from three windows on the south and east.

"This," said Cassie, leading me into the corner, "is my latest painting."

It was a desert landscape, with jagged mountains against a pale sky, a ravine running from back right to front left, and a giant saguaro cactus dominating the right third of the canvas.

"That's great," I said. "Inspiration?"

"More like the constant thought in my head," she answered. "It took me a whole afternoon to do the needles on the cactus."

"I think I'd have gone for a barren wilderness," I said, moving to look at some of her other works. Most of them still unframed, they covered the walls.

"I'm thinking of trying to sell some, if I can find a market," she said. "Any little bit helps."

I stopped in front of another mountain scene. "Tetons?" I asked.

"Um-hmm. From an old calendar. You think twenty-five a painting is too much?"

"I think it's too little."

"Really?"

"Really. These would go for a hundred easy at one of those shops in the Haymarket."

"I couldn't ask more than fifty," she said. "Not in good faith."

"Sold," I said.

Cassie smiled.

"No, I mean it. I'll buy this one for fifty bucks. If it's for sale."

"You aren't buying my painting."

"Why not?"

"Because it'd be a pity buy."

"Yes, my walls are pitiful and I need something to jazz them up a little."

Her hands went to her hips.

"I'm serious, Cass."

"You're sure you're not doing it just to help me out?"

"Two birds with one stone," I said.

"Okay," she said. "But I'm framing it first."

"If you get less than a 3.0 at ASU I want my money back."

We looked at the rest of her paintings then went outside. We wandered over toward the small shed-turned-stable that housed Forsberg, Nicky, and Tomas. Cassie, a huge hockey fan, had named her horses after Swedish hockey stars. I said a better hockey-themed name for a horse would be OffthePipe or StickSaveAndABeauty, something like you hear at the Kentucky Derby. But they were not my horses to name.

Forsberg (you could tell by the white on her nose) was hanging out by the fence, and Cassie placed her hand under the horse's cheek and stroked her forehead. Forsberg whinnied softly, and I gathered that they were both content to while away the afternoon together.

Cassie suddenly turned my way. "You want to go for a ride?"

I felt like Bob Wylie from the movie *What About Bob?* He had been afraid of going sailing, and I was afraid of getting onto a wild animal that I would only in theory have control of. A bit in the mouth of a horse is kind of like a BB in the behind of a buffalo, in my opinion — if he doesn't want to let it bother him, it won't bother him.

I had ridden once before. I hadn't been thrown, hadn't had the horse suddenly start sprinting, and hadn't been incredibly sore for the next week. And so, despite my fear, I told Cassie, "Why not?" I would just let the horse do the work, I told myself.

"Horses are like shrinks," Cassie said as we entered the stable. "They can tell what you're feeling even if you can't. Relax, be soothing, and you have nothing to worry about."

Implying that if I wasn't relaxed — which I wasn't — or if I wasn't soothing — not my defining quality by any means — that I did have something to worry about?

Cassie walked me over to Nicky, named for legendary Swedish defenseman Niklas Lidstrom. She showed me where to place my hands, how to stroke the horse, and had me talking to her like she was a baby and I was one of those annoying "goochie, goochie, goo" women. But Nicky seemed to like it.

We saddled up Forsberg and Nicky and, after a brief horseback riding refresher course from Cassie, we clop-clop-clopped out into the pasture. The first five minutes were terrifying, like being behind the wheel of a car for the first time. Only the car was a dump truck. But then I settled in, and we slowly worked our way to a canter. I wanted to scream in terror and shout in exhilaration at the same time. But I was too busy concentrating to do either.

At the back end of the pasture, we slowed to a trot and then a walk. I finally felt comfortable to ride and talk at the same time. "Ask you a question?" I said.

"Mm-hmm."

"What are your thoughts on 'being in love' with God?"

"You mean am I for or against?"

"I mean as opposed to loving God?"

"Is there a difference?"

"Your parents love you," I said, "but they're in love with each other."

Cassie nodded. "So why wouldn't we want to be in love with God?"

"I didn't say we wouldn't. But the phrase has kind of bothered me, and I don't know if it's the phrase or if it is the tugging of the Holy Spirit."

We rode for a little ways, Forsberg and Nicky content to plod along. People could learn a lot from horses.

"Well," Cassie said at last, "we are the bride of Christ, which sort of leans toward the idea of being in love."

I thought about that for a minute. "I guess the problem with being in love is that people fall in love."

"So?"

"So if you can fall in love, you can fall back out, can't you?"

"The divorce rate would certainly suggest so."

"So should we really be in love with God?"

"Should my parents or your parents be in love with each other?" Cassie asked.

"Isn't that different?"

"I'm not sure it is. To make a good marriage, you have to be in love, but you also need to have love that isn't based on feelings. You can't fall out of that."

"So it's the idea of loving God with heart, soul, and mind?"

"Don't forget strength," Cassie said. "Strength is the engine that drives the other three. At least that's how I see it. It implies loving God with your will, even when it's hard."

I looked at her, trusting Nicky not to do something stupid. "You're just full of nuggets of wisdom, aren't you?"

She shrugged, and we turned so as not to run into a fence. It was a beautiful afternoon, only in the low 80s and dry. The sky was a vivid blue and the clouds like billows of pure white smoke. A gentle breeze blew out of the south and reminded me why I liked summer.

"Ask you a question?" Cassie countered.

"Sure."

"Are you in love with Erica or do you just love her?"

Sometimes Cassie doesn't pull her punches.

I swallowed. "I'm not sure I'm ready to use the word love."

"Okay, well whatever toned down version of love you would use."

I thought for a few strides. "More in love than love," I said. "But isn't that natural early on?"

"You're asking me?" Cassie said. "The closest I've had to a boyfriend is apparently putting Tyler Harte's brother's shoes in the ladies' room at church."

"Which was purely platonic, I hear."

"Unless you want me to reach over and kick Nicky in the flank."

"Yep, purely platonic."

"I only ask because I want to make sure that if something does develop between you and her, it's the right thing."

"So do I," I said.

Cassie nodded. "Canter again?"

"Sure."

And so we urged our steeds on, and soon were flying—or so it seemed—through the knee-high (to a human, not a horse) prairie grass. We slowed at the corner, then trotted and walked the horses back to the stable.

Just like Bob Wylie, I survived in fine shape.

Chapter 16

"As they talked and discussed these things with each other . . ." Luke 24:15

The four of us ate apple pie with ice cream on the porch. It was a slice of Americana, a throwback to lazy summer Sundays of yesteryear. Mrs. Larson creaked in an old glider. Mr. Larson sat in a wicker chair, a contented smile on his face. I was in the second wicker chair, and Cassie sat on the porch railing. We listened to the rustling of leaves in the giant maple tree in the front yard and the chirping of various insects. It beat any spa or beach resort in the world.

This came on the heels of a game of Scrabble around the kitchen table that had Mr. and Mrs. Larson having another of their intense but friendly arguments, this time over whether worship was awarded a second "P" when a suffix was added. It had finally been determined that the answer was maybe, and the play with two P's had been allowed.

"How are your parents doing, Josh?" Mrs. Larson asked.

I swallowed a bite of pie. "Pretty good. The church is strong, and they're getting accustomed to life in Oklahoma."

"Hot there this week?" Mr. Larson asked.

"One-oh-seven."

"One-oh-seven?" Cassie mouthed.

"Tell your mother I've been meaning to write her," Mrs. Larson said. "It's just one thing after another."

"She actually told me to tell you the same thing," I said with a grin. "They're keeping pretty busy."

"Well you can also tell them we're praying for them," Mr. Larson said. "I'm sure this can't have been an easy transition for them."

"No," I said quietly. "And thank you."

I was making a list, just in my head, of people on my parents' side. Of course I had always known Cassie's parents weren't in favor of Dad's firing. Still, a guy could forget there was anyone in his corner. A modern day Elijah. (Now there was an Old Testament guy who wasn't a pervert.)

"Can I ask you both a question?" I said after watching a chickadee on the porch railing investigate Cassie's empty plate.

Mr. and Mrs. Larson both nodded.

"What do you think of the changes at church lately?"

"What changes are you referring to?" Mrs. Larson asked.

"The songs we sing and how we sing them, the fact that the worship team wears ripped jeans, the whistling and taking off of shoes . . ."

"Things not sitting well with you?" Mr. Larson asked.

"No. And I can't tell if it's just that it's not the way things used to be, or if there's something more."

Mr. Larson nodded. "You know when your father first arrived here, he and the elders of that day made quite a few changes people didn't like too. We used to say the Lord's Prayer every Sunday, but he sort of felt like it was just rote recitation—which I think it largely had become. So we stopped staying it. He also originally wore a robe."

"I remember that," I said, doing so for the first time in a long while.

"Thing is, no one knew why. It was a tradition with no purpose." Mr. Larson shrugged. "So we made some changes. Your father stopped wearing a robe, and we stopped saying the Lord's Prayer every week. We used to have an old, somewhat out of tune pipe organ. When it was exchanged for a standard piano, you'd have thought by some people's reaction that we'd torn the Old Testament out of our Bibles." He shrugged again. "Anyhow, the point is, things changed quite a bit, and that didn't sit too well with a lot of traditionalists."

"So they left."

"Eventually. And there were other influencing factors."

"So what's that got to do with now, dear?" Mrs. Larson asked.

"When the church split, it was hard on everybody. Your father more than anybody, but I don't need to tell you that."

I shook my head.

"And a strong church, anchored on the Rock, can go through a split — they can survive. But a second split is awfully hard."

"You think the church is splitting again?"

"I think people are afraid of that. A dozen years ago, a chunk on one side fell off. Now they're afraid a chunk on the other side will."

"Who?"

"You," Mr. Larson said.

"Me?"

He nodded. "And Cassie, and Scotty, and the other twenty-somethings. There are plenty of statistics showing that kids are graduating from high school and leaving the church — not Morgan Bible, but the Church in general — and even leaving the faith."

"So we're wearing ripped jeans and singing contemporary songs and doing quirky stuff to keep millennials from leaving?"

"I don't have the official word," Mr. Larson said with a nod, "but that's what I gather from the conversations I've had."

"So if they're trying to keep the young crowd from leaving by being contemporary and moderate and quirky," Cassie said, "what's going to happen to the group of people who like things the way they were?"

"Like I said, the split was painful for the church," Mr. Larson said. "And I think they're betting that the veterans won't want to go through it again, that they stuck with the church once, and they'll stick with it again, because they are the true core."

"Risky," Cassie said.

"Maybe. But I think they're also willing, if they have to lose somebody, to lose the older crowd instead of the younger crowd."

I frowned. "Why's that?"

"Because they think the younger crowd needs to be reached yet. Or because they think the younger crowd will have a greater influence on the world today. I don't know exactly."

"Or the older crowd will be dead soon anyhow?"

"Cassie," Mrs. Larson said with a shake of her head.

"So where does that leave me?" I asked. "I prefer hymns, don't like whistling and taking off my shoes, and think the pastor and worship team

144

should dress better than a guy hoeing weeds. But none of those things are outlawed or forbidden in Scripture. So is it just a matter of style, or does there come a point when you have to do things the right way, and if that means people are going to be upset and leave, then let them be upset and leave?"

"Those are good questions."

"And are we at that point or not?"

"And whose way is the right way?" Cassie added.

"I don't have all the answers," Mr. Larson said.

"Since when?" she asked.

"Yeah. It sounds to me like you should be on the elder board," I said.

"He was nominated a couple years back, but declined," Mrs. Larson said.

"I didn't know that," Cassie said. "How come?"

"Candace," Mrs. Larson answered.

"The Bible teaches that an elder needs to be able to manage his own family well and that his children need to respect him," Mr. Larson said in his firm, quiet manner. "I didn't feel that was the case, so I respectfully declined."

We were silent for several minutes.

"But in answer to your questions, Josh, I think you should talk with the elders. Tell them your concerns. Let them hear the millennial position."

"Yeah, but I have nothing concrete. I mean, something feels wrong about all this, more than just the style of music or quirky behavior. But I can't put my finger on it."

"Sounds like you have some soul searching to do."

"Yes, sir. But my soul's pretty good at hide-and-seek."

We sat for a while longer, just enjoying the summer breeze. Eventually Mrs. Larson cleared away the plates and Mr. Larson went to check on the Cardinals-Cubs game. He'd grown up listening to the Cards on the radio, and still followed them when he could. I couldn't blame him—they had the sharpest uniforms in the Majors, and their colors were red and white.

"Josh, do you want to stay for dinner?" Mrs. Larson asked, peeking through the screen door. A hundred pounds heavier and with a screech in her voice, she could have been Aunt Bea. That would have made me Andy, or more accurately, Barney. Maybe Goober. It really didn't matter.

"There's leftover chicken for sandwiches," she said as I looked at Cassie. Her blue eyes were wide, urging me to stay. I began to think maybe she hadn't invited me over today as much for me as for her.

"Sure," I said, knowing it wasn't an imposition. If Dirk was my second father, then Cassie's folks were kind of like a third set. I'd grown especially close to them during the tenuous year when the rebels were splitting away to form True Way. Mom and Dad had spent many a night meeting with different church members, and I, being nine, had needed a babysitter. It was also the year when I was going through a strange "I'm scared to be away from Mom and Dad" phase, and playing rummy with Cassie and her mom or helping Mr. Larson feed the cows had had a calming influence on my worried little brain. The bond had always sort of remained.

We played another game of Scrabble, this time without any disputes. I spelled loquacious, using our modified method where you could have ten letters, but also couldn't make a word that was less than four letters. Loquacious pretty much put me over the top and had Cassie sticking her tongue out at me. Her mother scolded her, and I grinned smugly.

After dinner, Mr. Larson watched *60 Minutes* while Mrs. Larson busied herself in the kitchen. Cassie and I took a walk. The afternoon had turned to evening, the sun lower in the sky, creating long shadows on the Nebraska fields. It was beautiful.

"You doing all right?" I asked as we strolled along the pasture.

Cassie reached her hand through the fence, felt some grass on her palm. "Yeah, why?"

"I don't know. You just seem a little . . . somber."

"I thought I was being cheery and playful."

"You are," I said. "But I sense somberness underneath it all."

"I can't stop thinking about ASU."

"I thought it was in God's hands."

"It is."

"But you're not sure He can handle it?"

"No, I'm just afraid He won't handle it the way I want him to." She looked at me, the breeze stringing a few strands of hair across her face. She swiped them away. "I know that says a lot about me, but it's something I struggle with."

We took a few steps. "I think it says you're human."

"It says I have a lack of faith. I don't trust that God knows what's best."

"Like I said, human. But I'll pray for you."

"Thanks."

"I mean, I could tell you that God knows best and you'd rather Him give you what you need than what you want but wouldn't want once you got it, but you know that. It's the application of the theory that's the tricky part."

Cassie nodded.

"Like trusting that the woman of your dreams won't come back from Haiti engaged to a former orphan-turned-rescue worker."

"Are you really worried about that?"

"I'm me, Cassie. I'm worried about everything."

"I'll pray for you too."

I sighed.

"That's why I like horses," she said. "They don't worry about anything. They're kind of like hockey players. They'll charge into battle or dive in front of a puck or whatever they're asked to do. They don't worry that maybe they'll get shot and George Washington will have to jump to another horse or that maybe the puck will break a cheekbone. They just do what they're supposed to do, without asking questions, without . . ."

Cassie stopped and turned back to where I stood a few paces behind her. "What?" she asked.

I shook my head. "Nothing," I said as I resumed walking again. "I'm just really getting lost in all these metaphors. Golf and horses and hockey and George Washington. And the disciples thought Jesus' parables were confusing."

"I thought I'd seen it all," I told Dave the following Tuesday. It was July 3, hot and muggy, and we were between loads of hay (seven this time). "Then they pulled out their 'instruments.'"

"It certainly was creative," he said.

"That's one word for it."

The worship team on Sunday, instead of using guitars and drums and a piano/keyboard (which they didn't really use anymore) had pulled out their smartphones and tablets and used different apps and programs to make "music." One guy played a virtual guitar. Another a virtual electric drum. The other members of the team hadn't even been using instrument apps, instead calling upon various noises their different phones and tablets made, supposedly keeping in tune. It had been hailed as another "fresh" way to encounter God. Baby diapers were referred to as "fresh" too.

Since then, I had been thinking about my conversation with Cassie's parents the previous Sunday. Week after week, I was witnessing a new way the church was coming up with to be modern and contemporary. I asked Dave what he thought.

"I'd say that's accurate. It's certainly unconventional, but if that's what appeals to the younger generation, that's what they're going to try to do."

"But playing video games in church would appeal to the young crowd too," I said. "Is that what's next?"

He shrugged.

"And what do you think of it?"

"You mean as an old fogey?"

"I mean not being part of the Twitter-Twitter, text-text generation."

"I find it unconventional and a little off-putting, to be honest."

"But?"

"But I'm not ready to leave the church over it."

I took a deep breath. "So what do I do? I go to church every Sunday and just get more and more frustrated. I don't like the style, but there's more to it than that."

"Like what?"

"I don't know exactly. I see red flags waving, and Cassie's dad said I should take my concerns to the elders."

"That's a good suggestion."

"But I've been trying to figure out exactly what it is that's bothering me. It feels like it's more than style and being contemporary, but I can't exactly place it."

Dave nodded and refilled his lemonade.

"I went to college hoping to grow spiritually, and the environment wasn't what I expected and the Bible classes I took didn't bowl me over, and then I come home and find my lifelong church turned into a circus and I'm not growing. And Erica's been in Haiti for like four years."

Two weeks and three days to be precise, but you try being in puppy love and have half a country, a large sea, and possibly a hurricane between you and the girl of your dreams.

"So what have you been doing to grow?" Dave asked.

I shrugged. "The same as always. I read my Bible every day . . . almost every day. Try to have 'devotions.' Pray. I go to church, go to Sunday school, which by the way isn't doing wonders for my soul."

"It's not church and Sunday school or Vernon-Bedford's responsibility to make you grow," Dave said.

"It's mine," I said.

"Yeah, and ultimately God's. Paul told the Corinthians that it was God who made the seed grow."

I nodded.

"And I don't want to sound harsh or condemning, but reading your Bible every day and praying—having devotions—they're all good things. But it's easy to let those become a habit, a daily chore that you do because you're supposed to do it."

"Which it's become. Like even going to church." I turned my head. "Do you think we're supposed to be in love with God? And if we are, can you fall out of love? And what happens then?"

Dave smiled at my onslaught. "I tell you what," he said, slapping my knee. "Let's run another load."

"Okay," I said a little reluctantly.

"Your mind's going a mile a minute," he said. "Some physical exercise might bring clarity."

"Are you just stalling?"

"That too. Come on."

We unloaded the third wagon of the day, a chore that took half an hour. It was the middle of the afternoon, one I had gotten off by promising Wendy I'd work the morning and afternoon on the Fourth. That was okay—the real fun in Morgan didn't start until suppertime anyhow.

Around the lemonade cooler, Dave and I resumed our talk. "When you think of all God's done for us, all the love He's shown us, it's pathetic that we become apathetic toward Him. But that's exactly what happens, to every one of us at some point and time. Devotions, Bible reading, prayer, service, church, Sunday school—they all start to feel like work."

"So what do we do?"

"Let me ask you something. Assume this thing with Erica pans out— you date, get engaged, get married."

"So far, so good."

He nodded. "You have a couple of kids, they're adorable, life is going great."

"Okay . . ."

"And then you wake up one morning, and she's lying beside you with no makeup, hair a mess, breath a little foul, and you're in the middle of a stretch of days where it's nothing but work, taking care of the kids, going to bed and starting over. And you don't feel like you love her anymore."

"Aside from the work part you mentioned, I can't imagine any of that other stuff being true."

He smiled.

And I tried not to imagine lying in bed next to Erica, because I didn't think it would stop there.

"I know it doesn't seem like it, but it happens. What do you do?"

I took a deep breath. "I have a bowl of Cheerios, go to work, and come home to the wife and kids."

"Right. You keep living, keep plugging along. As a Christian, divorce isn't an option, and it isn't an option with God either. And a good thing, because you could never make the alimony payments."

I nodded. "Point made. Keep at it."

"The point isn't over. Because while you have to keep plugging along, plugging along is what got you into the trouble. Sometimes you have to change things up a little. Maybe it's something as simple as sending her some flowers or a box of chocolates, or maybe you suddenly take the kids to Grandma's and treat yourselves to a romantic weekend."

Down, boy.

"You schedule date nights, commit to eating meals together, give up TV. Throw a curve ball and do something to change the routine."

I nodded, trying to slow my heart and my mind at the idea of a romantic weekend with Erica. That thought wanted to hang around, and I wanted it to as well.

"So how do I send God a box of chocolates?" I asked.

"Another load," Dave said.

"Fair enough."

When we reconvened, I was sweating like I'd been standing under a hose. I wished I had been. We took our positions on hay bales again, wiping foreheads on sleeves and chugging lemonade.

"You mentioned reading your Bible," Dave said. "Ever study it?"

I shook my head. "Not much."

"That'd be a good place to start. And if I may, I'd suggest a study with others. You do it yourself, it's easy to put it off a week or start to slack. You join a group, you have accountability."

"I don't mean to be contrary, but I think it's going to be hard to get a group together. The Sunday school class is dwindling, and I don't know who we'd have to teach."

"You," he said.

"Me?"

He nodded. "You're more than qualified, from what I know of you. And the best way to learn is to teach."

"Me?"

Dave drained his glass. "You."

I pondered that for three more wagons full of hay.

Chapter 17

"Save me, O God, for the waters have come up to my neck." Psalm 69:1

I pondered Dave's suggestion some more while scooping ice cream on Wednesday, July 4. We were busy, so my thoughts were somewhat interrupted. Me, leading a Bible study. On what? With whom? When? Where? It was too much, and I thought about shrugging the idea off.

But I couldn't. And that told me something.

I hiked home and changed into new clothes—a Husker T-shirt and brown shorts—and checked the weather online. They had been predicting a chance of storms during the afternoon and evening, but now all was clear. So I called Scotty. He had taken Cassie golfing while I was working. It was her first time, and I was anxious to hear the report. We agreed to meet at the park and I set out on foot.

The Fourth of July in Morgan is like the Fourth of July in most small towns on the Plains, I would imagine. The local clubs and businesses come out to grill hot dogs and hamburgers and brats, and sell beer and soda and chips and candy at their various booths. It's all for a good cause, club projects or community this or that. Whatever, it's dinner.

There are games for everyone, from the mud pile tug-of-war to the dunk tank to various carnival games like the ring toss or high striker. Plus you have kids playing pick-up baseball—just like in *The Sandlot*—footballs and Frisbees flying across the park, and a wide variety of lawn games being contested by families and friends and random groups. Some years they bring in rides, including a Ferris wheel once. I didn't see a Ferris wheel as I approached, but I was sure they had a Tilt-A-Whirl or a Zipper.

And there's entertainment. Live music, piped in music, dancing, and fireworks. The best place to watch them, if you don't mind the noise and the risk of a stray one going sideways, is from the bleachers of the ball field. Otherwise, there's a hill north of town that provides a good view of not only Morgan's fireworks, but those of several surrounding communities as well.

I arrived at the park just as Scotty and Cassie were getting out of his Blazer. "How'd it go?" I asked.

"We threw away the scorecard after the third hole," she said.

"That bad?"

"And I ran out of balls after the seventh hole."

"You ran out?"

"Four in the water," she said. "One off a tree on five. I don't know where the rest went."

"My ankle," Scotty said.

Cassie made a face. "That's right, I hit him once too."

"Twice."

She closed her eyes. "Twice."

"I'm sorry I missed it," I said.

"Wouldn't have been so bad if not for those guys swearing behind us."

"Yeah, but you put them in their place," Scotty said.

"I told them if they didn't watch their language, I'd play the last three holes with my putter."

"Probably would have helped your score," he said.

She punched his shoulder. Girls hitting guys in Morgan was apparently an epidemic.

"How were things at the ice cream parlor?" Scotty asked.

"Another day, another dollar."

"Let's go blow our money on overpriced hamburgers."

And so we did. And sodas. And candy bars. The local 4-H and Kiwanis better not be asking for donations from us anytime soon.

We ate walking, observing several of the carnival games, debating a ride in the Tilt-A-Whirl, and watching some clown — actually dressed as a clown — get dunked a few times. We were about to move on when I saw a posting of who would be perched above the dunk tank and when. I couldn't believe my eyes. Curtis Teasdale would be manning the chair from six until six-thirty.

"How much money you have on you?" I asked Scotty.

"Not nearly enough."

"You guys are terrible," Cassie said.

"Relax, I'll buy you a ticket too."

"Okay."

We finished our dinner and bought tickets. Five dollars bought three baseballs. Three baseballs were plenty.

Teasdale took his spot promptly at six. He was wearing swim trunks, a black T-shirt with "I live to praise!" stamped on it, and an inflatable floaty around his waist. Of especially high fashion was the rubber duck in the middle front of the floaty.

"What a goof," Scotty muttered.

"Shh. He's a man of the cloth," Cassie whispered.

"He's wearing a rubber ducky," Scotty said.

Cassie's shoulders fell. "He is."

We were not alone. I saw a number of familiar faces waiting to dunk Teasdale. Many were kids from Morgan Bible, but there were a handful of young adults and not-so-young adults too. I wondered for how many of them this was personal.

At least one, I noted with a smile, as Mike walked by. He was cradling a dozen baseballs in his left arm. Mike the All-Conference pitcher.

"At what point does dunking a guy who's soaked lose its appeal?" Cassie asked. "I mean, he's already wet."

"You want a ball or not?" Scotty asked. She held out her hand.

A little tyke excitedly eyed the three baseballs in his hands, and we let him go in front of us. He was no more than five or six, and I doubted he could even throw a ball hard enough to trigger the release mechanism. But the tongue curled around his lip said he was eager to try.

His first throw had a surprising amount of sizzle and sailed over Teasdale's head, causing the pastor to duck.

"No, Son," the tyke's dad said. "You don't throw at him."

The kid frowned, as if his dad was a moron, and heaved another ball directly at Teasdale. I nearly bought him three more balls.

The dad stepped in before the third throw, offering a wave as an apology to Teasdale. He replied by adjusting his personal flotation device. I wondered what my father was doing at that moment. Certainly not allowing a bunch of Sooner fans to dunk him at the Norman city park.

After his dad explained where he was supposed to throw, the little pitcher-to-be wound up again and fired a fastball that just missed the target. He stomped at the dirt and trudged off after his father.

"Next!" the teenager manning the dunking booth called.

"You're up, Rosie."

I licked my fingers. Then I rubbed the ball, just like the big-leaguers do. *This is for taking my dad's job.*

I went full wind-up and fired a strike, right at the bull's eye.

Clunk, spring, splash!

I raised my hands above my head as the crowd cheered. Vengeance is mine!

Teasdale climbed back onto his seat, he and the duck both dripping. I rubbed the second ball.

This is for singing lame songs to tunes I couldn't carry in a slop pail.

Clunk, spring, splash!

I felt like Peter Pan's son smashing clocks on *Hook.*

"We have a ringer," the teenage kid manning the booth announced to the clapping crowd.

No, we have a guy with motivation. The ringer was waiting patiently with twelve baseballs.

I readied my third ball, waited for Teasdale to get back into his seat, and avoided eye contact with him. I went into the wind-up.

For whistling and making me remove my shoes and iPhone services and whatever nonsense we do next week.

Clunk, spring, splash!

"I have avenged my honor," I said to Cassie in my best Scarlett O'Hara voice. It wasn't very good.

Scotty went next, dunking Teasdale once and missing once. Then Cassie threw her ball, missing just left.

We stayed around to watch the ex-pitcher Mike throw. Twelve balls. Ten strikes. Teasdale and his duck looked like drowned rats. If he was worth his salt as a pastor, he'd find a sermon illustration in this.

We left the dunk tank and wandered toward the ball field. I popped the question.

"What would you guys think of starting a Bible study?" I asked.

"Just the three of us?" Scotty asked.

I shrugged. "Not necessarily."

"You have someone else in mind?"

"Well, she'd be welcome, but I wasn't thinking of anybody in particular."

"I'm in," Cassie said. "If I can make it work with my schedule."

"Sure," Scotty said.

We walked a little farther.

"So what brought this up?" Scotty asked.

"I was talking with Dave yesterday," I answered. "He mentioned it might be a good idea for me—might help me grow."

"Any book or topic you have in mind?" Cassie asked.

"Still chewing on that. I'm open to suggestions."

"I'll let you know."

We found a softball game just getting going at the ball field. It was a game for young and old, athletic former-pitchers (who weren't allowed to pitch) and short girls who kept tripping over their golfing khakis. We shared gloves or played without, shared bats, and lost track of the score by the second inning. We eventually lost track of innings and teams too, and just rotated batters in and out.

Before we knew it, the sun had set and they cleared us off the field in preparation for launching the fireworks. It was okay—we couldn't see anything anyway.

Sweaty and thirsty, Scotty, Cassie, and I grabbed drinks from an area Knights of Columbus booth and headed for Scotty's Blazer. We rode with the windows down, blasting along country roads, headed for the big hill north of town. We weren't the only ones with the idea, and the prime spots were already taken.

Scotty circled around and parked on the southern slope, facing Morgan. We got out and sprawled on the hood and windshield, three across, waiting for the fireworks to begin.

There was magic in the air. Maybe it was just patriotism coursing through me. Maybe it was small-town Americana. Perhaps it was good friends, or the pleasure I'd taken in dunking Curtis Teasdale three times, or even the triple I'd hit down the line in our baseball game. But something made me feel alive, like I hadn't felt in a while.

I sighed. How much more alive would I feel if it was me and Erica laying on the hood waiting for fireworks? (That was certainly acceptable, wasn't it—laying on the hood of a Chevy Blazer to watch fireworks? I mean, what was going to happen with windshield wipers digging into your backs?) Not that I didn't enjoy being with Scotty and Cassie, but a night like this would be so much more magical with Erica by my side. We'd hold hands as we walked through the park, share some cotton candy or ice cream, cuddle a little closer together when the cool night breeze came.

Okay, so the breeze was warm, but kids in love don't need a reason to cuddle. (Assuming cuddling on the hood of a Chevy Blazer is acceptable for Christian kids in love.)

"I wonder if they shoot fireworks in Arizona," Cassie said.

"Probably not," Scotty said. "Too dry. They're afraid it'll start a fire. It's the case down in Texas a lot."

"Yeah, but they have trees down there," I said. "And grass. What's going to burn in Arizona?"

"Cactuses," Cassie said.

"You mean cacti."

"Cactuses," she repeated.

"And tumbleweeds," Scotty said.

"Who cares if a tumbleweed burns?" I asked.

"Your parents," he said. "Because that's where they all end up."

"What a rotten place to live," I said. "Oklahoma."

"Even Texans don't like Oklahoma," Scotty said.

"You guys better watch it," Cassie said. "God will send you to Oklahoma as missionaries."

They sent up a beacon, a warning that the fireworks would start in five or ten minutes. Maybe fifteen. Kind of a useless beacon, unless it was in the shape of a number. Maybe it was like the admonitions in Scripture, about being ready for the rapture. The virgins and their oil, and all that. Whatever. I didn't want to think about the end times and the rapture and Petey right now.

"Do you guys ever think about where you'll be in five years?" Cassie asked.

"Scooping ice cream," I said.

"I'm serious."

"So am I," I answered. "I have no clue. I have no degree, no idea what to go to college to get a degree for, and no money to go to college and get a degree, if I had an idea of what degree to get. I think I'm a Morganite for life, unless I make the jump to an ice cream parlor in the big city."

"Maybe you could become the next pastor at MBC," Scotty said. "A father and son deal. Sort of like two Bushes on either side of Clinton."

"Don't compare Pastor Teasdale to Bill Clinton," Cassie said.

"Besides, you can't be a pastor if you don't sing in church," I said. "And I haven't sung in weeks."

"Your wife can play piano and lead the singing," Scotty said.

"Do you think I should just propose when she gets back? I mean, why mess around with dating? We could get married and by next Fourth of July, bring Josh Jr. to see the fireworks."

"You could maybe ask about her trip first," he answered.

"I still say don't rush things," Cassie said. "If it's right, it'll happen."

"Unless he drags his feet," Scotty said.

"I thought you were in the don't rush things group," I said.

"It's been a couple of months. Give it another . . ."

"Even if he does drag his feet, God can put a little ramp in front of him to lift them off the ground," Cassie said.

I needed to find friends and parents of friends who didn't employ quite so many metaphors.

"What about you, Cass?" Scotty asked. "What'll you be doing in five years?"

"If I get in at ASU?"

"Yeah."

She stared placidly up at the sky. "I'd love to work in a museum, or maybe some sort of historical art gallery or something—after I disprove everything in *The Da Vinci Code*."

"You gonna get married?" he asked. "We know about Rosie, but are you going to be a single curator and disprover?"

"Married," she said. "I hope. But I think I could live single if I had to." She turned her head to Scotty. "How about you? Where will you be in five years?"

"Does this remind anyone of *¡Three Amigos!?*" I interjected. "The three of us, laying here in a row, talking about our futures."

Another beacon exploded before either of them could answer.

"I don't know," Scotty said. "And I don't care. I'll figure it out when I get there."

"Married?"

"Not in five years."

"Seeing anyone?"

"Maybe."

"Still living with your dad?" I asked.

"Nah. I'll get my own place eventually."

"Remember, rent, don't buy."

"I'll take your place when you and Erica buy the little house in the country."

I was lost for a few minutes with thoughts about the two of us and our own place—about winter evenings by the fireplace and summer nights on the porch, about bringing kids home, and nights when Grandma would take the kids . . .

The start of the fireworks interrupted me just in time.

Chapter 18

*". . . I hear that when you come together as a church,
there are divisions among you . . ." I Corinthians 11:18*

I had never attended church with so much relish as on July 8. Sadly, there was no hot dog to go with it.

There really wasn't church either, by the standard definition. No sermon (I wondered if Curtis Teasdale took a pay cut compared to what Dad had made) and the music came and went. They were singing as we filed in, and they had a few songs interspersed. And of course they made time to take the offering. But July 8 was "Fellowship Sunday."

It had been announced the week before, with mention of a potluck lunch afterwards. More on potlucks later. But I hadn't anticipated that the entire service would consist of fellowship. Or that the pews would have all been moved to the sides of the church, facing the middle. The lights were off, and ad hoc curtains covered the windows. Dozens—perhaps a hundred—candles lit the sanctuary, albeit poorly. I sniffed, expecting to smell incense. Smell it or not, I was incensed.

"I've never been to a séance before," Mike said as we entered the sanctuary.

We were encouraged to mingle, to talk, to pray with one another. Sing if you want. Maybe get together and read a passage of Scripture with your friends. Smoke 'em if you got 'em. I'd never seen anything so absurd in my life.

"At least we get to keep our shoes on," Cassie said as she, Scotty, and I stood dumbfounded where our pew normally was. Instead it was just old green carpet beneath our shod feet.

"Well, what do you want to hit first?" Scotty said. "Prayer booth, Scripture booth." He leaned forward to Cassie. "Want to dance?"

"I think we should maintain a little decorum," she said.

"How can you pray when they're playing grunge music at a hundred decibels?" I asked.

"It certainly doesn't fit with the mood lighting."

"All that's missing is people speaking in tongues," Scotty said.

"Don't give them ideas," Cassie said.

"The glory of the Lord is in this place!" Teasdale shouted.

And then two people started dancing. Not the cha-cha or the tango, and not the naughty things they do in clubs and I only see on TV. But more like grooving in place. I recognized one of the dancers as Sandra Teasdale. Strike that. It was her spitting image, twenty years younger.

"You guys want to sit down?" Cassie asked. She nodded to our left, to the back corner of the church, where the senior citizens were seated, fiddling with their hearing aids and not-whispering to each other and probably wondering if the folks at True Way were so bad after all.

"Either of you see an attractive, well-tanned brunette good at analyzing run defense?"

"Nope," Scotty said.

"I saw Geoff on the way in," Cassie said. "The team must be back."

"I'm going to circulate."

"Careful you don't get pulled into crack-the-whip or something," Scotty said.

"That's only on ice."

"He means a conga line," Cassie said.

I mingled. I did not dance and I did not stop to pray or read my Bible because the worship team was screaming that asinine song about being undignified again. At least it was fitting.

I ran into Tim. And his shoes.

"You think this is what the apostles did in Acts two?" he asked.

"If so, it would explain why people thought they were drunk," I answered.

"I've never seen anything like this."

"Wait till next week."

"Why, what's next week?"

"I shudder to think."

"I miss your dad."

"So do I."

"I've got to find Kevin. He took my iPod to Haiti. Be careful out there."

I made my lap, saw no sign of Erica, and returned to Scotty and Cassie. They were sitting with the old folks, as were a lot of not old folks. The dancing had stopped, and Teasdale called everyone to sing for a few moments. So it wasn't just a fellowship service. Nor were we free to worship as we saw fit after all.

We started the old Fanny Crosby classic, "Redeemed." It was one of my favorites, and despite the circumstances and atmosphere, I thoroughly enjoyed singing it.

Until they changed the tune and the meter and the rhythm and the words halfway through. I couldn't believe it.

"That's not the tune," I heard an old woman behind me say.

"It's quarter of," a man replied. "We should be done soon."

"I said the tune."

"What about the tune?"

"They've changed the tune to the song."

"What's wrong?"

"The TUNE of the SONG!"

"Well, you don't have to shout."

I nudged Cassie subtly and could see she was straining not to laugh. I nudged her again. Spontaneous laughter at hard-of-hearing old people had to be as much worship as whatever it was that everyone else was doing.

"Amen," Teasdale said when the song was finished. "Amen? Let's give the Lord a clap offering. Can we do that?"

Light applause followed.

"Shoot, that was just a good lag putt," Scotty said to me.

"We want to fellowship with Him and with each other," Teasdale said. "That's what this is all about—His church coming together. The Bible tells us that the early church got together to break bread in their homes, to eat together with glad and sincere hearts—like we'll do a little later. And they praised God and enjoyed the favor of all the people. That's what this morning is all about." He exhaled.

"So take the remainder of this hour—we've got about ten minutes left—and enjoy the favor of one another."

I turned to my right to face Scotty and Cassie. "So theoretically we could have gone for breakfast today?"

"I'm with you on this one," Cassie said. "I mean, this isn't a church service. Isn't that the point of the potluck, to cover the fellowshipping part?"

"Wow, that's cold analysis, Cass," Scotty said.

"I mean, whistling and clapping are one thing, but . . . I don't come to church to talk to you two smart alecks. And how can I meet with God when I can't hear myself think?"

"Say, that dunk tank was really fun, wasn't it?" I said.

"It's not just him," Cassie said. "The elders had to sanction this, didn't they?"

"Who are our elders now?"

Cassie bit her lip. "I think Greg de Boer's one. And . . . I should really know this."

"Maybe it's posted somewhere," Scotty said. "They post the attendance, for crying out loud."

"I'd look in my worship folder, but I didn't get one this morning."

"Let's investigate," Cassie said.

"Blow early?" Scotty asked. "When'd you become a rebel?"

"One of those dancers stepped on my foot."

"See, it is a good thing we got to keep our shoes," I said.

We snuck out early. I couldn't believe what my nice, normal, once-split church had become. Every week was becoming a "Can you top this?" Switching from hymns to choruses and appealing to youth was one thing. This was . . . I didn't know what this was.

We searched the foyer but did not see a list of elders. We found a worship folder/bulletin at the welcome center, but they weren't listed.

"Figures," Scotty said. "I'd want anonymity too."

"Church office?" I said.

"Or Teasdale's office," Scotty said. "He's got to have contact info somewhere."

"We've got a few minutes," I said.

"Guys," Cassie said. We were already down the hall. "Guys, I don't like this."

Scotty tossed his cell to her. "We'll call you. Be our lookout."

Lip securely locked in her teeth, she nodded.

Scotty and I entered the church office. From Teasdale's phone extension, I dialed Scotty's cell number. "Hey, Cass."

"Clear so far."

I turned to Scotty, who was scouring Teasdale's desk. "Anything?"

"Not yet."

"Look for future sermon notes too."

"I think he just wings it."

"Guys, people are coming out of the sanctuary," Cassie said.

"Copy that," I said. I snapped my fingers at Scotty.

"Got it," he said. He showed me a list and I scanned the names, trying to commit them to memory.

"Guys!"

Scotty returned the list to Teasdale's desk and we slipped into the adjoining work room. We exited from there, just to be safe, and rejoined Cassie in the hallway. She breathed easier and returned Scotty's phone.

"There was no one close," Scotty said, looking up and down the hallway.

"I had to give you time to get out, and I don't like this sort of thing. Did you get the names?"

"Yeah, but not here," Scotty said.

It was raining, so instead of heading outside, we went to Room 104. A Bible was on one chair, but the room was empty.

"Greg de Boer," Scotty said. "Larry Iverson, Charles O'Reilly . . ."

"Dale Ten Pas," I finished.

Cassie frowned. "Who?"

"I only know Greg," I said.

"Well who nominated these people?"

"Don't blame me, I was at college. What'd you two let happen to this church while I was gone?"

Gia entered the room and smirked in our direction. I could smell the perfume from our place in the back row.

"They let you back into the country, huh," Scotty said.

"Sorry," she said. "And sorry, Josh."

"Huh?"

She continued smirking and took her seat.

"Sorry for what?" I asked.

Gia simply turned over her shoulder and smiled.

What did she mean? Had Erica been so captivated by the Haitian children that she stayed with them? Had she been stricken by some tropical disease? Or had my worst fears come true—had she fallen for a fellow short-term missionary?

Amy was next into the room, shaking her head as she walked. "That wasn't a waste of time or anything."

"Don't let Petey hear you say that," Scotty said.

"I don't care if Curtis Teasdale hears it. I can find better things to do with my time." She looked down at Gia. "You're all back?"

"Um-hmm."

"What's church like in Haiti?"

"Primitive."

"Do they dance?"

"Sometimes."

Amy huffed and sat down.

I waited, anxious to see Erica appear through the doorway, maybe in a nice sundress and bare, tanned ankles and with an extra-bright smile directed at me. Instead I got Tim, Brad, and Geoff who shot a cheesy smile at Gia. And Cora a minute before Petey. No Erica.

Petey cleared his throat. "First, welcome back to those of you who were in Haiti. I understand it was a bit of a hassle getting back into the country, but we're glad you're here."

A hassle? What had gone wrong? Had Erica been detained? I could picture it, her being singled out for her faith, left behind in a Haitian prison. Scotty and I would have to go all *A-Team* and rescue her. And I didn't even own a gun!

"Well, today is Fellowship Sunday," Petey said, "so we will not be having a lecture tod—"

Scotty led the applause.

Petey stiffened. "Instead, we're free to spend the hour fellowshipping."

"We just did that," Brad said.

"Can we spend the hour making a Wieskamps' run instead?" Tim asked.

"I haven't made a Wieskamps' run in years," Cora said.

"What is a Wieskamps' run?" Amy asked.

"Back when Mr. Patrick taught, he'd often take us to Wieskamps' in the summer, buy us each a candy bar," Tim answered. "We'd talk about something on the way, but it was more fun than anything."

"Sounds like fellowship to me," Cora said.

"I think we're supposed to remain in class," Petey said.

"Says who?" Scotty asked. "We can fellowship anywhere, can't we?"

"Theoretically, yes, but—"

"Wieskamps'!" Tim said.

"Do they still make Mambas?" Cora asked.

"What's a Mamba?" Amy inquired.

"How old are you, anyhow?" Scotty called.

"It's like a Starburst," Tim replied.

"Except way better."

"They still make them," Scotty said.

"It's raining," Amy observed.

"So what if it's raining," Tim said. "We can drive."

"I really believe the leadership of the church would like us to fellowship in class," Petey said.

"The leadership of the church had us dancing in the sanctuary," Tim said.

"Man, woman, and child," Scotty said, imitating the legendary Nebraska radio announcer Lyell Bremser. He had retired long before our time, but we still knew his trademarks from an era gone by: "Man, woman, and child, did that put 'em in the aisle" and "They're dancing in the streets in Lincoln." His calls applied to touchdown runs as well as worship services at Morgan Bible.

"Who wants to drive?" Amy asked.

"My Blazer'll seat five," Scotty said.

"Who's going?" Tim asked.

Six hands shot up. Petey's was not among them. Nor were Gia's and Geoff's.

"We can all fit in my minivan," Amy said.

"You drive a minivan?"

"Shut up."

"I don't trust lady drivers."

"Shut up."

"I can't support this decision," Petey said.

"Objection noted, counselor," Scotty said. "Let's go."

And so the six of us filed out of the room, leaving a stunned Petey, Gia, and Geoff in our wake. The rain was really coming down, and we got more than a little wet getting to Amy's minivan and getting inside Wieskamps'. We were like little kids, free from our parents, running through the candy aisles. Only without Mr. Patrick to pay.

Cora found her Mambas, I grabbed a Snickers bar, and as we were lining up to check out, Tim asked, "Did anyone bring anything for the potluck?"

"That's the old people's job," Scotty said. "Amy, you bring anything?"

"Shut up."

"Is it me or is her vocabulary shrinking?"

"Shut up."

"We should bring something," Cora said.

"Like what?"

"How about more Mambas?"

"Let's just buy some chips," Tim said.

"Go grab some," Amy said.

"I'm not paying."

"We'll all chip in," Scotty said.

"I didn't bring any money," Cassie said. She was also not holding any candy.

"Not even thirty-six cents?" I whispered. She elbowed me back.

"You're with me," Scotty said, just before I offered to pay for her. "Now go grab some candy."

"It's terrible for my teeth."

"Your teeth are great; go get some candy."

She did, while Tim selected chips. We paid, got wet on the way back to the minivan, and snacked as we drove back to church.

"We haven't discussed anything spiritual," Cora said as Amy parked.

"God causes His rain to fall on the just and the unjust," Tim said.

"Right, so it's raining on Petey too," Scotty said.

Cassie slapped his arm and he threatened to take back her Rolos.

We returned to Room 104 in no mood to share. Petey, Gia, and Geoff were still there, talking in a circle when we came in.

"We reached a decision," Petey said as we took our seats. "Where's Tim?"

"Running chips to the basement," Cora said. She unwrapped a Mamba.

"Decision on what?" Scotty asked.

"We're going to mention your behavior to Sandra Teasdale."

"What behavior?"

"Leaving class like this," Geoff said.

"You're out of your mind," Scotty said.

"We have every right to leave," Tim said.

"That's not how this class is supposed to work."

"Are you going to rat on people who skip church too?" Scotty asked.

"Josh wasn't here the third of June," Cassie said. I elbowed her, banging her elbow, and sending Rolos flying everywhere.

"Skipping is your prerogative," Petey said. "But when you come to participate in class and then cause a rebellion like this . . ."

"Your mom caused a rebellion."

"That's out of line," Geoff said.

"Your mom's out of line."

He walked into that one.

"I don't think this is appropriate," Petey said. "We should —"

"Why Sandra Teasdale?" Scotty asked.

"A.k.a. Jezebel," I whispered to Cassie

"Shut up and help me find my Rolos."

"Cassie just said 'shut up' in Sunday school," I reported.

She elbowed me, but my Snickers was already safely in my gut.

"Please," Petey said.

"Why Sandra Teasdale?" Scotty asked again.

"She oversees all of the fellowships," Petey answered.

"So what's she going to do, give us demerits?"

"I have a feeling she'll want to talk with each of you," Petey said.

"Isn't there a Bible verse about not snitching?" Cora asked.

"I don't know," Tim said. "I tried to read my Bible this morning but it kept vibrating out of my lap."

"What's your problem with the service?" Geoff asked.

"It wasn't church," Tim said.

"Just because it wasn't what you're used to doesn't mean it's not church."

"Same deal with Sunday school, Les Paul," Scotty said. "Wieskamps' runs may not be your SOP, but they're still Sunday school."

"Why is there a Rolo under my chair?" Cora asked.

"Because Josh is a putz," Cassie answered.

"People, please," Petey said. "This is absurd."

I raised my hand.

"Yes, Josh?" he sighed.

"Uh, this may not be the best time," I said, "but I did sort of have an announcement to make, if I could, Pe — uh, Derek? A legitimate one."

"Go ahead."

I cleared my throat. "I'm . . . thinking of starting a Bible study, and I just wanted to see if anyone was interested. I'm not sure when, how often, or on what yet, but if anyone would like to join, please let me know."

Nobody said a thing. Petey actually frowned.

"Maybe you should concentrate on attending class first," Geoff said.

"Maybe you should get off your high horse before you get knocked off, Francis."

"You threatening me?"

"I'm saying that just because your dad's an elder and you went to Haiti doesn't make you some super Christian and everyone else a schlep."

"My father has nothing to do with this."

"You do not know what you are talking about," Gia said, turning around to shoot a few daggers at Scotty.

"Stay out of this, Estée Lauder," Scotty said.

"What'd you call her?"

"Sorry, I insult your new girlfriend?" Scotty asked. "What exactly was your mission in Haiti anyhow?"

"How dare you!"

Petey stepped forward. "That's enough of this! We are supposed to be a light shining in the darkness, and this is how we act and how we treat one another? I'm ashamed! Class is dismissed, and I don't want to hear another word from anyone."

Geoff glared at Scotty for a minute, then stood and ushered Gia out of the room. Petey sent the back row an intense look and followed them.

"He's right," Cassie said quietly.

"I'm not the one who started making personal attacks," Scotty said.

"I think this whole church has flipped," Amy said.

"You think your dad would come back?" Tim asked. "Maybe if we did a write-in campaign?"

"Not if he had any common sense," Amy said. "I'm going to go get in line before all the little snot-nosed kids go through everything."

Scotty, Cassie, and I closed down the room.

"This isn't good," Cassie said.

"Did you want me to just let him rip Rosie?"

"I don't mean just you. I mean this church. I don't like where things are headed."

"What can we do?"

"I don't know. And that's the worst part."

"It'll come to a head," I said. "Either they'll keep doing crazy things and there will be a split, or they'll realize the majority of people are against crazy things and tone it down."

"I'm afraid it will be the former," Cassie said.

"Wouldn't that be ironic," I said. "Trying to avoid a split, they create one."

"I don't think it will be so much a split as a wedge," Scotty said.

"Not more golf metaphors."

"I mean just a small slice off the rock," he said. "And maybe a new pastor."

"We should pray," Cassie said. "A split is not a good thing."

"Depends who's splitting."

"Still, there are better ways."

Scotty and I looked at each other, and then bowed our heads while Cassie prayed for the unity of the church. When she was finished, we headed downstairs to the potluck.

I hate potlucks. You never know what you're eating. It's bad enough not knowing who—and thus whose snot-nosed kids—made a dish. But not being able to identify the food, the soupy and mushy textures, people who use kale—it's just all too much. There's a reason the word "luck" is used.

But a potluck meant free food, and I was on a budget. The desserts were usually okay at least. And I was hoping that Erica might show up after all. She didn't, and even the desserts were lousy.

I hoped it was just jetlag, or she was sleeping in after a long, tiring three weeks. Maybe that was why Gia had said "Sorry, Josh." But I had a sinking feeling in my gut that there was more to it, that something had happened to Erica or that maybe Geoff and Gia weren't the only couple to form under the tropical sun.

Chapter 19

"I have been sent to you with bad news." I Kings 14:6

Sydney was in a foul mood to start the week, the result of a potential relationship that had gone south. I could theoretically empathize. Wednesday afternoon we were slammed with customers, candy shortages, and a malfunctioning waffle cone maker. When I finally got off some twenty minutes late, I was looking forward to a leisurely walk home.

I only took a dozen steps before spotting Scotty leaning against his Blazer.

"Hey," I said.

"Hey. You walked?"

"Yeah."

"Give you a lift?"

I frowned. I lived four blocks from work, and it was a beautiful summer afternoon. I sensed trouble.

"Sure."

Scotty nodded and we got into the Blazer. "What's up, dude?" I asked.

Scotty just looked at me, and I knew.

It was true.

The rumor.

Erica had a boyfriend.

I'd been tormenting myself since Sunday, replaying Gia's words over and over in my head, looking for hidden meaning. I concluded that since there were no prayer requests for a member of the team left behind in Haiti or who had contracted dengue fever that her cryptic apology could only have meant one thing.

And now Scotty's eyes told me it was true.

"Who?" I asked.

"Mark."

I took the news with a slow nod. I remembered Tom Hanks in *Cast Away*, and reminded myself to breathe.

"How do you know?"

"I ran into Gia today," he said. "She confirmed it."

Hope, albeit small, surged in my breast. Gia had started this whole mess — Was it possible she was just messing with Scotty, and thus me.

"What'd she say?" I asked.

"She asked how you were taking the news. I asked what news. She said, 'Hasn't he heard? Erica and Mark hooked up in Haiti.'" Scotty shrugged. "I made a nice frown and a shrug and asked why you would care. She just smirked and left."

I nodded again. We hadn't moved from the curb.

"She say anything else?"

"We exchanged unpleasant greetings, but no."

"Where'd you meet her?"

"Wieskamps'."

I nodded yet another time. And stared out the window.

"You all right?" Scotty asked.

"I don't know. It's still sinking in."

"You want to come over, hang out?"

"Yeah, I guess."

"I'm sorry, dude."

"Yeah."

We drove back to Scotty's and crashed on his couch. I made him repeat the conversation with Gia again, word for word. I looked for loopholes. There weren't any.

I hated irrational fears. They'd plagued me all my life. Was that cumulous cloud the forerunner of a supercell that would spawn a tornado that would level our house? Were all of those Y2K kooks right and everything would go haywire at the turn of the century? Might Nebraska actually lose to McNeese State? Would Erica go off to Haiti, bond with her fellow short-term missionaries, and come home with a boyfriend to ruin my life? That was the worst part of irrational fears—not the time they wasted by making you worry over nothing, but the once in a blue moon that they came to fruition. On one hand, it was sort of vindicating—I had been right to worry. But it was also a sickening punch in the gut, and guaranteed I'd have to worry about the next dozen or so irrational fears with added fervor.

Only I couldn't imagine much of anything mattering in the future.

I've heard about all the stages of grief—anger, denial, acceptance. I didn't know the order and didn't know what stage I was in, but after about fifteen minutes, we got up and went outside to shoot some hoops.

"If it's any consolation," Scotty said, "these types of relationships never work."

"No?"

"No." He passed on a shot and bounced the ball to me. "They're all built on emotion, on the heat of the moment. Three weeks together, alone, strange things are bound to happen. I mean, de Boer fell for Gia."

Clang.

Scotty tapped the rebound back through the hoop and passed it back to me.

"I liked Mark," I said.

"So did I."

"You can still like him."

"He stole your girl."

"No, he just beat me to her. It was completely legal."

"Still."

I clanged another one off the rim and batted the rebound to Scotty. I was sick of shooting. "No, I appreciate that, but this is my deal," I said. "You and Mark can still be pals."

We continued to shoot, me slipping into the stage of grief. Grief. Stages. What a bunch of nonsense.

To Scotty's credit, he didn't hand me some line about "maybe it's for the best" or "her loss" or whatever nonsense I had just been telling Sydney. He tried to encourage me with reasons their relationship would fail and even suggested ways we could try to split them up.

It was a nice gesture, but it didn't help.

"Let's rent some movies," Scotty said.

"I don't feel like movies."

"I know you don't feel like it, but it will distract you. And that's what you need right now, a distraction. You can deal with this tomorrow. Tonight, we forget."

"Isn't that from 'Hotel California'?"

Scotty shrugged. "Liam Neeson fest?"

"What'd you have in mind?"

"*Taken*. Maybe *Unknown*. *A-Team*? *K-19*? That airplane one. Whatever they have."

I came around. "Sure."

We stowed the basketball and got back into the Blazer. The only place to rent videos in town was Don & Flo's, and their selection was somewhat limited. We rented *Unknown* and *Non-Stop* and grabbed some quick, microwavable dinners.

"I'm telling you, Rosie, we can break this thing up," he said as we drove back.

"Yeah, and it will just strengthen their resolve and love." I sighed. "It's out of my hands now."

Dirk was puttering in the kitchen when we arrived home. He took one look at my hangdog face and knew there was trouble. I briefed him on Scotty's conversation with Gia and my billowing depression.

"Ninety-eight Masters," he said. "Fred Couples led the whole way, but Sunday at thirteen, he puts the ball in the creek. Made a seven. Tourney over." He sat down. "Except he came back and made eagle at fifteen, right back in the thick of things."

"Dad, O'Meara won the Masters in '98," Scotty said.

"Yes, but Freddie had a chance."

"Is this good news or bad news?" I asked.

"It's a 'hang in there,' kiddo. There's still golf to play."

"Yeah, maybe."

"Let's go watch Liam kick some tail," Scotty said.

I shrugged. "Why not?"

And so we did. And for a few minutes here and there throughout the double feature, I forgot that the girl of my dreams was now spoken for. But when the memory returned, it did so with double force, and I found myself, as a twenty-year-old man, wanting to go home and cry.

Those stages — there might be something to them after all. Sunday I was in full-fledged denial. I went to church practically whistling (I know, right — whistling) and clinging to the hope that somehow my intel was wrong. Gia was still the only source, and she was dubious at best. Maybe Erica and Mark weren't a couple. Maybe she was finally back from Haiti and we were ready to begin our wonderful romance.

This fanciful euphoria followed on the heels of the most depressing three days of my life. All I could think about was Erica, Erica with Mark, Erica without me, me without Erica. I was convinced I could never be happy again.

Not helping matters was the rain. It started Thursday afternoon and finished late Saturday night. It was accompanied by severe storms, heavy winds, and a cold front that dropped temps twenty degrees Friday evening. The farmers were thrilled. I was not.

I was eleven minutes early as I wanted to see people come in. Cassie arrived a minute later and gave me a hug. "Are you all right?" she asked.

"Scotty tell you?"

She nodded.

"I'm okay. It's still just Gia's word," I said.

Her face showed pity, but I blocked it out. The crowd filed in. I didn't see Erica. Or Mark. Were they going to some church in Panama now? Would I never see her again? Why hadn't a tornado hit my apartment?

Erica arrived thirty seconds after Scotty slid into our pew. She was alone, thank you, and took a seat in the second row on the left. I tried very hard not to stare, but she wasn't making it easy. She wore a white, pleated skirt, and a pink V-neck shirt under a three-quarter-sleeved denim jacket.

Her hair was in a ponytail. Somewhere, the cover of an *American Girl* book was blank.

Scotty nudged me. I looked to him, then left to the middle aisle. Mark sauntered toward the front of the church, looking cool and casual in jeans and a white button-down. He slid into the row behind Erica, immediately chatting up Kevin Sprague. I realized that all the Haitian team had assembled front left. We were due for a briefing.

The service started without fanfare, with the pews in their proper places, with everyone wearing shoes. There was no whistling or clapping or anything terribly strange. We sang a song, had brief announcements, and then were seated by Curtis Teasdale.

He then invited the Haiti team up to the stage, led by Greg de Boer. There was some mild applause. Medium-length par putt, if I had to gauge it.

Erica was the first to speak, and I cherished every word. She recounted how the team had conducted a Vacation Bible School with the Haitian children, although it really wasn't vacation for them. She detailed the difficulties communicating through lingual and cultural barriers, but reported with a bright smile that three young children had accepted Christ as a result of their efforts. She thanked us for our prayers and financial support, and then glided back to her spot in the row.

I tuned out the other speakers, keeping my eyes on Erica without staring. She was more beautiful than ever. Forbidden fruit?

When Greg de Boer closed after almost fifteen minutes, the team stepped down off the stage. I watched Erica carefully again, noting her graceful movement, natural poise, and . . . Mark's hand on the small of her back as he followed her down.

They sat together this time. Or rather stood, as we sang three more songs. I kept my eyes on Mark's hands, but they stayed in his pockets or on the pew in front of him.

We were seated again for the offering, a piano and flute duet. It was lovely. Mark and Erica sat side-by-side, and I tried to cling to hope that they were just good friends. His gesture could be explained by that, right? I mean, if they had just started dating, they'd be all over each other, holding hands, bumping arms, anything. Right?

After the offertory, Curtis Teasdale invited us to open our Bibles to Malachi. I did so, and for the first few minutes of his sermon, really tried to pay attention. But my eyes kept cutting over to the front left of the sanctuary, to Mark and Erica. And then it happened.

Somewhere around the part about breaking favor with the wife of your youth, he floated his arm behind her head. It was very casual, but instead of resting it on the pew back like a guy who was stretching, he curled his hand around her shoulder. And she leaned ever so slightly into him.

I nearly rent my garment.

Cassie squeezed my arm. She apparently saw the same thing.

I raised my chin. I had to be a man about this.

The sermon was over for me. I focused on the possibilities:

One, Erica and Mark could be, like Scotty said, the product of three weeks together — working together, eating together, being away from home and comfort together. Bonding happened. It could be mistaken for romance.

Two, they could be legit, but destined to fail. A lot of relationships failed. What were the odds that this was one that made it?

Or three, they could be the real deal, and I was left out in the cold.

It reminded me of the parable of the sower and the seed and the birds that ate it up and the thorns that choked it out. Thorns were Scotty and Sydney, both of whom had offered to try to break up Mark and Erica for me. That was a last resort.

My grandpa always had a saying, one of those down-home things old-timers say. Whenever someone said, "You get used to it," he'd reply with, "You get used to hanging too, after a while."

As I trudged to Sunday school, now that reality had set in, I was getting used to hanging. I was starting to figure out coping mechanisms — considering ways, if it was option three and Erica and Mark were the real deal, that my life might still have meaning and purpose. Or at least trying to consider them. It was still very early in the coping stage.

Scotty bailed on class. He figured he was in for a sermon from Petey and possibly Geoff and maybe even quiet time with Sandra Teasdale. Besides, it was sunny at last. He and Dirk were playing eighteen. He said he'd call later. I told him I'd be on my balcony contemplating a jump. "Funny," he said. And, "Later."

Cassie and I sat in the back row, her chattering on and on about nothing, trying to keep my mind occupied. I appreciated the effort and felt a little better.

That lasted for five minutes, until Erica and Mark entered the room, hand-in-hand. Seriously, where was Petey to enforce a little decorum?

I was too distracted to mention the Bible study again, as had been my plan since maybe this week's class would actually be a class and not a Wieskamps' run and near fistfight. I was also too distracted to focus on Petey's lecture on the seventh seal and the trumpets. I didn't even get into the rapture discussion that evolved from a question about whether the trumpets in Revelation 8 were the trumpets that would sound Christ's return.

All I did was think about Erica. I was in the moping stage of grief. Why did God let us meet and fall into love or whatever it was we fell into for nothing? Why couldn't Mark have found some nice Panamanian girl?

Petey gave the last five minutes of class to his new BFF Geoff de Boer. Geoff wanted to take an offering, not just this week, but in coming weeks, for the new Haiti church. They were meeting in a crooked building with one room, dirt floors, no plumbing, and a leaky roof. They only had homemade instruments and no hymn books or projection system or anything. So could we sacrifice a little, save, maybe work some odd jobs, organize a carwash, anything to raise a little money?

It wasn't a bad idea. Even if Haiti was now a swear word to me, I figured I could pitch in.

Until he said the money would go to buy the Haitian church a drum set, an acoustic and an electric guitar, and an amp they could plug into their outdoor generator.

Since Erica was sitting in front of me and I didn't want to ruin any chance we'd have if she and Mark fizzled, I kept my mouth shut. But why in the Sam Hill should we buy instruments for a church that didn't even have a floor? Wouldn't a sanitary toilet be a better first step than an amp? And why, in the name of Chris Tomlin, Matt Redman, and Lincoln Brewster, couldn't we just once sing a song without a band? *A cappella,* even. Maybe we could buy Bibles for the little converts before an air guitar? It was stupid, and I said a quick goodbye to Cassie and started for the door.

"Hey, Josh!"

I turned around. It was Mark. I summoned every ounce of restraint and gave him a non-non-friendly nod.

"Hey man, you doing anything this afternoon?"

"Why?" I asked with typical caution and trying very hard not to look at Erica, who was standing peacefully behind him, smiling, gorgeous as ever.

"I'm getting together a group of guys to play some football."

Erica cleared her throat.

"And girls," he said with an exaggerated sigh.

She lightly backhanded his side. I remembered when she used to backhand me.

"You in, man?" Mark asked.

"I can't today," I said. "I've got some other stuff going on."

Stuff like moping and complaining and writing a few "why me" Psalms.

"You sure?"

"Yeah, I'd love to, but you know how it is."

Mark nodded. "All right. Well, if you change your mind, I'm shooting for the high school around four. Take care, man."

Erica offered a brief smile as she passed. I thought about our banter just a few weeks ago, when she had said she'd have to show me how she could play football. That promise had lost its luster.

Then again, so had life.

Act II

Chapter 20

"Blessed is the man who perseveres under trial . . ." James 1:12

My first week A.E. (After Erica) dragged. By mid-week, I was getting through my daily routine without thinking about her. But the first moment my mind was idle, she flooded it. And almost anything triggered a thought of her. A customer who vaguely resembled Mark. A brunette walking down the street. Just when I started to think I would never get over her, I realized that I was starting to acclimate to the idea of life without her. This was my new normal.

Because it was officially the dog days of summer and because I had nothing to do and because my life lacked meaning, I took a shift at Nebraska Novelties on Saturday. It was a mistake. Late in the afternoon, the happy couple came in for some ice cream. Erica looked cute as you please as she bit down on her lip, trying to choose between chocolate fudge and peaches 'n cream. Mark made a crack about her taking too much time, earning him another backhanded slap to the arm. To make matters worse, they decided to dine in, sharing ice cream from each other's spoons and flirting all the while. It made the last four hours of my afternoon and evening shift miserable.

I walked home, debating playing video games long into the night. Instead I got into my car and drove to the Morgan Family Restaurant. I parked next to Cassie's Chevy Cavalier and went inside.

At half past nine on a Saturday night, the Morgan Family Restaurant was mostly empty. The hostess was Brianna, a girl I'd gone to school with, but whose last name I couldn't remember. It was okay — she didn't appear to know me from Adam.

"Is Cassie still working?" I asked, a stupid question since her car was outside. Conversation starters had never been my thing.

"Yeah, till ten."

"Can you see if she has a minute?"

Brianna gave me the once over and then nodded. I stuck my hands in my jeans and waited. Cassie rounded the corner and paused when she saw me. "What are you doing here?"

She wore khakis and the blue MFR polo that all staff wore. Her hair was wadded up behind her head, and she looked exhausted.

"You work till ten?" I asked.

"I actually just have to roll some silverware and then I'm out," she said. "Why?

"Buy you dessert?" I asked.

"It's almost ten o'clock," she said. "On a Saturday. And I'm beat."

"I know. But you've had a long crummy week, and mine hasn't been so grand either, and I thought we could commiserate."

"Did they teach you that word in college?"

"Learned it on my own."

She bit her lip. "I shouldn't eat dessert."

"Just a small slice of pie," I said.

"Mmm. What kind?"

"You pick."

"Cherry."

I nodded.

"But no ice cream."

"Okay."

"Give me fifteen minutes."

I nodded, waited ten, and then ordered two slices of cherry pie, no ice cream, from Brianna.

When Cassie came back out, her hair was down, her shirt untucked. I held up the boxed slices of pie and suggested we eat elsewhere.

"Okay . . ." she said, following me outside.

"My car?" I said.

"Where are we going?" she asked as she twisted her hair into a ponytail.

"The park," I said.

She nodded and walked around to the passenger side. She held the pies and I drove, into the park and along the maintenance road that led beyond the ball field and to the brow of a small hill at the western edge of the park. Ringed by trees on three sides, sort of like an old, balding man's haircut, the hill looked down on the railroad tracks and out at the Morgan water tower and west across the plains. At night, the view was somewhat limited, but it still beat the Morgan Family Restaurant parking lot.

"Okay, what's the real reason for this dessert?" Cassie asked as we got out.

I climbed onto the hood of my Escort and took the pies from her as she clambered up. "No pretenses," I said. "It's just been a while since we talked."

"You could have called."

"I know, but you were busy working and I was . . ."

"Moping?"

"Yeah."

"Are you still?"

"Moping? Yeah."

Cassie took a bite of pie.

"Mark and Erica came into the shop today," I said. "For ice cream. They're a very cute couple."

"I'm sorry."

I nodded and dug a fork into my pie.

"Newly dating couples are the worst," she said. "I was planning on avoiding you for about a month if the two of you hooked up."

"Yeah, well, you don't have to worry about that now."

"Sorry, I didn't—"

"It's okay."

We ate for a few minutes. Off in the distance, a train whistled. The sound hung in the air, low and mournful. Amen, brother.

"I'm sure Scotty and Dirk have given you plenty of advice," Cassie said, "but I'm going to give you some more."

"Okay."

"You may not like it."

"That's okay."

"You need to concentrate on being her friend."

I nodded.

"Assume for a moment that you had no romantic interest in Erica."

"I only have so much imagination."

"Try," Cassie said, stabbing some pie. "Would you want to be her friend?" She took a bite and chewed while I deliberated.

"Yeah, I guess," I said. "Of course."

"Okay. So then if it never works out between the two of you, if she and Mark fall in love and get married and have adorable children, you can still be her friend."

"I don't know that it works that way, Cass."

"It does if you choose to let it. And I'm not finished, anyhow."

"Go on."

She licked off her plastic fork. "And if this thing doesn't go well with Mark, Erica's going to need a friend, and the best way you can position yourself to be the next guy in her life is by being a friend."

"That sounds very cold and calculating for you."

"I'm trying to think like a guy." She dug into the pie again. "Either way you slice it, Josh, the best plan is for you to be her friend."

The train was getting closer.

"I know," I said. "But it's hard to be just a friend with somebody you have feelings for."

"I'm sure it is," she said.

I stabbed a cherry and studied it for moment. Down the hatch.

"And I didn't say it would be easy. But I bet I know where you can get some help."

"Are you being spiritual now?" I asked.

"I am."

I nodded.

"And you know what else?" she said.

"What's that?"

"Some time off might do you some good."

"I just had three weeks off."

"I mean off as in where she isn't available."

"And how might that do me good?" I asked.

"Right now, being apart from Erica feels like agony, right?"

"That'd be a fair description, yeah."

"Well, give it a few weeks. A month. See if the agony is still there. You might find you actually get over her, as absurd and even insulting as that sounds."

"And if not?"

"Then maybe that's a sign that the two of you are meant to be together."

I exhaled. "That's all good advice, Cass."

"But?"

"But, it's hard."

"I know it's hard. So next time, don't go two weeks without talking to me."

"We talked in church."

"Barely."

"Sorry."

"I mean, where do you think I came up with all this good advice? I've been planning what to say to you since Scotty told me."

The ground was rumbling now from the approaching train, and its whistle pierced the night as it thundered across Main Street. I saw the lights on the front of the locomotive a hundred feet ahead of us and down a few dozen yards. I watched them disappear and then listened to the clackity-clack-clack of dozens and dozens of empty coal cars following the locomotive.

When the train was finally gone, I turned to Cassie. She was savoring her last bite of pie.

"Thanks, by the way," I said.

"You're welcome."

"I really mean that."

"I know you do."

I nodded. "So how about you?"

"How about me how?"

"How are you doing? Any word from ASU or the grant companies?"

She smiled. "They're not grant companies."

"Whatever."

The smile faded. "No, no news. And I've been taking on all these extra hours, but it's not going to matter. If I don't get the financial aid, I won't be able to afford to go. Of course, if I don't get accepted, none of that will matter."

"Why wouldn't they accept you? You're a great student."

"I may be good, but I'm not great. And there are a lot of good students who apply. And I didn't help matters by waiting so long."

The train whistle sounded at the next intersection south.

"Sell any paintings yet?" I asked.

"One. A mountain landscape."

"It looks great in my living room, by the way."

"I haven't even painted in a week or two. Too busy."

"There's tomorrow."

"I plan on it."

"And you should really find a place to sell them, Cassie. I'm not just being your friend here. They are good."

"Thank you."

I nodded, enjoyed the breeze blowing through my hair. It was due for a cut.

"Speaking of tomorrow . . ." Cassie said. "It's getting late."

"Yeah."

We climbed down off the hood and drove back to the parking lot. I parked right beside Cassie's car, and she paused before opening her door. "Thanks for the pie."

"Thanks for the therapy."

"Any time."

"Night, Cass."

"I'll see you tomorrow?"

"Yeah, I'll see you tomorrow."

Chapter 21

"A despairing man should have the devotion of his friends . . ." Job 6:14

I did not see Cassie tomorrow, because I didn't attend worship services at Morgan Bible Church. I woke up on time, but kept thinking about sitting behind Mark and Erica and watching them hold hands and cup shoulders and do all of the other little nervous-energy flirty things they did, and I couldn't take it. Besides, the previous week's service had been relatively normal, so I figured we were due for some Bobby McFerrin cheek-popping and chest-slapping or spiritual duck, duck, goose or some other nonsense.

As I showered, I thought about what Cassie had said last night. She was absolutely right. It had been a week and a half since Scotty had broken the news to me, and I really needed to come out of the funk. And the best way to do that was to accept that Mark and Erica were together and Erica and I were not and get on with my life. But having a pity party just sounded better, and so as I poured a bowl of cereal, I planned on giving in to the depression.

I have no idea to this day how or why I got into the car and drove east on Main Street. I don't know what compelled me to get out of the car and walk up the front steps, or what force dragged me into the sanctuary and had me sit down in an unpadded pew near the back. But I was there. And I stayed for the entire service.

At The True Way Church.

They sang all hymns, all ones I knew, with just an organ for accompaniment. The pastor wore a suit and tie. He stood behind a regular old pulpit, wooden, with intricate detailing. There was no whistling, no clapping, no dancing, no oddities of any sort.

And no sign of the Spirit.

There was no outright blasphemy or heresy, but there were undertones. The prayers were more recited than prayed. We uttered no less than three creeds or declarations. The bulletin (at least they called it a bulletin) reminded us to attend several confirmation services in the following weeks. Nothing wrong there, at least on the surface.

But there was more. All Scripture was read from the King James Bible, which was openly declared to be the only accurate English translation. During communion, they spoke about the sacraments as if they played a role in a person's salvation instead of harkening back to the work of Christ on the cross. There was mention in the sermon about a person justifying himself before God, through obedience to the Scriptures. And the capper, a reference — albeit off-handed — to making sure we were saved by adhering to the Ten Commandments.

Make it overtones. Heretical ones.

I shook the hands of a smiling middle-aged lady and a scowling old man, and hightailed it out of there before sulfur fell from the sky.

I didn't know where this left me with Morgan Bible. With some things to think about, maybe. But in math class, being closer to the right answer didn't get you any points. At least not at Vernon-Bedford.

Erica wasn't suddenly available either. So while I had some food for thought to go along with my delicious lunch of Ramen noodles (third time that week), I still didn't have a ladder out of my pit of depression. And I wasn't yet in the mood to pull myself up by my bootstraps, despite the soundness of Cassie's advice.

I walked home from work Tuesday and found Scotty and Cassie leaning against my apartment door.

"Hey, guys."

"See, I told you he was still alive," Scotty said.

"Yeah, I wasn't in church. Sorry."

"You promised," Cassie said.

"I meant well."

She stepped aside and I opened the door.

"Your phone broken?" Scotty asked.

"Huh?"

"We left you messages."

"When?"

"Last night," Cassie said.

"Yesterday afternoon," Scotty said. He kicked the door closed behind them.

"I was getting groceries last night, and I turned off the ringer Sunday. I never thought to check for messages. Really guys, I'm sorry."

"Forget Mark and Erica," Cassie said.

"I'd like to."

"Forget about them. We're worried about you," she said. "We know you're frustrated with church — so are we. And there's nothing in the Bible that says you have to go every week, but . . ."

"I went this week," I said.

"What?"

"Yeah. I, uh . . . I went to True Way."

They looked at each other. For several seconds.

Then at me.

Cassie turned back to Scotty. "I think we should maybe call the elders to pray over him."

"Or else an exorcist."

"Maybe we should just stone him."

"You two want to cut the routine and let me explain?"

"If we just flog him, will that work?" Scotty asked. "Or beat him with rods, maybe?"

"Blows and beatings purge away evil," she answered. "It's in Proverbs."

"Abbott, Costello, do you mind?"

"All right, Rosie. But we aren't converting."

"Neither am I," I said. I told them about the service, about the red flags and air raid sirens that had popped up and clanged everywhere.

"So what does that mean?" Cassie asked.

"I've been thinking on that," I said. "Gives my mind something to dwell on other than Erica."

"And . . ." Scotty goaded.

"And, while I still think Teasdale might be fruitier than a package of gummy bears, and while I think we may still be missing the mark in some ways at MBC, our key doctrine is still sound. And that is what ultimately matters. The rest matters too, but . . . not as much. No one's eternal destiny hangs on whether we sing or whistle or don't."

I frowned. "Actually, it might still. I mean, if an outsider comes in and thinks we're a bunch of nutjobs, they might not come back, might miss hearing the gospel . . . Anyhow, that's a worry for another day."

"Okay, so you're not possessed," Scotty said. "You still need a kick in the pants."

"Really?"

"Not a punishing kick, but a get-you-going kick."

"And that's the purpose of this tag-team?"

"Cassie told me about your pie on the hood therapy session the other night."

"And?"

"And, she's exactly right."

"I know."

"And yet you sit over here and play video games all day."

"How do you know?"

"What else would you do? But that's beside the point. We know that knowledge isn't your problem. It's application."

"Okay," I said.

"We're here to help you apply."

"How?"

"However it takes. For starters, we're going to keep you occupied tonight."

"Occupied."

"That's right."

I looked at Cassie. She nodded.

"Okay, occupy away."

"Not here," Scotty said.

"Where?"

"My place. Change of scenery."

"Can I change clothes first?"

"Sure." Scotty nodded at Cassie and she darted into the bedroom.

"What are you doing?"

"Making sure there's nothing sharp or noose-like in here."

I shook my head. "How long'd you guys practice this routine?" I asked when she emerged. "It gets an A."

She smiled and curtseyed.

"And thanks. But I am turning the corner."

"Yeah, well, you're rounding it a little bit," Scotty said.

I nodded. "I'm going to change, not hang myself or jump out the window. You guys rehearse your next funnies or figure out how this occupation is supposed to work."

"We've already got that planned," Scotty said.

I started to close the door. "You're not parading all of the available young bachelorettes through your living room, are you?"

"No."

"Okay. Because if you were, I might be able to deal with that."

"Go," Scotty said.

"Assuming they were the available, young, attractive bachelorettes."

"Go!"

I smiled as I shut the door. I actually smiled. That was progress, I figured. Now to figure out what Fric and Frac had planned for the evening.

We started by digging out Scotty's old Nintendo and playing *Donkey Kong* and *Punch-Out!!* for a while. Cassie, while not a video gamer per se, kicked our butts, especially at *Punch-Out!!* Scotty said it was because Nintendo didn't require much skill. Cassie claimed it was because she was sound with the fundamentals. I argued that they were arguing the same side of the coin.

After gaming, we made dinner. Dirk had a date—which Scotty claimed was really more of a business venture—and we would be eating alone. We made quesadillas, which, with the three of us novices in the kitchen, was something of an adventure in and of itself. We dined on the deck with chips and salsa, enjoying a brilliant summer evening.

"So I've been thinking more about this Bible study," I said. "Are you guys still in?"

"Yeah," Scotty said.

Cassie nodded.

"Okay, well since you guys appear to be the core, what days work for you?"

"Any," Scotty said.

"Monday, Tuesday, or Wednesday nights," Cassie said. "Just let me know so I can let work know."

"How many hours are you working?" Scotty asked.

"Full time at D&N, and twenty to thirty at MFR."

"That's crazy."

"Yeah, well . . ."

"We should figure out some other way to make money," Scotty said.

"Like what," she asked, "the Send Cassie to Arizona fund drive?"

"Something along those lines."

"We could do odd jobs, bake sales, carwashes," I said. "Compete with Geoff's Haiti fund."

"His what?" Scotty asked.

"You didn't hear about that? They're trying to get our class to raise money to buy electric guitars and amps for the church in Haiti that doesn't even have a floor or a bathroom."

"That's practical."

"I think Cassie's just as noble of a cause," I said.

"As amps for Haiti? She's way more noble."

"Guys, I'm right here."

"Seriously," I said, "people like to give to charities. Especially the True Wayers—they think it gets them in tight with God. We can prey on that, dress it up a little."

"I'm with Rosie," Scotty said. "We can pull down a grand easy if we do this right."

"I don't want dirty money," Cassie said.

"We'll wash it first."

"Great. Dirty, laundered money. I think I'll stick to my day job." She sighed. "And my night job."

"Geoff de Boer's a putz," Scotty said.

"He's in his father's camp," I said.

"Which is Teasdale's camp. They're the problem."

"So let's talk church a minute. You guys both agree something's off at church?"

"Yeah," Scotty said. "Like you said, it's not doctrinal, but something's not right."

Cassie was a little more reticent. "I'm not sure it's wrong, because I'm not sure it's anything yet."

Scotty looked at her. "Meaning?"

"Meaning, I think they're experimenting. I don't know that it's always going to be this way."

"If it is, they're going to lose a lot of people."

"Where will they go?" I asked.

"True Way."

"For one week."

Scotty shrugged. "There're a lot of churches around. You just have to drive a few miles. And people are. Have you seen the attendance numbers? Dropped an average of twenty over the last few weeks."

"It's summer," Cassie said. "People—"she cleared her throat "—skip in summer."

I took a drink of my iced tea. "What do you think we should study?"

"Huh?"

"In our Bible study."

"New Testament," Scotty said.

"Definitely. And not Hebrews," Cassie added.

"Why not Hebrews?"

"It's complicated."

"Doesn't that make it a good book to study?"

"Yeah, and you can have Petey lead it," Scotty said.

"Point made."

"I'll think about it," Scotty said.

"I'll pray about it," Cassie said.

Scotty shot her a glare.

She stuck out her tongue.

I was thankful that, while Erica-less, I had good friends.

And then, after dinner, because Scotty and Cassie hadn't planned this evening as well as they thought, we drove to Kansas.

It was about an hour drive, one we had first taken shortly after getting our driver's licenses. We'd been bored one night, excited about having our licenses, and had taken turns behind the wheel of Cassie's Cavalier. We'd driven first to Beatrice, and then, since we were close, to Kansas. For no reason whatsoever. Just because we could. We'd done it a few times since, when we were bored and bumming through the countryside on a sunny summer evening seemed like a good way to spend time.

Like tonight.

We talked about life, about our childhoods, about how we'd changed and about how we hadn't. And whether, in another twenty years, we'd be three single residents of Morgan still driving our corn-powered cars to Kansas for kicks. Talking about our futures was as close as we came to talking about Erica all night.

And it was the best night I'd had in weeks.

Chapter 22

"Today God has delivered your enemy into your hands." I Samuel 26:8

I was in church (Morgan Bible Church) the following Sunday. I was even early, so there would be no concern from Scotty or Cassie.

We started by singing "And Can It Be That I Should Gain," one of my favorite hymns. We didn't jazz it up (although I still preferred piano to guitar music for hymns) or add a bridge or change the words or anything. We just sang it straight up. I nearly dropped to my knees and repented for attending True Way the previous Sunday.

Then we were seated for announcements, immediately followed by the offering, during which we had a special little performance. Annabeth Hissink took the stage dressed in some sort of white frock, and proceeded to twirl and pirouette and otherwise dance to canned flute music. It was *Swan Lake* mixed with Marcel Marceau. It was complete nonsense.

They called it interpretive dance, and Teasdale urged us to applaud afterwards. Dance is one thing. The interpretive part is where I draw the line. What makes Annabeth Hissink any more qualified to float around the stage for four minutes than me? Why couldn't Scotty and I do interpretive football tossing for four minutes, to marching band music? We could do one-handed grabs and behind the back passes and everything. It would be just as worshipful.

The rest of the service went by without any oddities—or any normalties as I had come to know them. The sermon wasn't exactly Spurgeonesque, but it wasn't fluff either. And it wasn't Scripturally inaccurate like last week's at True Way.

I didn't see Mark and Erica, but I also didn't spend the entire service craning my neck to find them either. I did spot her after the service while I was in line for coffee and a cake donut, as my morning bowl of Cheerios wasn't going to tide me over until lunch. Mark wasn't beside her, or anywhere, for that matter. I quelled the rising irrational hope that maybe they broke up, and took my coffee and half donut to Room 104.

Cassie saw my donut. "That looks good."

"They have more."

"Any more with chocolate frosting?"

"I think so."

"I shouldn't."

"Want me to get you one?"

"No. I should walk it off."

I wasn't sure on the logic of a walk down the hallway and back justifying half a chocolate-frosted donut's calories, but what did I care?

Cassie left, and a minute later Erica walked in. I tried to ignore her, but it wasn't easy. For one thing, her form-fitting skirt and blouse combo magnetically drew my eyes. For another, she walked directly over to me and Scotty, after stopping to talk with Cora for a moment.

"Hi," she said with a smile.

"Hi," I replied. Scotty nodded.

She extended a postcard to each of us. "I'm having a party Saturday, for my birthday. You're both invited."

I scanned the postcard.

"It's a pool party, but that sounds like an eight-year-old's birthday with a clown or something. We'll be grilling, and there's plenty of room at my parents' house for football or volleyball or whatever."

Erica tilted her head to the side, then tucked loose hair behind her ear. "Will you come?"

"Next Saturday?" I asked, trying to be casual. "Sure."

Scotty nodded again.

"Starts around two, three, whenever, and you don't have to bring any food, don't have to bring any gifts. Just come for a good time."

"Okay."

She looked around. "Is Cassie here today?"

"She will be."

Erica handed me another postcard. "Will you give that to her?"

"Sure. You not staying?"

"I can't. Mark's taking me to brunch with his parents."

I nodded.

"Valentino's."

I hated him so much.

Erica smiled again as she turned and scouted out a few others in class. She was right, a pool party was sort of juvenile. And yet it was somehow perfectly suited for Erica, the girl with the inner child and sound football analysis. Who was off to meet the parents at Val's.

"Meeting the parents," I whispered to Scotty. "That's the next step, isn't it?"

He shrugged. "Head up, Rosie."

I nodded and tucked the postcard into my Bible. I had been invited. That was good. It meant she valued me as a friend. But just a friend, because she had invited Scotty too and was having the aforementioned brunch with Mark's folks at Valentino's.

I sighed as Cassie returned. "Here," I said, handing her the postcard.

"Munt's at?" she asked, covering her mouth so donut didn't come tumbling out.

"Pool party at Erica's," I said. "Saturday."

She swallowed. Twice. "I have to work."

"How unusual."

"Besides, I don't exactly have a pool body."

"And I do?"

"Maybe you guys should pack in a few more donuts," Scotty said.

"Terminate," Cassie said, pulling off a hunk of donut.

Petey started to call the class to order. We had a pretty good crowd, and I put my hand up. Petey reluctantly recognized it. "Josh?"

"Um . . . I just wanted to mention as I did a few weeks ago that I'm looking at starting a Bible study, probably evenings mid-week. What we study is still to be determined, so if you're interested, please let me know, and let me know when works for you and any druthers you have about a topic."

I nodded and Petey cleared his throat. You'd think by the look on his face I'd just tried to organize a junket to a strip club.

Cassie gulped down a bite of her donut. "Did you just use the word 'druthers'?"

"It might have slipped out."

"I wanted to make an announcement too," Geoff said. I turned my eyes to Scotty to see if he was ready for another fight.

"We're having a carwash at Wieskamps' Saturday morning," he said, "from nine till noon. All proceeds are going for the Haiti church, so if you can be there to help out or if you can donate any supplies, please contact me. We're also open to any other money-earning ventures, so please be in touch."

Scotty raised his hand. Petey sighed audibly. "Scotty."

"What's the money for?" Scotty asked with complete innocence.

Cassie slid her foot into mine. Hang on.

"It's for the church we ministered to," Geoff said. "They have nothing, so we want to buy them some instruments—drums, a guitar or two, an amp."

"They have electricity?" Scotty asked. He was good.

"A generator."

Scotty waited a beat, until Petey was ready to speak. "Didn't you guys say that these people couldn't even afford Bibles?"

"Yeah, that's right."

"Wouldn't buying them Bibles be a better use of the money then? I mean, you can sing without instruments, and you can certainly worship without them, but it's hard to grow without a Bible."

"Unless the Holy Spirit guides you," Gia said.

"But how are you going to know if it's the Holy Spirit or the spirit that guides Monique the voodoo lady unless you can compare the guidance to what's in Scripture?"

"There are a lot of Christians who mature without Bibles," Geoff said.

"You got proof of that?"

"I've heard stories."

"Yeah, well, I've heard a story too, Gibson, about plants that withered because they had no root."

"People, this is not the place for this," Petey said.

"It's exactly the place, prof. He's asking people in this class to give time and money for a cause, and I'm saying we shouldn't be putting lipstick on a pig."

"How can you call them pigs?" Gia said. "You are so insensitive!"

"It's a metaphor, Elián."

"And you're saying instruments aren't essential?" Geoff asked.

"No, not compared to the Word of God," Scotty said.

Geoff shook his head.

"That an admission of defeat?" Scotty asked.

"This isn't about winning," Petey said.

"Of course it is. Agreeing to disagree is fine if what you're arguing about doesn't matter," Scotty said. "But when it does matter, winning is absolutely critical, especially if you're right."

"Who says you are right?" Gia asked.

"The Bible, for one," Scotty said. "And probably the Haitians, if they had a choice."

Geoff turned around with a smirk. "They did have a choice. They asked us for instruments."

"Over Bibles?"

"Over everything."

Scotty nodded, letting Geoff gloat for a second. "Then you ever consider that maybe their priorities might be off? That maybe the culture they're in values music a lot, values the arts, and thus skews their perspective?"

"What do you know about the culture in Haiti?" Gia asked.

"I don't. I'm just suggesting." Scotty shook his head. "You guys can buy them whatever you want, but don't expect me to give money or time. I'll donate to the Gideons instead."

"Fine. We don't want your help," Geoff said.

Poor Petey was tasked with starting the class in the silence that followed. Fortunately, he had an outline and delved right into his lecture on Revelation 10.

Petey's lectures never lent themselves to a ton of discussion, and there was even less this time. Until he was finished, three minutes before class was to be adjourned. Amy shot up her hand from the seat in front of Scotty.

"Yes, Amy?"

"Is there any way we can possibly understand Revelation? I mean, I know you've put in all this work and studied it, but . . . an angel standing on land and sea, seven thunders, an edible scroll. Can we really know what all this means?"

"It's in the Bible for a reason."

"Yeah, but so is a lot of stuff in the Old Testament about not having sex with animals and where to bury poop and stuff. I mean, wouldn't our time be better spent studying other stuff that we can understand?"

"Like Hebrews," Cassie whispered.

"We've been given eyes to see and minds to understand," Petey replied. "Of course we should study Revelation. It may be difficult, but nobody ever said the Christian life was easy."

I had to give it to him. I could tell by the redness in his cheeks and neck that he was about to burst. But he gave a composed answer, and before Amy could answer, closed us in prayer. And another crazy Morgan Bible Church Young Adults Fellowship was in the books.

Tuesday afternoon Mark came in to Nebraska Novelties. He ordered a small sundae from Sydney, and as she was preparing it, he noticed me stocking candy.

"Hey, Josh," he called out.

I turned, acting as if I'd just recognized him instead of having identified him as he approached the front door and turned my back to the door to focus on Tootsie Roll packages. "Hey," I replied.

"I was hoping you'd be working today, man."

"Why's that?"

He looked over his shoulder to see how Sydney was coming. She wasn't exactly a speed demon when it came to sundae making. "You got a minute?"

I nodded.

"I've been trying to figure out what to get Erica for her birthday. I'm not really the kind of guy who can walk into Kohl's and pick out a blouse, you know?"

I nodded again.

"You got any ideas, man?"

"Me?"

"Yeah. You've known E for a little while, seem to be good friends with her. I thought you might have an idea. I've got nothing."

I didn't know "E" well enough to go by initials. So I sighed as Sydney walked around the counter and delivered the sundae to Mark. He nodded his thanks and took a spoonful. He looked up at me. "If she was your girlfriend, what would you get her?"

A, that was pathetic. B, stabbing me wasn't enough, you have to twist the knife too? C, this would be a great chance to sabotage the relationship by telling him to get her an authentic German beer stein or a girly glittery T-shirt. But I decided against that. It might reflect back on me. Besides, I was a man, not a mouse. And I liked Erica. I didn't want her birthday to be crummy.

But I didn't know what to get her, and said as much to Mark. "I really don't know her all that well," I explained. "What does she like and dislike?" I asked, as much to find out for myself as to help him.

"She loves her Huskers," he answered. "And music. Singing, playing, listening."

"Playing?" I asked.

"Yeah, she plays the piano."

"Well?"

"She says no, but I disagree."

Great. She was giving him concerts.

"And Erica loves stuffed animals."

"Stuffed animals?"

"Yeah, she's got a huge collection of them."

That was kind of cute. "That's a possibility," I said.

"Yeah, but she's got every animal known to Noah. And if I did that, I'd want it to be something special, not just another teddy bear."

I nodded agreement and thought for a minute. Mark ate.

"Maybe . . ."

Inspiration was hitting, and I was kind of mad at it.

"Maybe your gift shouldn't be a thing," I said.

"Meaning?"

"Instead of giving her a thing, give her an experience. Take her somewhere. Do something. Girls like experiences, I hear. Surprises too."

"Hmm." He licked off his spoon. "That's not bad, man." He took another bite. "An experience. Any ideas?"

Must I do all the work? Could I get the kiss on the cheek for my thoughtfulness if this worked out?

"If it was me," I said, allowing that thought to consume me for just a second (and hoping the look on my face didn't give away the desires of my heart), "I'd take her to the Haymarket."

"The Haymarket?"

"Yeah. At sunset, for dinner. Or maybe to browse the shops before dinner. And then, take her to see a concert. Maybe a classical pianist, or some artist she likes if he happens to be in town."

"What are the odds of that?"

"This week, not high. But you could get the tickets, and then you have something to look forward to in the future. It's like she gets the gift twice."

"That's not bad."

No, it wasn't. And now I was talking about their relationship in a future tense.

"That's not bad, man," Mark said yet again after another scoop of his sundae. "Good thing I ran into you."

I nodded. "Yeah." Sure was.

Chapter 23

"I also want women to dress modestly, with decency and propriety." I Timothy 2:9

As Saturday approached, I grew less and less excited about Erica's pool party. For one thing, I don't swim. It looks like fun, but unless you have an Olympic-sized pool, there isn't much point. Two strokes and you're at the end of the pool, and then what? It's a lot less like actual swimming and much more like taking a bath. And don't even bring up ponds and rivers.

For another, I don't have the most athletic body in the world, and thus I'm not real fond of displaying it in front of a lot of people. And since I don't display my body in front of a lot of people, I also don't display it to the sun, meaning it is rather white. As a result, I'm even less fond of displaying it in front of a lot of people.

But most of all, I would have to deal with being around Mark and Erica again. I was doing better since my talk with Cassie and my little intervention with her and Scotty. But being around them still wasn't easy, and I doubted a swimming pool would hinder their flirting any.

That brought up another issue. Swimwear. I've never considered myself to be a prude, no more than any other Christian guy. But spending hours in the company of girls in bikinis didn't seem like the most spiritual use of my time. Especially since there was one girl there that I really wanted to see in a bikini. I couldn't help it—I was attracted to her, and that's where attraction naturally goes as a guy. Even if you are relatively self-controlled and living by the Spirit, that desire is still there.

And so several times throughout the week I was tempted to come up with an excuse and opt out. But despite the fact that I wanted Erica to be more than just my friend, she was my friend. And when a good-looking girl invites you over to her house—whether by yourself or with a church full of people, whether on a date or just as a friend—you accept. Especially when you've already told people you're going to go. And so I decided to man up, suck it up (or in my case, suck it in) and try to have a good time.

Thunderstorms had pummeled the state all day Thursday and Friday, but Saturday dawned bright, clear, and hot, and the party was on. I spent the morning at Scotty's, and we thought about driving by the carwash to see how it was going. We decided against it, and instead watched *SportsCenter* and played Nintendo and just chilled.

The postcards Erica had passed out said the party began at two, and she had said to come at two or three. We decided on three, and after killing it at *Bases Loaded* on the Nintendo, headed over. Erica's parents' house was within reasonable walking distance from Scotty's house, but we drove anyhow. Several other cars were already parked in the driveway or by the curb as we arrived, so we would be spared the awkwardness of being the first ones there.

Erica had left a message while I was at work Friday—I listened to it three times—telling us to come around back when we arrived. So we did. The Chamberlains had a huge deck behind their house, in the center of which was a spacious, rectangular pool. The terrain sloped in such a way that the deck on the other side of the pool was elevated over a patio and the entrance to a walk-in basement.

"Hi, guys!"

I turned to see Erica approaching, and a wave of heat came over me. She wore a red bikini top and a pair of white shorts, her brunette hair in a bouncy ponytail. Her smile was wide and bright, as were her eyes, which seemed to twinkle. I practically stammered my hello.

Scotty, as always, was cool. "Hey."

Erica explained to us that there were Frisbees, footballs, a croquet set and lawn darts down on the patio, a ping-pong table and regular darts in the rec room in the basement, and a cooler full of drinks on the hot tub. I looked and saw that there was indeed a hot tub, not that anyone would be using it on this day. Despite the cars out front, we were among the first to arrive, and she invited us to make ourselves at home. We headed over to a couple of chaise lounges beside the pool. So far, it was empty.

I watched Erica as she went to the edge of the deck and peered over it at something or someone. I couldn't hear what she said because Tim chose that moment to pull up a chair beside me.

If I was white, Tim was an albino. He had cleverly thought to wear sunglasses. Scotty had his hat to shield his eyes. I was forced to squint, particularly when I looked at Tim, who had already removed his shirt.

Tim wanted to talk Royals. They had just won four of six over the Tigers and Twins, but were still nine games out of first place in the division. What was the point?

Mark rescued us when he ascended from the patio. He was holding a Nerf football and lobbed it in our general direction. Scotty snagged it effortlessly.

"You guys wanna play?"

Scotty nodded, effectively for all of us. Lightning quick, Mark whipped off his shirt—he did have an athletic and tanned body—and nodded toward the empty pool. Scotty got his meaning and lobbed the ball over the turquoise water. Mark leapt out over the water, snatching the ball out of the air just before splashing into the pool.

With what could only be described a as a war whoop, Tim jumped out of his chair and dove into the pool. Scotty shrugged and pulled off his shirt, knocking off his cap in the process. He picked it up, turned it backwards, and crammed it down on top of his shaggy hair. Hoping Erica wasn't watching, I peeled off my shirt, sucked in my stomach (Monday through Friday, I had observed a strict regimen of crunches and pushups in the hopes of adding some quick muscle tone—I got only a pulled stomach muscle) and kicked off my old, untied tennis shoes. Then I joined Mark, Tim, and Scotty in the pool.

Mark matched Scotty in laid-back coolness and in athletic ability. They "cancelled" one another in our two-on-two game, and I liked to think that I outplayed Tim. It was hard to keep score because it was hard to score in a twenty-five foot long pool. What transpired was more of an aquatic, football version of 21.

We were eventually joined by Damon and Mike, who had the worst farmer's tan I'd ever seen. We played for another half an hour, and other than for the time when Mark, Mike, and I all went up for a pass and my forehead and Mark's elbow collided, I had a blast. I was so caught up in the game that I even forgot that Erica was lolling poolside in a red bikini.

After a few hand slaps and fist bumps after the game, I climbed out of the pool, dripping water and sweat in equal proportions. The party was in full swing, with at least two dozen people in lounge chairs, standing around in circles on the deck, or entering the pool now that it was devoid of violence. An iPod had been rigged to a pair of speakers and was blasting what sounded like ABBA. Nope, it was just an old Newsboys hit.

I heard giggling coming from over the deck railing, and went to see that a group of girls were playing some game with what looked like croquet balls. But it wasn't croquet. They were throwing the balls into the grass and then throwing other balls at the first ones. I spent a few minutes watching them, primarily because Erica was one of the players, and couldn't figure out the object of the game. Was it just to throw croquet balls close to other croquet balls? At any rate, it was not un-entertaining.

Scotty tapped my arm with a very cold can of lemonade. I took it, popped the top, and gulped half of the contents down with one swig.

"How's your head, dude?" Scotty's hat was still backwards and closer to its original dark purple shade now that it was saturated with water. He was still shirtless, tan, and fit, and reminded me that I was still shirtless, white, and unfit.

"I don't know, how many girls are down there?"

"Four."

"Then it's fine."

He grinned. "Jay Cutler over there has challenged me to a game of ping-pong," he said, nodding at Tim. He had thrown half a dozen interceptions in our little game, earning the comparison to the oft-beleaguered Chicago Bears quarterback. "You wanna join a round robin?"

"Maybe later," I said. "I'm going to hang out up here."

"All right."

"Enjoy your game," I called over his shoulder, and then went back to find a chaise lounge before they were all full. As it turned out, the only available seat was next to Mark, who was in the process of crushing a Mountain Dew. As if he weren't dating the woman of my dreams, I sat down beside him.

"You play a nice game, man," he said. "You play in high school?"

"No. With this body?"

"You could have been a receiver, d-back." He took another chug of soda. "Course it's hard to tell in a pool." He looked around. "And considering you were being covered by that white kid."

I smiled, mostly in relief that there was another guy at the party that looked worse with his shirt off than I did. I sipped from my lemonade and lay back, wishing I had brought some shades. Mid-afternoon midsummer sun was kind of bright.

Newsboys had given way to something I didn't recognize on the iPod, which in turn segued into some seriously old school Switchfoot. I closed my eyes and rocked inwardly to "Meant to Live" and enjoyed the feeling of warm sun on my still wet skin. When Jon Foreman stopped and Bart Millard began, I opened my eyes and sat up. The game of hand croquet was over, and Erica and her friends were ascending the steps of the deck. She gave a little half wave that I wished was for me and then ducked into the house. Two minutes later, she scampered over toward us, and I felt my heartbeat accelerating.

Mark sat up in his chair and spread his legs, affording her a place to sit. I once again inhaled and held my breath, imagining my gut to be twice the size it really was.

"How was football?" Erica asked, glancing over her shoulder with a sparkle in her brown eyes. "Did you win?"

"Shoot, I don't even know if we scored," Mark answered. "How was bocce ball?" He leaned forward and rested his chin on Erica's very bare shoulder. "Did you win?"

She wrinkled her button nose and shook her head slightly. The motion caused her ponytail to flop back and forth. Why was it that such little things could make a guy go crazy?

Erica leaned back into Mark and I turned to scan the deck, seeing how many people I recognized. Brad, Brett, Cora, Geoff, Kevin—wearing some sort of a scuba suit that looked like an Under Armor T-shirt and bicycle shorts in one—and a few girls I recognized from the Haiti team. A couple others I did not. Notably absent was Gia, which was fine with me.

I turned back as Erica tapped Mark's knee. "I'm going to go for a swim," she said. "You want to?"

He gave her a quick peck on the cheek. "Naw, football wore me out. I'll stay here and chat up Josh."

"Fine, big strong football player," she said. Then she stood up and very flirtatiously pushed on his sternum, knocking him backward onto his chair. With a wink at him and a smile at me—as if I enjoyed this disgusting display—she quickly stepped out of her shorts and headed toward the pool.

Mark sat back up and drained his Mountain Dew. He watched Erica enter the pool and acclimate herself to it. She ducked under the water a few times and emerged, wiping the sheen off her face.

"You want another?" Mark asked me.

I got my head around in appropriate order. "No, I'm good."

He nodded and tromped over to the cooler. I was left, momentarily, with no one to talk to and nothing to do except watch Erica in the pool. A volleyball game had started, with a small net stretched across the center. The shrieks of the players blended with the tunes from the iPod and the murmurings of several conversations on the deck. I had to admit, this wasn't so bad after all.

However, I did feel a little guilty watching Erica play. I wasn't sure how the rules of fidelity worked when someone was only dating instead of married, but I felt kind of bad eyeing somebody else's girl. Especially since Mark wasn't the scourge of the earth like the guy who stole my dream girl ought to have been. He was a decent guy, and if I had met him before Erica, I wouldn't have thought about her for a second.

I also felt guilty because of the role Erica's red bikini played in my desire to watch her. God had given her a beautifully sculpted body, and quite a bit of it was on display. While I tried not to stare and to keep my eyes from inappropriate places, I still realized her overall attraction was heightened by her skimpy clothing. Looking at her was appealing to me, and that swimsuit was a large reason why. Did that mean I was lusting? And if so, how could I avoid doing so at a pool party full of girls in skimpy swimsuits? Was the answer to not look at any girls? That seemed a little over the top, and I continued to monitor the pool volleyball action. I also continued to have a knot in my stomach.

"How long have you been going to MBC?" Mark asked as he straddled his chair momentarily blocking the sun. Then he sat down and cracked open a second Mountain Dew.

"I was raised in the church."

"Really?"

"Yeah. My dad was the pastor for twenty years."

"Was?"

"They had a . . . parting of ways. He's in Oklahoma now."

Mark sat forward. "I've always thought pastors are like football coaches."

"Football coaches?"

"Yeah. Coaches are always switching schools, getting fired, getting re-hired, moving cross-country. Same with pastors. Even youth pastors and music pastors get promoted to senior pastors." He took a swig.

I'd never heard it put like that, but it wasn't inaccurate. "Yeah, twenty years in one place is kind of unusual."

"How long have you worked at the ice cream place?"

"Just this summer. How about you? How'd you get into the world of home security?" I asked. Might as well know as much as possible about the competition.

"After high school I just started filling out random applications. They called first. Pays pretty well."

"So you have to go around selling the things?"

"Yeah. Usually you spend an hour chatting with a lady and she gives you the 'I've got to check with my husband' brush-off and you never hear from them again."

"That's got to get old."

He nodded and chugged more Dew. I determined that if he died of a caffeine overdose or a super sugar buzz, I would wait an appropriate amount of time before moving in on Erica.

"Yeah, but I service a lot of the small towns, so I spend a lot of time driving and listening to ESPN Radio. All reimbursed."

"Nice."

"Yeah." He crushed the empty can in his hand. "You go to college?"

"Sort of."

"Sort of? Online classes or something?"

"I've taken four semesters, but I'm taking a break."

"Money?"

"Direction," I answered.

"How long a break?"

"That is a very good question," I said, and had another sip of my lemonade. "I guess until I get tired of scooping ice cream."

Mark grinned. Then he winced at the music. It was some girl music, Superchick or BarlowGirl or somebody. "Hey, did you know Erica's dad used to have a band?" he asked.

"Like a real band?"

"Yeah. They played at state fairs and stuff. It was just like *That Thing You Do* movie, you know with Tom Hanks, Steve Zahn, and Liv Tyler."

He raised his eyebrows at "Liv Tyler" and I nodded.

"What'd he play?" I asked. I couldn't pick Erica's dad out of a lineup, didn't even know his name. But thinking positively, I figured I should get the scoop on my future father-in-law.

"Bass guitar. The guy was good. Still is, actually."

Great, Mark was treated to bass concerts by Erica's dad, in addition to piano performances by her. Maybe the whole family put on a show for him.

"He works at Union Bank, right?" I asked, looking away from the pool at Mark. We had both been glancing at it regularly during our conversation. At first I was afraid he would think I was ogling Erica, but then I realized there were other girls in the pool too. He had no idea I was checking out his girl. Was that how King David started?

Mark scratched his jaw, then his leg. "Yeah. President of the local branch." He leaned toward me. "There's a reason they've got a place like this."

I nodded and drained my lemonade.

We watched the rest of the volleyball game, the finish of which was very spirited. Every point was punctuated with girlish screams of excitement. When it was finished, new players entered the pool. Erica stepped out, toweled off, and came over and sat on the front end of Mark's beach chair.

Breathing heavily, she wiped wet strands of hair out of her eyes. Her eyes again flashed with vigor, but they were aimed at the wrong guy. "We won this time," she said, leaning slightly in toward Mark.

"I'm glad."

Erica put her hand on his arm. "Are you properly rested so you can join me in the next game?"

He smirked. "I think so."

Her head, and her wet ponytail, whipped around. "How about you, Josh?"

"Uh, I'm not a big volleyball fan."

"Aw, come on. In this state?"

She was only kidding, but even so, I found her pleading seductive, and wished her smile and her eyes had more than just casual friendship in them. I couldn't help but grin, and admit that perhaps I would be up for one game of pool volleyball.

Mark got up to get another can of Mountain Dew, and Erica took over his seat and lounged back. I allowed myself, for just a few moments, to enjoy the view. I was almost nauseas, and I wasn't sure if it was excessive infatuation or guilt that caused it. I convinced myself that enjoying a good-looking girl, without impure thoughts, couldn't be sinful. Could it?

Jennifer Knapp's "Undo Me" was next on the iPod, and I wondered if that was some sort of a sign. I asked God to help me be pure, without being a prude. After all, if it was a sin to look at a girl in a bikini, wasn't it a sin for a girl to wear a bikini? Erica's smile wasn't the smile of someone who was sinning.

Mark returned with another can of lemonade, which he tossed to me. Then he stood over Erica. "You're in my chair, missy."

"Finders keepers."

"Is that so?"

"Uh-huh," she said, flirtatiousness etched on her lips and in her eyes.

Mark shot me a quick smirk as he set down his can, and then reached down and began tickling Erica's sides, just above her waist. She squealed and giggled, and lowered her elbows to try and stop him. He raised one hand to her neck; she fought off with a raised shoulder. Eventually, she curled into the fetal position to fight him off, and he easily lifted her out of the chair.

Mark sat back down, a big grin on his face. Erica sat in front of him, his arms loosely wrapped around her mid-section. I found myself longing to be in his place, wishing that it had been my fingers tickling her skin.

Mark and Erica were lost in flirtatious puppy love, and I got up. I grabbed my new can of lemonade, found my shirt, and headed for the basement. I figured the best way to avoid lusting was to play ping-pong with Scotty and the albino.

Chapter 24

"Watch and pray so that you will not fall into temptation." Matthew 26:41

The Chamberlain's basement was not the safe haven I had hoped for. Scotty was still at the ping-pong table, with half a dozen people seated on the floor or leaning against the wall watching him. His opponent was a girl named Christie, one of Erica's friends I was pretty sure didn't go to Morgan Bible. I would have noticed.

Christie stood at least six feet tall, with short, straight blond hair and a pixie face. Her thin, lithe body was accentuated by a navy blue halter swimsuit top and incredibly short orange shorts. Several other girls in the basement were similarly dressed, although without a WNBA frame. Where could I put my eyes?

I kept them on Scotty. His face was a mixture of tense focus (I gathered without looking at her half of the table, that Christie was a pretty good player) and utter calm. He never missed a shot, and ultimately won the game.

"Four in a row," he said with a smirk.

"I'm next!" several voices announced.

"Sort it out," he said, flipping his paddle. He nodded in my direction. "Rosie, you're up."

"What?"

"Take my place. I need a drink." He handled me the paddle and looked toward the group of people clamoring to be his next opponent. "He's my proxy. I'll be back to whip the winner."

I took the paddle from him and assumed my position at the end of the table, praying my opponent would not be wearing a bikini. Hardly. It was Kevin, still in his Aqua Man costume. After a quick warm-up volley, we began, with Kevin serving first.

Scotty and I played a decent amount in his basement, and I was proficient enough to hold my own against most people. Kevin was not most people, and I could have taken him left-handed. The final score was 21-7, and I spent the last half of the game trying to make trick shots.

Two girls I didn't recognize began to argue over who got to play me next.

"Uh-uh-uh," Scotty said, stepping through the sliding glass doors. "The king is back."

I wiped my hands on my shirt, and switched the paddle from hand to hand. Scotty took a long pull from his can of Dr. Pepper and took the other paddle from one of the girls. He was wearing his white T-shirt again, his hat still backwards. He smirked in my direction as he nonchalantly flipped his paddle in the air. "You ready, Rafa[12]?"

"Let's go."

I had beaten Scotty before, but it was so rare that I never really let myself hope that I might. Today, I held my own, getting a couple of fortunate bounces and a few lucky returns of great shots by Scotty. The score was 14-10, Scotty leading, when Erica walked in.

She was still in her swimsuit, but her hair was out of the ponytail and hung in wet strands and clumps beside her cheeks and on her shoulders. She came with several other partiers—not Mark—and took a position directly behind Scotty.

Maybe it was my intrinsic desire to impress her. Maybe it was my acute focus on the game, driven by a desire not to look at her for fear that lustful thoughts would ensue. Or maybe it was because she declared that she had the winner and I wanted a chance to play her — and eye her — some more. Whatever the reason, I became Roger Federer in his prime.

I began hitting amazing shots, smoking balls off the corners, and slapping everything Scotty hit right back at him. I tied him at 17, and then scored three straight to force match point. He turned his hat forward, and then back backwards.

"Your serve," I said confidently, tossing him the ball. He scooped it, eyed me, and aced one just out of my reach.

---

[12] "Rafa" is a common nickname for professional tennis player Rafael Nadal.

By now there were close to a dozen people watching the game, clapping and cheering, most of them for me. I gathered that Scotty had defeated half of them and they wanted someone, anyone, to take him down. I was someone.

After a spirited volley, I skimmed a shot over the net and off the side of the table, just out of Scotty's reach.

I dropped my paddle and raised my hand, wiggling my fingers in a smart-aleck, Hawkeye Pierce sort of wave. Scotty scraped his hat off his head and then turned to hand the paddle to Erica.

I couldn't very well play without looking at my opponent, and I wasn't going to beg off with some excuse. I was stuck playing a game of ping-pong against my dream girl while she wore a very revealing swimsuit. I said a quick prayer for help and tried to ignore sex appeal and to focus on table tennis.

It wasn't easy. For one thing, I'm ultra-competitive. And here I was playing a girl. I couldn't lose—it would damage my male ego. And I couldn't beat the snot out of her, because then I'd look like a chauvinistic bully. I had to win, but not dominate the game. Talk about pressure.

Having a table in her basement, Erica was pretty good. Having a table in my friend's basement that I used frequently (not to mention a student union at college), I was better, and eventually beat her. Then I lost the next game, to Brad, primarily because I couldn't get the image of Erica out of my head.

I left the basement and headed back upstairs, into the house, and into the bathroom. I sat down on the closed toilet and put my head in my hands. What was going on? I'd seen girls in swimsuits before, even revealing two-pieces. So what was it today that was making it so hard? And was the fact that it was so hard a good thing? Did it mean I was more conscientious and trying harder not to sin with my eyes, or did it just mean I was being bombarded?

And how much did Erica have to do with it? Christie and Cora looked pretty good in their suits too. Was I just a sex-crazed guy, hot for Erica because of the physical attraction I felt? Forget Erica. Was that the only reason I felt anything for any girl? And if so, was I any different than any other guy?

Realizing I'd been in the bathroom for quite a while, I got up with a sigh. Sure it was a pool party, but I hadn't expected an ambush at a gathering of Christians.

I left the bathroom with one thought in mind: eye contact. I would, to the absolute best of my abilities, try to look girls only in the eye. It was a flawed plan, thanks to depth perception, peripheral vision, and the desires of the flesh. But with plans to spend the night praying when I got home, I tried to have a good time and not spend every minute analyzing if my eyes and thoughts were where they belonged.

It worked, sort of. A couple of guys were tossing the football in the lawn, and I joined them. As expected, a game eventually broke out. A few girls joined us, and fortunately put on clothes first. Trying to figure out just where exactly it was kosher to two-hand-touch a girl was bad enough when they weren't dressed for a Victoria's Secret catalog.

After the game, we cooled down with another quick dip in the pool, and I used the water to help me keep my eyes north of the Mason-Dixon Line. It was see-through, as is most water, but at least distorted the objects beneath it.

Erica's parents—who had so far remained out of sight—emerged from the house to serve dinner. After hours of activity in the summer sun, hamburgers, grilled chicken, fruit salad, pasta salad, several kinds of chips, and more cold drinks hit the spot. We lounged on the deck and around the pool, eating until we could eat no more. I sat between Scotty and Mark, who regaled us with stories of their crazy teenage years, odd athletic feats, and impressions of various celebrities. After half an hour of listening to them, I wasn't sure if I was mad that my best friend was fraternizing with my sworn enemy—even though I'd given him permission—or if my best friend was in jeopardy of being replaced by my sworn enemy.

After dinner, Erica's dad built a bonfire and everyone put on a few clothes to fight the evening chill. We gathered around the fire pit and the story telling and can-you-top-this resumed. Erica had donned a red Nebraska Cornhuskers hoodie and the white shorts she had worn earlier, and still looked adorable in the glow of the fire. I tried not to stare at her, and not to think about what I knew she was wearing under her hoodie.

I turned my eyes down to the fire, spending several minutes watching the flames lick at the perfectly stacked logs. What was wrong with my mind? Why couldn't I appreciate a good-looking girl without my thoughts always wandering toward impurity? Perhaps because girls wore swimsuits that left little to the imagination. Then again, my imagination was doing just fine with a thick, bulky, hooded sweatshirt. I had always considered myself a pretty good person, and yet I felt as if the warm tongues of fire were burning my conscience.

So when Tim absentmindedly began rolling a football back and forth between his hands, I nodded at him to toss it to me. We stepped away from the fire, were joined by Brad, and played a three-way game of catch for a while. I had not come to Erica's pool party to hang out with Tim Harte and Brad Ostrander, but it beat wrestling with my conscience.

When Erica's mom brought out marshmallows and skewers, Tim and Brad both beelined for the fire pit. Realizing it would be pretty lame to stand in the middle of the lawn tossing a football up to myself, I ambled over as well. Scotty and Mark were still going at it, the current topic bonfires they had built, contributed to, or seen explode. I sat down, impaled a marshmallow, and wondered if—lustful thoughts aside—it was wrong for me to steal glances at my sworn enemy/new best friend's girlfriend. But I did, and thought about how much I'd like to cuddle with her around a cozy fire sometime, perhaps while Scotty and Mark were blowing something up.

Scotty tapped my arm. I had been admiring the way Erica's mostly dry hair fell over and hung up on the ridges of her hood, and hoped he wasn't tapping me because my staring had become obvious. I looked his way and grunted a very casual, "Huh?"

"You about ready, dude?"

"Yeah, I suppose."

I swallowed my mallow and handed my stick to Kevin. Erica stood and thanked us for coming, her smile purely sociable and yet heartwarming. We thanked her back, and thanked her dad, who was still hanging around the fire and seemed to be enjoying the crazy juvenile stories being told, almost as if he missed his own rambunctious youth. Then Scotty slapped/shook hands with Mark, I nodded at Tim, and we headed across the yard, up onto the deck, and past the now dark, tranquil pool.

Scotty grabbed one more drink from the cooler and we strolled toward his Blazer. "You have a good time?" he asked, popping the top on his soda.

I debated telling Scotty the truth, how I had battled impure thoughts for six hours. But as close and open as our friendship was, I still felt weird talking about it with him. Especially since he seemed so calm and unaffected around girls. Who knew, maybe his head was swirling with tempting thoughts too. Maybe he just knew how to handle them better, or wasn't affected by them, or didn't have as aggressive of a conscience as I did. Or wasn't in love with a spoken-for woman. At any rate, I took the easy road and answered with a, "Yeah."

Scotty dropped me off, and worn out physically, mentally, and emotionally, I headed straight to bed. It took me a while to fall asleep, in part because I was lying on sunburn, and in part because my mind was still in hyper-drive. I couldn't erase the feeling of guilt that was for some reason so strong today.

Nor could I erase the image of Erica in her red bikini.

Chapter 25

"How can a young man keep his way pure?" Psalm 119:9

"Turn with me in your Bibles to First Corinthians chapter six," Curtis Teasdale said the following morning. We'd sung a series of songs on the topic of purity and excellence in living and being filled with the Spirit. At least, I think that was the gist of it. I'd been having trouble focusing, because a night's sleep had not calmed my mind. I was still tormented—and at the same time delighted—by images of Erica from the day before. And by once again wondering why this particular temptation had been so much stronger than previous ones.

If singing the morning songs had been difficult, the offertory had been excruciating. Special music again, by one Erica Chamberlain. She hadn't mentioned at the party, at least in my company, that she would be singing, so I was surprised to hear her announced. Then I was floored when she stepped up onto the stage.

Erica's hair was beautifully styled, even more so than ever, falling upon bare shoulders that were revealed by the spaghetti straps on her bright pink dress. A few strands of hair curled over the front of the dress, as if to draw attention to the silver locket around her neck. It was matched by silver hoop earrings, and hung just low enough to draw the eyes toward the crease slightly exposed by the cut of the dress. The dress hugged her figure all the way down, which wasn't that far. It was cut above the knee, and as Erica stood on pink high heels at the front of the stage, her long legs were completely visible.

In short, she was stunning. And while the dress might have been a little immodest for church—although not really compared to what a lot of other women and girls wore—it wasn't slinky or slutty, even by typical "Christian" standards. But for me, on this day, it was a stumbling block.

A huge one. With spikes on top. And a pop-up boxing glove like in the cartoons. My eyes were drawn to the edges of the dress, and each time I looked, it was as if I could see a little more of her, as if the dress was shrinking.

There I was, in church, listening to her beautiful solo, and I was being dragged away and enticed like never before. What was I to do? If I turned my eyes away from every girl who dressed like Erica, I'd be better off blind. And my great idea of eye contact didn't work when she was fifty feet away on stage. The eyes weren't that far removed from other features at that distance.

And so by the time Curtis Teasdale asked us to open our Bibles to I Corinthians, I felt as if every eye in church was on me, as if God was pointing out my obvious sin to the entire congregation. And I wasn't even sure I had sinned. Being dragged away and enticed was a description of temptation. And yet, I hadn't exactly gone kicking and screaming.

My hands found Corinthians on autopilot, and I followed along as Teasdale read from his Amplified Bible.

"*'Everything is permissible for me, but not all things are beneficial. Everything is permissible for me, but I will not be enslaved by anything [and brought under its power, allowing it to control me]. Food is for the stomach and the stomach for food, but God will do away with both of them. The body is not intended for sexual immorality, but for the Lord, and the Lord is for the body [to save, sanctify, and raise it again because of the sacrifice of the cross]. And God has not only raised the Lord [to life], but will also raise us up by His power. Do you not know that your bodies are members of Christ? Am I therefore to take the members of Christ and make them part of a prostitute? Certainly not! Do you not know that the one who joins himself to a prostitute is one body with her? For He says, "THE TWO SHALL BE ONE FLESH." But the one who is united and joined to the Lord is one spirit with Him. Run away from sexual immorality [in any form, whether thought or behavior, whether visual or written]. Every other sin that a man commits is outside the body, but the one who is sexually immoral sins against his own body. Do you not know that your body is a temple of the Holy Spirit who is within you, whom you have [received as a gift] from God, and that you are not your own [property]? You were bought with a price [you were actually purchased with the precious blood of Jesus and made His own]. So then, honor and glorify God with your body.'"*

Teasdale closed his Bible and took a few steps to the side. "In his second letter to Timothy, the Apostle Paul wrote, *'run away from youthful lusts.'* This isn't avoidance. This is full-fledged retreat — it's the antithesis of pursuit. Run away!"

I swallowed hard. I hadn't exactly been running from sexual sin yesterday. But what did that mean? No mixed pool parties or beach trips? What about summer barbecues where girls wore tank tops and short shorts? Or sang solos in moderately revealing dresses? Or for that matter, wore blue jeans and a heavy sweater? Did running mean avoiding girls all together, or was there an obvious line somewhere between bikinis and burkas?

It was a slippery slope either way. Once you started avoiding girls in tank tops or T-shirts or shorts cut above the knee, you weren't far from joining a monastery. And yet, if you justified short shorts and bare midriffs, pretty soon you were back to two-pieces at pool parties.

"Let me be clear," Teasdale continued. "Sex is a gift from God. He created it. He likes it. He wants us to have it, but in the context of marriage. Paul uses the analogy of food. It's a good metaphor. Food is necessary for survival. But food, eaten at the wrong time, say when you're sick, can have dire consequences. And that is the admonition here — not to defile our bodies with premarital or extramarital sex. They were not made for it. Sex was not made for it."

Maybe there really was something to those arranged marriages in the Old Testament. Isaac never lusted after Rebekah because he never saw her until they were married. But who arranged your marriage when your folks moved to Oklahoma? I was not marrying some Sooner girl.

I realized I was sweating, and tried to fan myself with my worship folder. It drew a look from Cassie, and I was sure half the church could see me squirming under this sermon. And the only person who squirmed under a sermon, be it on sex or anything else, was the person guilty of the thing the sermon was speaking out against. I had to stop squirming. But the cooler and calmer I tried to look, the more anxious and nervous I felt.

"The entire theme of this passage is the intended use of our bodies. They were made to honor God. Sex outside of marriage isn't honoring to God. Sex inside of it is." Teasdale looked up, making eye contact with the congregation. "Are you honoring God with your body?"

Hmm. I hadn't sinned with my body. Except for my eyes, maybe. And my mind, which was part of the proverbial temple. But was that what the passage meant, or was it talking about actual sex?

And wait a second. Was wearing a bikini honoring God with your body? How much of this was my fault and how much was Erica's and Cora's and Christie's? And did it matter what they did? Wasn't I called to be pure no matter what?

Forget swimsuits. Should girls sing solos in pink spaghetti strap dresses that didn't conceal as much as they could? Should they wear shirts that rode up their back when they bent over? Should they be showing so much leg with their shorts? Pretty soon I'd have them back in burkas.

Maybe it was just me. Maybe the average guy didn't struggle the way I did. I mean, how did a Christian guy in Miami survive, when every girl was rollerblading on the sidewalk in a bikini? And did guys in Alaska struggle with lust when all the girls wore parkas all day? Would they find a girl in a long-sleeved Henley to be a temptress?

Maybe I should become a monk after all.

Teasdale didn't provide any of the answers to my questions. He just stomped on my toes for thirty minutes, and after we closed with a reprise of one of the purity songs, I filed out of church feeling dirty and even more confused than ever.

"That was fun," Scotty said.

"Yeah," I answered.

"You going to Sunday school?"

"I wouldn't miss that party for the world."

On the way to class, I stopped to check the signup sheet I had posted in the Church Happenings Center — what normal people called a bulletin board. I had stopped in on Wednesday and been granted permission to advertise my Bible study. I had made the executive decision to have it Wednesday nights, starting the next Wednesday (because it had already been over a month since Dave suggested the study). Scotty had offered his basement for a location, and all the details were on the sheet, which had only three names—mine, Scotty's, and Cassie's. And I had forged their names, since they had already given me a verbal agreement.

Wonderful.

Sunday school was no great shakes. We talked about the two witnesses and the seventh trumpet, and avoided any major arguments. Which means we also avoided any real fun.

Erica was there, and her dress was as revealing and alluring from the back as from the front. I decided that I may very well be a prude, but there were certain things a girl—even a wonderful Christian girl who may be considering being a missionary nurse—shouldn't wear to church. At least without a stole.

Fortunately Mark draped his arm over her largely bare—from my view—back to restrict the view. Lucky arm.

I tried to "flee" by keeping my eyes buried in my Bible. It sort of worked, and when class mercifully ended, I made one last announcement for Bible study. Topic, sex. (I did not say that; only thought it.) I got a similar response as the two previous times, which is to say, zilch.

"You want to come over for lunch?" Scotty asked.

It beat being alone with my thoughts. "Yeah, sure."

"Cass?"

"I think we're headed to Nebraska City this afternoon."

"Have fun."

She nodded and we said goodbye. On the way out, I checked the signup sheet again. One name had been added. Gia Torres.

Doubly wonderful.

"Maybe it's a practical joke," Scotty said.

"Hmph. Maybe."

Scotty and Dirk had walked to church, as had I, and so the three of us strolled back to their place. "You all right, dude?" Scotty asked when we got there. Dirk had gone into the bedroom to change. Scotty, wearing shorts and a polo shirt, didn't really need to change. "You seem a little off."

I nodded.

"Erica?"

"In a manner of speaking."

Scotty went to the fridge, found a couple of cans of cream soda, and held one up toward me. I nodded, he tossed it. "You want to talk about it?"

"Yes and no."

He nodded and popped the tab on his pop can, then led the way onto the deck. It was a beautiful morning, light breeze, birds chirping, a squirrel darting across the lawn. Scotty pulled out a chair and sat down. Waiting.

I sighed and took the chair next to him. "Promise not to think I'm a perv?"

"Unless you tell me you found Kevin attractive in his wetsuit."

"No, not Kevin. Erica, Cora, Christie—all the other girls."

"You feel guilty for cheating on Erica or something?"

"No. I feel guilty for leering."

"I didn't catch you leering."

"You were busy playing ping-pong."

He shrugged and took a slurp. I finally summoned the courage to open my can. It foamed a little but wasn't bad.

"I wasn't leering . . . I don't think. But it's like I'm being ambushed by sex. Girls in bikinis, Erica in that dress today . . ."

"This come on from the sermon?"

"No. Before that. The sermon just drove it home. It really started yesterday at the party."

"Do what I do. Eye contact."

"Yeah. Make eye contact with me while I peek over the TV at you during an LSU-Alabama game."

"Didn't say it worked," he said with another shrug.

"So it's not just me? You struggle too?"

"Why do you think I spent the day playing ping-pong?"

I nodded, took a drink.

Dirk peeked out the door. "What do you boys want for lunch?"

Scotty shrugged again.

"Some fruit of the Spirit," I said.

Dirk frowned.

"You got advice for a couple of guys who can't stop looking at girls in their bikinis?" Scotty asked.

Dirk stepped onto the deck. *"'It is better to marry than to burn with passion.'"*

"Really?" Scotty asked. "That's it? No golf analogy."

Dirk squinted. "You got a deep bunker in front of the green with a pin tucked just off the front edge. So play to the back of the green."

"I think that means no pool parties," I said.

"Or lots of table tennis."

"Or someone could buy these girls a decent piece of swimwear," I said.

"Great," Scotty said. "Next year all the girls will be dressed like Kevin Sprague."

"That'll get rid of the temptation at least."

Dirk shook his head. "I'm going to stick a couple of pizzas in the oven. Then I'll tell you a story."

We swilled pop and waited. Dirk was back in three minutes and sat down across from us. "Before I met your mother, I dated a girl named Lindsay Taylor."

"Not Lindsay again," Scotty said.

"This is a different story," Dirk said.

"Why, what's the deal with Lindsay Taylor?"

"You don't want to know," Scotty said.

"Lindsay was a tall, blond Texan," Dirk said. "Texas women are not overrated, by the way. I met Lindsay through her sister, Loraleigh. Loraleigh was possibly the most beautiful woman I've ever seen, to this day, but she was a year older than me, and well . . . out of my league."

Dirk had himself a pop as well, and he took a drink before continuing. "I had just been washed in the blood, and one of the things I struggled with was lust. And Loraleigh was my Road Hole Bunker[13], so to speak. Try as I might, I couldn't help undressing her with my eyes every time I saw

---

[13] The Road Hole Bunker is a particularly deep sand trap in front of the 17th green at the famous Old Course at St. Andrews.

her. It helped that it was a hundred degrees in Texas and there wasn't all that much undressing to do. Anyhow, then I met her sister, a fair-looker in her own right, and we started dating."

Dirk took another drink. "It got sort of serious, to the point where I was starting to think about Lindsay and I getting married. I wasn't buying a ring or anything, but it was in my head. And I realized, if I'm going to be married to Lindsay, I really can't be struggling with Loraleigh like this. And it dawned on me that as I fell more for Lindsay that Loraleigh wasn't 'on the market' anymore. I started to view her as a friend, as a future sister-in-law. Once that happened, I found the temptations diminishing, because I no longer saw Loraleigh as a potential sex object, but as a person."

"So I should marry some other girl not quite as good-looking as Erica?" I asked.

"No. I'm saying that maybe the issue is you're viewing Erica sexually—viewing all these girls sexually—because although you're a good Christian young man, you're also a young man, and every young man's ultimate goal is to win a girl's heart and to take her to bed. It sounds terrible to say, but that is how guys work and it is how God designed us to work—to have sex, in marriage."

"Maybe you should relate this to golf, Dad," Scotty said with a frown.

Dirk leaned on the table, looking between us. "It's simple. If you consider a girl, even subconsciously, to be potential girlfriend—and thus a potential wife and thus a potential sex partner—your mind is going to go to sex. If you see her as just another person, a friend, a sister-in-law, a coworker—whatever the case is—your mind is somewhat less likely to stray there."

I nodded.

"It's a theoretical thing," Dirk said. "I still struggled with Loraleigh from time to time, and if your sister-in-law's built like Brooke Shields and dresses like a swimsuit model, you're probably still going to have troubles. But the mindset you have toward a person helps, at least in my experience."

I turned to Scotty. "Who's Brooke Shields?"

He shrugged.

I thought about what Dirk said. It made sense. I'd never once had a sexual thought about Cassie. She wasn't built like a model, but she was cute in the little sister sort of way. I just had always thought of her as a friend, nothing else. Maybe that's where I needed to go with Erica.

"Anyhow, that's my take," Dirk said. He took another drink and pushed back from the table.

"So what happened with Lindsay?" I asked.

"Hmm?"

"You didn't marry her. What happened?"

"He met some other girl, fell hard and fast for her, and dumped Lindsay," Scotty said.

"You did?"

Dirk nodded. "Scotty's mother."

Chapter 26

"'So I have called on you to tell me what to do.'" I Samuel 28:15

For the next few days, I tried to think of Erica just as a friend. Not as a potential girlfriend—and thus, according to Dirk's logic, as a potential sex partner. It was, after all, the strategy Cassie had suggested on the hood of my car while eating pie in the park. But I had begun to employ the idea of being Erica's friend as a means to an end. Now I tried, as hard as it was to give up the idea of someday being a couple, to consider her as just a friend. No more looking at friendship as a stepping stone.

Wednesday was our first scheduled Bible study. Sans the study. As I still had no idea what to pick for a topic or who would be coming, I thought we could meet, get to know one another—if we didn't already—and decide what to study.

Scotty, Cassie, and I hung out at Scotty's before the study, and shot buckets in the driveway until we started to get sweaty. We quit as sweat wasn't viewed as great ambiance for a Bible study. Even just an informative opening session.

Gia arrived at 6:32, two minutes after the time posted on the signup sheet at church. I tried my best to be peaceable and greeted her politely.

"How long is this study going to last?" she asked.

"Over-under two weeks," Scotty mumbled.

I shrugged. "An hour or so."

She nodded and inched her purse a little higher on her shoulder. It was clothed, like a good shoulder should be, and she wore jeans. I'd found—as a corollary to Dirk's friends-don't-ogle-friends theory—that my impure thoughts were not limited to girls I liked. But today, Gia was not an issue.

230

We stood around awkwardly for several minutes, not saying much. I was about to suggest we head inside when a dark blue minivan pulled to the curb. Amy got out, in what could only be described as a fluster. Simultaneously she pulled her hair into a ponytail, dug through her purse for something to bind it with, beeped her doors locked, and nursed a frozen coffee drink of some sort.

She looked up as she started up the driveway. "What, there's five of us?"

"That's a twenty percent increase," I said. "I'm excited."

"Does anyone know the name of that girl at Nebraska Novelties — the one with all the tattoos and crazy hair?"

I gulped.

"She totally screwed up this drink. It is supposed to be a frozen cinnamon latte, and there is no cinnamon and I think this is caramel."

Sydney did not mess up coffees. Not accidentally anyhow.

I noticed that the inferior caramel drink was two-thirds of the way gone.

"Should we get started?"

We headed down into Scotty's basement, my old room. In addition to the couch/my old bed, there were two old armchairs, a beanbag chair, and a glider. Plus folding chairs at the ready. They could stay there.

I took the couch. Cassie joined me. Scotty and Gia opposed each other in the armchairs, and Amy plopped into the glider and immediately gave it a peculiar stare as it creaked. "What are we studying?" she asked. Slurp.

"That's what we have to decide," I said. "I thought this first night could be a chance to figure that out, decide if Wednesdays at six-thirty really work best for everybody, discuss anything else."

I got four blank stares.

"Should we start with prayer?"

More blank stares. So I prayed. I prayed like some of those guys in church who take big pauses between sentences. I figure they're just wrestling with the right words and not stalling. I was stalling. We would be done at quarter to seven the way this was going.

My "Amen" was punctuated by a clap, and I looked up to see Amy returning a bottle of lotion to her purse. She rubbed it into her hands while asking if I was the teacher.

I shrugged. "I was planning on starting as such, but this isn't a lecture circuit. I thought we'd all contribute."

"I don't think Petey liked your Bible study idea," she said. "Every time you made an announcement he tensed up."

"Petey came out of the womb tensed up," Scotty said.

"Yeah, but what does he care if Josh has a little Bible study? It's not like we took over the nursery and recruited young adults away from his class."

I cleared my throat. "I thought we could also take a few minutes to get to know each other."

"We all know each other," Gia said.

"Yeah, but I meant on a deeper level. You don't need to bare your deepest secrets, but I thought we could just each share a thirty-second or minute-long testimony of where we're at in life. And I'll start."

Eight eyes turned toward me. I swallowed. Leading classes was not my thing, even if it was just four other people, two of whom were my best friends.

So to shut up the nerves, I started talking. I explained how I'd been a Christian most of my life but was lacking direction. I told them about college, my sense of floating along as a Christian, and a desire to grow deeper. I did not bring up Erica or sex, but it still took me almost three minutes. Forty-eight to go.

I turned to good sport Cassie, and she mentioned her desire to go to Arizona State, and her attempts to save—

"Arizona State?" Amy asked. "Why on earth would you want to go there?"

Cassie was taken aback and took a moment to regain her composure. "They have one of the best art history programs in the country—"

"Better than UNL? Or anywhere this side of the continental divide?"

"And I've always wanted to go to Arizona," Cassie said. Amy tisked as if a desire to go to Arizona was the most ludicrous thing she'd ever heard. "It's been my dream for years," Cassie continued. "I'm still waiting to hear back on several fronts, so right now I'm trying to be patient and trust God, and not worry about what happens if this door closes."

Gia went next. She talked about the Haiti trip and how it had really impressed on her the need to reach the lost—particularly children, for whom she'd always had a soft spot. She was also in the boat of not knowing what her future held, but speculated it might be in the mission field.

While she spoke, she sounded smug, almost as if she were delivering the Sunday school answer that would shame us all. But I sensed she was genuine, and had to admit that one of my adversaries might not be the horrible wretch I'd always thought.

Scotty didn't talk long. Life was life, he was fine, but agreed with me that his walk with God was somewhat casual, and maybe a Bible study would help.

Forty-three minutes to go. I was reminded of an old Johnny Cash song about a guy on death row, counting down the minutes. Only I couldn't wait for the clock to reach zero. We all turned to Amy.

She shrugged. "There isn't much to say. I'm still living in Morgan, which is a total surprise, and working part-time at Union Bank and part-time at Menards in Lincoln. And let me tell you, I'm getting sick of that drive." She took a deep breath. "I've been going to MBC since I was in diapers and I have to say I think they've gone around the bend, but I'm certainly not going to the quack church, and until somebody tears the oil and gas companies a new one, I'm not driving halfway across the county to some other church, so I guess I'm stuck with it." She looked at me. "Is that what you want to know?"

"It'll do," I answered, trying to get the image of Amy in diapers out of my head.

Amy sat back in the creaking glider and sucked the last bit of not-cinnamonized latte out of her cup.

"Okay. I forgot earlier, but I wanted to ask if anybody has any prayer requests?"

"Can we not do prayer requests?" Amy said.

"Why not?" Cassie asked.

"It'll turn into my senior high Sunday school class. Every week we'd take prayer requests and it would take half an hour praying for everybody's uncle's job situation and grandma so-and-so who broke a hip. It was ridiculous."

"If people are in need, we should pray," Gia said, somewhat sternly. I sensed she and Amy may have a flare-up before all was said and done.

"But people think they're in need when they're not," Amy said. "Aunt Meemie has lung cancer, but it's because she smoked three packs a day all her life. I don't want to take time to pray for her. Or a friend of a friend of a friend is in trouble because he's not paying the rent and his girlfriend walked out on him. Do we really need an update on his crisis every week so we can pray the same canned prayer that he'd get his life out of the toilet?"

"Let's do this," I said. "We won't take formal requests each week. But if you have something legitimate that you want prayer about, let us know."

"Fine, but I'm calling people on any crap they try to pull."

Great. Prayer abolished based on Amy's crap-o-meter.

I took another deep breath. Thirty-nine minutes. I felt the same way I felt when Nebraska's defense was trying to hold a lead late in the fourth quarter. That is, sick to my stomach.

"Now the hard part. What should we study?"

"Anything but Revelation," Amy said.

"That *would* make Petey mad," I said with a smile.

"I vote Revelation," she replied.

"Something New Testament," Cassie said. "Something practical."

"Are you saying the Old Testament isn't practical?" Gia asked.

"I didn't mean it like that. It's just . . . The New Testament was written largely for us."

"It was written to the people of the day."

"Yes, but it also has a lot of commands and principles that apply to us too."

"And the Old Testament doesn't?"

Amy huffed. "The Old Testament is all wars and concubines and strange commandments. I don't want to study who slept with who and who attacked who and a bunch of feasts and festivals."

If only she'd share her opinion.

"Is New Testament okay with everybody?" I asked. No one disagreed.

"Or do we want to study a topic instead?"

"Like what?" Amy asked.

I shrugged.

"I'd rather study a book of the Bible," Gia said.

"Me too," Cassie seconded. "Otherwise we're just studying what somebody else said about the Bible. It's secondhand."

"Okay, what book?"

"John," Cassie said.

"John is way too long," Amy said.

"How about Third John?" Scotty asked.

"Why would we start with Third John?" Gia asked.

"It's short."

"Mark is shorter than John," she said. "What about that?"

"Mark is still too long," Amy said.

"Are you planning on quitting soon?" Scotty asked.

"No, but big books make you feel bogged down."

"You have any ideas?" I asked.

"Something not long. Galatians, Philippians, Colossians, Thessalonians."

"Which one?" Scotty asked.

"I don't know. Pick one."

"I meant which Thessalonians."

"There's two?" Amy asked.

He nodded.

"I thought that was Timothy."

"It's both."

"What about Ephesians?" I asked.

"Galatians comes first," Cassie said.

"Galatians has a lot of law talk," Scotty said.

"So?"

"So, I think in this town we've pretty much gone through the law versus grace debate."

"So start with Ephesians," Amy said.

I looked around. Ephesians, perhaps, it was.

"Anybody else want to teach?" I asked.

"You passing the buck already?" Amy asked.

"I thought nobody was really teaching," Gia said.

"Okay, not teach. Lead. And no, I'm not passing the buck. I just want to know if somebody else would rather me not lead."

"You lead," Scotty said.

"Okay," I said. "Next week, we'll start Ephesians 1."

They nodded. It beat blank stares.

"Between now and then, try to read through the book in prepa—"

"The whole book?" Amy asked.

"Yeah."

"It's only six chapters," Cassie said.

"But why the whole book?"

"Context," I answered.

"I'm glad we didn't pick John," Amy muttered.

Our no-study study was essentially over, some twenty-five minutes early. I thought about closing in prayer, but instead just mentioned everyone could feel free to hang around if they wanted. Amy and Gia were gone within two minutes.

"Well, that went well," I said.

"It was the first class," Cassie said.

"And next to last. I think Scotty was right. Five people?"

"Five's not bad."

"It is when three of us are essentially one."

"Maybe we should have studied the Trinity," Scotty said.

"Let's dig out the Nintendo," I said. And so we did, and for a while I forgot about the poorly attended first Bible study.

Chapter 27

"'Bring the fattened calf and kill it. Let's have a feast and celebrate.'" Luke 15:23

On the second Saturday in August, Scotty and I watched golf on his couch. The PGA Championship was shaping up for an exciting finish, with a bunch of big names in contention. While watching, we debated whether or not to order a pizza for dinner or drive to Wieskamps' and pick up subs. We also debated skipping Sunday school the following day, hitting the links early, and being back in time to watch the final round.

So many decisions, so much lethargy.

At 5:23, a time that would forever be ingrained in my mind, the doorbell rang. It was followed by a prolonged pounding on the door.

With a frown at me, Scotty got up to answer the racket. I glanced over my shoulder as he opened the door to reveal a short blonde in long jeans and a gray T-shirt.

"I got in!"

"What?"

"ASU. They accepted me!"

I muted Jim Nantz[14] and stood. "You're in?"

Cassie beamed. And nodded. And beamed some more. "They called while I was at work, and I just got the news. I'm going!"

She initiated a hug with Scotty. I followed after him, and about had the soup squeezed out of me.

"What about the money?" I, ever the pragmatist, asked.

"Well, there's one grant still pending," she said, coming in and sitting down on the couch. We bookended her. "But I'm eligible for the Pendleton Scholarship, which covers about a third of tuition. With what I have saved

---

[14] Jim Nantz is a sports broadcaster who typically anchors CBS's golf coverage.

up already, if I work full-time while I'm there, and during breaks, I should be able to afford it."

"Cass, that's great," Scotty said, putting a hand on her back. "Really."

"I still can't believe it's true."

"What's all the racket?" Dirk asked as he emerged from the hallway.

"Cassie got accepted at ASU," Scotty said.

"For this fall?"

She nodded.

"Cutting it close," he said with a wink.

Cassie exhaled. "Tell me about it. I was late to apply because I was worried, and well—" She exhaled again. "I'm in."

"Well, congratulations."

"Thank you."

"You know, college is like Q School. You—"

"Dad." Scotty gave Dirk a look.

"Well, never mind." He looked at us. "You two going to just sit there, or are you going to take this girl out and celebrate?"

"Of course," Scotty said.

"Isn't this the Major Championship or something?" Cassie asked.

"It's almost done," I said.

"We'd rather take you out and celebrate anyhow," Scotty said.

I nodded.

Cassie grinned from ear to ear. "Okay. As long as it involves food. I was so excited I came over without eating any supper."

"Scotty's treating," Dirk said as he turned back down the hallway. "It'll involve food."

After five minutes of deliberation, we made the noble choice to let Cassie decide what to do. We headed for Lincoln, and after making a few laps around the southern half of the city, settled for a Red Robin at the corner of 27th and Pine Lake, across from the SouthPointe Pavilions mall.

"What'd your parents say?" Scotty asked as we waited for our burgers. Business was picking up, and the restaurant was loud. It was all ambient noise to the three of us in our booth.

"I haven't told them yet," Cassie said.

"You haven't told them?"

"They're in Hastings all day for some family reunion."

"And you didn't go?"

"I needed the hours, and besides, it's the kooky side of the family."

"What do you think they'll say?" Scotty asked.

"They'll say that they're proud. Dad will ask me, 'Is this what you really want, sweetie?'" She imitated her father's deep voice pretty well, pausing to take a drink of Diet Dr. Pepper. "Then Mom will worry about me moving to Arizona."

"Are you worried about it?" I asked.

"Not yet," she answered. "I've been so focused on getting there and worried that I wouldn't, that I haven't had time to think about it."

"You gonna live in the dorms?" Scotty asked.

"That's the cheapest option," Cassie said. "I just hope I can find a job close by."

"You said you were going to have to work full-time?" I asked.

"Probably. Depends what kind of job I can get."

"That's rough," Scotty said.

"Yeah, but I'm used to it." She slurped some more Diet Dr. Pepper.

Our burgers arrived and we prayed—hard with the noise—and then dug in. Despite snacking on junk all afternoon, Scotty and I were famished, and the food hit the spot.

"How far is Tempe from here?" Scotty asked as he munched on a fry.

"About fifteen hundred miles."

He looked up at the ceiling as he did some math. "What's that, like twenty-two hours?"

"Depends how fast you drive," I said.

"We should take a road trip to see you sometime," he said.

Cassie protested. "It'd be way too expensive."

"What's money between friends," I said. "I'll just scoop more ice cream."

"Like I said, road trip." Scotty looked at Cassie. "I'm serious."

I nodded too.

"Where are you going to stay?" Cassie asked.

"If you have a boyfriend, we'll crash at his place," Scotty said. "If not, the back of my Blazer."

"Terrific," I muttered.

We spent the rest of the meal talking about school and the classes she might have to take first semester and whether a road trip with gas prices at whatever they'd be at in a few months was in any way viable.

Scotty and I combined to pick up the tab, and we headed across the street to the mall. On a complete whim, Cassie wanted to try on dresses from Von Maur—dresses she didn't need and could never afford. We humored her for half an hour as she tried on a series of gowns. She modeled every one with a hesitant, "I don't know" sort of look on her face, but we told her she looked great. She did, largely due to the glow that hadn't left her countenance all night.

I did not lust at all.

We browsed at Old Navy, then walked through Scheels and rode the escalators upstairs and bought some fudge. Then we went mini golfing. A hot day had turned into a beautiful evening, with a hazy orange sunset playing out over the western sky. Bubbling fountains, playful squeals and screams of children and teenagers, and the contemporary music pumping through the speakers combined to create an energetic atmosphere.

Cassie wasn't much better at mini golf than actual golf. She played while trying to keep her crocheted purse out of her way and while balancing her putter, the ice cream cone I had bought her, and the scorecard she insisted on keeping. For sentimental reasons. It would be something to hang on her wall in her dorm room, she said.

Scotty kept draining putts while crunching on a sucker, and I tried desperately to keep pace while working on an ice cream cone of my own. At the "turn," Cassie announced that I was only four strokes behind Scotty.

"Where are you?" he asked.

She replied by biting on her lip.

"How many?"

"Thirty-nine."

Scotty had sixteen strokes so far.

"Do you know all the things I'm going to have to buy?" Cassie asked as we continued playing. "I don't even have a computer."

"You can get one pretty cheap these days," Scotty said. He turned his attention to his ball for a second and rolled in a fifteen-footer over a brow and around a hazard.

"Cheap for who?" she asked. "I'm scraping over pencils and notebooks."

"Don't forget Ramen noodles," I said.

"Ugh. I'm going to put on the freshman fifteen, aren't I?"

"Not if you eat Ramen noodles," Scotty said.

"I don't think the standard meal plan even includes breakfast. Maybe I'll lose fifteen."

She putted and the ball missed the hole, clacked off the rock at the back of the green, and headed for a water hazard. "No—" she said, reaching out with her putter and stopping the ball. In doing so, she lost her balance and nearly plunged into the water. But Scotty extended his putter for her to grab onto, and she managed to stay on the green.

We laughed.

"Shut it off," Cassie said. She swiped wisps of hair out of her face, placed her ball, and hit her next putt. It missed, as did the follow-up, and finally she tapped it in.

"Bogey?" Scotty asked.

"Is there a penalty for stopping a moving ball?" Cassie asked, squinting, head tipped to one side.

"Two strokes."

"Then nine."

"Six is the max," Scotty said.

Cassie studied the scorecard. "Don't see that here."

"It's understood."

"I'll take my nine," Cassie said. "What's typical par for eighteen holes?"

"Less than you have now," Scotty said, and she shot him a glare as we moved to the next hole. "But at least you're dry," he added.

"Josh, remember when Scotty fell into Holmes Lake while we were paddle boating?"

"I didn't fall. I was shoved," he answered.

"That's right. By Dana McMahon."

"Dana?"

Cassie nodded. "Remember? She went to church for about two months? Just long enough to break Scotty's adolescent heart."

"Dana . . ." I said. "Long red hair, beguiling smile."

"That's her."

"So why'd she shove you off the boat?" I asked.

He hit his putt. "Because she was a psycho."

"So why'd you have a crush on her?"

"I didn't."

"That's not what I heard," Cassie said with a huge teasing grin.

"From who, Tyler Harte?"

She gasped. Then whacked Scotty in the leg with her putter.

"Ow."

She whacked him again.

"Hey."

"Did you tell him?" she asked, turning to me.

"I didn't say a thing," I said.

"The whole church knew," Scotty said.

"What?"

"It was kind of obvious."

"How?"

"You baked him brownies, Cass."

"Yeah, for his birthday."

"I never got any brownies," I said.

She brandished her putter and I buttoned my lip.

"Somebody should putt," Scotty said.

Cassie kept staring at him, so I rolled my little blue ball toward the hole. It lipped out and I went ahead to tap it in and get out of the way.

Cassie was next, and her ball smashed into Scotty's, knocking it into the rocks and clear away from the hole. "Ha," she said, removing the scorecard from her mouth, where it went during each shot.

"Sure, now you can aim," Scotty said.

Cassie hit him with the putter again.

"Easy, Elin[15]," he said. "They're going to kick us off the course."

"Maybe I should just throw you into the water."

"Or hide my brother's shoes, maybe?"

She gasped and swung the putter again, but this time he got out of the way.

"Hey!" an authoritative female voice called out. "No horsing around on the course."

We all turned and nodded at a sturdy female in jeans and a tank top. There was a tattoo on her neck. A relative of Sydney's?

"Sorry," Scotty said.

Cassie's lip was zipped until the woman turned away, then it burst into a giggle.

"As I recall, Dana got kicked off the lake too," Scotty said.

"Terminate."

We finished the round without any more mayhem, or without any discussion of my junior high crush, one Kelly Herron. Leaning against the side of Scotty's Blazer, Cassie tallied the scores.

"Thirty-four," she said to Scotty.

"Hmm."

"Thirty-seven," she said to me with a wince.

"How about you?" Scotty asked.

"Hold on," she said.

"Need a calculator?"

"Button it." She mumbled under her breath. "One-oh-two."

"That thirteen on the eighth hole really hurt."

"The twelve on seven wasn't a big help either," she said.

"No."

"You want us to sign that?" I asked. "For memory's sake?"

She handed the card to me and I scratched my name with the dull pencil. Scotty followed suit.

---

[15] Elin Nordgren is the former wife of Tiger Woods. Some speculated she attacked him with a golf club, precipitating his vehicular crash in 2009.

"Who is Rickie Fowler?" she asked.

Scotty smiled. "He's the guy who's going to win the PGA tomorrow."

"What's the PGA?"

"Let's go."

We drove home through the dark, reliving our past adventures and memories. Like the time we had decided to ride our bikes to Firth one summer afternoon, only to have a thunderstorm sweep us off the road halfway there. Our parents had found us huddled in the ditch, and had taken our bikes away for a month.

Then there was the time four-year-old Cassie had been playing with her mom's pearl necklace in church, and had tugged it off her neck and snapped it, sending pearls rolling across the sanctuary floor. My dad had paused mid-sermon to help pick up the pearls, made a remark about pearls before swine, and resumed preaching. Cassie's mom had blushed for a month.

And there was the snowball fight when Cassie had thrown a snowball at Scotty, missed, and pegged old Mrs. Grady in the shoulder, knocking her and her sack of groceries into a snow bank. Fruit and cans and boxes had tumbled into the snow and rolled down the sidewalk.

"You never could aim," Scotty said, and she leaned forward and punched him in the shoulder. He served into the other lane, on purpose, and Cassie screamed, punched him again, and yelled at him to get back on the right side of the road.

"Remember when your mom accidentally bought prune juice instead of grape juice for communion?" I asked Cassie.

Scotty turned around. "What?"

"Watch the road." She pointed out the windshield. "You don't remember that?"

"He probably skipped to play golf," I said.

"You should talk," Cassie said. "At least he didn't go to True Way."

"True Way wasn't there at the time."

"Hmm. Anyhow, Mom was in charge of preparing communion, and for some reason, she bought prune juice instead of grape juice. She blamed it on Dad, but he asked her to pinpoint when he had ever gone to the grocery store."

"Does Don & Flo's even carry prune juice?"

"In this town?" Cassie said. "They probably get a wholesale discount."

As we bummed along the old country roads, one memory led to the next, one laugh was followed by another, and for a while I forgot that Cassie would be leaving.

As happy as I was for her, I was also just a little depressed at the thought of her going to Arizona. As our stories reminded me, the three of us had been best friends forever, and now she was leaving. I had left for college twice, but that had seemed far less significant than her going cross-country. Maybe it was because I had been the one to go away then. Or maybe it was because I had the feeling Cassie would be going on to bigger and better things. Whatever it was, ever since she had broken the news to us in Scotty's living room, a part of me had been a little gloomy.

What was next, I wondered. First Erica came back from Haiti with a boyfriend, dashing my dreams. Then the pool party and my struggle with lust. Now one of my best friends was moving across the country. And all this was on top of my uncertain future and spiritual quagmire. It wasn't exactly the summer I had hoped for.

But as Cassie shifted a conversation about the time her spilled coffee may or may not have caused the sound system at Morgan Bible to crash to a deliberation on how she could afford a computer for college, I realized again how much this meant to her. My dreams were lying shattered along the side of the road, but hers were just taking off. Focusing on that, I couldn't help but be happy for her, and that happiness blocked out my sadness.

We dropped Cassie off at a still dark house, her wondering where her parents were. We conducted a quick sweep of the house at her behest to make sure that there wasn't a Charles Starkweather[16] hiding in the closet. There wasn't, and we said goodbye and promised to all be in church tomorrow. Scotty drove me home, and I went to bed with a smile on my face but a little bit of a frown on my heart.

Cassie was leaving.

---

[16] Charles Starkweather was a Lincoln, Nebraska, native who went on a killing spree in Nebraska and Wyoming in the 1950s.

Chapter 28

". . . so come, let us confer together." Nehemiah 6:7

Wednesday I worked until four, giving me a few hours to have dinner and make some final preparation for our second, but actually first, Bible study. Ephesians 1 wasn't long, but it was meaty, and I was actually a little excited as I prepared, ate, and headed over to Scotty's.

On an invite from Scotty, Damon had joined us, ready to "carve up the Word." Scotty, Cassie, Gia, and I all returned, which was something, I guessed. Gia looked even more sullen than usual, and Scotty had been rambunctious that afternoon. I was a little worried.

We were about to start when Amy arrived, looking as if she had just stepped out of the gym. Her blond hair was in a ponytail, and like her face and bare arms, it glistened with sweat. She wore a tight-fitting spandex tank top, running shorts, and athletic shoes, and carried a squirt bottle of lemon water. No glasses. Instead of sitting, she proceeded to complete her post-run stretches.

"Go ahead, we can start," she said.

And so I opened in prayer, our Bible study of one black man, one Cuban woman, and four plain white people, one of whom was standing spread-eagle, fingers extended to the toes of her right running shoe. Yeah, prayer was a good idea.

I led, asking God to guide our study, lead us into truth, and bless our conversation. I closed the prayer and opened my eyes to see Amy bent over, still stretching, her spandex tank top revealing far more than was fitting for a Bible study. Or a boudoir.

Lord, what am I supposed to do?

I opened my Bible. "Let's look at Ephesians chapter one."

"I forgot a Bible," Amy said.

"Maybe next week you can bring your Richard Simmons Study Bible," Scotty said.

Amy shot him a glare.

I started by glossing over the greeting in verses one and two, a greeting that various sources I'd looked up online had flowing dissertations about. I concluded it was a greeting, and we hit the high points in a minute.

Then I asked for a volunteer to read verses three through fourteen. Blank stares. Cassie finally started reading.

"'*Praise be to the God and Father of our Lord Jesus Christ, who has blessed us in the heavenly realms with every spiritual blessing in Christ. For he chose us in him before the creation of the world to be holy and blameless in his sight. In love he predestined us to be adopted as his sons through Jesus Christ, in accordance with his pleasure and will – to the praise of his glorious grace, which he has freely given us in the One he loves. In him we have redemption through his blood, the forgiveness of sins, in accordance with the riches of God's grace that he lavished on us with all wisdom and understanding. And he made known to us the mystery of his will according to his good pleasure, which he purposed in Christ, to be put into effect when the times will have reached their fulfillment – to bring all things in heaven and on earth together under one head, even Christ.*

"'*In him we were also chosen, having been predestined according to the plan of him who works out everything in conformity with the purpose of his will, in order that we, who were the first to hope in Christ, might be for the praise of his glory. And you also were included in Christ when you heard the word of truth, the gospel of your salvation. Having believed, you were marked in him with a seal, the promised Holy Spirit, who is a deposit guaranteeing our inheritance until the redemption of those who are God's possession – to the praise of his glory.*'"

I had some notes, but first I asked what stood out to everybody. More blank stares. This was really going smoothly. Great idea, Dave.

"I like the idea of adoption," Cassie said. "My sister was adopted, so in one way, she wasn't originally part of the family. But by adopting her, Mom and Dad made her part of the family . . . as much their daughter as I am."

"I didn't know Candace was adopted," Amy said.

"Not a lot of people do. I remember once when I was little, and Candi did something—I don't even remember what it was, but it got her in trouble. And Mom and Dad handled it really well, and I asked Dad about it, and he said that he was trying to treat Candi the way God treated us. What she did was nothing compared to how we sin against God, and He adopted us after our sins. That's always sort of stuck with me."

I thought of how, now that Candace was doing whatever it was she was doing in Las Vegas, it was an even better example. And even more painful.

"So if we're predestined, does that mean we don't have free will?" Amy asked.

"Of course we have free will," Damon said.

"Then how do you explain verses four, five, and eleven?" Scotty asked.

Damon shrugged. "Teach?"

"I'm not the authority," I said.

"What, didn't you prep?" Amy asked.

"I did prep, but I'm not the answer to all the questions."

"Then what is?"

I raised my Bible slightly.

"And that says we're predestined," Amy said. She swigged some lemon water.

"Doesn't it say we have free will too?" Damon asked.

"Where?"

Cassie pulled her feet up under her legs. She was on the couch beside me, like the week before. "I don't know that it comes out and says it in those words, but we're told to believe, and there are plenty of times where Jesus says those who believe are saved, and those who don't aren't. So it implies the choice is necessary."

"But maybe God predestines some people to believe and some people not to," Amy said.

"So God sends people to hell?" Damon asked with a frown.

"I found another verse that might be helpful," I said and flipped to Romans 8. "'*For those God foreknew he also predestined to be conformed to the likeness of his Son, that he might be the firstborn among many brothers. And those he predestined, he also called; those he called, he also justified; those he justified, he also glorified.*'"

"Meaning?"

"God did predestine us, but He predestined those He foreknew."

"Foreknew?" Damon asked. "The ones He knew would choose Him, right?"

"Right."

"But if he knew it, how is that not predestination?" Amy asked.

"Because knowing something's going to happen and causing it to happen aren't the same thing," Scotty said.

"Yeah, but we're talking about before the creation of the world. Isn't that in there somewhere?"

"Verse four," I answered.

"So if God knew before He even made us what we would do, then how do we have a choice?"

"Because we do," Scotty said. "God could see every choice and decision that every person would ever make. He knew before creation that you would put lemon in your water today. But that doesn't mean He made you do it. You could have chosen not to put lemon in your water, in which case He would have known that choice before the creation of the world too."

"Yeah, but doesn't God create us to be smart or stupid or stubborn or whatever?" she asked.

"To an extent, maybe," I said, not ready to acknowledge that my stubborn behavior was God's doing. Although, it would be a nice excuse.

"So He makes some people more trusting, accepting, willing to change, and other people stubborn old cusses who will never bend or be flexible or willing to trust another person. So how is that not predestination?"

"Because sometimes stubborn old cusses come to Jesus," Damon said. "Like my granddad before he died."

"But most of them don't," Amy argued. "And they're certainly not as likely to as sweet, trusting, happy-go-luckers."

"What about kids in Haiti?" Gia asked.

"What about them?"

"They seldom hear the gospel. It's not even part of their life. Here, you can't find a town that doesn't have at least one church that preaches Christ. We have a lot better chance here than they do of ever coming to faith."

"You're forgetting the Holy Spirit," Cassie said.

"No, I know. But the Holy Spirit can work in all lives, so all things being equal, their odds are much worse."

"So what are you saying?" Amy asked.

"That it may not be completely fair, that some people are better suited to receive Christ than others. But the Haitian children have the choice just like we do."

"And I think that's the point," I said, trying to somehow steer us back to Ephesians. "We'll never be able to completely understand how free will and predestination intersect. But Scripture is clear that the people who do come to faith in Christ have been predestined to be adopted as sons, to be redeemed and forgiven, to an eternal inheritance, and to be sealed for the day of redemption. That should blow our brains," I said, borrowing a phrase Dave had often used in Sunday school. That and how the *Shekinah* Glory "would melt our faces like in *Indiana Jones*."

I touched on a few more thoughts from the "Spiritual Blessings" section of the chapter, and then moved on to the final nine verses of Ephesians 1. They highlight the riches we have in Christ and give us a model for prayer for one another. The study turned more into lecture than I had hoped, but apparently everyone had exhausted their brains on predestination. Everyone but Amy, who kept leading us on various rabbit trails—Scriptural and otherwise. At least she sat up straight.

I asked Scotty to close us in prayer—two minutes before our hour was up—and he did a nice job tying the study together. He closed by thanking God for saving both Huskers and Texans and poor little Haitians. Unique phrasing, but not, I determined, off the mark.

"Poor little Haitians?" Gia asked when he was finished. She hadn't said a word the last half of study, just fidgeted with the pages of her Bible. Now her eyes flashed again.

"Easy, Shakira, I didn't mean anything by it."

"You are always so flippant," Gia said. "And I am sick of your insulting nicknames."

"I nickname everybody," Scotty said. "Ask Rosie."

"It is kind of insulting," I said.

"Isn't Shakira Colombian?" Amy asked.

I shrugged. Shakira was the last thing I needed to think about right now.

"I gotta split, man," Damon said, slapping my hand. "We're runnin' some ball at the high school. I'll see you next week."

"Yeah, thanks for coming."

He nodded and was gone. Amy was on his heels.

"Don't forget to pump your arms when you walk," I said. Was I flirting because I'd seen a little cleavage? Was I a complete degenerate?

I turned back, thinking of thanking Cassie for getting the ball rolling. But I saw that Gia and Scotty were still going at it.

"I am more than just a Cuban," Gia said.

"I'd hope so."

"What is that supposed to mean? What do you have against Cuba?"

"Nothing. I hear they make great cigars, and they're excellent raft-builders."

"You are such a bigot."

"So I'm anti-Communist. Shoot me."

"Sometimes I would like to."

"Guys," I said, stepping between them. I was nearly impaled by lasers shooting out of Gia's eyes.

"I have to go," she said, breaking the stare down first.

"You and Geoffie have a little studying to do too?"

"We broke up," she said.

"You broke up?" Scotty asked.

One missions trip romance down. One to go?

"Yes," Gia snapped. "We broke up. Happy?" She turned with a flick of her hair and strutted for the stairs before Scotty could utter a retort.

The front door slammed. I looked at Cassie and she at me.

"Did I start that?" Scotty asked.

I sighed. "No."

"Why are you down?" Cassie asked me. "I thought it went well."

"Except when I wasn't just lecturing like Petey, we got way off topic."

"But it was good discussion," she said.

I nodded. It had been.

"And six is better than five."

"Yeah, but I have a feeling one of them isn't coming back," I said.

"Sorry," Scotty mumbled.

"Not entirely your fault. But if Gia doesn't come back, we're at five." I turned to Cassie. "Then you leave . . ."

"When do you head out?" Scotty asked.

"A week from Saturday. And I may need a ride to the airport."

"Why's that?"

"Mom's got a women's retreat that weekend, and Dad has the men's breakfast at church."

"He can't skip?"

"He's leading it," she said. "He might be able to get a sub if he had to, but . . ." She bounced a foot on the floor "Can one of you take me?"

We both nodded, and I remembered my various reasons to be down. My best friend was leaving, my Bible study was flopping, I wasn't allowed to dream about the girl of my dreams because my dreams turned naughty, and even at Bible study, I was attacked with sexual temptation.

Maybe I should just move to Oklahoma and be my parents' third wheel for life.

Chapter 29

"Listen to my instruction and be wise . . ." Proverbs 8:33

It was haying time, so Thursday was hot as the dickens. It hadn't rained much of late, and the crop was a little thin. Five and a half wagons full of hay. During a break, I mentioned to Dave that we had started a Bible study, but that it wasn't going so well. I gave him the details, and he advised me to hang in there. His first college Bible study had been him and one other guy for six months before it blossomed into a group of four. I figured I could give ours a few more weeks before declaring it a complete failure.

"How are things going otherwise?" he asked. "Any progress with Erica?"

"Haven't you seen?" I asked. "She's got a boyfriend."

"I wondered."

"Met him on the Haiti trip. I never liked short-term missions trips," I said.

"If it's anything like summer camp romances, it won't last."

"Even if it doesn't, I'm not sure I'm suited for girls."

"What do you mean?" he asked, wiping sweat off his forehead with his forearm.

I took a big drink of lemonade and told him how, ever since the pool party, I'd been struggling with lust. "I always sort of battled it," I said. "I mean, it is *Every Man's Battle*, isn't it?"

He nodded.

"But lately it's been really bad. It's like I'm ambushed. The girl I work with, who frankly I've never given a thought to, yesterday was dressed like . . . well, never mind. And then at our Bible study last night, a girl bends over and I'm staring straight down her shirt."

I looked up into Dave's eyes, expecting the judgment I felt in my heart. It wasn't there.

"What am I supposed to do, Dave?"

"I wish there were an easy answer," he said. "But I haven't found one."

"I mean, I feel like I'm sinning and yet I don't see how there's any way I can avoid it most of the time. My eyes are drawn like magnets, and when you tell yourself not to think about sex, it just programs it into your head."

"The pink elephant."

"Huh?"

"Try not to think about a pink elephant, and it's all that's in your head."

"Exactly. And I'm sure there are times when I'm giving in to the temptation, but there are other times when I don't feel like I have a choice." I frowned. "We talked about predestination in our study last night."

"God doesn't predestine us to sin," Dave said. "And He isn't the only one that can stir feelings of guilt in our hearts."

"The devil?"

"He is the accuser."

"Why would he convict me of sin?"

"Conviction is the work of the Holy Spirit," Dave said. "Guilt is the devil's domain."

"What's the difference?"

He shrugged. "Largely semantics, I suppose. But at the core there is a difference. Conviction is how God deals with legitimate sin in your life. Guilt is how the devil takes legitimate sin—and sometimes things that aren't sin—and tries to ruin your life with them. He reminds you of things you've done that you've long since dealt with; he brings them up and makes you feel like scum. And he can also take temptation and try to make you think you're a horrible wretch for being tempted."

"Why?"

"Because it does this to you," he said, pointing. "You feel rotten and miserable, like you can't possibly be of service to God. Believe me, I know. And pretty soon you've taken yourself out of the game. Inactive Christians are the devil's greatest asset. They're also useless targets, so the fact that he's attacking you is a pretty good sign you're on the right track."

I thought for a moment. "But how do I know if it is the devil or if it's God?"

"Ask yourself if you made a choice. Sin involves choosing to partake in sin, after being dragged away and enticed."

He wiped some more sweat. "For example, let's say — using this idea of sexual temptation — that I were to come into your house one night, throw you over my shoulder, and take you down to a gentlemen's club and set you in front of the show, which being a man, you found very enticing. You didn't go on your own — I dragged you — and you didn't choose to be enticed — it's a natural response — but you'd probably feel guilty. But if you got up and left, you wouldn't have sinned. However, if you stayed and watched a while, you would have given into that temptation and crossed the line into sin. Then you'd feel convicted. And I'm betting, Josh, that deep inside you'd know the difference."

I looked out at the haze floating in the southern sky. "Yeah, I think so."

"Another thing," Dave said, "and then we'd better get back at it before our muscles atrophy. There are times when sitting there and analyzing whether or not you just lusted after a woman or had an impure thought is only ingraining it further in your head."

"Pink elephant."

"Right. The best thing is to just forget about it and move on. Remember, all sins are covered by the blood of Christ. We're supposed to keep short accounts, but that doesn't mean we have to obsess over every thought, every flick of the eyes. If there's something you need to deal with, trust that God will bring it to your attention and you'll know it's Him. And I know you, Josh. More often than not, I suspect you're doing the right thing."

I nodded. "Let's go sling some hay."

We slung some more hay. I asked Dave another question during our next break. Wasn't some of the responsibility on girls not to dress provocatively? Yes, he answered, and it drove him nuts the way women and even young girls dressed. Not just at the beach or a summer barbecue, but around town or to church. Like pink spaghetti strap dresses, for example?

On the other hand though, he said, our job as guys was to be pure no matter what. Did some females make it harder? Yes. But that wasn't an excuse.

We finished the final wagon and a half and cooled down with some more lemonade. "How's church?" Dave asked.

"Still a little weird," I said.

"How so?"

"Have we talked since Fellowship Day?"

"Said hello in the hall, I think."

"That was strange."

"A little."

"And last Sunday with the healing service."

"You're not a fan?"

"I don't have a problem with prayer and healing, but for a whole service it's kind of a drag for those of us in good health."

"I still think they're experimenting," Dave said. "Trying to keep it fresh."

"Yeah, well, it feels like gimmicks. And it's just so frustrating, coming to church trying to worship and trying to learn, and not really being able to do either very well."

"A suggestion?"

I took a drink and nodded. "Please."

"Try to focus exclusively on the vertical — you and God. As if you're in a silo."

"Doesn't that kind of put a kibosh on corporate fellowship and worship?"

"To an extent, maybe. But the most important thing is your relationship with God. Focus on that, block out the horizontal stuff — the whistling, the odd services, whatever it may be. Focus on God, focus on your walk with Him, and let everything else float around. If it sticks, great. If not, focus on God."

I nodded.

"It may not be easy, but that's my advice. For the time being."

I nodded again.

"And stick with the Bible study," he said. "If nothing else, you'll grow from the work you're doing preparing each week."

"I'll give it a try."

"Good." We picked up the lemonade and cups and headed for the house. "You talk to your folks much?" he asked.

"Once a week or so we talk."

"How are things going for them?"

"They've kind of hit the wall a little," I said. "But overall, things are good I think."

"You talk to them about things here — Erica, church?"

"Not much. I didn't want to say anything about Erica until something happened, which it didn't. And, I don't know, I feel like they've moved on and my running down the old church wouldn't do them any good."

"That's a valid point."

"But?"

"But, I think they'd like to know how you're doing. They know you better than anyone, and can help you better than anyone."

"*That's* a valid point," I said.

"Besides, I'm going to have to start billing you pretty soon."

Sunday wasn't too weird. Except that I realized, as I sat next to Cassie and listened to a pretty good sermon on faith like a mustard seed, that this was the last Sunday I would sit next to Cassie. Saturday she would be off to Tempe, Arizona. I was trying not to think about it.

Several well-wishers stopped Cassie, who had always been popular with the adults in church because she was generally well behaved (except for when she threw snowballs at old ladies or hid people's shoes). As a result, we weren't first to Room 104. Erica was.

She sat in her usual place, in front of Cassie's seat, blowing on a Styrofoam cup of coffee. She wore a red flared skirt that came to the knee and a white blouse. Her hair was in a low ponytail, and she looked beautiful. And Huskerish.

"Hey," she said.

"Hey," I greeted. I really loved our highbrow conversations.

"Two weeks," she said with a wink-like grin. "Southern Miss."

"Piece of cake," I said.

"I hope so." She blew some more and tried a sip of the coffee.

"Where's your worse half?" Scotty asked.

"Not here," she said through a sigh. "I'm not sure why not."

Was that frustration? Signs of trouble in paradise?

Erica turned around, resting her arm on the back of the chair in front of me. "So, what's your prognosis?"

"For the season?"

She nodded.

"Roses."

"Really?"

"We've got the defense for it."

"We had the defense last year, too."

"And we do struggle against the power sets," I said.

Erica looked at me for a moment, then smiled in a way that made me want to renounce my vow of friendship. "I think so too. This is the year."

"Yeah," Scotty said, "the year you get creamed in Florida by some SEC team on New Year's Day . . . again."

"Like LSU?" Erica asked.

"No, we'll be playing for the national title."

"We? You aren't even from Louisiana."

Scotty shrugged. "You don't play for the Huskers."

She stuck out her tongue. I've always had a thing for mature women.

Petey called the class to order before their repartee could continue, and we settled down to a discussion of the beast out of the sea. Petey's lecture went unimpeded until he concluded verse ten. Then Brad's hand shot up.

"Brad?"

"Doesn't this pretty much indicate the pre-tribbers are wrong?"

"Why's that?" Amy asked.

"Because verses seven and ten talk about the saints. How can there be saints if the rapture has taken place?"

Several heads turned to their Bibles. Amy's rose defiantly. "Because they'll be saved by the witnesses."

"The two witnesses or the 144,000 witnesses?" Brett asked.

"Both."

"I thought we could only be saved by Jesus," Tim called.

"Do you want your shoes to go back into the women's bathroom?" Amy asked.

"We're straying here, people," Petey said.

"Did it say anyone would get saved by the two witnesses?" Brad asked.

"Of course it did," Amy said.

"I don't see that anywhere," Rena said.

"I thought you were pre-trib," Amy said.

"I am."

"You don't sound like it."

"I'm just saying that Revelation doesn't say anyone will be saved by the two witnesses."

"So how can there be saints if the rapture has already come?" Brad asked.

"Do you really think they're going to testify for three and a half years and not save anyone?"

"Kind of reading into the text, aren't you?"

"Only Jesus can save," Tim said.

"Can we get back to Revelation thirteen?" Petey asked.

"There's still the 144,000 witnesses," Cora piped up.

"What chapter are they in?" Brad asked.

"Eight."

"Six."

"Seven," Petey said with a sigh.

Pages rustled.

"It doesn't say anything about them saving anyone either," Brad said.

"I'm telling you, only Jesus can save," Tim said.

"Shut up!" half the room shouted.

"Let's keep it civil," Petey said.

"Let's keep your mom civil."

"Don't you think the 144,000 are saints?"

"They're Jews."

"Jews can't be saints."

"My grandpa's Jewish."

"Your mom's Jewish."

"Call him and ask him."

"He's dead."

"Was he a saint?"

"He was a Christian."

"Are saints the same thing as Christians?"

"Not if you're Jewish."

Erica turned around in her seat, her eyes wide, eyebrows raised in disbelief. "Has this church always been like this?" she whispered.

"More this age demographic," I said.

"Was there something in the water?"

"So you don't think anyone will get saved during the tribulation?" Amy asked.

"Sure," Brad replied.

"Well?"

"But that's before the rapture."

"When's the rapture?"

"At the end of the book."

"The end of the book is the thousand-year reign."

"Right before that."

"So no one will get saved after the rapture?"

"They won't have time."

"Is that true, Petey?"

Petey's head was in his hands, his elbows resting on his little music stand of a pulpit.

"Josh?"

I looked to see who had called my name. Amy.

"You teach Bible study. What's the scoop?"

"Well, I'm pre-trib."

"See."

"He's not canon," Brad said.

"You don't even know what the canon is," Brett called.

"It's the books that are part of the Bible, instead of the Maccabees and the Apocraphy."

"Apocrypha," I said.

"See," Amy said again.

"That doesn't prove anything."

"I thought we were still going to be witnessing to people during the millennium," Rena said.

"No way," Amy said. "Do we ever get to relax?"

"Geoff says you get to sing praise songs forever," Brett said.

"And play football," Tim added.

Petey's sigh this time was more of a moan and a scream and a sigh all rolled into one. As a fellow teacher/leader, I could sort of relate. I almost felt sorry for the guy. His class protocol was a little strict, but this was over the top the other way. And not going anywhere.

Eventually everyone petered out and Petey was able to conclude the class with a weak speech on the beast out of the earth. I wondered if our church might split again, not because of ripped jeans and whistling and one-themed worship services, but based on the tribulation. I was pretty sure it wouldn't have been the first church to do so.

Erica sighed as she stood after class. "Well, I am off to Wahoo," she said.

"Wahoo?" Scotty asked.

"I'm meeting Mark and his brothers to go four-wheeling."

261

"Is that why he's not here?"

"It's where he is," she said. "I'm still not sure why he's not here, though. Isn't an afternoon of riding around in the dust enough? I think they're all a bunch of thrill-junkies. He wants to go bungee jumping sometime."

"You must like the guy to put up with all that," Scotty said.

"Yeah," she said with another sigh. It was far from convincing. "I'll see you around."

I watched her leave, shot a glance at Cassie, then turned to Scotty. "Subtle."

"I thought so."

Cassie punched my arm. "Friends, remember?"

"Yeah."

All too often.

Gia did not show up for Bible study Wednesday. Amy, Damon, Scotty, and Cassie (for the last time) did. So too did Gerhard Van de Kamp. He's seventy-six.

Gerhard had stopped me in the hall after Sunday school, said he saw my Bible study and wondered if an old man could join. I had told him we were open to all demographics. Wednesday night he arrived at Scotty's fifteen minutes early, dressed in a tweed blazer with elbow patches and carrying the oldest, most worn Bible I had ever seen.

Gerhard had gone to Morgan Bible as long as I had, so I knew of him. I think my parents might have even had him over for lunch after church once or twice. He'd never been married, to my knowledge, and I didn't know why not. He was friendly, smiled a lot, I assumed had been handsome back in the day, and he smelled good. He wore cologne of some kind, strong enough to be noticed, but not strong enough to overpower like some people's I knew.

The six of us sat down and opened to Ephesians 2. It was more meaty material, how we were alive in Christ, saved by grace, and united in

Christ. They were verses that were easy to gloss over if you were just reading, but that had a wealth of information if you took the time to study them. We did, for almost an hour and a quarter (Damon left early to play ball again). We pulled several good insights from the text, such as how we were not only saved by grace, through faith and not by works, but also saved for the purpose of doing good works. During a discussion of what those works could be, Amy tried to sidetrack us with a debate about helping the poor and letting them help themselves, but we steered the train back on the tracks.

After the study, Amy announced that she wouldn't be able to make it next week. She didn't say why. Gerhard, however, announced with a twinkle in his greenish-brown eyes that he would be back next Wednesday.

"That is, if you don't mind an old geezer being part of your study."

"Not at all," I said. Gerhard had added several good points to our discussion, in addition to providing a different age group's point of view.

"And that wasn't an admission that you are an old geezer," Cassie said.

Gerhard winked. "It's okay. I am." He headed for his Volvo with a wave, Bible tucked under his arm. Scotty, Cassie, and I were left.

"I should go pack," Cassie said.

"So is this goodbye?" Scotty asked.

She shrugged, her hands in her jeans pockets. "Well, Mom leaves for her retreat Friday afternoon, so the three of us are having our farewell tomorrow night. You guys want to do something Friday?"

"Sure," we said in unison. "What?" Scotty asked.

Cassie shrugged again. "Whatever. Hang out. And . . ." She twisted the toe of her shoe on the pavement ". . . I do sort of need a ride to the airport Saturday."

"I can take you," I said.

"So can I," Scotty replied.

"I thought you had to golf with your dad."

"We can move it back."

"Why bother? I can take her."

"I love it when you guys talk like I'm not here."

"We're practicing," Scotty said.

"I have to go. Call me about Friday."

"We will," we said in unison again.

We stood there until she got into her car and drove away.

"This needs to be epic," Scotty said.

"So not mini golf and modeling dresses at Von Maur?"

Chapter 30

"Dear children, this is the last hour . . ." I John 2:18

Scotty and I debated taking Cassie to Worlds of Fun in Kansas City, but determined it was just too far away. A Royals game was eliminated for the same reason . . . and because at twelve and a half games out of first place, the Royals weren't really fun. We thought about the world-famous Henry Doorly Zoo in Omaha, but even that was a little too far. Cassie's flight was early (back in Omaha) and she didn't want to be out late.

Just driving to Kansas was mentioned, but it was hardly epic. It was sentimental, and got some more play, but we decided against it. Thursday night, we got together at my place and scoured the internet. We found a few options, figured out how to make them work, and hodgepodged together an itinerary. While maybe not epic, we knew Cassie would enjoy it. So after rearranging our schedules, we checked the timing with her. She said it was fine, begged to know what we were doing, and pouted when we told her it was a surprise. Mock pouting, we knew.

Friday I got off at one, much thanks to Sydney who came in early to cover for me. I owed her, she said. I'd find her a date, I said. Find yourself one first, she said. Grrr.

Scotty's boss was super flexible, so we picked up Cassie at quarter after one and headed for the capital city. It was a warm summer day, with the threat of thunderstorms that could hamper our plans. But for the moment, it was just a bit overcast.

We headed into town on what became 56th Street, then took Highway 2 west and ultimately north—where it became 10th Street—to downtown.

"Where are we going?" Cassie asked.

"We should have blindfolded her," Scotty said.

"Right, and driven a blindfolded woman through town. You want her to spend her last night in Nebraska bailing us out of jail?"

"You worry too much."

"Yeah, you don't worry enough."

"Great," Cassie muttered from the backseat, "I get treated to a fight. Is this how you guys are going to be when I'm gone?"

"After the weeping," Scotty said. "Yeah."

Scotty parked and we set off on foot.

"Something at the Lied Center?" Cassie asked.

"Nope."

"There's not a football scrimmage or something, is there?"

"We could only hope."

"Will you please tell me where we're going?"

"Right up there," Scotty pointed.

Cassie frowned. "Panera?"

"The Great Plains Art Museum," he answered. "You've been saying for a year how you wanted to go and never had the time."

"We thought it could serve as inspiration for those eight a.m. classes," I said.

Cassie clapped like she was back in church.

Opened in 1981, the museum houses various works of art and literature pertaining to the Great Plains region. We let Cassie lead the pace, perusing sculptures and Remington bronzes and paintings. The rotating collection even had some names I recognized: Rockwell, Pollack, Byxbe— okay maybe I only knew that name from the original *Incredible Hulk*.

Cassie could have lingered for hours, but we tried to hurry her along. We had another stop to make before five.

A thunderstorm had passed over while we were in the museum, leaving the pavement wet and the smell of rain in the air. We strolled several blocks north, past the Lied Center for Performing Arts and onto the campus of the University of Nebraska.

"Not Sheldon, is it?" Cassie asked.

"It is."

She squealed in delight.

Founded nearly a century before the Great Plains Art Museum, the Sheldon Museum of Art contains both the Sheldon Art Association collection and the University of Nebraska collection. The combination comprises over 12,000 works of art, including a wide variety of paintings. We had over ninety minutes before the museum closed, and needed every one of them to make our rounds.

"Oh . . . look at those clouds," Cassie said as we stopped in front of a piece titled *River Landscape*. It was an oil painting by a guy named Bierstadt—vaguely familiar, probably from talking with Cassie—that showed a bank of trees by a river at day's last light. The moon had already risen, and the wisps of clouds in the sky were dotted with pink and orange by the setting sun.

"Almost as good as that Teton painting you made."

"Don't even say that."

"It's true."

"It reminds me of that time we all went out to Mahoney."

"You mean when Mike Baxter decided to see if he could walk across the Platte?" Scotty asked.

"Didn't he get trapped on a sandbar?"

We nodded.

We also moved on, taking our time as Cassie oohed and ahhed over more paintings. She especially liked a pair by John Henry Dolph—*Beagle Puppies* and *Horse's Head*.

"You should paint your horses," Scotty said.

"I tried. They wouldn't stand still."

"Horses?"

"I think they knew they were standing for a portrait."

"Paint them when they're asleep."

We continued to the north gallery. This time Scotty stopped us. We were looking at a white canvas with a series of colored circles and squares. It looked like a *Twister* mat.

"You're not going to school to do this, are you?" Scotty asked.

Cassie only sighed.

"What I want to know is why people paint a bowl of fruit," I said, nodding at a painting on the adjacent wall. "Why not just set out a bowl of fruit?"

"You two are impossible."

Meandering through the museum, we made our final stop in front of a seascape on a rocky cove, clouds flitting across the late afternoon sky, a single sailboat out in the middle of the sea. It was one of the more lifelike paintings I had seen that day, and from a distance, resembled a photograph more than a painting.

"I never could understand why someone would stick a sailboat in the middle of their painting," Cassie said. "It just seems to ruin the tranquility."

"Artist's opinion, isn't it?" Scotty asked.

Cassie shrugged. "Yeah, but it just doesn't seem to fit. It's like all those Bob Ross mountain landscapes . . . He always put a little shed in them."

"Who's Bob Ross?" Scotty asked.

"Come on. Bob Ross? 'Happy trees'?" She turned to me. "You remember him, don't you? We'd sit on my parents' couch and eat fruit snacks?"

"Your mom allowed fruit snacks?" Scotty asked.

"Hush it."

"Was he that guy with the afro?" I asked.

Cassie nodded.

"Who talked to squirrels?"

She nodded again.

"And he put sheds in his mountain landscapes?"

"A lot of them."

"Isn't there a famous picture of the Tetons with a barn on it?" Scotty asked.

"Not the one on my wall," I answered.

We moved on from the seascape with the unnecessary sailboat. It was five before five, and Cassie looked around, making sure we hadn't missed anything. Satisfied, we headed outside. "Okay, what's next?" she asked.

"Next?" Scotty asked.

"Come on, I know you have something else planned."

He smirked and looked at me.

"Dinner."

"Where at?"

"Guess."

"I can't."

"Good effort, at least," Scotty said.

"Will you tell me where?"

"Tico's," I answered.

"I love Tico's."

"We know."

"Are you blowing all your ice cream-scooping money on me?"

"Not all. The museums were free."

"What about my money?" Scotty asked.

"You're loaded," she said with a wave.

"Then why am I working maintenance at a golf course?"

"Free golf," we both answered at once.

"What time's our reservation?" Cassie asked.

"Five-thirty."

"Can we walk? I'm going to need the practice."

Scotty and I both looked up at the sky. It was dry for now, and actually mostly sunny. Tico's was five blocks south and five blocks east, but we had time and decided with a pair of nods that, yes, we could walk.

And so walk we did, through the heart of downtown Lincoln. On a Friday afternoon turning into evening, crowds were flocking out of businesses and into the bars and restaurants. Compared to the real big cities—New York, Chicago, L.A.—Lincoln was just a dot on the map. But compared to Morgan, where the main hangout was Wieskamps' convenience store, Lincoln was a happening place. Especially once the college crowd returned in a few days.

College kids reminded me that I was walking beside one, that this was the last hurrah for the three of us. When would I see Cassie again? Thanksgiving? Christmas? Next summer? The rapture, whenever it was?

Bright sunshine highlighted the Hispanic look of Tico's, reflecting off the stucco exterior and the clay tile shingles. Inside, the atmosphere was dark and still quite Hispanic, with intricate stained glass windows and a circular chandelier in the lobby that was straight out of a Spanish mission. The hostess led us to a table near the back wall, and for the moment, we were by ourselves. On a Friday night, Tico's wouldn't be half-full for long.

We studied our menus while plying ourselves with chips and salsa. After we ordered, Cassie excused herself to the ladies' room and Scotty and I did some serious damage on the chips and salsa.

"You think she liked the museums?" I asked.

"Mm-hmm."

"You think she'll like the park?"

"Mm-hmm."

"You want to take a break to breathe?" I asked as Scotty dipped another chip into the salsa.

"Considering our time constraints, we did all right," he said. "Besides, she'd be happy sitting at home on her porch." He crunched on the chip.

Cassie rejoined us and we spent some time talking about her upcoming schedule. She would arrive in Phoenix late morning (their time) tomorrow. Orientation started Sunday afternoon, and classes began Tuesday. She would be meeting her roommates, learning her way around the campus—which had her freaked—and adjusting to hundred degree heat and the desert culture.

"More nervous or excited?" Scotty asked.

"Mmm . . . Tie." Cassie reached out for the salsa. I nudged it toward her. "But in about eighteen hours, nervous wins."

"So what time do we have to leave tomorrow?" I asked.

"How long's it take to get to Omaha?"

"To the airport, an hour and a half," I said. "Ish."

"My flight's at 8:55," she said. "And I'm supposed to be there at least ninety minutes early."

Scotty waved. "They overcompensate. You can be there half that."

"Um, I'm not getting this close only to miss out because I'm late for my plane.

"I don't think this is the last flight ever to Phoenix," Scotty said.

Cassie glared and he shut up.

"Pick you up at six?"

"No later."

"I'll be there at quarter till," I said.

"Here we go," our waitress said, delivering sizzling plates of chimichangos, burritos, tamales, and Ticorittos. It all looked, smelled, and tasted delicious.

"So I get off December 14," Cassie said midway through the meal. "We are doing something that weekend."

"Okay."

"Is that the next time we'll see you?" I asked.

"I'm hoping to come back for Thanksgiving," she said. "Depends how much flights cost."

"Have you lined up a job out there?" Scotty asked.

"No. There's a job fair or something on Monday. And I talked with one of the guidance counselors." She paused to lick sauce off her thumb. "He gave me some advice on finding a job on campus and I made a few phone calls, but nothing so far." She winced. "I'm kind of nervous, because I have to get something on or close to campus since I don't have any wheels."

"Buy a horse."

She looked up at him from her plate. "Don't remind me I won't see my horsies for four months."

"You want to go home and take one more ride?"

"We did last night," she said. "Mom, Dad, and I. And, oh, I talked to one of my roommates yesterday," Cassie said.

"Let me guess, a spoiled brat valley girl named Shay," Scotty said.

"No, she's from Montana," Cassie said. "Her name's Shelly."

"A cowgirl?"

"She lives on a ranch. And rides horses."

"Maybe you can all go calf-roping sometime," Scotty said, cutting into his tamale.

"I don't think I'll have time for a lot of roommate bonding activities."

Scotty chugged some of his pop. "What's your course load like?"

"Monday, Wednesday, Friday I have Art Prehistory Through Middle Ages at eight," Cassie answered, reaching for a couple of chips. She dipped them in the salsa. "Then I've got Photography and Art, Renaissance to Present at nine and ten; and then . . ." She paused to think, head tilted to one side, and stuffed the chips into her mouth. "Art of Africa, Oceania and Americas at one."

"Is that it?"

"I wish. I've also got a late afternoon Photography lab Mondays and Thursdays, and then two hours of 3-D Design on Tuesdays and Thursdays at nine."

"What is that, forty credits?"

"Eighteen."

"That's not too bad," I said.

"I do my homework," she teased.

"That was one class, okay?"

We relived high school memories as we ate, laughing at all the good times we'd shared and forgetting that most of our good times were in the past. We declined dessert, planning on grabbing something later. Maybe. We were all stuffed.

Heading for the lobby to pay for our dinners, we heard a strange sound. We couldn't identify it until we stepped outside.

Rain.

Heavy rain.

Cassie made a horrified face.

Scotty peeked out from under the arched canopy that was keeping us dry. He was drenched in seconds.

"It's beet purple to the northwest," he said.

"Beets are red," Cassie said.

"They're purplish red."

"Does that mean good weather or bad weather?" Cassie asked. "I can't remember."

"Red means good weather tomorrow," I said. "But this is purple."

"Then it's not beets."

"I guess we wait," Scotty said. "Our after-dinner plans kind of depended on good weather anyhow."

"What's that?"

"Pioneers Park," I said.

"Oh," she groaned.

"These are isolated storms," Scotty said. "Once this one's gone, we might be in the clear."

"But won't it last a while, what with it being beet purple?" she asked.

He flicked some water off his hand at her.

Then we waited, enduring a few vivid lightning flashes and several startling rumbles of thunder. After about ten minutes, the rain began to slacken, and in another five minutes it was down to a light shower.

"Should we send out a dove?" Cassie asked.

We waited two more minutes. Scotty's beet purple sky had turned to light gray, white, and some holes that looked up at pale blue. We started walking.

We made it two blocks before it started raining again, from out of nowhere. Scotty whipped the cap off his head and handed it to Cassie. She looked good in LSU purple turned lavender.

We reached 13th and M before it started to come down with force again. We quickly crossed M Street, then 13th against the light and huddled against the side of the U.S. Bank building. With the wind from the west, we were shielded from the rain.

Until the wind shifted.

"I'll go get the car," Scotty said.

"You'll get soaked," Cassie said.

"I'll dry." He plucked his cap off her head and took off jogging down the sidewalk. We moved under the small canopy by the front doors, which kept us reasonably dry.

"This reminds me of that bike trip to Firth," I said.

"Reminds me of the time you and I got stranded in the barn," she said.

"Oh yeah." A severe drought had hit the plains, and after five weeks with one day of rain, the jet stream or El Niño or something had moved, and it had rained for four straight days. The last of which had seen an absolute donnybrook that had temporarily turned the Larson's driveway into a river. Cassie and I had been in the barn tending to "her" calves, since her nine-year-old mind had thought they would be afraid of the rain. Who knew, maybe they had been. At any rate, we had been stuck there until her dad came and carried us back to the house.

"I spent all summer praying for rain," Cassie said. "I was scared to pray for a month."

"That would have been a good illustration for Teasdale's sermon last Sunday."

Thunder rumbled again, this time rolling and echoing across the sky.

"Will you promise me something?" Cassie asked.

"What's that?"

"Look after Scotty."

"Are you worried about him?"

"No, but . . ."

"Are you going to give him this same speech later?"

"It's not a speech."

"That's not a denial."

"Scotty's just a little . . . aloof. Sometimes aloof people become . . . more aloof."

"I'll keep an eye on him."

"Thank you."

"And you still didn't deny it."

Cassie looked me in the eye, then turned out to the rain. "I think it might be letting up."

A flash of lightning lit up the street, the thunder cracking almost instantly.

"I could be wrong."

Scotty arrived in the Blazer just as the rain was indeed letting up. We climbed in mildly wet. He was drenched. "Looks clear west of here," he said. "You guys want to hit the park?"

"You'll catch pneumonia," Cassie said.

"From going to the park?"

"You're drenched."

"I'm drenched in here too."

"Maybe we should run to Shopko or something to get you some dry clothes."

"Yeah, that would be a memorable sendoff."

"Josh, make sure he doesn't get too sassy when I'm gone."

"Putting the fox in charge of the chickens?" Scotty asked.

"See."

"I'm not even sure that analogy fits," I said.

"Park or not?"

"Park," I said. "Then to CVS to get you some anti-pneumonia pills."

I turned to see Cassie's evil eye. I knew it would either be that or a stuck-out tongue.

We journeyed west of Lincoln to Pioneers Park. By the time we reached the bison statue near the entrance, the sun was glistening off its bronze head. East, the sky was dark purple, almost black. Beyond beetish. South too. West and north it was clear blue with only a few tufts of cotton floating along.

We drove slowly through the park, past the Pinewood Bowl (an outdoor, grass-seat amphitheater) past the golf course, and to the Pioneers Park Nature Center. Since the weather had improved, we parked and strolled around the grounds. We checked out the snakes and turtles and the art wall in the Prairie Building, then went outside to walk a nature trail amid a herd of elk. We also headed to the top of the hill to check out the bison, none of whom were interested in approaching the fence.

None of us said much as we strolled. We just took in the scenery and enjoyed being together. I guessed that Scotty and Cassie were too busy swallowing the lumps in their throats to say much of anything. I know it was the case for me.

We left the park and stopped at McDonald's for ice cream cones, then cruised on the back roads back to Morgan. The sun was setting, casting an orange glow over the corn and soybean fields. Way off in the distance, I could still see the remnants of the storms that had ruined our post-dinner walk (Scotty's clothes were just drying out). Behind us, I noticed another row of clouds, maybe more storms, maybe just clouds.

"Hey, isn't that what's-her-name's house?" Cassie asked, pointing to a rambling farmhouse on a hill.

Scotty nodded.

"Who's what's-her-name?" I asked.

"Scotty's prom date. Mallory?"

"Melanie. Melanie Wilterdink."

"Oh yeah," I said. "The 'hottest girl in the history of the world.'"

"That's her. Unfortunately her dress size and IQ were the same."

"Why'd you go with her?" I asked.

"You already answered that question," Cassie said out the side of her mouth.

"What else was I supposed to do, go stag?"

"Hey, I wasn't going to go at all but everyone told me I had to," I said.

Proms were for high school sweethearts, I had figured. I hadn't had a high school sweetheart, or any girl I had been particularly interested in. But staying home hadn't been an option, everyone had told me, so I had gone with the intention of sitting on the side, looking cool, drinking inordinate amounts of punch, and copping as many hors d'oeuvres as possible.

"How long did it take you to try to pawn her off on me?" I asked.

"About four syllables," Scotty said. "Which was about four sentences."

"What excuse did you give her again?"

"I told her I was a eunuch."

Cassie slapped his shoulder.

"It's okay. She thought it was a religion."

"You know, you guys could have taken me," Cassie said.

"Both of us?"

"One of you."

"Yeah, but which one? We actually talked about it, but couldn't decide which one would ask you."

"Yeah," I said. "The other would have been left to . . . Melanie."

"We should have just dressed the same and taken turns with her," Scotty said.

"Taken turns with me? I'm not a new toy you got for Christmas."

"I suppose I could have let Josh take you."

"Now you make it sound like you're letting the dog out to pee."

I frowned. "Why me?"

"Since I took her . . ."

"Took her where?" I looked to Scotty, then back to Cassie. "Took you where?"

"Scotty took me to my prom."

"You did?"

He nodded.

I didn't say anything.

"You were off meeting girls at college," he said.

"I didn't know that."

"We were afraid you'd get jealous."

"Jealous?"

"Not in that way," Cassie said. "But you know . . . If there's three friends . . . Scotty?"

"Think *Bandits*," he said.

"They made it work in *Bandits*," I said.

"But they almost killed each other first."

"That was part of the act."

"Not in the bank, before that. And they ended up living in that vineyard in Mexico."

"Hmm, there is that."

"What's *Bandits*?" Cassie asked.

"Sort of like *Two Guys, a Girl and a Pizza Place*, only without the pizza place."

"It was nothing like that," I said.

"What are you even talking about?"

"I wonder what ever happened to her," Scotty mused.

"Who, Melanie?"

He nodded.

"Why, you want to make another run at it with her?"

"She was hot."

"Yes, but your children wouldn't be able to read until they were twelve."

"Yeah, but they'd be cute."

"I don't know. Heather Donaldson's kids aren't cute."

"Who's Heather Don . . . You mean Heather de Smit?" Cassie asked.

"Yeah."

"What does that have to do with anything?" Scotty asked.

"Don't you remember? She was his first crush."

"She was not."

"I thought his first crush was Kelly what's-her-name."

"Herron," I said.

"That's right."

"No, it was Heather," Cassie said. "It was kind of weird. She was like twice his age."

"I was eleven, she was seventeen, and I didn't have a crush on her. I just realized that maybe there was a future for me with the opposite sex."

"Crush."

"Was not. Honest, I'd tell you if she was."

"So who was?" Scotty asked. "Kelly?"

"Well, depends on what you mean by crush. Cassie and I sort of engaged ourselves when I was five."

"I remember that," Cassie said. "I even picked the flowers I was going to wear in my hair."

"So what happened?" Scotty asked. "I came along and broke you two up?"

"Something like that," I said. "Then you took her to prom . . ."

He looked into the mirror at Cassie. "Told you he'd be jealous."

"Um-hmm."

We skirted around Morgan and arrived at Cassie's house just as the sun disappeared beyond the horizon. We all got out, stood around awkwardly for a few moments, and then Scotty and Cassie hugged goodbye. It was emotional just for me to watch, and I dreaded saying goodbye to her the next morning.

"Don't get into too much trouble, okay?" Cassie said, wiping a tear from her cheek.

"Sure. Don't marry any Starbucks-guzzling sun-worshipers in Birkenstocks until we can meet them and approve."

She grinned. "Deal."

"Quarter to six?" I asked, looking at Cassie. She nodded, then gave Scotty one more hug. She turned and went inside, and he drove me home.

"It's going to be kind of weird, dude," he said as he turned into my apartment's parking lot.

"Was it weird when I left?"

"No, that was just depressing."

"I'm touched."

Scotty shrugged. "What can I say? You're my Trapper, the Cory to my Shawn, the George Costanza of my life."

I frowned as he braked in front of my door. "How come you guys didn't throw me a going away celebration?"

"Because you were coming back, dude."

"You think she's not coming back?"

"Yeah, for Thanksgiving, Christmas, spring break. After that . . ." He shrugged. "I don't think she's going to get an art history degree to come back here and keep us sane."

I stared straight ahead, letting reality in. I had really hoped we could all stay twenty forever.

"Get some sleep, dude," Scotty said.

"Yeah."

I got out of the car and leaned back in through the window. "Hang out tomorrow, when I get back?"

He nodded. "Sure."

I nodded back. "See ya."

"See ya."

Chapter 31

"I, even I, am he who comforts you." Isaiah 51:12

I did not get some sleep.

As I was entering my apartment, the phone rang. Cassie, I figured. Make it five-thirty. Or I've changed my mind and don't want to leave you and Scotty. No, that couldn't be it.

I kicked off my shoes and grabbed the cordless phone. "Hello?"

"Josh?"

It was Erica. My heart stopped, then made up for it with several rapid beats.

"Yeah," I answered brilliantly.

I heard her sniff. "Are you by any chance free tonight?" she asked.

"Um . . ." More brilliance. "Yeah, what's up?" A hundred thoughts pushed at the front of my head, but none of them had time to formulate.

"Mark and I broke up. I need someone to talk to."

It took a few seconds for words to form. I hoped they were the right ones. "I'll be right over."

"Thank you."

I hung up, my mind racing almost as fast as my heart. It had happened! They had broken up!

But Erica did not sound happy. So could I, in good conscience, be happy?

Of course! My dream girl was now available again!

But my dream girl was my friend, and my friend was hurting.

But I could ease the pain!

She didn't need a Casanova slipping his shoulder under her tears; she needed a real friend.

Could one be the other?

And so back and forth it went while I quickly reapplied my deodorant—but not cologne, as that might send the wrong message. I also gargled with some mouthwash. After all, if we were going to be talking . . .

Then I stepped back into my shoes, didn't bother to tie them, and headed for the door. I stopped, remembering my alarm clock. I didn't know when I would be back or in what condition my brain would be in at the time. So I set the alarm for five so I would be sure to wake up in time to take Cassie to the airport. Then I headed out.

The night was still balmy, breezy, and I got the feeling more storms might be building. As I drove, I tried to figure out what I should say. Calling up a guy friend probably wasn't normal in this situation, but Erica had said before she found girls annoying. And she was sort of new to town. Maybe she didn't have a lot of available girl friends in whom to confide. And what did I know about normal girl breakup behavior? And that was just the point. I didn't know squat. What was I to say to make her feel better?

And for that matter, what exactly was my responsibility? This was an opportunity here. But, I determined, even if my ultimate goal was to win Erica's heart, tonight was not the time to work toward achieving that goal. Tonight Erica just needed a friend, and I resolved that a friend was all that I would be.

But being a friend could actually help me achieve my goal, whether it was my motivation or not. So wouldn't it be just as well to be honest with myself going in and have that as a secondary intention? No. I resolved again to deal with Erica just as a friend. But that would sure be easy if she wasn't so incredibly beautiful and alluring.

About the time I turned onto 8th Street, it dawned on me to pray. So I did. I had no idea why they had broken up, what sort of mental and emotional state Erica was in, or what she would need from me. So I just prayed for help in general as I pulled into the driveway.

Erica met me at the door, opening it just before I could ring the bell. She wore blue jeans and an orange Henley top, her hair down. Her eyes were red, but she wasn't crying anymore. Before I could say anything, she reached out and hugged me.

We'd had brief physical contact before, the accidental stuff that happens when two people are around each other and one backhand in the candy aisle. But this was the first interaction of any sort, and it gave my focus on friendship a standing eight count.

It was a short hug, and before I could wrap my arms around her, Erica pulled back. "Thanks for coming, Josh. Mom's at the ladies' retreat and Dad's in Omaha on business, and . . . I needed someone to talk to."

"No problem," I said.

"Do you mind if we go somewhere?" she asked. "I need to get out."

"Sure."

Erica nodded. "I have to get my shoes. Come on in."

I followed her into the entry of the house, noticing that she was barefoot. The lights were low, her parents were gone — yeah, leaving was probably a good idea.

Erica slipped on a pair of flip-flops and grabbed her purse, and we headed back outside. I got her door for her, closed it behind her, and circled around to my side of the car. My heart was breakdancing and I wasn't sure I could string more than three or four words together without them colliding into each other and piling up on the end of my tongue.

I forced myself to take a deep breath as I got into the car. I reached for my seatbelt. "Where do you want to go?"

"Anywhere," she said.

I nodded and started the car. I followed 8th Street north. The only sounds were my tires on the asphalt and the slight hole in my exhaust pipe. At Ash, I turned west, heading for the park. As good of a place as any, I figured.

Unless Erica wanted to go to Kansas.

Neither of us spoke as I drove up the same path Cassie and I had taken not so long ago. I parked in the same spot, at the crest of the small hill, and put the car into park. "You want to get out? Stay here?" I asked.

She nodded, which wasn't much of an answer to a multiple choice question, but I cut her some slack. Then she unbuckled her seatbelt and reached for the car door. I shut off the engine.

We got out and slowly walked around the front of the car. We stood looking out across the railroad tracks and the empty fields, all a wash of black under the night sky. There was no way to be prepared for what came next.

"I had a brother," Erica said. "His name was Zach."

I noticed, after a moment, that she had used the past tense.

"Five years ago, he was on his way home one Friday night when a drunk driver swerved into his lane and hit his car. He and his best friend were both killed."

I swallowed, not wanting to just utter an "I'm sorry" but not knowing what else to say.

"The driver said he didn't even remember it. He was so drunk that . . . he didn't remember killing my brother."

I put my arm around her, with no romantic motivation whatsoever. She responded by turning and burying her head into my shoulder and crying. Hard. I wrapped both arms around her and held her as she sobbed. At some point, her arms embraced me. I really wasn't paying attention to such things.

Instead I was trying to link up her brother's death to her breakup with Mark. I didn't have it, and decided to let her tell me at her own pace. Selfishly, I was glad she was crying because I didn't have a clue what to say after a bombshell like that.

Finally, she pulled back, apologizing and wiping her eyes. She reached into her pocket for a tissue and blew her nose, then turned back to me. "I'm sorry."

"It's fine."

"I should totally be bawling on some girl's shoulder, but girls just gossip and trash guys and . . . That is not what I need right now."

"I understand."

"I guess you're the closest thing I have to a confidant in this town," she said. I guessed that was sort of a compliment.

I rubbed her back, like a friend.

She wiped tears from her cheeks again and ran her fingers through her hair. She exhaled. "Mark and I . . . We went out for pizza tonight." She looked at me. "He ordered a beer."

It was starting to link up.

"It's one thing to drink," she said. "But we were in Lincoln, and he had to drive back. And last week he and his brothers—I don't know, they just sort of . . . They reminded me of the type of guys who would be careless enough to drink and drive. And then Mark did. Legally, I'm sure, but still."

I nodded. "Did he know?"

"I told him about it a while ago, but he apparently never put two and two together. When we got back tonight, I said something about it. He said it was just a beer and that I was a little uptight. I kind of lost it then."

I was no genius, but I knew telling a girl she was being uptight about a personal tragedy wasn't a great move.

"Before I knew it, I told him it was over."

She started to cry again, and I wrapped my arms around her again. I didn't know if the tears were for Zach or for Mark—probably for each—and I didn't much care. I also, in that moment, didn't have one thought about romance or about how the girl of my dreams and I were locked in another embrace. All I wanted to do was make her feel better, and I didn't have clue one how to go about it.

I have never, in my life, audibly cursed. I have wanted to on several occasions, never more than Saturday morning when my alarm went off at five a.m. My head hurt, every movement created intense nausea, and my limbs were unresponsive to my brain's commands.

I managed to roll out of bed and stagger into the shower. It was there that I remembered, with relative detail, the night before. Or rather, the night that still was.

Erica had finally cried herself out on my shoulder, and we sat for a long time on the front edge of the Escort talking. Mark's alcohol consumption was just a small part of the reason she had broken off their relationship, the proverbial straw that broke the camel's back. She told me everything, how she had seen a lack of spiritual commitment in Mark—

how he was just "along for the ride." In Haiti, she'd seen the way he interacted with the kids and the passion he seemed to have for Jesus, and it had drawn her to him. After a month and a half of dating, she realized what she had mistaken for passion was just Mark's enthusiasm for life and not a desire to grow in and serve God. Truthfully, she said to me, she'd been contemplating ending things for several weeks.

She had found more tears, ultimately laying her head on my shoulder again. For a long while more, we had sat side by side on the edge of the Escort, her head on my shoulder, watching the stars disappear behind a bank of clouds, then watching faraway lightning as another storm rolled in.

Lost in thought, I let the water in the shower beat down on my face. Realizing I was behind schedule, I slammed off the faucet, not sure if soap had been introduced to my morning cleansing or not. I would have to make up for it with extra doses of deodorant and cologne.

I arrived at the Larson house at 5:47. Cassie was waiting on the porch in the dark. She greeted me with a quick forced smile and we loaded her luggage into the trunk. She explained that she had already said goodbye to her dad, who was probably brewing coffee for the men's prayer breakfast as she spoke. Cassie was stoic as we backed out of the driveway and headed away from the only home she had ever known.

"How'd you sleep?" I asked.

"Not good. You?"

"Great." For four hours.

"Something wrong?"

"No, why?"

"Because you've got a weird look on your face."

I nodded. "Erica and Mark broke up," I said.

"Serious?"

"Very."

"When?"

"Last night."

"Last night?" she asked, frowning. "When?"

"She called me just after I got home."

Cassie had already removed her sneakers, and she pulled her left foot up onto the seat, tucked it under her knee, and turned toward me. "Why you?"

"Huh?"

"Why'd she call you?"

"Her parents were gone and girls gossip and she needed someone to talk to."

"So did you talk?"

I nodded. "We went to the park, where you and I went, and she unloaded everything."

Cassie switched positions and looked out the window. "So now what?" she asked.

"Huh?"

"Now what, with you and Erica?"

I looked at her, and she turned back from the window. "I don't know," I said. "What do you think?"

"I think you should be careful, Josh."

"I'm always careful."

"I mean it. The last thing she needs is someone trying to pick her up, and the last thing you need is to mess things up by being that someone."

"You're awfully smart for six in the morning."

"And I'm serious. Be patient."

"I'll try."

"You've made it all summer."

"She wasn't available all summer."

"Consider her still unavailable, for now. Just be her friend. It's what she needs, and long term, it will be best for your relationship."

I sighed. "I'll try."

"And it's probably the best way for a relationship to start too, as friends. I mean, what's a better foundation, a first date or months or years of friendship?"

I thought about that as we continued north, through the town of Bennet, then jogged west for a half a country block on Highway 2. Then it was north again to Waverly, where we backtracked a few miles west to catch I-80 east. Once on the interstate, it was a straight shot to Omaha. The sun was at least high enough in the sky that I wasn't staring straight into it.

Cassie looked back out the window. "So why'd they break up? No, wait. I don't need to know. It's none of my business."

I looked her way.

"No, I don't need to know."

"So let's talk about you then," I said. "You excited?"

She grinned. "Very."

"More excited than nervous?"

"Yes."

"More excited than sad?"

The smile faded, but only for a moment. "Yes. I have to grow up sometime."

"I think you've done quite a bit of growing."

"Thanks a lot."

"You know what I mean."

Her scowl turned into a smile. "I get to see mountains, Josh. Real, jagged, huge mountains."

"Now you're making me sad."

"I'll send you a postcard."

We picked up breakfast sandwiches at a McDonald's in Gretna before hitting rush hour Omaha traffic. We encountered a bit of a jam near the 680 exit, but then cruised at a pretty good speed to Eppley Airfield. By the time we arrived at twenty past seven, Cassie had nearly tied strands of her hair into knots. I sensed the nerves were taking over the excitement.

Burdened down with Cassie's luggage, we headed into the terminal. It was as empty as I had ever seen Eppley, and we quickly checked in and found the appropriate concourse. We stopped just short of the security checkpoint, as far as I could go without a ticket.

"I guess this is it," she said, hoisting her backpack higher onto her shoulders.

I nodded. "It's going to be weird without you."

"Weirder for me," she said. "I know one person in Arizona, and she's from Montana."

"Well, if you get lonely, don't hesitate to call."

"If I can afford it."

"Collect."

"If you can afford it."

"We'll bill it to Scotty."

She smiled through tight lips, and we stood there for a second.

"Well . . ."

"Yeah."

I reached down to give her a hug, and she squeezed back tightly. "I'll be praying for you," I whispered in her ear. "You'll do great."

She responded with another quick squeeze, and I thought about kissing her forehead as we backed away. It was the type of thing I always saw on television, and that was the reason I didn't do it.

"Bye, Cass."

"Bye."

I watched her through security, feeling like my kid sister had been released to the world. Cassie wasn't naïve or immature, but she had lived at home her whole life. She was not used to the big city, to the liberal wackos that I was sure existed at Arizona State, or to being on her own. But she was smart, and I was sure she would make it. To be surer, I prayed.

Once through the metal detectors, Cassie turned back, and seeing that I was still standing there, issued a little half wave. I returned it and watched until she was out of sight.

Her flight didn't leave for another hour, and since I had nothing else to do anyway, I decided to wait around until it left. If something happened to go wrong and her plane couldn't leave, she wouldn't be stranded.

I bought an expensive coffee and a copy of the *Omaha World-Herald* and sat down in front of the arrival and departure monitors to read about Husker football that was only one week away. When United flight 1621 to Phoenix's status was changed to departed, I folded up the paper and trudged back to the parking garage.

The drive home was long and sad, broken only by a stop because I had forgotten to pee in the airport. I thought back on all the fun Cassie and I had had, usually with Scotty, over the last fifteen years. I thought again of her forging her way alone in the world, scrambling as always to make ends meet. Then I thought of Scotty's words from the night before, how she probably wouldn't be coming back to us.

I am a grown man, and do not cry unless there is a darn good reason. As I cruised the lonely interstate, I shed a few tears.

Act III

Chapter 32

"This day is a day of distress and rebuke and disgrace . . ." II Kings 19:3

Scotty and I saw no reason to sit in a separate pew anymore, so Sunday we joined Dirk a little farther toward the back. Then catastrophe hit. Some sort of electrical problem kept the amps from functioning. A very somber Curtis Teasdale sadly announced at the start of the service that they had been trying for about twenty minutes, and the sound system just wasn't cooperating.

"I'm afraid we don't have much of a choice," he said. "We won't be able to worship our Lord this morning."

Several people groaned. Several old people behind me probably did mental cartwheels. I just stood there, wondering what was prohibiting the worship team's larynxes from functioning. Since the guitars didn't work, we couldn't sing? I'd heard some doozies in my day, but this one . . .

"Maybe we should keep the carwash money in house and let the Haitians fend for themselves," Scotty whispered.

"I wonder if God knocked out the amps at True Way too," I said.

"They don't use amps, remember? They're of the devil."

"Oh yeah, that's right."

"He could have clogged the organ's pipes though."

"Perhaps."

Teasdale took a few moments to compose himself. I think he may have shed a tear. Then he said since we couldn't sing, we might as well start the sermon.

For the second week in a row, it wasn't bad. It wasn't Moody quality, but it wasn't bad. It was certainly in line with Scripture. (Fortunately, Teasdale was able to preach without mechanical amplification.)

He dismissed us twenty-four minutes early, since the amps still hadn't come around. I wondered if amp failures like this could be prayed for, like when a guy was hoping to get home early to watch football or something.

"Funny how tribes in Borneo can worship in the jungle, but we can't sing without amps," Scotty said.

"Yes, but they have bongo drums."

"So do we."

"Ours plug in."

"Ah-ha."

"Maybe the worship team can't carry a tune," I said. "Maybe they need the guitars and drums for cover."

"That's possible."

"Or maybe the whole world has gone daffy."

"That's possible too."

We turned into Room 104. Only Tim was there, and he had his eyes shut, his iPod buds in his ears. We left him alone.

"You talk to Erica last night?" Scotty asked. He and I had hung out Saturday afternoon, and I had briefed him on the breakup and my being there to catch the pieces.

"No," I said. "I didn't see her this morning, either."

"Maybe she's so grief-stricken that she went to True Way. I hear some desperate people try it."

I gave him a glare.

Tim apparently heard us talking, because he sat up and looked around. Then he lowered his ear buds. I could hear Skillet coursing through them from the back row.

"Dude, how are you not deaf?" I asked.

"It's Skillet," he said. "You're not supposed to listen to it pianissimo."

"They should have had you play it in church," I said. "Pipe in the music."

"Skillet's not exactly worship music," he said.

"Around here lately it might be," Scotty replied.

The words were no sooner off his lips than Petey entered the room. He was followed by Sandra Teasdale. She wore a black skirt to the knees, a dark green blouse, and a bead and jade necklace that looked like it was used by jungle tribes to summon the dead. Her hair was darker than I had ever seen it, darker than blackest space, in fact. It was not of God.

She eyed the three of us suspiciously and took a seat in the opposite back corner. She crossed her legs and opened a notebook on top of them.

"You auditing?" Scotty asked.

"I beg your pardon?" she said, looking up.

"The class. You auditing it?"

"No. Derek has asked me to say a few words."

I sent Scotty a look out the side of my eye. Petey had threatened, and now he was making good.

For the next ten minutes, Scotty, Tim, and I compared Skillet to other bands of their generation, Christian and secular, as well as contrasting their current style with the early years. It killed time and helped us avoid the evil eye of Sandra Teasdale. Frau Frump.

Erica arrived a few minutes before class was due to start, wearing black slacks and a red scoop-neck blouse. She smiled in my direction. I held up a hand as a wave.

"Hey, Tiger," Scotty said.

She stopped.

"Tiger Woods. Wears red on black on Sundays."

"I see. Mind if I sit here?"

She pointed at Cassie's seat. Cassie was probably worshiping Alpha Centauri with the rest of the New Agers out in Arizona. I said, "Sure."

Erica sat down and I smelled lilacs. I liked lilacs, especially without the bees.

"How are you doing?" I asked, quietly enough that the rest of class didn't hear. I didn't think the breakup was for public consumption.

"I'm all right," she said. "I'm kind of anxious for Mom to get home this afternoon. I could use some girl talk."

"I thought you didn't like girl talk."

"Mom's different. She's . . . sane."

I nodded. And decided to take one step forward.

"Well, if you need any guy talk, you've got my number."

"Thank you, Josh," she said, placing her hand on mine for just a second. Gia picked that exact moment to walk in. "And thank you for Friday night."

"Of course."

Gia briefly made eye contact with me as she took her seat, across the room from Geoff, I noticed. So now in addition to splitting the room based on rapture timing beliefs, we were also divided by love spats. Pretty soon we'd have tape down the middle of the floor like Brother and Sister Bear.

Petey called the class to order. He kind of needed a Radar to his Colonel Blake. But he got us settled down. "I've asked Mrs. Teasdale to address the class for a few moments before we begin," he said. He nodded at her, and she stood and strode to the front of the room.

"Brace for impact," I whispered to Scotty.

Sandra Teasdale had her notebook with her, but it was closed. "When this class was formed in the spring," she said, "it was done so with the intention of helping young adults grow spiritually. Derek was chosen to lead the class because of his excellent knowledge of the Scriptures and his desire to fulfill the Great Commission by making disciples."

She looked up, scanned the room. "However, it appears that he is one of the few in this class who shares that desire. The majority of you, it seems, would rather horse around and make his task difficult by cracking jokes and steering the conversation anywhere but on topic."

Brett's hand shot up.

"Please wait until I'm finished," Sandra said. I glanced at Scotty. Then at Erica. But only for an instant. I didn't want my knuckles rapped for looking away from the teacher.

"I'm not here to tell you not to be lively, animated, fun-loving young people," she said. "But there is a time and a place for that sort of behavior, and it is not in an in-depth Bible study class designed to help people grow in their walk with Christ. So from now on, please refrain from making jokes and sidetracking the class during the study hour. I've told Derek to please let me know if this sort of behavior continues."

She looked us over again, and her eyes settled on Brett. "Do you still have a question?"

"Yeah. Do we now get demerits or are you going to call our parents or something?"

I was raised to respect my elders, which definitely prohibited sassing them in Sunday school. But I couldn't hide a smirk at Brett's question.

"Mr. Baker? I wonder if I might have a word with you in the hall."

"Um . . . I'll pass."

"It wasn't really a request."

"And all due respect, but I don't believe you have the authority to tell me what to do."

Sandra's eyes blazed.

"And I don't see why you're lecturing us about our behavior in class," Brett continued. "Petey's finished every one of his lectures on time, and we've had some really good discussions — Ask anybody. Are we a little out there sometimes? Sure. But we're not promoting heresy or blasphemy. We're fellowshipping. Isn't that a big thing around here?"

Sandra's eyes widened. I thought fire might actually shoot out of them and consume Brett. I leaned over slightly, so as not to be caught in the crossfire.

"Your tone is completely out of line, Mr. Baker. I'm going to have to ask you to step outside so we don't disrupt the class any further."

"And I'm going to decline," he said. "I think the entire class should be in on this discussion. Unless you just want to scold me."

"Would you like me to bring Pastor Teasdale in here?" she asked.

"Not particularly."

"Then please come with me."

"Are those two mutually exclusive?"

"Mr. Baker," she said, raising her voice.

"What? I'm sorry if you're offended by a little joke, but we are 'fun-loving young people.' And frankly, I don't think I'm alone when I say we find it offensive that you come in here to tell us how to behave like we're a bunch of rowdy kids."

"He's right," Amy said. "We didn't lecture your husband after that dancing in the aisles service. That was way more rowdy."

"Or after we had to dig through shoes like at Goodwill," Tim added.

Brett continued. "After all, you're the ones who segregated us in a 'young people's fellowship' or whatever we're calling this group. Maybe if you'd let us sit at the adults' table you wouldn't have to come down here to read us the riot act."

And then Sandra's eyes took it to a whole new level. So did the vein in her neck, which threatened to pop and spew blood at everyone, like a Horned Frog from Texas Christian. "That is completely out of line," she said, "comparing your behavior in this class to expressions of worship."

"What do you know about expressions of worship?" Amy asked. "You can't even sing without amps!"

"That's it!" Sandra said. "You are all out of control. You've been warned. I'm going to get Pastor Teasdale."

"Oooh," several in the back half of the class said at once. Somebody coughed, "Tattletale."

Sandra stormed out of the room. Erica turned to me. "This is getting ridiculous."

"Why do you think we sit in the back? Best seat in the house."

"I think I'm going to leave," she said. "I've got enough on my mind already without getting involved in a church squabble."

"Don't you want to see how it ends?"

"I'll get the cliffs notes from you."

Implying a future get-together?

"You trying to avoid a scolding?" Scotty asked as she stood.

"I just don't think anything productive is going to come from it. And it's been one of those weeks," she said with a sigh.

Scotty didn't let on that he knew what had made it one of those weeks.

"I'll see you later," Erica said.

"Bye," I returned. She walked to the door, getting a few looks from others in the class. I thought several of them would follow her, but none did.

"I don't think you should leave right now," Petey said.

"Sorry," she said, not slowing down for a second. Then she was gone. I wondered if Sandra would notice the absence.

The Teasdales returned in unison, and Curtis played the role of good cop. Hey, we all just want you to mature in Christ, and a little structure is what's necessary. And we enjoy and embrace your fun-loving side, but couldn't you tone it down a little bit during class?

Nobody spoke. We hadn't made any plans, but as if by agreement, we all remained on our best behavior. Perfect decorum. No argument. Sandra Teasdale seethed. I couldn't help but feel that maybe we were being a touch bratty, and I sort of tuned out Curtis while working to straighten out some things in my mind. Was respecting elders just a command for kids, or did it apply to adults too? If it was for adults, where was the age discrepancy line? Could a forty-year-old born in June not sass another forty-year-old born in May? Or was sassing covered by another command entirely? Did anyone ever just deserve a good sassing? And was I on the side of those being sassy because I agreed with them wholeheartedly, or because I wanted the people who had replaced my parents to be sassed?

The Teasdales eventually left and a blushing Petey got up to teach a shortened class. Nobody said a word or asked a question, even when we got to the part about harvesting the earth, which certainly could have sparked another rapture debate. Petey closed by praying himself, and the strangest Sunday school class yet was behind us.

Chapter 33

"What advice you have offered to one without wisdom!
And what great insight you have displayed!" Job 26:3

It was a hot, muggy morning, the kind that makes you eager for autumn to arrive, and I twirled my keys as I strode through the parking lot, impatient to get home and put on some shorts. I looked up when a horn honked.

It was Mark, idling in his Honda Accord. He looked as if he hadn't shaved in several days—or slept for that matter—and he was dressed in jeans and a T-shirt, casual even for him on a Sunday.

"Hey, Josh."

"Mark."

"You got a minute?"

"Yeah," I said, caution and curiosity mixing and surfacing.

"Hop in."

I did not hop in, but leaned in through the open passenger window. "What's up?"

"Come on, I'll buy you lunch."

It wasn't even eleven o'clock, but I was already feeling hunger pains tickling at my stomach. They were matched by nerves. Mark had a friendly smile on his face, but I sensed it was plastered there. Did he suspect I had something to do with the breakup and want to—for lack of a better term— knock me around? It couldn't be. If he had suspected my feelings for Erica, he would have confronted me long before now. And he wouldn't have buddied up to me at her birthday or invited me to play football with him or sought my advice about a birthday present for her.

And yet . . .

My hesitation showed. "What, you got plans or something?" he asked.

"No, no." I dropped my keys back into my pocket and opened the door. I caught Bon Jovi's "Have a Nice Day" as I slipped into the tan seat and buckled in.

"Morning Glory okay?"

"Yeah, sure."

The Morning Glory Diner is the other eating establishment in Morgan. It's a small little place that looks like an overgrown mobile home—the silver spacecraft kind. It's on the west edge of town, across the street from Wieskamps'. Open only for breakfast and lunch, it caters largely to the old folks who like to eat early, drink lots of coffee, and complain about the weather. I plan to frequent the place in a few decades.

Mark and I rode without talking, allowing me plenty of time to wonder what was going on. We did indeed drive to Morning Glory and not to some back alley where he could thrash me for stealing his girl. I tried to convince myself that my fear was absurd. Mark wasn't going to pound me.

And yet . . .

True to his word, Mark bought me an early lunch. Scotty and I were having pizza and nachos and all sorts of other food most parents (not Dirk) would frown upon later, so I took it easy on Mark and just ordered an appetizer of some cheeseburger sliders. He ordered a steak sandwich and a double portion of fries and we took a seat in the relatively empty dining room.

Mark waited until our orders were up, which wasn't long. He took the first bite of his sandwich and finally broke the tension. "It's about Erica."

Big surprise. I nodded.

"I hear you were with her the other night," he said.

I wasn't sure where he'd heard that, unless Erica had told him. Were they talking already? Was she reconsidering? I realized he was waiting for me to say something, so I nodded again, and tried swallowing the lump in my throat. It was too big.

"How much did she tell you?" Mark asked. "About the breakup?"

"Quite a bit," I said.

He nodded and chomped on a handful of fries. At least the breakup hadn't taken away his appetite. He swallowed and made eye contact with me. It was then that I realized he wasn't angry, but sad.

"I want to get her back, Josh," he said. "I thought . . . I thought maybe you could help me, you know, since you're kind of . . . I thought maybe she told you why she broke it off."

It was my turn to add a dramatic pause by taking a bite of a slider. Then I needed a drink, and took a slug of my pop. "She didn't tell you?"

"Yeah, sort of. But she's a woman, man. I couldn't understand what she was trying to say."

Bingo, genius.

I finished the first slider while trying to figure out what to tell him. Should I just give him the facts, painful as they may be? Should I tell him he had no chance, exaggerating the facts slightly? I certainly didn't want to help him win her back, if it was possible he could.

I decided to play psychiatrist and deflect. Go-betweens get burned. "Why do you think it was?" I asked.

"I don't know, man. I know she was upset because I had a beer at dinner, and we got into an argument. But I can't believe she dumped me just because of that." He shook his head and looked away for a moment. "She said something about spiritual maturity . . . I don't remember exactly what. But that was it."

I may have winced.

"Come on, Josh, I can take it."

I nodded. "She said you were immature spiritually and that she didn't see any signs of improvement."

"It was only a few months."

Yikes, he was really forcing me to twist the knife. I wondered if I should tell him everything, if there was some ex-girlfriend and friend confidentiality. But he did deserve an explanation for being dumped, and had probably gotten one and just not understood it.

"She said it didn't seem to bother you — that you weren't trying to grow or mature, that you were just 'along for the ride.'"

Mark looked out the window. "That just seems . . . It was literally two months." He shook his head again. "Be honest, Josh, was the beer the big thing?"

"I think it was the kicker, yeah."

"I'm not a drinker," he said. "I have an occasional beer now and again. It's not a big deal."

"It was to her."

He sighed. "How is she?"

"She's okay," I said, trying to be as nebulous as possible. I started on another slider.

"So do you think . . . there's any chance? What would I have to do to get her back?"

The knot that had been twisting in my stomach since the conversation started tripled in size. On the one hand, here was my chance to run Mark off for good. Erica would be free, and since she had chosen me as her confidant, I would stand a better shot than anybody of winning her affections. But on the other hand, shouldn't I do what was in her best interest, not mine? The fair thing to do would be give Mark good advice and let the chips fall where they may. Then again, back on the first hand, if Mark was spiritually immature with "no hope for improvement," wouldn't the best thing for Erica be for me to bury him?

I decided to shoot straight. First I took another bite, chewed carefully so as not to choke, and swallowed. Swig of pop.

"I don't think you can right now," I finally said. "I think you'll need to show her that you have matured spiritually, first. Or at least that you are maturing significantly."

He nodded.

"But you can't just mature with the intent of winning her back. You have to mature because it's what you want, even if she's gone for good. Which means if your goal is to get her back, it's probably not going to be genuine maturation."

Sort of like being a friend to be a friend and not to position oneself for a move at a romantic relationship when a romantic relationship was the ultimate goal?

"And I'd recommend you not drink beer anymore too," I added.

"It's just beer. Lots of people drink beer. And I don't get drunk."

"No, but to her, the line is too fine."

Mark sat back. "You think it'd be okay if I tried talking to her?"

Was he even listening to me? I weighed the question for a minute. "I don't see why not," I said at last. "But I'd give her a few days first. Give her some time."

He nodded and picked up his sandwich again. I finished my sliders and drained my pop. The after-church crowd (from both local churches — I hear they have some lively Sunday lunch debates) was starting to trickle in, and Morning Glory was getting busy.

I decided to bend over backward with kindness. I wanted it put in my record that I went above and beyond the call of duty. "If you're interested, a few of us get together every other Wednesday for a Bible study. We meet at Scotty's around six-thirty. We're going through Ephesians right now." I shrugged. "If you're interested."

Mark nodded, but didn't commit. We sat there for a couple of awkward minutes, and then he thanked me and drove me home. His last words were, "Take care of her." I didn't tell him that I planned to. Instead, I was struck by the fact that while he may be a beer-swilling spiritual baby, he did care for Erica.

Chapter 34

"... to the most distant land under the heavens ..." Deuteronomy 30:4

I spent the week debating. The following weekend was Labor Day, the unofficial end of summer (it often continued for another month or two in these parts) and the start of the football season. It was also when the Richmonds usually had a big party at their farmhouse, open to the entire church. Softball, volleyball, football, lots of food, and the pond behind their house all beckoned people. I considered the likelihood that Erica would go, the possibility that Mark might, and what could happen if I wasn't there to guard against it. I didn't think she was in the reconsidering phase, but I hated to take the chance.

On the other hand, I hadn't seen my parents in months and had sort of been planning on taking the extended weekend to make the seven-hour trip to Norman, Oklahoma to visit them. I could leave Friday after work, and since I had off Monday, stay through mid-afternoon and still be back in time to work Tuesday.

In the end, I sided with Mom and Dad. I seriously doubted Erica was ready to take Mark back so soon—if ever—and decided to trust God that if that's what happened, then that would be what happened. I prayed that that would not happen.

My Friday shift ended at four. By four-fifteen I was flying south in my gassed up Escort, three PB&J sandwiches in a Ziploc and a can of cream soda in the small cooler on the passenger seat. I hadn't spoken to Erica since Sunday, which either meant she was doing well or had found another confidant. I also hadn't spoken with Cassie, but had received a short e-mail from her. She had arrived safe and sound and was busy as a beaver, but so far things were going well.

People who say Nebraska is a boring state haven't been to Kansas. There's just nothing there. Highway 77 took me to Florence, where I caught Highway 50 west to Newton. In Newton I joined Interstate 135 to Wichita. I stopped on the south edge of the city to fill up on gas and pee before the final leg to Norman.

The sun was setting into an orange haze as I crossed into the Sooner State. It made Kansas look like paradise. How people lived in these parts, I didn't know. Then again, their forebears had also cheered for Barry Switzer and Brian Bosworth, so . . .

I had a lot of time to think as I cruised south, about Erica and Mark and Cassie and the gang in Room 104 and the Teasdales and my worship preferences and biblical mandates for worship preferences and my Wednesday night Bible study, among other things. I didn't reach any conclusions one way or the other, but I did work out some talking points for the weekend.

Bible study Wednesday had been interesting. With Cassie gone, and Amy absent, our group had been down. Damon had called on Tuesday to let me know he would also be gone—tournament time in his little basketball league. That had left me and Scotty as the only for-sures.

To my surprise, Gia had come back. So had Gerhard. That was it, just the four of us. But we had a good study, good discussion, and no arguments. Gerhard had provided valuable contributions, particularly when we had come to the mystery of the gospel in Ephesians 3. He had given every indication that he would be a regular, and while it threw off our age demographic, I was happy to have him.

Interstate 35 was desolate, even on the Friday before Labor Day. Finally traffic began to pick up as I neared Oklahoma City. I was shocked at how huge the city was, and at how long it took me to get through it. Suddenly it was feeling late.

Norman is about twenty miles south of downtown Oklahoma City, although the suburban sprawl never really stops. Its population, according to the sign along the highway, is almost 111,000, making it less than half the size of Lincoln. I didn't have to, but I cruised along Lindsey Street, right through the heart of the University of Oklahoma and past their Memorial Stadium. (Ours is way cooler.)

Mom and Dad's house was less than a mile east of the campus, and I arrived two minutes before eleven. Not bad time, I thought. Mom and Dad were both thrilled to see me, and I was just as excited to see them. Both of my parents drink coffee religiously, and Mom made a fresh pot. We sat up past midnight, catching each other up on the goings on in our respective lives. I saved the heavy stuff until daylight, and at twenty to one, my head finally hit the pillow. I was out before the soft little thup reached my far ear.

Dad was mowing the lawn when I woke up. He was one of those strange people who enjoyed such things as mowing the lawn, and so I thought nothing of taking a long, slow shower instead of putting on old clothes and going out to take over for him. After the shower, I walked into the kitchen, where Mom—as if Central Casting had put her there—was waiting to make me some eggs. She had some errands to run, so I took my eggs into the living room and watched the guys on ESPN's *College GameDay* break down college football's opening weekend matchups. I had driven over four hundred miles to eat breakfast in front of the TV, alone.

Dad entered just as Lee Corso put on the headgear[17] (Crimson Tide over Tigers). Dad was dripping with sweat, his gray T-shirt soaked, and grass clippings covering the socks he still wore far too high. At least Mom had talked him out of the Thomas Magnum-length shorts.

"Morning." He was smiling.

"Hey, Dad." I watched Corso smack Kirk Herbstreit with the trunk of the elephant that served as Alabama's mascot.

"Mom out?" Dad asked as I picked up my plate and carried it into the kitchen.

---

[17] Lee Corso is a former college football coach most famous for picking games at the end of *College GameDay*, when he dons paraphernalia (usually a mascot head) of the team he picks to win the day's biggest game.

"Running errands."

He nodded and wiped sweat from his forehead onto his shirt sleeve, and vice versa. "I'm gonna shower, then maybe you can tell me about this girlfriend of yours."

Dad winked and I grinned, mostly because I found my forty-nine-year-old father to be goofy. Goofy, but in a good way. He disappeared down the hall, the smell of sweat and murdered grass following behind him. I rinsed dried egg yolk off my plate and let the knot in my stomach churn. Dad's mentioning Erica made me wonder again if I should have left her behind in Morgan, a sheep among potential wolves.

Florida was playing some patsy, but it was the best game on at the time. I watched without watching until Dad rejoined me fifteen minutes later, smelling like the personal care aisle at Target. "So, Erica . . ." he said.

"Yeah."

"Any developments?" he asked. I had called them last weekend and told them she and Mark had broken up. That was about all they knew.

"Not since last week," I answered. "I'm heeding everyone's advice to take it slow, not rush in while she's on the rebound."

"That's wise."

"And decent, I figure. But the problem is, when does a rebound become a loose ball?"

Dad frowned.

"I mean, it's hard enough to figure out when to make your move when a girl isn't coming off a bad relationship. How am I supposed to know when it's 'okay' to move in? And just because I thought we were nearing that point before her and Mark and Haiti, does that mean we're still there? I feel like I'm back at square one, but it isn't even square one. It's square minus-one."

"You need to take some time to breathe now?" Dad asked.

"Sorry. I had the state of Kansas to think things over yesterday. That's a boring drive."

"Why do you think we haven't been back to see you?"

We both grinned. For a moment.

"Maybe you should take the approach your mother and I took," he said.

"You mean wait for her to ask me out?"

"It worked," he said.

"Yeah, but isn't the man supposed to take the lead?" I asked. "What if I wait for her and she thinks I'm a wuss and gets sick of waiting and goes for some other guy who does know when to make his move?"

"Then it's meant to be."

"You really believe that? What if we're meant to be and I drag my feet?"

"Then are you meant to be?"

"Meant by whom?"

"By God."

"I don't know," I said.

"If He means for it to happen, it will happen."

"But what if He lets something else happen?"

"Then it's meant to be."

I sighed. This was starting to sound like Sunday school.

Dad tapped my knee. "My advice," he said, "is if you're wondering if the time is right, it probably isn't. When the time is, you'll know it. Then it's just a matter of working up the courage to do something about it."

"You think it will be that clear?"

He nodded. "When you have to go from talking yourself out of it to talking yourself into it, it's probably time."

I frowned. "So what were you talking yourself into when Mom asked you out?"

"I was more focused on whether the giant 'PC' I saw in the sky meant 'Preach Christ' or 'Plant Corn,'" he said.

I sighed and sat back. "Seems to be the advice I get from everybody. Take it slow."

"Isn't that a clue?" he said.

"Yeah, I suppose. But it's hard to drive forty on the interstate."

Dad reached for the remote and muted the announcers on the TV. "Is there more to that metaphor?"

"Meaning?"

He shifted on the couch. "Is . . . waiting giving you problems?"

"You mean sex?"

Dad nodded.

I suddenly wanted the announcers back on. "Yes and no."

He pursed his lips.

"I'm not afraid that if Erica and I are alone together we're suddenly going to throw twenty years of puritanical living to the wind."

"But?"

"But . . ." I sighed and explained about the pool party and the subsequent temptations. I hadn't brought it up before because it wasn't the type of conversation I wanted to have over the phone. I wanted my parents to be able to look me in the eye and see that I wasn't a complete degenerate.

I also told him about my talks with Scotty and Dirk and with Dave. He agreed with their general sentiment, that there was no surefire game plan for fighting lust. He also seconded their tips and suggestions, and added his own piece of advice. Pray like the dickens. Before anticipated situations. And for the ones you couldn't anticipate, pray each day.

We turned the TV back on and watched until Mom came home and made us sandwiches. We ate in the living room, talking about little things like life in Norman, the summer storms we had both experienced, and Cassie. She'd been gone a week, and it still felt like she was just away on vacation or at summer camp, and that come next Sunday she would be back in church.

The afternoon football slate featured a couple of good games. We weren't able to get the Nebraska game, but Dad did tune in on the radio, which drove Mom nuts. The TV showed one game — or rather three games we kept switching between — and the radio broadcasted another. She couldn't take the chaos and left the two of us to root against OU and Notre Dame, both of whom pulled out close wins that shouldn't have been close. (Nebraska creamed Southern Miss 38-7.)

After Oklahoma's victory was secure, we headed out for dinner. We ordered, and Mom leaned on the table. "So what is it about *this* girl?" she asked. During lunch, I had recapped the high points of the first part of my morning conversation with Dad. Mom had agreed . . . Take it slow, bide my time, blah, blah, blah.

"I don't know," I said as I reached for my water. I took a sip, wondering what *this* girl was doing right now. I shrugged. "She just seems perfect."

"I know the feeling," Dad said as he buttered some bread.

Mom rolled her eyes at him. "Come on, Josh. You must have reasons."

"Well, she's beautiful for one thing. Ashley Judd meets Jennifer Lawrence meets that girl from *Who's the Boss.*"

"*Who's the Boss?*" Dad asked. "Have you ever even seen that show?"

"Scotty and I got hooked on reruns one summer."

He nodded.

Mom took a drink of her water. "Is there more to it than looks?"

"Yeah, but I can't describe it. I just know that when I'm with her . . . It's like everything around me becomes a blur."

"How old is Ashley Judd?" Dad asked, frowning at his now buttered bread.

"She looks like a young Ashley Judd."

Mom shook her head—more in disbelief than frustration—before looking at me. "Is she a Christian?"

"Yeah. A strong one, I think," I said. "She sings in church."

"Not sure that's a guarantor," Dad said.

"What else?" Mom asked.

"Well . . . She's funny—not in telling a lot of jokes or being a prankster, but just the way she is. And she's fun to be with. She's herself. And she's a diehard Husker fan."

"Sounds like a winner to me," Dad said.

"Are you yourself around her?" Mom said.

"I try to be. But I haven't done or said anything really stupid, so I can't say as that I am."

Mom gave me that disapproving 'you're my son and you're not a failure' look.

"All I know," I said, "is I've been around cute girls before, and I've had cute girls that I liked before. None have ever made me feel the way she does. If this is just infatuation, it's the strongest case of it ever."

"Well, I trust you, Josh. We both do. You may not think so, but you're the best judge of your feelings for her—why you have them and whether or not she's a girl worth pursuing as a girlfriend now or someday as a wife."

"So we're back to me interpreting my hormone-driven feelings," I said. "Wonderful."

Chapter 35

*"Listen, my son, to your father's instruction and do
not forsake your mother's teaching." Proverbs 1:8*

The First Community Church of Norman met at nine o'clock for an hour and a quarter worship service, followed by thirty minutes of fellowship time, and then another hour to hour and fifteen minutes of what they called the instructional hour. Codeword for Sunday school.

As he had at Morgan Bible, Dad led the singing and Mom played the piano. But they were joined by a dude in (non-ripped) blue jeans playing the guitar and a drummer. They sang two hymns—including "There is a Fountain Filled with Blood"—and two choruses. The drummer got a little carried away during one of the choruses, but it wasn't bad. Or overly loud.

And they didn't whistle.

Dad, wearing a tie but no suit coat, preached from Hebrews 4. Unlike Cassie, he apparently had the courage to tackle the author-unknown epistle. There were a few moments of unease around the part about the "double-edged sword" that "judges the thoughts and attitudes of the heart." It reminded me of my conversation with Dave, about knowing whether my eyes and thoughts were lusting or merely being enticed. It also made me wonder, as had Cassie and Mom, whether I was in love with Erica or in love with her body. I was convinced it wasn't just physical, but yet, the physical sure played a big part of it.

Between the service and the instructional hour, Dad introduced me to a few people, including a middle-aged guy named Harry who was Boomer Sooner to the core. Amazingly, Dad joked in front of Harry, he was also a devout Christian. I chatted with Harry for a few minutes, discussing the Game of the Century (which neither of us had been alive for) and Sooner

Magic (which I hadn't been alive for) and the "Black 41 Flash Reverse Pass"[18] (which I had been alive for and remembered vividly) and how it was too bad Nebraska and Oklahoma didn't still play every year. I left the conversation realizing there might be a few decent Sooner fans. I was like Abraham praying over Sodom.

Dad, who had taught Sunday school for most of his two decades at Morgan Bible, did not teach at First Community. So I sat with my parents during a discussion on, believe it or not, the end times. It was part of a series on Thessalonians, and we did not drift to a debate about the timing of the rapture or the cast of intergalactic TV shows. Nor were there any slapfights or lectures by a stern pastor's wife.

We headed home where Mom had a roast in the oven. Since the NFL didn't start for a week, Dad and I hung out in the dining room — and out of Mom's way — while she finished preparing lunch. Then we sat down to a delicious meal that made me pine for the days of living at home.

"Something on your mind, Son?" Dad asked halfway through dinner.

"I'm just thinking about church," I said.

"Here or back in Morgan?"

"Both."

He nodded and broke open a second roll. "Anything in particular?"

"Church back home has been really frustrating," I said. I explained about the whistling, clapping, singing, ripped jeans, odd services, and the aura that I couldn't quite accurately describe. I also recounted my talks with everybody about it, and how I hadn't said anything to Mom and Dad because I hadn't wanted to rip open the wound.

"You don't have to worry about that," Mom said. "We've both accepted what happened and moved on. This is where God wants us now."

"Not to say it wasn't difficult at the time," Dad said. He finished the roll. "But your mother's right—"

"Eat, then talk," Mom said.

Dad swallowed. "She's right. You don't have to be afraid to come to us."

---

[18] "Black 41 Flash Reverse Pass" is the name of a trick play used by Nebraska to defeat Oklahoma in 2001.

I nodded. "So do you think this is all just bitterness on my part, that I'm angry because you got fired?"

Dad looked to Mom before answering. "No, not all of it. I think that certainly could play a part if you're not careful. A lot of it is an issue with styles, which is one of the reasons we were let go."

"I thought they didn't tell you the reasons."

"Not in so many words. But reading between the lines, we put the pieces together. Morgan Bible is looking for a younger, less traditional vibe."

"They got it."

"Youth and young adults leaving the church is an epidemic—in Morgan, Norman, and everywhere. I think they wanted to be sure to guard against that."

"So they fired you? Couldn't you be less traditional?"

"I think they wanted a fresh start."

"Why? Do they really think contemporary songs and services without shoes are going to change the demographics that much? And if they do, do we want the change? I mean, if we watched R-rated movies instead of sermons we'd get more people too, but do we want that?"

"That's a bit drastic, don't you think?"

"Yeah, but the principle is the same. Where's the line?"

"That's a fair question."

"So what's the answer?"

Dad cleared his throat. "Are they preaching the gospel?"

"More or less."

"More or less?"

"It seems to sort of be a watered down version of the gospel," I said. "Except for lately, the sermons haven't had any real meat to them. It's kind of like one of those Bible translations that puts everything in modern language to the point that you don't even recognize the Bible anymore."

Dad frowned. "But the preaching is still in line with Scripture?"

"Yeah."

"Is the mission still the same, to equip believers to reach the lost?"

"Yeah."

"Those are the main points."

"Yeah, but what about the methods? I get that there are different ways of doing things, but that doesn't mean that all methods are equally viable."

"No, it doesn't."

"So just because the focus is right, that doesn't necessarily mean that the actions are right, does it?"

"No, but you have the same foundation. You disagree on the style of the building, but you're building in the right place, on a sure Foundation—Foundation with a capital F, by the way."

"So I just grin and bear it?"

"I wouldn't say that either. I think you ought to bring your concerns to the elders."

"The same elders that canned you."

Dad didn't respond to that particular remark. "Let them know your thoughts," he said. "Let them know you're the target audience and the method they're using to reach you isn't effective in your case. You may be the aberration, or you may find out—and they may find out—that you're more like the rule. At least it gives them something to think about. Just remember to be respectful, disagreeing in love."

I nodded. "That's what Cassie's dad said too."

"Wayne Larson's a good man," Dad said. "His advice is probably as sound as you'll find."

I nodded again. Talk to the elders. Express my concerns. I wasn't convinced it would have many results, but I surmised it was worth a try.

"How's your Bible study going?" Mom asked, beginning to collect the dishes. Reminding me I still had a third of a cut of cooling roast on my plate. I sawed into it with my knife.

"Okay," I said. "Our attendance kind of fluctuates, but the study is going well."

"Ephesians?" Dad asked.

"Yeah."

"And you're teaching?"

"So far."

"You like it?"

"Yes and no. It's a lot of work for what seems like very little benefit on Wednesday evenings. But I think the real benefit comes throughout the week, while I'm preparing."

"That's good," Dad said. "They say the best way to learn is to teach."

"That's what Dave said too."

"Well, you're getting all sorts of advice. You don't need us to tell you what to do."

After cleaning up and doing dishes, we went for a drive. Mom and Dad showed me around Norman and some of the surrounding countryside. They told me stories about arriving in town and being greeted by members of the church, adjusting to life in Oklahoma, and a few of the problems in the early weeks of the new pastorate. I in turn told them more details about my few interactions with Erica (Mom said things sounded promising) and hit the high points of my summer. A summer that was almost over. I couldn't believe it.

We returned home without seeing a single trailer park (my Uncle Bill may have placed a few thoughts about the quality of life in Oklahoma in my head) and relaxed in the backyard, checking out the flowers Mom had planted, drinking lemonade on the swing, and just being together. Come late afternoon, Dad fired up the grill and we had hamburgers for dinner. Even Mom's hamburgers tasted incredible.

After dinner we rented a movie and spent some more time talking about church and my spiritual progress and my future plans. Mom and Dad both agreed—as they had in the spring—that my decision to take a break from college until I had a major in mind was a good one. However, like me, they wondered what I would do with the rest of my life. They promised to pray for me, which was about all we could do at the time. I was learning that life was largely a waiting game.

I left for home Monday after lunch, with admonitions from Mom to watch out for other Labor Day travelers and with Dad making me promise to call when I got back to Morgan. I said I'd see them at Thanksgiving, if I could stomach the drive through Kansas and half of Oklahoma again.

For the first hour of the drive home, my mind was pretty much occupied with navigating Oklahoma City and its traffic. Once I was cruising through nowhere on I-35, my thoughts were free to wander to the things Mom and Dad and I had talked about over the weekend.

I also thought about Erica, picturing her at twice the weight, with blotchy skin and thinning, tangled hair. Would I still be wooed by her? I doubted it.

But the thing was, God had made her. He had created the DNA that would turn into a beautiful young woman. Appreciating and being drawn to that beauty couldn't be a sin any more than appreciating the grandeur of the Rocky Mountains or the brilliance of a sunset over the prairie. And hadn't God also created sex, and thus physical attraction between a man and a woman? So the physical appeal couldn't be sin either. Rather, it had to be an abuse of that appeal that turned it dirty. As with so much in life, it came down to lines. Problem was, they were often very thin and covered by a bunch of dust and dirt.

My thoughts gradually turned to Ephesians, and I reflected on what I'd learned so far. God had adopted me as His son, blessed me with "every spiritual blessing in Christ," saved me, made me alive in Christ, and made all the resources of His power available to me.

I crossed into Kansas praying that God would continue to help me appreciate all that He had done for me . . . and was doing for me. I prayed that He would help me to live my life — whatever it entailed — in a way that pleased Him. It was the least I could do in response. I prayed for help discerning my future, in dealing with church and my attitude about it, and in my relationship — whatever status it was in — with Erica. I determined to be pure with my eyes and my thoughts and my actions, but I knew I would need some help. So I prayed for that as well.

Morgan was still four hours away, and I thought of Ephesians again, about God's "incomparably great power for us who believe." Could that power also find me a wormhole to avoid the rest of the drive through central Kansas?

Chapter 36

". . . so that you also may know how I am and what I am doing." Ephesians 6:21

My first foray into having a better attitude at church despite the quirkiness was tested during the opening prayer, which immediately followed the announcements. I had my eyes closed, as usual, but for some reason—maybe a sound, maybe an itch—I opened them. They spotted a man, who had been seated in the pew in front of me, now on the floor under the pew, crawling from his aisle to my aisle.

I quickly closed my eyes again, figuring watching such a thing was rude. A grown man, crawling under the pews during prayer time. Had he dropped something? Realized he was in the wrong church and tried to make an unobserved getaway? Was he just mixing things up?

The prayer finished and I opened my eyes to see nothing out of the ordinary. Houdini had disappeared. Whatever.

There was no singing this Sunday. It was another themed service. We'd done singing, prayer/healing, and now apparently, a sermon service. Pastor Teasdale just preached for the entire hour, broken with a few videos from noted speakers, all addressing the topic of forgiveness. It was pretty good, albeit long.

I ran into Dave on the way to Sunday school. It was a coolish morning, and we were both getting some coffee. "How's your Bible study going?" he asked, grabbing a packet of creamer and a coffee stirrer.

"Good," I said. We stepped to the side, out of the way. It also gave us some privacy. "We've had about five or six people most weeks."

"That's good."

"It's not what I've expected."

"Oh?"

I explained about Gia, Scotty's arch-nemesis, being one of the regulars. She had come again the previous Wednesday. Amy and Damon had both been back, as had Gerhard. And Bobby, his senior citizen pal. Seven was our high-water mark, and our median age had doubled since the start of class. Checking over my shoulder to make sure we weren't being overheard, I told Dave as much.

"Well that's good," Dave said. "Having a varied age group is good for you, I think."

"Me?"

"You in general." He finished stirring and took a drink of his coffee. "How's the study itself going?"

"Good. We're into the practical half of Ephesians."

"Practical?" he asked, giving me the same look Gia had when I said the same thing to introduce the study Wednesday.

"Chapter one through the first half of four is more theology. The rest of the book is instruction on how to apply that theology."

He nodded.

"We're having good discussion."

"I'm glad."

We chatted for a few more minutes, then I asked, "You going to have a fourth crop?"

"Hope to," Dave said. "The weather's been cool so far. We'll see."

"Well, you have my number."

"On speed dial."

We said so long, and I headed to Room 104. I had no idea if the class was even still meeting or what sort of punishment the Teasdales had handed down to its members. It turned out things were back to normal, whatever that was, and Petey lectured on the Seven Bowls of God's Wrath. There was some discussion, a few rabbit trails that tried to fan out, but by and large, it was a standard Sunday school. Whether that was a result of Sandra Teasdale's lecture or just the nature of this week's material, I wasn't sure.

Erica did not sit by me. She showed up late, a sheepish smile on her face, and slid into the front row. Petey, to his credit, didn't admonish her in front of the class.

After the closing prayer and an announcement from Geoff about another fundraiser for the Haitians, Scotty tapped my shoulder. "I gotta go, dude. Bobby and I are going to get a quick round in before the Cowboys game."

"Bobby Van Engelenhoven?" I asked. The seventy-nine-year-old from our Bible study?

He nodded. "I'll call you."

"Okay."

I was punched in the other shoulder. I turned to see Erica. Red sundress, sleeveless, but not immodest. Hair in a low, loose ponytail. Smiling.

"Hey," she said.

"Hey," I rejoined.

"How you been?" she asked.

"Good. How have you been?"

"Pretty good." She leaned against the back of the chair in front of her, a posture that said she expected to be here a while, talking. I didn't mind. "How was Labor Day in Oklahoma?" she asked.

"Good," I said. "I hadn't seen my folks in months, so it was nice to visit for a while."

"How are they doing?"

"Good," I said. My fallback answer. I nodded, trying to stay casual. "How about you? Do anything?"

"Went to the Richmonds' on Monday afternoon," she said. "No football."

"Too bad."

"Mark was there too," she said. She looked over her shoulder. We were alone. "We talked for a while."

I swallowed.

"He said he wanted a second chance, wanted to prove to me that he could change."

I didn't have the spit to swallow again. I was able to make my head nod, barely.

Erica held her Bible against her waist, hands clutched underneath it. "I told him no." She looked up at me. "I said I didn't want him to change for me. I wanted him to change because it was the right thing to do. I said it was over between us."

I shushed the "Hallelujah Chorus" playing in my head and asked, "Are you okay?"

"I'm fine," she answered quickly. "My breakup wasn't a spur of the moment decision, and I've known it was the right thing to do. It's just hard after giving away a portion of your heart."

Had it been that serious? It had only been two months. Then again, people got married in less time. Like Dirk.

Erica smiled. "That sounds schmaltzy. But you know what I mean. Even when it's just casual dating, you open yourself up to that person, you consider possibilities . . ."

I didn't really know. Like I said, I've had three dates in my life, none with the same girl. To call that dating would be a stretch. I certainly hadn't opened my heart or anything like that. We'd had pizza and watched *The Monuments Men*. I had never considered the possibility that those girls would turn into anything other than maybe a second date. Maybe.

"So . . ." Erica said. "Two and oh."

Nebraska had outgunned Washington on Saturday for their second win of the season. It had been a nerve-racking first half until the Blackshirt defense had gotten it going. The Huskers had pulled away in the second half, and the latter part of the afternoon had been a blast.

"I told you, Rose Bowl," I said.

"Wait till we play the Badgers."

"They barely beat UTEP yesterday."

She grinned. "I am trying to temper my enthusiasm."

"Are you kidding? The enthusiasm's half the fun," I said. "It's like Christmas. The month-long anticipation of all those presents is more fun than the actual opening of the presents Christmas morning."

"We open Christmas Eve."

"Whenever."

"You still have a month-long excitement for Christmas presents?" she asked.

"Depends on the year."

Her smile turned to a sigh. "I should get going. I have to work today."

"Where do you work?"

"Administration department at Bryan Hospital," she said.

"In Lincoln? That's quite a drive."

"Yeah. And it's not even actual nursing, but it's a start." We started walking for the exit. "I tried to get in at the clinic in town, and I may be able to get some part-time hours, but not enough to pay room and board."

"I thought you lived with your folks."

"I do," she said with a sigh. "For now. But Daddy says he won't let me turn into a freeloader. I have to pay rent and chip in for groceries. And heat in my room come winter."

I smiled, not at her father, but at the fact that she called him Daddy. It was cute.

"I suppose if my folks hadn't been shipped to Sooner country, I'd have to pay my way too."

We stepped out into the hall.

"So, Mom and Dad are going to be gone next weekend, and the house gets kind of lonely. You want to do something, maybe?"

"Sure," I said, trying not to let my enthusiasm fly out of my mouth and slap her in the cheek.

"That sounded bad. I didn't mean that you're like a save-me-from-boredom failsafe or something."

"I didn't think that," I said. "But now that you mention it . . ."

"I'll give you a call?" she said with a grin.

"Sure."

We said goodbye and I stopped walking. Had she just asked me out on a date? If not a date, a pre-date? I'd even take her initiating hanging out.

"You certainly don't let the grass grow under your feet," Gia said.

I turned to her, wondering if I'd been staring after Erica with a dumb smirk on my face. "Just talking," I said. "Like you and I are now."

"Uh-huh."

"By the way, nice work with the idiom," I said. "Shows improvement."

Gia made a face and brushed past me. I resolved to do a better job of controlling my expressions when around Erica. And maybe only talk to her in back alleys in the fog after midnight, when nobody but a stray cat could observe us.

Wednesday was a beautiful late-summer day, more like a pre-fall day that was just warm enough to still be summer. A few of the trees in town were starting to turn, the ones that always did so way too early. Still, it was nice to see. Football had started, kids were back in school. Autumn was here.

My lesson on Ephesians 5 was pretty much ready, so I warmed up a pair of turkey potpies in the microwave and sat down in front of the computer. I checked my e-mail while the potpies cooled and then clicked my way to my favorite website for tracking the Huskers. Before I could read the latest scuttlebutt, a message appeared on my screen.

cassiemay1014: hey josh!!!

I stared at the screen for a moment while blowing on my fork before comprehending that Cassie had sent me an instant message. (It may be an antiquated form of communication, but I wasn't rich enough to afford a texting plan and had yet to join the Facebook revolution, so it was the best method available to us.) I set down my plate and the fork and reached for my keyboard.

softspeakingstickcarrier: Hey, Cass.

cassiemay1014: you know i never understood that screen name

softspeakingstickcarrier: Teddy Roosevelt quote.

cassiemay1014: hmm

cassiemay1014: so how are you

softspeakingstickcarrier: I'm good. How are you?

cassiemay1014: good

cassiemay1014: busy

cassiemay1014: tired

cassiemay1014: and i really miss home

cassiemay1014: ☹

I felt a pit in my stomach. I didn't know what to say — or rather, type — to make her feel better. I settled on the old male fallback, a change of subject.

softspeakingstickcarrier: How are your roommates?

cassiemay1014: um...

cassiemay1014: eclectic

cassiemay1014: theyre nice

softspeakingstickcarrier: That's good.

cassiemay1014: nobody uses punctuation in chats josh

cassiemay1014: or capitalization

softspeakingstickcarrier: And our society is in decay, too.

cassiemay1014: ☺

cassiemay1014: so whats new

softspeakingstickcarrier: Not much. Bible study tonight.

cassiemay1014: hows it going

softspeakingstickcarrier: We had 7 people last week.

cassiemay1014: thats great

softspeakingstickcarrier: Including two old codgers, Gerhard and Bobby Van Engelenhoven.

cassiemay1014: thats good

softspeakingstickcarrier: It is. They bring good insights.

cassiemay1014: has gia come back

softspeakingstickcarrier: Last two weeks.

softspeakingstickcarrier: No more fights.

cassiemay1014: whats up with erica

softspeakingstickcarrier: We may be having a date this weekend.

"May" was the operative word. She hadn't called me yet, and I was trying not to be nervous.

cassiemay1014: what?!?!?!

softspeakingstickcarrier: She and Mark are officially off.

softspeakingstickcarrier: He tried to get back with her over Labor Day, while I was in Oklahoma.

softspeakingstickcarrier: She rebuffed him.

cassiemay1014: and...

cassiemay1014: who says rebuffed

softspeakingstickcarrier: Guys who carry sticks.

cassiemay1014: the date!!!

softspeakingstickcarrier: She asked if I'd want to do something this weekend.

softspeakingstickcarrier: I said sure.

softspeakingstickcarrier: I guess it's technically not a date.

cassiemay1014: its a good sign

softspeakingstickcarrier: I thought so.

cassiemay1014: just be careful josh

cassiemay1014: shes still vulnerable right now

cassiemay1014: dont mistake needing a friend for wanting another boyfriend

cassiemay1014: sorry to be a downer

softspeakingstickcarrier: You're not a downer. I know to take it slow.

softspeakingstickcarrier: But this is still exciting.

cassiemay1014: i hope it works out for you

softspeakingstickcarrier: Me too.

softspeakingstickcarrier: So tell me about ASU.

cassiemay1014: i am loving it

cassiemay1014: great weather

cassiemay1014: 92 yesterday

cassiemay1014: perfect blue sky

softspeakingstickcarrier: How are classes?

cassiemay1014: ugh

cassiemay1014: hard

cassiemay1014: but also informative

cassiemay1014: im learning a ton

softspeakingstickcarrier: Is your soul staying uncorrupted in Liberal City?

cassiemay1014: i did watch that new vince vaughn movie with my suitemates this weekend

softspeakingstickcarrier: (Gasp!)

cassiemay1014: well half of it

cassiemay1014: it got gross

cassiemay1014: and i had homework

cassiemay1014: and...hang on a sec

I hung. And ate potpie that was cooling quickly.

cassiemay1014: so a bunch of girls are heading to dinner...

cassiemay1014: they invited me along

cassiemay1014: im looking for bonding opportunities

softspeakingstickcarrier: Go.

cassiemay1014: im still looking for the perfect postcard

softspeakingstickcarrier: It doesn't have to be perfect.

cassiemay1014: ill try to be in touch soon

softspeakingstickcarrier: Okay.

softspeakingstickcarrier: Have fun.

cassiemay1014: will

cassiemay1014: miss you

softspeakingstickcarrier: Miss you too.

I sat there for a few minutes as my screen told me that cassiemay1014 had left our chat. Then I reread the chat while eating, looking for words between the words telling me how she was doing. She sounded like the old Cassie, but it was hard to tell from an instant message.

I had to reheat the second potpie. I wolfed it down and then hurried over to Scotty's to report on how our girl was doing in the big city.

Damon, Gerhard, and Bobby joined Scotty and me for Bible study. All guys, two of them decades-long members of AARP. Whatever.

We studied Ephesians 5, focusing primarily on the early part of the chapter since we were all single.

"Either of you ever been married?" Damon asked our elder statesmen when we got to the part on submitting to husbands and loving wives.

Gerhard laughed. "Not yet."

"Yet?" Scotty asked.

"Bobby here's got himself a girlfriend."

We all turned to Bobby. I glanced at Scotty. If their golf outing Sunday had revealed such news, it hadn't been passed to me.

"Her name's Adeline," Bobby said.

"How long have you been seeing Miss Adeline?" Damon asked.

"Oh . . . going on twelve years."

"She's a Van de Kamp," Gerhard said, chuckling again. "Natural-born fear of commitment."

"You're related?"

"She's my cousin."

"Bobby, man, you gotta make a move," Damon said. "Give her an ultimatum."

"How's that?"

"An ultimatum, man."

"Make her choose," Scotty said.

"Dadblastit, I know what the word means. The boy mumbles."

Gerhard leaned over and peered in Bobby's ear. A moment later he pulled something out. I was horrified at first, until I realized it was just his hearing aid.

"You've got the blame thing turned off, Bobby."

"Must have forgotten to turn it on after church. That music's so cottonpickin' loud."

"We didn't sing this past week."

"How's that?"

Gerhard made a turning motion with his hand and waited until Bobby had turned on his hearing aid and replaced it in his ear.

"We didn't sing last week."

"Not? Hmm. Can't say why it was off then. Would explain why I haven't heard a blessed thing all week. What were we talking about?"

"My mumbling," Damon said.

"Your girlfriend," Scotty said.

"Ephesians five," I said.

"Whatever it was, we might as well start over," Gerhard said. "This daft old codger hasn't heard a word."

"You should talk after that poor woman at the grocery store last Saturday," Bobby said.

"You guys shop together?" Damon asked.

I interjected before this got completely crazy. "Do you all mind if I ask you a question, since we're already off topic?"

They all turned to me. Bobby fiddled with his hearing aid.

"Off the record, doesn't leave this room," I said. "What are your thoughts on Morgan Bible Church? Be honest."

"How do you mean, man?" Damon asked.

"General impressions."

"It's too cottonpickin' loud," Bobby said.

"I miss the old hymns," Gerhard said. "And I miss preaching through a book of the Bible. We're jumping all around like a frog on a blacktop road in the summer. I'd like a little continuity."

I nodded.

"I just wish we'd settle down," Damon said. "Every week it's one thing after the other. I can't remember the last time church was just church."

"I miss fellowship dinners," Bobby said.

"We had one this summer," Gerhard answered.

"I mean when we'd go to people's homes."

"We haven't done that in a decade."

"Well, I miss it."

"I thought you always complained about the food."

"I didn't go just for the food."

"Why on earth did you go then?"

"Mostly to see Adeline."

"You can see her any time."

Bobby stared at Gerhard for a moment, as if he had lost his mind. Then he shrugged. "I guess I don't miss the dinners all that much then."

"Forget us," Gerhard said with a wave. "They're appealing to you people."

"Us people?"

"Young adults," he said.

"You hear something?" Scotty asked.

"It's obvious. They don't sing new-fangled songs and play drums to win over the old people. They figure we're stuck here anyhow."

"You're not."

Gerhard shrugged. "This is home."

I turned to Damon and Scotty. "You guys feel appealed to?"

Scotty shrugged his face.

"I don't know, man," Damon said. "No more than I did before they started whatever it is they started."

I nodded and glanced at the clock. We had five minutes left, even though we really didn't have a defined closing time. "One more week of Ephesians," I said. "Any thoughts on where we should go next?"

"What comes next, Colossians?" Damon asked.

"Philippians," Gerhard said.

"Are you sure?"

"Yeah," Scotty said. "Galatians, Ephesians, Philippians, Colossians."

"That's right, Go Eat Pop Corn," Damon said.

We all looked at him. "What?" I asked.

"Go Eat Pop Corn. G-E-P-C. Galatians, Ephesians, Philippians, Colossians."

We all looked at him some more.

"I can't," Bobby said. "Cottonpickin' stuff gets stuck in my throat."

We turned our eyes to Bobby. He fiddled with his hearing aid.

"Colossians is good stuff," Scotty said.

"You want to skip over Philippians?"

"We skipped over Galatians."

"Philippians is after Ephesians," Bobby said.

"That's what we said, you old coot," Gerhard said.

"How's that?"

Gerhard waved him off.

I tabled the discussion until next week.

Damon closed us in prayer, and Gerhard drove Bobby home. At seventy-nine, he golfed and dated, but didn't drive. But who was I to judge? Damon, Scotty, and I shot hoops until sundown, and then Scotty and I headed inside to chill for a while.

"Josh, how goes it?" Dirk asked. He had been golfing when I arrived earlier.

"It's going," I answered.

"I hear your girlfriend broke up."

"Uh, yeah."

"Happy to hear it."

"Me too."

"So you shooting for the green or laying up?"

"I think I'm still on the tee. I'll see if I land in the fairway or the rough."

"Smart man."

"Ask you a question?"

He popped the top on a cream soda and sat down beside Scotty on the couch. "Sure."

"How'd you know when the time was right?"

Dirk stopped, the can almost to his mouth. He looked at me. "Just so we're clear, the time was right for what?"

"Shooting for the green," I said. "How do I know when I should go from being a shoulder to cry on to asking her out?"

"Are you a shoulder to cry on?"

I nodded.

"Then you're in the fairway, Josh. Striped down the middle."

I nodded again. "Okay. But metaphors aside, it's been a couple of weeks. How do I know when the time is right to . . . escalate things?"

"I had a surefire method," he said. He took a swig. "If the girl said 'yes,' then I knew the time was right."

Scotty shook his head. "That's great, Dad. Very helpful."

"No, but seriously, we had a code back in San Antonio when I was growing up. You wait at least half as long as they were dating, up to six months. Six was the cap. Unless the guy was your friend, then you'd better clear it with him first and double the length."

"What if he was just sort of a friendly acquaintance?"

Dirk took another drink. "No permission, but wait two-thirds."

If my math was correct, that meant about a month from the breakup. Or another week or two. So not this weekend, if indeed Erica did call back. But that was the minimum time, and I didn't want to rush things. I also didn't want to let somebody else swoop in either. I liked Dad's advice better, about how I would know when the time was right. But what if I didn't?

"You're worried too much," Scotty said, reading my mind. "Just stop thinking about it all. Let it happen."

Great, from the San Antonio Code to the Confuciusism of a fortune cookie.

Chapter 37

". . . after I have enjoyed your company for a while." Romans 15:24

According to Dave, a neighbor farmer once saw a mountain lion at his brother's farm south of Crete. This is the closest, to my knowledge, that a living cougar has ever come to Morgan. And yet, the folks in charge back in the day selected the cougar as the mascot for Morgan High athletic teams. I guess it sounded ferocious.

Erica had called me Thursday night, as I was going to bed. Wanna go to the Morgan-Louisville game tomorrow night? Sure. Come on over around six and we'll eat dinner and head over. Great.

I spent all day Friday pondering whether or not this constituted a date or not. Sydney voted yes. Dinner and an activity was definitely a date. Scotty voted no, because going to a high school football game was a lame date. Either way, I wasn't so much concerned with the technical definition of the evening as I was with Erica's definition. Did she mean for this to be a date? If not and I made my move, I would look like a jerk trying to move in on a friend in need. If so and I dithered, I might lose my chance. And what about the status of her recently broken heart? Even if she did intend for this to be a date, was it too soon? Should I resist any advances out of decency and not wanting to take advantage of her still-on-the-rebound heart? And given the fact that it was just a high school football game, would there be any opportunities for advances?

I kept hearing Dad's voice telling me I'd know the time and Cassie's voice telling me to take it slow and Sydney's actual voice telling me to make my move. In the end, I decided to take Scotty's advice. Sort of. I was just going to let it happen. Whether it was a date or just a friendly outing, I was going to spend the evening with Erica, the girl of my dreams. What did I care if it was a date or not?

I walked home from work and showered, not wanting to take a risk that a day of malt-making and ice cream-scooping had given me an off smell. I also prayed, as I realized I should have long ago, for God's wisdom and guidance—not just for the night, but for the near future with Erica. Then I resolved not to think about all this stuff again. At least not for tonight.

I dressed in jeans and a gray Husker hoodie. Then I switched to a plain black zip-up hoodie over a Husker T-shirt. I had always thought it would be cool to offer my letterman's jacket to my cold date, and since I didn't have a letterman's jacket, I figured a zip-up hoodie was the best bet. Erica was probably too sensible to dress in a way that would lend itself to getting cold, but I wanted to be prepared, just in case.

At ten to six, I couldn't wait any further. Her exact words had been "sixish" anyhow. I drove over, parking at the curb across the street from her house. The sun was still above most of the treetops, but it cast long shadows across the street and her lawn, contrasting with the otherwise brilliant yellow glow of late afternoon in the autumn. I couldn't help but think how nice the Haymarket would look in similar light.

Erica opened the door before the echo of the doorbell had died away. She wore a red hoodie—the one from the pool party, if memory served—and blue jeans. Her hair was down, cascading around the hood and spilling onto the front of her shirt. Her cheeks were bright, her eyes vivid.

I really wanted this to be a date.

"Hey. Come on in."

I followed her inside, feeling that odd sensation that came over me when I was alone with a girl. Maybe it had something to do with danger, since we were un-chaperoned, even though nothing was going to happen. Or maybe it was just the insinuation—guys and girls who were alone together usually were more than just a guy and a girl—they were a couple.

"I hope you like runzas," Erica said, stirring me from my thoughts.

"I do."

"They're just coming out of the oven," she said, leading me into the kitchen. It was very modern, with stainless steel appliances and an Italian theme that worked especially well with late afternoon sunlight flooding in through the window.

Erica bent over, tucking her hair behind her ear as she peeked into the oven. "Yeah," she said. "They're ready."

I looked at the counter. Two plates, two forks, and two glasses were set out. A bowl of lettuce salad sat between them, along with several bottles of dressing.

"There's water, pop, I think some tea in the fridge," she said. "Grab whatever you want."

There was indeed a pitcher of tea, and I lifted it out. "What do you want?" I asked.

She swung the pan of runzas out of the oven and looked at me. "Tea's fine."

I poured two glasses and left the remaining tea on the counter. Erica slid a spatula under a runza and lifted it to my plate. Her eyes glanced up at me as she held a second runza in the air.

"One to start with," I said.

She nodded and dropped the second runza onto her plate. She set the pan down and came around the counter to join me.

"Did you make these?" I asked as she took her seat.

"Try it first," she said. "If you like it, yes."

"And if not?"

"Leftovers I just heated up."

"Wow, throwing your mom under the bus?"

"We'll say they're from a family gathering."

I nodded and cut into my runza. Steam wafted out as beef and cabbage tumbled onto my plate. I scooped as much as I could onto my fork, blew once, and deposited the mixture into my mouth.

"Well?" Erica asked.

I swallowed. "So who all was at this family gathering?"

She backhanded me in the arm and I grinned. "They're good."

"Yeah, well, I made them the other night," she said, cutting into hers. "Part of that earning my keep bit."

"Well, they are good. Serious."

"Yeah, yeah." She took her first bite, then stopped and spat it onto the plate.

335

I raised my eyebrows.

"Didn't pray," she said.

"I'm not spitting mine up."

"Just bow your head."

I did.

"God, we thank You for these incredibly tasty runzas. Thank You for sending Josh into my life to be my friend. Please watch over us tonight. Amen."

"Amen," I said, wondering how much meaning I should glean from a three-sentence prayer.

"Have some salad," Erica said, passing it to me. I did. "So tell me about the Morgan Cougars. Are they any good?"

"So-so," I answered. "Made it to state back in '06. That was the high point."

"Will they win tonight?"

"Against Louisville? Maybe."

"I went to Southeast," she said. "It was pretty much a given every night."

"You have us outclassed a little," I said.

She took a bite of salad. "Did you play?"

"Look at me."

"I didn't ask if you were a nose guard."

"No, I didn't," I said, not volunteering that I had been scared of having my medium-sized frame destroyed by stronger, faster, meaner guys my age but not my size. Pointing out that you're a wimp isn't a great way to win a girl, I figured.

"Did you play any sports in high school?" I asked.

"No. Unless you count powder puff football."

"I bet you kicked some tail."

She glanced at me. "Some serious tail. I laid this one girl out. She came across the middle and caught a slant, and I was playing linebacker."

"You?"

The glance became a glare. "I stuck her, Josh. They made us play touch after that." She looked down at my plate. "You want another one?"

"Maybe half."

"And what am I going to do with the other half runza? In or out, Rosie."

"Then out. Only because I want to save room for nachos or a pretzel at the game."

"Fair enough. Finish the salad?"

"Okay."

I finished it, we cleaned up, and Erica excused herself to the bathroom. I found a mirror in the hallway and made sure there was nothing in my teeth. Then I crunched a mint quickly and waited for her to return.

She returned, stuffing some cash into the pocket of her jeans. "Ready?"

"Ready," I said. "If you don't mind bumming in the Escort, I'll drive."

"Actually, I was hoping we could walk."

I glanced at the clock. We had time. "Sure."

"Oops," Erica said at the door. "Keys. Be right back." She ran upstairs and I smiled at a girl as poised as Erica who spat out food because she hadn't yet prayed and who still forgot her keys.

"Let me guess," she said, bounding back down the stairs, "you small town folks never lock your doors."

"Did you pick up these home security tips from Mark?" I asked before thinking.

Erica stopped and looked at me.

"Sorry," I said. "Didn't mean to bring up a sore subject."

She shook her head. "No, it's okay. Come on."

Feeling like a dope, I followed her out of the house. She locked the door behind her and we started across the lawn. Her street teed into Cherry, which curved to run straight east-west at the southern edge of town. Cherry ran into 6th Street, and across 6th was Morgan High School.

"The truth is," Erica said as we joined the sidewalk, "I've been sort of avoiding talking or thinking about Mark. I mean, I'm over it and everything, but I've kind of been afraid to dredge up too many memories."

I nodded.

"I only really had one other 'relationship' in high school, and it didn't end so well."

"How so?" I asked as gently as possible.

"There was this guy named Willie. We'd been dating for about a month, and I thought he was a pretty solid Christian. Then one night after going to see a movie, he suggested we go for a drive. We headed out of town and found a nice secluded spot where he proceeded to suggest we slip into the backseat of his Chevy Tahoe and . . . well, you get the idea."

"Yeah."

"He didn't like the word 'no' either, so I had to give him a bloody nose with my elbow to get my point across. I got out and walked four miles back to town where I called Daddy to come get me. That sort of soiled the dating experience for me for a while."

"I believe it."

"Worse yet, his sister was one of my best friends. I thought she'd understand, take my side. Instead she spread the word that I had come on to him, tried to compel him to have sex with me, and then attacked him when he rejected me."

Erica looked down. "The people who really knew me didn't believe it, but . . ."

"Yeah."

"So, when I found out Mark wasn't the guy I thought he was, I was afraid we were headed down the same sort of a path as with Willie. I'm actually kind of mad I didn't break it off sooner."

"I know it probably doesn't mean anything, but I'm sorry for what you've gone through."

She turned my way and smiled. "No, it does mean something."

I smiled back. And breathed a prayer of thanks that I had friends and parents who had advised me to take things slow. This wasn't the girl to rush into a relationship with. I also prayed that Willie Whatever-his-name-was would be impotent for life.

"I, um . . . I have a confession to make," I said as we rounded the curve on Cherry. We were walking straight into the sun, and were both squinting.

"What's that?"

"Mark came to me the Sunday after you broke up. He wanted my advice on how to win you back."

"What'd you tell him?"

"The truth," I said. "That he would have to show signs of spiritual growth, and that it couldn't be motivated by a desire to show you he'd grown spiritually." I winced. "I hope you're not mad. I don't think he quite understood why you broke up with him."

"I'm not mad. And you're right, he didn't understand. I had to explain it in very painful terms on Labor Day. It was sort of like the rich young ruler and giving away his wealth. He went away sad."

I nodded.

"Not that I'm comparing myself to Jesus."

"I think the more accurate parallel is eternal life," I said.

"That either."

We walked in silence a little further.

"So how about you?" she asked. "Any crash and burn romances in your past?"

"Nope," I said.

"Any smooth landing romances?"

"None of those either."

"None?" She asked.

"Well, my parents had a rule about not dating until I was eighteen."

"Mine said sixteen."

"And to be frank, there weren't many candidates around here at the time. I had a few dates at college, but nothing serious."

She nodded, chewing on the corner of her lip. "Okay, this is sort of depressing," she said. "Let's not talk about love. Let's talk football."

"Okay."

"Any traditions I should know about? Do you guys release balloons or 'jump around' or anything?"

"The students like to stamp their feet on the bleachers," I said.

"Besides that."

"All the parents think the referees are nearsighted idiots with a bias against their kids."

"Besides that."

"We use Southern Cal's fight song," I said. "'Fight on, for Morgan High . . .'"

"That's pathetic."

"The singing or the song?"

"Both."

"Sorry."

"Do you play that annoying little ditty after every first down or defensive stop?"

I hummed a few notes. Maybe half a measure. "That one?"

She nodded with a wince. "This could be a long night."

"I think our defense is down this year, so there may not be a lot of stops."

"Why Southern Cal?"

"Beats me. Trojans, Cougars? I guess 'There is No Place Like Morgan' would have been a little much."

"Okay, so where's the best seat?" she asked.

"Anywhere but the back corners. Then the light poles get in your way."

We crossed 6th Street and joined the throng headed across the parking lot to the football field, which sat on the southwestern edge of the school property. On the east side were the home bleachers, built permanently into a hill that was higher than they were. A tunnel led through the middle of the bleachers, under the hill, and into the basement of the school and the locker room. The visitors had their own pathetic little stand of bleachers on the west side, butting up against a cornfield. Their locker room was a maintenance shed.

Admission was a paltry three dollars, and Erica had trouble getting her money out of her jeans pockets. I quickly slapped a ten on the counter. "On me," I said. For some reason, paying for her made me feel more like a man. And more specifically, like *her* man.

"I owe you one," she said as we headed for the bleachers. The band was in the middle left, and the parents in the middle right. Same spot they had always been in. I guided her a little further right, down far enough that the light pole wouldn't block our view.

I also kept an eye out for familiar faces. I knew how the rumor mill worked—the wrong person (like Gia) saw us together, and pretty soon word was around town that we were a couple. Part of me wanted that rumor floated because I liked the idea. But the other part of me didn't want to deal with it, and figured Erica wouldn't either. Come on, couldn't two friends just enjoy a ball game?

The visiting Louisville Lions wore white jerseys with purple and gold trim. They warmed up on the south end of the field, their helmets glistening in the setting sun. Morgan stretched and dry-ran plays on the north half of the field, decked in royal blue jerseys, bright yellow (gold was the official term for it, but it was yellow) pants and matching helmets. They looked sharp too, in the sun and under the lights.

It was a perfect evening for football, alive with excitement. Maybe it was the way every sound — from the yells and pad slaps of the players to the whistles of the coaches to the murmur of parents and family members — carried on the crisp night air. Or maybe it was the cool weather, a forerunner of the autumn to come. Maybe it was the sky, bright blue, tinged with purple behind us, on fire on the horizon in front of us.

No, it was probably the beautiful girl next to me, squinting with her hand over her eyebrow, trying to match players on the field with the paper program in her hand.

The players cleared off the field, adjourning to their separate locker rooms for last minute instructions before kickoff. The Morgan cheerleaders "entertained" us in the meantime, waving pompoms and clapping in rhythm. "Come on Morgan, let's go blue. Fight on Cougars, we love you!" Jump, kick, shout, clap, wave the pompoms.

I nudged Erica with my knee. "You ever a cheerleader?"

She gave me the dirtiest look two friends had ever exchanged at a football game.

"Did you ever beat one up?"

That cracked a smile.

A few minutes later, the cheerleaders formed a "tunnel" and the Morgan players burst out of the locker room, hailed by the band's rendition of "Fight On!" We all stood and clapped and stomped our feet. Some around us whistled. It was like being back in church.

The game commenced, and Louisville scored on the third play from scrimmage, a long pass to a wide open receiver. Their fans across the way smattered their applause.

Morgan tied the game four plays later on a long run by the fullback. He broke four tackles near the line of scrimmage and then raced away to a standing ovation. The band played "Fight On!"

"They could use you as a middle linebacker," I said to Erica.

For the rest of the first quarter, the teams traded punts. The sun set over the cornfield to the west, etching a magnificent scene across the sky. Cassie would have loved to paint it.

Come the second quarter, the scoring resumed. First Morgan drove for a touchdown and a 14-7 lead. Louisville quickly tied the game, then intercepted a pass to set up a second consecutive touchdown. They led 21-14 with four minutes to go in the half.

Morgan drove down to the goal line, and on fourth-and-one, decided to go for a tying touchdown instead of a field goal. They were stuffed and the crowd groaned as we hit halftime.

"Nachos or pretzel?" Erica asked.

"What are you having?"

"Whatever you're not so we can split them."

"Shrewd."

"Come on, I want to beat the lines."

I looked at her for a second. "If we're splitting, does it matter which one I pick?"

She licked her lips. "Fair point."

I started to reach for my wallet.

"This one's on me," she said.

"Thanks."

She nodded and disappeared up the steps, and I sat back and thought about how good my life was.

Chapter 38

"So the two of them sat down to eat and drink together." Judges 19:6

Erica returned just as the Morgan dance squad finished their interpretation of some hip-hop song. I wondered if Curtis Teasdale was in the process of booking them for Sunday morning. Erica handed me a tray of nachos and sat down, a soft pretzel in her lap. She broke it in half, handing a portion to me.

"Thanks," I said.

"That looks like fun," she said.

"What does? The dance squad?"

"No. That." She nodded at a group of little kids playing Nerf football on the hill. It wasn't organized, just a bunch of kids running around, occasionally passing a football, and tackling each other (and usually sliding down the hill as a result) without any adults to tell them to play two-hand touch because tackle was too dangerous. Yes, it did look like fun.

"I'll hold your pretzel if you want to play," I said. "I think you could take them."

She leveled her eyes at me and stuck a small piece of the pretzel into her mouth. "So what's your game plan, coach?"

"You mean the real game or if you join those kids?"

She kept her eyes leveled.

"Keep running Robards," I said.

"The fullback?"

"Mm-hmm."

She reached for a chip, dipped it in the cheese, and popped it in her mouth. "What about on defense?"

"Jump offside and hope the ref doesn't notice?"

"Ha."

I had a nacho myself. The referee blew his whistle and the third quarter began.

Morgan made it to midfield before throwing another interception, this one run all the way back to the four yard line. Louisville scored on the next play. Two holding penalties stalled the next Morgan drive and the punt was shanked out of bounds. The fix was in, the family section to our left declared. The refs had it in for our boys. Louisville kicked a field goal to push their lead to 30-14, and Erica nudged me.

"You want to go?" I asked.

"What? No." She frowned. "I want the last nacho."

I extended the tray to her. The cheese had long since clotted.

"Do you always give up this easily?" she asked.

"We are down by sixteen."

She just shook her head.

"And I'm not leaving," I said. "I thought maybe you wanted to."

Erica glared at me out of the corner of her eye while she chewed. She swallowed. "I work twelve hours tomorrow, Josh. I want this night to last as long as possible."

That made two of us.

"Then we'll stay," I said.

"Good."

"To the bitter end."

"Right. Unless Patrick Pick Six throws another interception," she said.

His name was Patrick McGee, and he actually threw two touchdowns, bringing the score to 30-27 (Morgan missed a two-point conversion after the first score) with just over five minutes to play. Now the Morgan defense needed to force another stop.

They didn't. Instead the Louisville running back broke around the right end for sixty yards, down to the nine. A yelling, clapping, stomping bunch of fans were suddenly drowned out by the whoops and hollers of a few across the way.

But the Morgan defense rallied and held Louisville to a field goal. Trailing by six with two minutes to play, they still had a chance.

"Do you like hot chocolate?" Erica asked.

"Huh?"

"Do you?"

"Yeah, I suppose."

"With marshmallows in it?"

I shook my head, not knowing where this conversation was going. "Sure."

"Maybe a whisper of cinnamon?"

"I can take or leave the cinnamon."

"Would you like a cup, after the game? Mom has this mix, made from scratch."

"Okay."

Erica nodded. Her hands were sucked into her sleeves. Hey, if you need somebody to hold those to keep them warm . . .

A freshman, forced to return kicks due to an earlier injury, muffed the ball, chased it back toward the goal line, kicked it sideways, and finally pounced on it at the one yard line just before the swarm of Louisville defenders fell on him. I felt sorry for the poor kid, especially when several of the angrier parents grumbled about how he shouldn't even be on the team.

"Jerks," Erica whispered.

The Morgan offense huddled under the shadow of their own goalpost. The scoreboard clock read 1:47. No problem for Aaron Rodgers and the Packers, maybe. But Patrick McGee wasn't Aaron Rodgers.

The Cougars lined up with two tight ends on first down, a fullback and tailback behind McGee. He took the snap and immediately plunged right, a quarterback sneak to get some breathing room. Only he kept sneaking. Louisville's defense was misaligned, and instead of falling on the back of his line for a small gain, McGee dashed forward, then bounced outside.

As one, the crowd stood. McGee was at the fifteen and he was kicking it into high gear. The entire Louisville defense rushed toward the near sideline, looking like a white and purple avalanche. And Patrick McGee was the skier, squirting down the sideline before the avalanche arrived. He cut back to avoid one defender, accelerated back to full speed, back toward the middle of the field, and was gone.

People in the stands began shouting, raising their hands, shouting some more. McGee was at the forty, with only a Louisville safety in position to catch him. At the thirty, McGee was dying. At the twenty, he was a goner. By the ten, the safety was on his heels. At the five, McGee dove for the end zone as the Louisville player lunged for him. McGee landed, ball outstretched, on the goal line. The referee signaled touchdown. The crowd went bananas.

Hugs, high-fives, war whoops. Even Erica and I, relatively disinterested bystanders compared to the parents and students, got into the action, slapping hands with strangers around us. Odd how people bond so much over a high school athletic competition.

The band forgot to play until after the extra point, which the poor kicker shanked and almost missed. One minute and twenty-nine seconds remained in the game. On the sideline, Patrick McGee had his head between his knees, gasping for breath. I couldn't believe it—we had just seen a ninety-nine-yard quarterback sneak.

"And you wanted to leave," Erica said, drilling me in the shoulder.

"I didn't want to leave. I thought you wanted to leave."

The game wasn't over. Louisville returned the kick to the forty, causing a nervous hush to come over the crowd. The students revived them, stomping on the metal bleachers, and the Morgan defense responded. They turned Louisville over on downs, and the crowd and players and cheerleaders erupted again. Two kneel-downs and the game was over.

We crossed the parking lot and headed back east on Cherry Street. The lights of the football field were still lit behind us, and our shadows stretched halfway down the block in front of us. We walked slowly, I know because two other groups passed us, one on our sidewalk, one on the sidewalk across the street.

"Thanks for agreeing to walk," she said after a while.

"Sure. It's a nice night," I said. The moon had risen sometime during the second half and contributed to the bright evening.

"Zach was killed on his way back from a high school football game," Erica said. "I know it's ridiculous, but I've just preferred to walk to games since."

"That's not ridiculous," I said.

Erica looked at me but didn't say anything. Behind us, the stadium lights flicked off and the moon alone lit our way. That and streetlights. But the moon was far prettier.

"Did Zach play?" I asked several strides down the sidewalk.

"Not football. He played tennis."

I nodded. We walked some more.

"He was good, too. He was hoping to play at UNL."

"Do you play tennis?"

"No. Not anymore."

Every guy — at least according to the books about guys — wants to save the damsel in distress. Fighting dragons and beating off guys named Willie and stuff. But it was emotional issues — scraping and saving to afford college, breaking up with four guys in one summer like Sydney, dealing with the death of a sibling — that caused the majority of the distress. And I either didn't have the genetic makeup or hadn't read enough guy books to know how to slay those dragons.

We turned onto 8th Street. "You still want some hot chocolate?" Erica asked.

"I do."

Our pace quickened. We entered the house and Erica flipped on lights on our way to the kitchen. She opened the pantry and pulled out a canister. "Cocoa mix," she said, handing it to me.

"The homemade secret recipe?"

"You got it."

She continued to dig around.

"Is it a two-part mix?" I asked. "Kept in separate containers for secrecy?"

"No, I can't find the marshmallows."

"That's okay."

"No, it is absolutely not. You can't have hot chocolate without marshmallows."

"I can deal."

"Word will get out that I'm a lousy hostess," she said. She began opening and closing random cupboards, exposing cups and pitchers and spices and dish towels. No marshmallows.

Erica turned to me, sighing heavily. "You think Don & Flo's is still open?"

"Are you serious?"

"Dead serious."

I shrugged. "No, but Wieskamps' probably is."

"You mind driving?"

"Not at all."

We left the lights on and headed for my car. "I can't believe we don't have any marshmallows," Erica muttered as I pulled away from the curb.

"I can't believe you're this obsessed," I said.

"I can't believe you have such low standards."

"I can't believe . . . I've got nothing."

"That's what I thought."

I was by no means an expert on flirting or signals or reading girls (maybe why I'd only had three dates thus far in life) but I was getting a positive reading from Erica's behavior. Then again, I was also starting to think she was just this way all the time. A little bit of a flirt, a little bit of a flake, an awful lot of fun.

Wieskamps' was indeed open, and somewhat to my surprise, sold marshmallows. Erica grabbed two bags to make sure this sort of thing didn't happen again. Then we headed back to her place. I used the bathroom—and made sure I wasn't dripping snot all over thanks to the cool weather—and returned to the kitchen to find her measuring cocoa mix into a pair of giant mugs. Water was boiling in a teapot on the stove. All that was missing were the frosty edges on the windows.

Erica returned the canister to the pantry and pushed the sleeves up on her sweatshirt. Her cheeks were still a little flushed from being outdoors, and her eyes sparkled with that combination of mischief and amusement and a whole bunch of other things I couldn't wait to find out about.

She flung the bag of marshmallows at me. "Open those, will you?"

I opened the bag while she got out two spoons. Then I handed it back to her and she poured out a handful of marshmallows. "That enough?" she asked, extending the handful to me. I pretended to be analyzing the number of mallows, but was really studying her hands. They were perfect in every way, and I envied those little puffs of sugar.

"What, are you counting them?"

I looked up at wide brown eyes. "Yeah, that's enough."

She dumped them into my mug, then poured a similar amount into hers. On second thought, she added a few more. The teapot whistled, and she poured water. We stirred. She grabbed a sleeve of shortbread Girl Scout cookies and we sat down at the dining room table. The living room would have been more comfortable, but I couldn't judge a girl who had almost been raped once by a thought-to-be Christian for avoiding getting too comfortable too fast with another guy — even if he was just a friend after a football game.

"How is it?" she asked after my first sip.

"Definitely not left over from a family gathering."

She smiled and nodded. I took another sip and wiped melted marshmallow off my lip.

"Thanks for listening before . . . about Zach."

I met her eyes and nodded.

"You're a good listener. You don't say too much. Most people want to try to fix my problems with a pithy paragraph. Otherwise they quote Romans 8:28 to me. I believe Scripture, Josh, but there's a time not to trot out verses like aspirin."

"I agree. And you're welcome. The truth is, I probably would have said something pithy but nothing came to mind."

"Well, at least you didn't force it."

I drank more cocoa. She dunked a cookie.

"So I've kind of unloaded all of the problems on my life on you — Zach, Willie, Mark. You need an attentive ear for any crises?"

Aside from wondering if you'll marry me?

"Well," I said, stirring my cocoa to make sure it didn't get nasty at the bottom. "I wouldn't mind some advice on what to do with the rest of my life."

"Even if it's pithy?"

"Even if."

"Even if I say, '*For I know the plans I have for you*'?"

I nodded and popped a cookie into my mouth. Delicious.

"Well . . ." She sat back. "What do you want to do with your life?"

I chewed for a moment. "I don't know."

"Come on. Dream scenario. You get paid and it's in God's will, what do you do?"

"Are you talking realistic dream or pipe dream?"

"What's the pipe dream?"

"Professional golfer," I said, reaching for another cookie. I really like shortbread cookies.

"Okay, realistic dream."

"I'd coach football," I said. "I love the game, I'm fairly knowledgeable about it, and I'd like to help mold young men, help them grow from boys to men . . . You know, once I figure it out myself, being all of twenty."

Erica's smile warmed me more than the cocoa. "That's nice," she said.

I shrugged and smiled back before inserting the second cookie into my mouth.

"You couldn't leave when the team was down by sixteen."

I narrowed my eyes at her.

"So why don't you become a coach?" she asked.

"It's not that easy. Unless you're the head coach at a major university, you probably have to teach something too, and I don't know what to teach."

"Hmm."

"And they say coaching burns you out, is hard on the family—especially if you ever make it big and coach at, say, Nebraska."

"So is that part of the dream?"

"Coaching at Nebraska? Yeah, but we're probably back to the pipe dream."

"I meant a family."

"Oh." I nodded. "Yeah, eventually."

Erica took a drink.

"What about you?" I asked. "Are you still in a holding pattern?"

She looked up at me. "What, were you hiding a tape recorder?"

I shrugged. "I've got a good memory." Especially when the girl of my dreams tells me her dreams.

"Technically I'm still holding," she said after a moment. "I'm taking some online courses in my free time—just generals to fill in some holes if I do decide to go for a nursing degree."

"And if not?"

"Then maybe I'll just get a plain old Associate of Arts degree, pad the résumé." She shrugged. "Otherwise, I don't know. I want to serve God, but I want to serve Him His way, not mine."

"Do you have any pithy thoughts on how to find His will?" I asked.

"If I did, I'd write a best-seller on it."

"You wouldn't be alone."

"So . . . in the meantime, I keep praying. I'll add you to the list."

"The list?"

"Of people with no direction that I pray for."

"Is it a long list?"

"Medium."

"Mine too," I said. "One less, now that Cassie's at college. I guess you can have her slot."

"Gee, thanks."

"I didn't—"

"I know," she said. She drained her hot chocolate. Mine was already gone. "I hate to tarnish my already tainted hostess rep, but I should probably kick you out. Six a.m. comes early."

"Yes it does. Ouch. I plan to sleep till noon and watch football with Scotty all day."

"Shut up."

I smiled. "Thanks for the hot chocolate. And the nachos and pretzel. And the runzas."

"You forgot the salad."

"Thanks for that too."

"Thank you for listening," she said. "I mean it."

"Anytime."

I stood and carried my mug into the kitchen, setting it in the sink. Erica walked me to the door and hung against the trim. "Tonight was fun," she said. "We should do this again sometime."

I nodded. "We should."

"I'll see you Sunday?"

"Yeah. Good night, Erica."

"Good night, Josh."

I strolled back to my car, still wondering if that had been a date or not. Maybe not technically, but it sure felt like one. Whatever it was, it had been a lot of fun.

And that's when it dawned on me. Dating was sort of like Christmas as a kid. As great as opening presents on Christmas morning was, the anticipation was almost as great. Sometimes better. I wondered if maybe the pursuit of Erica—the anticipation, the flirting and the backhanded shoulder slaps and just hanging out with no expectations—might not be worth savoring and enjoying.

I had a metaphor for Dirk. Forget Thursday at the Masters. It was December 1. I was listening to Bing Crosby and stringing garland around the house. I couldn't wait for Christmas. But the three and a half weeks leading up to it wouldn't be bad either.

Chapter 39

"When someone invites you to a wedding feast . . ." Luke 14:8

September went out like a lion. (That is, if "like a lion" is symbolic for hot, summer-like weather — the "out like a lion, in like a lamb" thing was another metaphor I never could figure out.) October came in similarly. Fall had been delayed a few weeks in southeastern Nebraska, but nobody seemed to mind. I certainly didn't, but then again I wasn't minding much these days. My life was humming along nicely, thank you.

For the better part of three weeks, I had meditated on the night Erica and I had shared at the Morgan-Louisville game. She'd been busy with online classes and work, apparently trying to imitate Cassie, and we hadn't seen each other much since then, other than at church. That was okay — the memory could last me a lifetime.

Speaking of Cassie, she was adjusting well to Arizona State. She was burdened under a mountain of schoolwork, so her correspondences were hurried and few and far between. But I guessed that was good.

Things at church were going better. Actually, they were about the same, but I had been doing a better job of trying to focus vertically — trying to concentrate on the important things. I was still planning on talking to the elders at some point, but first I was clandestinely taking the temperature of my generation. I wanted to be prepared when I did approach the church leadership, so as to make the most of our meeting.

But there hadn't been anything too crazy, just one more day of whistling. Sunday school had also calmed down, with a little more rapture talk but no more lectures from Sandra Teasdale.

And Nebraska was 5-0, having just manned up and stuffed the Wisconsin running game in a 21-9 victory that had Erica believing in our defense, even against power sets. Around the state, we were smelling roses.

It all combined to make me pretty happy, even if I was stuck working a nine-to-five on Wednesday the third of October. I was sort of in a rut at Nebraska Novelties, to the point where my job was no longer a challenge. There was nothing I couldn't handle (even the waffle cone maker). But it wasn't an unpleasant rut, because since my quarterly performance review at the end of August, I was pulling down twenty-five cents more per hour, thank you. It added up.

Bible Study that night was on Colossians 2 (we had indeed settled on Colossians after Ephesians). After work, I sat down to leftovers and reviewed my lesson plan. I had been elected to remain the teacher, and was glad. I sensed I was getting a lot more out of it by doing all the prep.

After almost two months, our group had pretty much rounded out. Scotty, Damon, Gia, and Gerhard were turning out to be regulars; Amy and Bobby came and went. By all indications, the study was going well. I had received several positive comments on the effects of the study, and had noticed growth in my own life as well. Ephesians and Colossians had reminded me of God's almighty nature and highlighted how much He loves me and how much He's done for me. The change was small, but I felt more appreciative and more in tune with my Heavenly Father.

It was boys' night again, with Gerhard and Damon joining Scotty and me. We attacked Colossians 2, studying "all the fullness of the Deity" living "in bodily form" in Christ, and His "having disarmed the powers and authorities" by making "a public spectacle of them, triumphing over them by the cross." It was good stuff.

Afterwards, Gerhard and Damon both asked if they could bring someone along next week, or if I was happy with our current dynamic. Our current dynamic changed from week to week, and I wasn't in charge anyhow. I said sure.

I walked home, grabbing the mail from the apartment's cluster box and carrying it up to my apartment. Slid between my electric bill and a credit card pre-qualification was a postcard, showing a silhouetted cactus backlit by the most beautiful orange, yellow, and pink desert sunset.

Inside the apartment, I closed the door, tossed the other mail toward the counter, and leaned back against the door to read the postcard.

Josh,

I'm really starting to like it here. I mean, I've always liked it, but you know. Temps are in the 90s every day (still) and it's only rained like once. And the mountains still amaze me, even if they are all brown. I'm getting along pretty well with all my roommates, especially Shelly (the cowgirl from MT). School is keeping me really busy, and I'm working almost 30 hours/wk. Ugh. How are things with you know who? I pray for you every day. Except for the day I had my first Middle Ages test – double ugh. And Thanksgiving isn't looking great, but I'm still hoping. I miss you tons. Postcards are too small. Love ya. Cass

I read the postcard four times before clipping it to my refrigerator.

Sunday and Monday the wind howled across the plains. The weather was cold and cloudy and raw and miserable, and my mood took a turn for the worse. Maybe it was just my rut at work getting a little deeper. Maybe it was the fact that Sydney had broken up with another guy and had been a bear. Maybe it was the fact that Erica hadn't been in church so I hadn't gotten my weekly fix. Maybe it was the fact that Nebraska had lost 27-21 at Ohio State Saturday night. It didn't destroy their Rose Bowl chances, but it sure took away some of the early season enthusiasm. Maybe it was the postcard still on my refrigerator, reminding me that my best friend was half a continent away.

Or maybe it was a combination of all of the above. Whatever the cause, I was in a funk as I drove to work Tuesday morning, the wind threatening to blow me off course. But it also finally cleared out the overcast skies, bringing in beautiful blue sunshine by afternoon. I don't know if it was the weather or just time taking its toll, but my mood started to come around. I left work (after doing my best to give a caring pep talk to Sydney) and drove home. Good thing the weather had been crummy and cool, or I might have walked and missed the phone call.

"Hello?"

"Hey, Josh. It's Erica."

The sun had come out a second time.

"Hey," I said. "What's up?"

"Don't hate me . . ."

"Are you going to give me a reason to?"

"It's short notice, but are you free a week from Saturday?"

For anything. "Yeah, why?"

"A friend of mine from high school is getting married. I completely spaced on the invitation, and I need to let her know if it will be just me or if I'm bringing a date."

My heart sounded like snare drums in my chest. I played it cool. "I didn't picture you for a space."

"I'm not a space. Call it a blonde moment."

"Yeah, I'm free."

"Great."

Great didn't begin to describe it. She had used the word "date."

"Just so you know," she said, "I'm not one of those girls who has to have a date so I don't look pathetic."

"But you need a date so you don't look pathetic?"

I pictured the look I was sure she was giving me, and it made me smile.

"Aside from the bride and the bridesmaids, I'm going to know like two people there," she said. "I'd rather not spend the day alone. Not a sterling invite, I know, but what can I say?"

"It's fine," I said. "What time?"

"Wedding's at two, at Sunken Gardens, and dinner's at six."

"We play Northwestern at two-thirty."

"Are you having second thoughts?"

"Nope."

"Okay, because I am. Anyhow, you'll go?"

"I'll go."

"Great. I've got to get back to work, but I'll see you Sunday? We can lay out plans."

"Sounds good."

"Thanks, Josh."

"Sure thing."

I smiled and hung up the phone. It rang a minute later.

"Hello?"

"Forgot to ask, chicken or beef tips?"

"Beef tips."

"Yeah, wedding chicken is usually dry."

"I'll take your word for it."

"See ya."

"Bye."

The phone didn't ring again. That was okay. I had a complete Bible study lesson to prepare. And my short-lived doldrums were completely gone.

Scotty, Gia, Amy, Damon, Gerhard, Bobby, and a guy named Georgie attended Wednesday night. Georgie was Gerhard's old pal and also a guy Damon knew from The Piedmont. He walked with a cane and his sweater smelled like vegetable soup, but he was there to learn. So be it.

I scanned the room after prayer. Two white guys, a white girl, a Cuban girl, a black guy, and three old codgers. This had to be the most diverse gathering in the history of Morgan.

Our study was on Colossians 3—setting our hearts and minds on things above, putting to death the earthly nature, putting on the new self, clothing ourselves with *"compassion, kindness, humility, gentleness and patience,"* and letting Christ rule and dwell in us. I closed by reading verse seventeen: *"'And whatever you do, whether in word or deed, do it all in the name of the Lord Jesus, giving thanks to God the Father through him.'"*

Or rather, I tried to close. Bobby had a question about verse sixteen. "What are spiritual songs? It says, '*Let the word of Christ dwell in you richly as you teach and admonish one another with all wisdom, and as you sing psalms, hymns and spiritual songs with gratitude in your hearts to God.'* So what are spiritual songs? Are they different from hymns?"

"And why don't we sing Psalms?" Gerhard asked.

"Because Hebrew music sounds lousy," Scotty said.

"I have The Message," Amy said, "and it says—"

"That's a paraphrase," Scotty said.

"So?"

"So it's not a translation."

"What message?" Bobby asked.

"Who says it's not a translation?" Amy asked.

Scotty shrugged. "People who know."

"Josh?"

"I don't know. I've read the NIV since I was three."

"You could read at three?"

"You couldn't?"

"Does *'spiritual songs'* mean these new-fangled praise choruses?" Bobby asked.

"Some of them aren't very spiritual," Gerhard said.

"Maybe it is just repetition," Gia said. "Stressing the point."

"So the Bible just wastes words?" Amy asked, apparently giving up on the wording in her translation/paraphrase.

"Repetition is used a lot," Gia said.

I nodded. "She's right. That could be it. Or it could mean psalms and hymns and other kinds of music—all kinds of music."

"So does that mean we're going to keep singing these new-fangled songs?" Bobby asked.

"What do you mean new-fangled?"

"The tune," he said. "They're . . . I can't sing them. And they're loud."

"That should help you," Amy muttered.

"How's that?"

"Whatever they were," I said, "I don't know that we have the same type of music two thousand years later. I think Gia's right—it's stressing the idea of singing to God, however you do it."

"Can't we do it with hymns?" Bobby asked.

"Or at least songs with a more fluid tune," Gerhard said.

"Or a tune at all," Amy mumbled.

"How's that?"

"We'll start a petition," Scotty said. That closed it. We prayed. Study was over.

"Can you believe this?" Amy asked. Gerhard and Bobby were on their way out, and Damon had already left, taking Georgie back to The Piedmont. "This study's turning into an AARP meeting," she said.

"I'd rather they come than nobody," I said. "And they contribute."

"Are you saying I don't?"

"No, I'm saying they do."

"I was going to bring bars next week, but maybe I'll bring pudding and Geritol."

"You should be happy," Scotty said. "Else we'd be calling you the grandma of the class."

"Only once," she retorted.

He smirked.

Amy looked at Gia warily, then back at me. "Is it true you're going to tell the elders off?"

"What?" I asked. Gia's head had whipped around, as expected.

"It's not true?" Amy said. "I heard a rumor."

"From where?"

"I don't know. I heard you took a poll at class a few weeks ago."

That lowered the possible moles to Scotty, Damon, Gerhard, and Bobby.

"I'm not going to tell the elders off," I said.

"Oh. Because if you did, I want to be there."

"I'll be sure to keep that in mind."

"The Bible says you need two witnesses. I'll be number two. Anyhow, I have to go. My friend raised somebody from the dead, so we're having a little party."

"Hold on there, Dorcas," Scotty said. "Run that past me again."

"My friend's an ER nurse, and she brought a guy back. Dead for two minutes."

"Sounds like a book deal to me," he said.

"Brownies and ice cream at least." She waved. "Bye."

That left Scotty, me, and Gia, who surprisingly had hung around. "How's Cassie doing?" she asked.

"I haven't heard much from her lately," I said. "But I think she's doing okay."

Scotty confirmed with a nod.

"Next time you talk to her, tell her I'm praying for her."

"I will," I said. "Thanks."

Gia flashed what amounted to a smile and left.

"She might not be pure evil," I said to Scotty as the door closed behind her.

"Might not."

Then I told him about Erica and the wedding. And hoped I'd get to tell him about Erica and a wedding again someday.

Chapter 40

"Does a maiden forget her jewelry, a bride her wedding ornaments?" Jeremiah 2:32

Saturday the 20th dawned overcast, but with a ribbon of blue on the southwestern horizon. By mid-morning, the blue had tripled in size as the cloud cover slowly moved out. It was looking like a spectacular autumn day.

I nervously debated my choice of attire. On one hand, this was an outdoor wedding. But that didn't mean hoedown. And while the weather appeared to be clearing, it wasn't going to be terribly hot. I settled on casual classy. White dress shirt, understated tie, a royal blue V-neck sweater that I was sure brought out my eyes. Light brown—almost khaki—pants, no pleats, but none of those wrinkly side pockets either. I rolled up the sleeves on my sweater and dress shirt to just below the elbow, and determined I looked quite dapper. Even my hair, which was styled with just enough product to make it behave, looked good. What a day.

I was picking Erica up at quarter to one. I had offered to drive, if she didn't mind showing up at the wedding in a twenty-year-old Escort. Not if I was a gentleman and got the door for her, she had said. I had lunch, nothing heavy, nothing to give me bad breath, and nothing that might fall on my royal blue sweater.

At twenty to one, I checked myself once more in the mirror, determined I had nothing in my teeth or any fuzz on my sweater, and headed out the door. The clouds were gone, a distant memory now over Iowa. Good place for them.

The afternoon was perfect. The sun was warm on my skin but the gentle breeze was autumn cool. The leaves around town were peaking, vivid oranges and reds. Fallen leaves were strewn across the lawns and sidewalks and collecting against the curb, crunching under your feet when you walked. I wished I could bottle it . . . In a few weeks it would be gone again for another year.

I parked in the driveway and strolled up to the front door. I had determined not to rush anything this day, but to enjoy every second of it. I also had determined not to analyze it, debating with myself whether it was a real date or a friend date or just two people going to a wedding. (Sydney voted real date, Scotty had only shrugged.) However, all of my determining was likely to go out the window the first time Erica spoke.

Her mom opened the door, introduced herself as Amanda, and said I looked sharp as she invited me in. "Have a seat," she said. "Erica will be right down."

She was just preparing lunch and asked if I was hungry.

"No thanks," I said.

"I was told to apologize to you for not keeping marshmallows in stock."

I grinned. "It nearly destroyed our evening."

Amanda smirked and picked up two plates. "Nick's got a game on, I'm sure. You're welcome to join us."

"I would, but I'm afraid I'd never get up if I did."

"I know the type. Why do you think we're eating in the living room?" She paused at the bottom of the steps, juggling the plates. "Erica!"

I heard a response from up the stairs but couldn't interpret it.

"She'll be right down," Amanda said as she took the plates into the other room. I stood up and leaned against the counter. A moment later, I heard footsteps on the stairs.

High heels appeared, followed by magnificent ankles, tanned legs, then a floral patterned dress that was sleek enough to be formal, but flared enough to be a little fun. The background was white, the flowers big and multi-colored. Red, maroon, orange, and pink. Pink dominated. The neckline was partially concealed by a bright, reddish-pink shrug, the sleeves down to the elbow. A silver locket hung just above the cut of the dress, matched by string earrings. A wide ribbon — also pink-red — ran through her hair, behind the ears and a fringe that was swept to the side of her face. The rest of her hair was down, wavier than normal, curling around her shoulders. I smiled as she descended; I couldn't imagine anything more beautiful.

"Hi," she said, smiling back adorably. She wore a trace of makeup, which was more than she needed. A small purse was over her shoulder, tucked under the arm.

"Hi," I returned.

"You ready?" she asked.

"Yeah."

Erica turned toward the living room. "Bye!"

"Bye, honey."

"Call if you'll be late."

"I will." She turned to me. "Let's go."

I held the front door for her, then quickly caught up to her so I could open her car door. A deal was a deal. I circled the front of the car, squinting into the sun, wondering how I'd gotten such a deal.

I settled into my seat, but before starting the car, turned to Erica. "I'd be remiss and a cad if I didn't tell you, you look great," I said.

Erica beamed. "Thanks. You don't look so bad yourself. But no one says cad anymore."

I smiled to myself as I buckled my seatbelt and turned the key in the ignition, thinking that if I had been analyzing, this would have counted as a positive exchange.

As I navigated out of Morgan and west toward Firth, we caught each other up on the last few weeks. Erica was busy working and busy doing homework online. Her courses were self-paced, which fit nicely into her schedule, but also made it hard to stay motivated. Why do homework tonight when I can watch *Friends* reruns on Netflix instead and do the homework tomorrow? she reasoned.

I didn't have much to tell her, as my life had been pretty routine of late. Rut-like, even. But that was okay—her voice was David's harp.

As we neared Lincoln, I figured I'd better bone up on the wedding party. "So what's your friend's name?" It had started with an R, I was pretty sure.

"Tara."

So at least it had an R.

"From high school?"

"We were close junior year. Then things got busy, she got a boyfriend."

"The husband?"

"No."

"Do you know the husband?"

"No."

I nodded. "Can I ask you something?"

"Yeah."

"It's kind of personal."

She looked my way. "Okay."

"Are you not getting them a gift?"

Erica's eyes got wide. "Josh." Wider still. "Josh!"

"Blonde moment?"

"Uh-huh."

"You know where they were registered?"

"Mmm, no time. Just go to Kohl's. Yankee Hill and 27th. It's sort of on the way."

I turned onto Yankee Hill Road a half mile later.

"I can't believe this," she said. "You must think I'm a total flake. Almost forget the wedding, forget a gift."

Maybe you just had other things on your mind. Like me?

"I cannot believe it," Erica said, digging through her purse. "Do you have a watch?"

"No." I pointed at the dash clock.

"One-twenty already?"

"It's five or ten minutes fast."

"We're going to have to divide and conquer. Can I trust you to buy a decent card?"

"Yeah."

"Nothing with butts on it or a *Far Side* cartoon or anything. Something nice, something serious. Generic."

"Must it be a Hallmark?"

"No. Just a nice card."

"And where will you be?" I asked as I turned into the access road to Kohl's.

"Candles and photo frames," she said. "You can never have enough of either."

I found the closest parking spot I could and we hurried inside. Watching women run in high heels is funny, even if they're just sort of fast-walking. But a gentleman doesn't laugh at his date (or whatever she was) in crisis.

"Remember, nice, nothing goofy."

"I got it."

We split up, then rejoined because the candles and photo frames at Kohl's were kept relatively close to the greeting cards. I perused the selection carefully but quickly, and found a Hallmark wedding card that was very pleasant but not too gooey. I sought out Erica.

She had a large wall-mount photo frame in one hand and cradled several sets of candles in her right, like a football. I took the frame from her and we headed for the checkouts.

"Wrapping paper," she said. We made an about-face and quickened our step.

"I hope we beat the bride down the aisle," I said.

"Shut up."

"Usually the girl frantic before the wedding is the bride," I said.

"Shut up."

I smirked and followed her back to the wrapping paper. She selected a roll in short order, grabbed some matching ribbon and Scotch tape, and we headed back to the front of the store again.

Erica quickly paid for the items and we hurried out to the car. I again got Erica's door for her, but she opened the back door and got in.

"If you didn't like the card . . ." I said.

"I have to wrap these while we drive. We don't have time once we get there, and that would look trashy anyhow."

"You should have just bought a gift bag."

She slapped her forehead. "Now he tells me."

I drove. She wrapped from the backseat. Or tried to. We had forgotten the scissors.

"Josh, I may say something very unladylike pretty soon. Do you have a pocketknife or something?"

"Afraid not."

"Don't you hunt and field-dress deer and pheasants?"

"No, and not on the way to a wedding."

"Are you enjoying this?" she asked, meeting my eyes in the rearview mirror.

Truthfully, I was having a blast. But I didn't think we were quite at the stage where I could tell her that she was cute as the dickens when frantic. Plus it would have likely earned me a candle against the head.

"I've got a little utility thingy in the door here," I said, reaching for it. "Might be something that cuts in there."

I handed back the combination pliers/screwdriver/file I'd gotten in my stocking one Christmas. Erica played with it, looked up nervously to see we were coasting to the stoplight at Old Cheney Road, and exulted when she found a knife.

I continued north on 27th Street. Fortunately the Huskers were playing in Evanston, Illinois, and I didn't have to deal with game day traffic. Not that anyone would be stupid enough to take 27th Street all the way north anyhow.

"How's it coming?" I asked.

"Fine."

I heard paper tearing and glanced in the mirror. "Am I going to have exposed stuffing in my seats?"

"Watch the road, Roosevelt."

I watched the road. We crossed Highway 2, then passed the country club, touring through some of the city's older, nicer neighborhoods. I knew Lincoln well enough to know we were getting close.

"Where am I supposed to park?" I asked.

"Surrounding streets," Erica said. She moaned.

"What's wrong?"

"Have you ever wrapped a round object in a moving vehicle?"

"Can't say that I have."

"I'm normally not like this, Josh."

"You mean a touch cranky?"

She gave me the evil eye in the mirror. "Forgetful. I don't know what it is."

"You a Freudian?"

"What's that got to do with it?"

"Maybe you're subconsciously forgetting on purpose. You didn't have a falling out with Tara, did you?"

"No. I don't think that's Freud anyhow."

I shrugged.

We caught a break, a red light at South Street. Another groan came from the backseat. Erica was working on ribbon now, around the photo frame and then binding the candles together. "She'll probably just take it all back anyhow," she said.

"Don't give her the gift receipt."

Erica looked up. "Didn't get a gift receipt."

"Problem solved."

At A Street, Erica announced that she was finished. She then asked me to pull over.

"What?"

"Pull over. I can't get out from the backseat."

I turned left onto B and pulled to the curb. Erica got out, got in the front seat, and we drove a few more blocks, parking at the corner of 25th and C. It was a nice day, so a walk of a couple blocks wouldn't kill us.

"One-fifty by the fast-running dash clock," I announced as I killed the ignition.

"And aside from a thoughtless gift and the fact that I'm sweating like a hog," Erica said, checking herself in the visor mirror, "we're in good shape." She reached back for the presents. I came around and got her door. To be a guy, I carried the gifts. Half a block later, I gave them to her and ran back to get her shrug.

And for some reason, that's when it hit me. The wedding was at two. The dinner was at six. We'd have at least three hours in between, at which time we could have purchased and wrapped the gift. Lots of people — most people — brought the gifts to the reception anyhow. Especially at an outdoor wedding. I decided not to say anything to Erica.

I rejoined her and she bit her lip. "I completely forgot the card."

I pulled it out from under her shrug with a bit of a flourish.

"Thank you."

"You're welcome."

She took a deep breath and blew it out. "And I'm sorry for all this chaos. Back to normal Erica now."

"Don't worry about it," I said. "It will be a story to tell our kids someday."

She looked at me.

"Not that we'll have kids. I mean, we might, but . . . I meant, we might each have our own kids . . . That's what I meant by telling kids —"

"You mentioned Freud a while back . . ."

"I really didn't mean it that way. It's an expression."

"Now you know how I felt dragging you into Kohl's," she said. Then she smiled. "Come on. We want to beat the bride down the aisle, after all."

Chapter 41

"Then maidens will dance and be glad, young men and old as well." Jeremiah 31:13

The wedding was lovely. The sun kept it warm, the flowers kept it fragrant and beautiful, and the pastor kept it short. And the best part was no receiving line afterwards. Everybody just filed out.

Erica regained her composure and sat pleasantly beside me throughout the service. She did not smell like sweat. Anything but. And she didn't need the shrug, either. Her bare arms glistened in the sun, and I had to remind myself to stay focused on the ceremony. The problem was, the male mind—or at least this male's mind—tends to drift to a few hours after the wedding, and then to my wedding, and then to kids, and how kids might come nine months to the day after said wedding . . .

Fortunately the message was, as mentioned, brief. Special music interrupted my derailing mind, and I too regained my mental and spiritual composure. I hung on to it for the rest of the ceremony.

"Now what?" I asked. "We've got over three hours till the reception."

"I have an idea," she said, perking up.

"Okay."

"But it's a surprise."

"Okay."

"Come on."

We started back for the car, me wondering what surprise Erica had for me, and not really caring. Any surprise would be a good one.

Back at the car, Erica asked for the keys.

"What?"

"I'm driving. It's not much of a surprise if I have to tell you where to go."

"Am I supposed to blindfold myself too?"

"No, just close your eyes."

I sighed and tossed her the keys. The sparkle in her eyes made it worth closing mine as I got into the car and she started driving.

"Can you at least turn on the radio?" I asked.

She did, and we listened to the local broadcast of the Nebraska-Northwestern game. It was early, but the Huskers had a 7-0 lead.

We drove north. I think. I'm pretty good with directions, but not with my eyes shut and not after Erica's seven-point turn leaving our parking spot.

"Are you peeking?" she asked.

"Nope."

We stopped at a light. Northwestern punted.

"This car's fun to drive."

"When it runs."

We accelerated.

"Can I ask you a question?" I said.

"I suppose."

"I get the feeling you've done this before."

"Done what?"

"Driven blindfolded people around in their car."

"You're not blindfolded."

"Technicality."

"Nope. First time."

We turned left.

"I did lead a blindfolded Chris Joseph down to the creek when I was twelve," she said.

"Who's Chris Joseph?"

"He was a twelve-year-old who lived down the street from my grandparents in Norfolk. My first crush."

"I thought you weren't allowed to date until you were sixteen."

"It wasn't a date. It was also why we snuck down after dark."

"So why the blindfold?"

"I was a little seductress," she said.

I nodded. "There more to that story?"

"We should have gone during the day. Chris slipped and fell in the creek."

"Kind of puts an end to romance," I said.

"Especially when your parents ground you for a month."

"We're not going near water, are we?" I asked.

"Not even close."

We turned left again, and a moment later, pulled over to the side of the street. I realized Erica had parked at the same time that she announced, "We're here."

"Good, because—"

I started to open my eyes, but her hand clamped over them. Slapped, was more like it.

"Sorry," she said. "But you have to keep your eyes closed."

"I'll need a walking stick or a black lab," I said.

"Wait here."

"Waiting," I said.

A moment later, my car door opened, and Erica took my hand. I sure loved surprises.

"Do I get any hints?" I asked as I stepped out of the car, trying to sound cool and calm. I was anything but.

"No. Come on."

She squeezed my hand a little tighter, and I wanted to never let go. We strolled for a dozen paces, then stopped. I assumed from the sounds around us that we were at a street corner.

"Maybe I should hold out a tin cup and see if I can make any money," I said.

Erica jabbed me with the elbow of the hand holding my hand. We resumed walking again. I enjoyed the breeze at my back, the warmth from the sun, and the cool hand in mine. No, it wasn't typical hand-holding, but I wasn't going to complain.

We turned and Erica announced we had to go up steps. "Lift your feet," she said. I did, counting the number of steps. Nine. Then a long, flat section, paved. We were facing into the sun, at least for a while. Then I felt the cool of shade on my face.

"More steps," Erica said.

"Can I open my eyes so I don't trip?"

"No. I'll guide you."

I let her. We climbed, step after step after step. I lost count. I stumbled only once before we reached the top.

"Okay, the doors might be tricky," Erica said. She had to let go of my hand for a minute, but then found it again. Without looking, I gathered, because it took her fingers a moment to locate mine. If only time could have stopped.

Erica's heels clacked and echoed—on a long, marbled hallway, I deduced. I smirked. "Please tell me we're taking the elevators."

Erica stopped. She dropped my hand. "You know where we are?"

I nodded.

She sighed. "Where?"

"Capitol Building, just inside the north entrance."

"You peeked."

"Did not."

"How'd you know? And how'd you know the north side?"

"The steps, your heels, and the shade."

"Open your eyes, Roosevelt. Now you just look silly."

I opened them and looked into a lopsided grin.

"I thought it would be a nice day for looking over the city," she said.

"I agree."

We took the elevators, up fourteen stories to the top of the Nebraska State Capitol Building. Sadly, we didn't hold hands during the ride.

We took our time in the screened in observation decks on each side of the Capitol. The sky was perfectly clear, with only a few wisps of white in the west. Below us, Lincoln was a mass of green, orange, red, yellow, and brown—a mixture of millions of trees in the midst of their autumn glory. Had I come alone, it would have been quite the experience. With Erica, it was incredible.

She shivered as we looked east, out of the sun. I very nearly put my arm around her, but fear stopped me. Fear of rushing things with a girl who had some unpleasant history. Fear that the timing wasn't quite right and I would blow things. And the biggest fear of all, that I was misreading everything and she wasn't really into me. If I stretched my arm around her and she wiggled free, I might jump.

So I waited. If this was going somewhere, I was content to take my time getting there. And if it wasn't, I wanted to take even more time not getting there.

We circled the top of the Capitol, taking in all the views. The grain elevators in the distance, the downtown skyline, empty Memorial Stadium, and the distant hills and wind turbines on the far horizon. People who rip Nebraska for being boring have never seen that view.

Nebraska led Northwestern 17-7 late in the second half when we returned to the car. The sun was low enough now in the sky that it was turning everything orange. Including Erica's dark chocolate hair, so beautiful as it fell on her tanned shoulders. I wanted to freeze time again.

"We still have a couple hours," I said as I merged into traffic on K Street. "Any preferences?"

"Mmm . . ."

"My turn for a surprise?"

"Okay."

"Close your eyes."

"Josh."

"Only fair."

She sighed and closed her eyes. I smiled and turned right at the next light. I took a meandering route through downtown, reasonably sure that Erica, if she had kept her eyes closed — and my glances indicated she had — didn't know which direction we were headed. I parked across from the water tower in the Historic Haymarket. Beaming, I told Erica to keep her eyes closed, and got out to get her door.

As I swung the door open, I figured the only decent thing to do would be to offer Erica my hand. So I reached for her delicate fingers, lifted her hand gently, and helped her out of the car. I closed the door and reluctantly released her hand. "Okay, you can open them."

Erica opened her eyes and smiled. "I thought so."

"You did not."

"Um-hmm. Although your circuitous route kind of threw me off."

"So how'd you know?"

She shrugged. "I asked where I'd take myself if I sort of knew me."

"It was here or Runza."

"Good choice."

We killed an hour strolling through the Haymarket, ducking into shops, peeking in at The N Zone to check on the game (24-10, Huskers) and talking about everything from families to weddings to football to life in general. As we talked, the sun dipped, the red bricks got a little more orange, and Erica donned her shrug. At five-thirty, I suggested we'd better be on our way. Erica agreed.

The reception was held at a former warehouse in north Lincoln. It had been converted to a hall perfect for reunions, get-togethers, and wedding receptions. Outside, the building wasn't anything to look at. Inside, it was designed with that old-fashioned pub feel, and actually looked like it belonged in the Haymarket.

We bypassed the bar, taking only the time to glance at the TV showing the Nebraska game (31-17). Since we didn't really know anybody and seats weren't assigned, Erica suggested we sit on the fringe. We did, and then I got her and myself some punch. We were joined by two other couples whom Erica didn't know but who apparently knew each other. Our table was one of the last to be served, but the meal was worth the wait.

I'd heard once that a guy should take a girl out to eat early in their relationship. It was one thing to spoon yogurt or pick at a salad, but get her to cut into a steak or bite into a burger (or deal with beef tips and mashed potatoes) and you'd learn quite a bit about her. I learned that Erica possessed great composure and poise, just by observing her dinner manner.

Under the auspices of getting her more punch, I checked the score of the Nebraska game again. I was in time to see the Husker's star running back break a fourth-down run for a touchdown, clinching the game 45-17. We were back on track.

After the toasts, which were a little maudlin, the cake was cut. I was about to fetch us a couple of pieces, but Erica excused herself to the ladies' room, saying she would bring cake back. So I stood as she stood, and then got some coffee.

I sat by myself, the other couples lost in each other. I allowed myself a few moments of analyzing. By no means was I an expert in reading females, and most of what I knew was from watching TV or my brief interactions at college. But unless Erica was one of those drivers who left their turn signals on for long stretches on the highway, I was pretty sure she was into me.

And yet, I wasn't one hundred percent positive. What if everything (the way she looked at me, her mannerisms when she was around me, the questions she asked and the things she shared, the fact that she had asked me to the wedding) that I had taken to mean she felt the same way about me that I felt about her didn't mean what I thought after all? What if her behavior wasn't a sign of romantic interest but just an outpouring of her bubbly, effervescent, somewhat flirty personality? Maybe it wasn't a turn signal but daylight running lamps.

I thought again of what Dad had said, about knowing when the time was right. So maybe all my questions meant the time wasn't right yet. Or maybe I was just messed up. I sighed, figuring waiting a little while longer couldn't kill me. Especially if waiting meant football games and wedding dates like this. But how long would I keep saying I'd wait a little longer?

"I hope you don't mind a corner," Erica said, placing a plate in front of me.

"It's fine," I said. "Thanks."

She smiled as she sat down, gracefully, and began eating her cake. The grace ended when she reached over and swiped a glob of frosting off my plate. I'm not a huge fan of excessive frosting, and had scraped off some from around the corner.

"Pardon my manners," Erica said. "I have cravings."

I edged my plate toward her.

She devoured the frosting.

"We could get you another piece," I said. "Or hit a Super Saver on the way home and buy some straight up."

"So I like frosting."

I held up my hands as everyone began clanking their glasses again, prompting the bride and groom to kiss. He dipped her, everyone cheered, and I wondered what combination of cutlery and glassware could induce Erica and me to kiss.

I got up to refill my coffee and get Erica some at her request. I returned to the table in time for the bride and groom's first dance. It was followed by Tara dancing with her father and her new husband dancing with his step-mother. That apparently concluded the organized dance card, and the bridesmaids and teenage girls took to the floor next.

After something that sounded like a knock-off of the Black Eyed Peas and an upbeat Elvis number, Celine Dion's "My Heart Will Go On" started playing, sounding somewhat tinny over the portable speakers.

"Oh, I love this song," Erica said, reaching out for my arm. "Want to dance?"

I made a face. "I'm not much of a dancer."

"Come on."

"I've never actually danced."

"What about your prom?"

"Nope."

"Come on, Josh. It's easy."

I looked into her eyes, and although I had never before danced (except when Big Suh intercepted that pass against Colorado[19]), had no idea how to dance, and was in no hurry to learn how to dance, it was over.

"I have no idea what I'm doing," I said as we got up and she led me to the dance floor.

"There's nothing to it."

"Where do I put my hands?" I asked, apparently out loud. The shoulder was for waltzes, the butt was for perverts, somewhere in between

---

[19] Defensive lineman Ndamukong Suh's interception return for a touchdown sealed Nebraska's 40-31 victory over Colorado in 2008.

was the line of her dress. South of the border was kind of low for just friends, and north of the border was bare back, and I thought of Colonel Blake's wife Lorraine dancing with some guy at the country club who didn't even put a handkerchief over his arm. It was a legitimate question.

"Well, I take this one," she said, clutching my right palm in her lefthand. "And then . . ."

I tentatively and loosely reached my left arm around her body, finding middle ground right at the top of her dress. The butterflies in my stomach were tachycardic as she wrapped her right hand and forearm around the back of my shoulder.

"Like that," she said.

I squinted the image of floor mats with numbered footprints out of my head and concentrated on shifting my weight from one foot to the other so that I was, indeed, actually dancing. I also tried to maintain the proper distance from Erica. Too close and I was getting fresh. Too far away, and I looked like a seventh-grader at my first dance. Then again, I certainly felt like one.

"See, it's easy," she said.

"When do we dip?"

She grinned, working magic on my nerves. I let myself relax, let my hand enjoy the absolute bliss of cradling hers, and allowed my eyes to look into hers. Tolkien's Lady of the Wood didn't possess such power.

The song lasted for some four minutes, during which I waddled back and forth like a penguin. Then Erica and I retreated to our seats and allowed the teenage girls to hop and twirl with one another.

We stayed for another half hour. On our way out, Erica stopped to hug and congratulate Tara. She looked at us with some inquisitiveness, but my relationship to Erica never got discussed. Shortly after eight, we left the reception.

Neither of us said much on the way home. I'd like to think we were both just enjoying one another's presence. I know I sure was.

"How late is your little ice cream parlor open?" she asked as we coasted into Morgan.

"On a weekend, ten," I answered.

"Feel like a sundae? My treat, to thank you for going today."

"You don't have to thank me."

"Believe me, Josh, I've gone to weddings for strangers before. It's no picnic."

"I know," I said. "But today was fun. Blind surprises, wrapping candles in the backseat, peeking at Husker scores in the Haymarket. I'm glad I went."

"In that case, let me top off your fun day with some ice cream."

"Okay."

We stopped at Nebraska Novelties, and to my extreme relief, Sydney wasn't working. It was a little chilly to eat ice cream outside, so we returned to the car, drove to Erica's house, and ate in the driveway with the heater on.

"I've always dreamed of an outdoor wedding," Erica said, slipping a spoon full of ice cream between her lips. "But I'm afraid instead of a day like this, I'd get one like a couple of weeks ago. Cold, windy, raining."

I swirled my strawberry topping in with the ice cream and took a bite.

"How about you?" she asked.

"How about me what?"

"You ever think about your wedding?"

"Isn't that kind of for girls?"

"Yeah, but don't tell me you haven't ever pictured it."

Down to the bride.

"Yeah, once or twice," I said.

"Well?"

"Well, it can't be in the fall, because Memorial Stadium would already be booked."

"Typical guy, can't be serious."

"I am. I'd come out of the tunnel to 'Hail Varsity!'"

She rolled her eyes.

"Okay, serious," I said.

Erica spooned more ice cream and reached over to tweak the heater.

"You know, we could go inside," I said.

"Dad's watching football, Mom's ironing his shirt, they're arguing about who to have over for dinner tomorrow afternoon. This is better."

"Okay."

"Your serious wedding?"

"It'd be small," I said. "Just family, close friends."

"I like that."

"It'd have to be in the late summer, in the evening, on a small hill in the country, overlooking a ripe field of corn, glistening gold in the setting sun."

"What if it rains?"

"We move it into the barn."

"The barn?"

"Well, a sanitized one. No livestock or cow pies."

"What if your wife has allergies?"

"Hmm. I guess that'd have to be in the pre-nup."

"Back to the barn . . ."

I nodded. "Those little white folding chairs, like they had today, and the hay and straw would be sort of a background." I frowned. "It's probably not terribly practical, but things don't smell bad and people don't have allergies in dreams."

"I think I prefer the hilltop anyhow."

"Yeah, but it's a little too *Field of Dreams*," I said.

"I was thinking *Napoleon Dynamite*."

"That hurts."

"Sorry."

Erica scraped her dish, cleaning out her ice cream. "I guess that's it," she said.

I swallowed my last spoonful. "I guess so."

"Josh, thank—"

"Hold on," I said. She had started to reach for her car door. "We had a deal, remember?"

Erica grinned as I got out and circled the car to open her door. I offered my hand to help her out. She took it, then released it. It had just been meant as a form of chivalry.

"I'll walk you to the door," I said.

Her heels clicked on the concrete walkway, and I took small steps, trying to draw out this magical evening a few more seconds. I thought about how great it would be to tell her to close her eyes, how I had one more surprise for her. Then I would lean in, touch my lips against hers, and we'd share a long, soft kiss.

Or she'd slap me.

"Thank you for today," she said as we stood on the stoop. "I would have hated to go alone."

"My pleasure."

"Yeah, mine too," she said. And then she leaned in, tilted her head, and brushed her lips against my cheek.

Electricity shot through my body. For just a moment, her hair dangled on my neck, and her citrus perfume wafted into my nose. I closed my eyes and opened them slowly as she stood back.

I was speechless. Despite having seen *Hitch* a couple of times, I had no idea what to say.

"I'll see you tomorrow?" Erica said.

"Yeah, tomorrow."

"Good night, Josh."

"Good night, Erica."

I could have floated home. But it would have been poor taste to leave my Escort in the Chamberlain's driveway. So I drove, thinking about nothing but Erica's kiss. I was pretty sure it had been more in the "Thank you" vein than the "How's that for a signal?" vein. But I was going to cherish it for a while anyhow.

And maybe the next kiss wouldn't be just out of gratitude.

Chapter 42

"For what do righteousness and wickedness have in common?
Or what fellowship can light have with darkness?" II Corinthians 6:14

Our weekly AARP meeting reconvened on a cold, rainy October evening. Scotty, Damon, Gia, Amy, and I were joined by Gerhard, Bobby, and Bobby's "girl" Adeline Van de Kamp. Adeline was Gerhard's cousin, which, I gathered from them, didn't distinguish her from the rest of the population all that much. Gerhard's father had had seven siblings and his mother ten. All had taken on the challenge of filling and subduing the earth.

Our study had moved to Titus, and our discussion was on the importance of good teaching and solid rebuke. At least, that was the primary topic. It had gotten off track when Amy wanted to hold up each of the MBC elders to see if they met the requirements for an overseer in Titus 1:6-9. In theory, it was the role of the church to do just that, we determined, but maybe not in the context of a witch hunt.

The phrase "witch hunt" had been Scotty's, and had opened up another can of worms entirely.

"Hey, can we cancel next week's study?" Amy asked.

"Why?"

"Because it's Halloween?"

"So?" I asked.

"So . . . I have plans."

"For the devil's holiday?" Gerhard asked.

Amy sent him a dirty look. "Did you know Christmas is a pagan holiday?"

"What?" Gia asked.

"Easter too."

"Even if that were true, it doesn't justify celebrating Halloween," Gerhard said.

"I'm not celebrating Halloween. I'm just having a celebration on Halloween."

"You say potato . . ."

"It's just a costume party," Amy said. "And I'm taking my sister's twins trick-or-treating."

"Don't you think making light of all this is a bad idea?" Gerhard asked.

"Making light of what?"

"Witches and devils and ghouls."

"I'm not making light of anything. I'm going as a Viking maiden."

"That should —"

"Shut it," she snapped before Scotty could finish his comment.

"Hey, man, I thought Paul said that we don't have to be caught up in this type of debate," Damon said. "I mean, isn't this sort of like that passage on food sacrificed to idols?"

"Yeah," Amy said.

"If your eating food sacrificed to idols causes someone to stumble," Scotty said, "then you'd better not."

"Is anyone stumbling because I'm going to a party dressed up like a Viking maiden?" Amy asked.

"Only if I see pictures," I replied.

"Shut up."

"What do you think, G?" Scotty asked.

"I think Halloween is another example of their eyes being blinded so they cannot see," Gerhard said. "It may be all fun and games to people, but the day is nothing to celebrate."

"So what if I went to a costume party on August 4?" Amy asked.

"Then it would be a costume party, not a Halloween party."

"That's stupid," she said.

"You wouldn't have a problem with these boys playing catch," Gerhard said, nodding at Scotty, Damon, and me. "But if they were doing it in the church sanctuary on Sunday morning, it would be a different story."

"So?"

"So, when and why you do things can matter."

"Listen to him preach," Adeline said. "He used to be a little terror on Halloween."

"That was a long time ago," he answered.

"He'd hire his pals to scare all the local girls crazy so they'd come and hold him for comfort."

"Worked too," Gerhard said with a smile.

"Yes, yes, Mr. Popularity." She shook her head. "Never lets me forget, the old Hickman High Hot Dog."

"I don't know, I have to agree with Amy," Damon said.

"Thank you!"

He shrugged. "I mean, it's not like we're worshiping the devil or channeling evil spirits or anything. It's just harmless fun."

"What do you say, Havana? You all practice voodoo and sorcery and stuff on Halloween?"

Gia bristled. "No. But I do not think trick-or-treating is some grave sin."

"Didn't you say you were going?" Amy asked.

Gia nodded.

"You're going trick-or-treating?" Scotty asked. "Aren't you a little old?"

"Hey, man, I go too."

"Dude, you're a grown man. Mostly."

Damon grinned. "It's fun."

"And you actually find suckers who will give you candy?"

"Yeah. And caramel apples, right, man?" he asked, turning to Bobby.

Bobby winked. "Adeline and I make them from scratch."

"You grow the apples, or what?" Scotty asked.

"I mean we don't just buy them at the store."

"You participate in Halloween?" Gerhard asked.

"Oh, Gerhard, calm down," Adeline said. "We're just giving the kids a treat."

"And grown men," Scotty mumbled.

"See," Amy said.

I held up my hands. "Hey, do what you want." I took a deep breath. "If everyone's going to be busy, I guess we'll call the study for next week."

"Count one for the devil," Gerhard said.

"Oh, Gerhard," Adeline said again.

"So what are you going as?" Amy asked Damon.

"Bob Marley."

"You'd better grow your hair out."

"What about you, Cha-cha-chá?" Scotty asked. "Little green painter's cap and a gray beard?"

"I was going to go as you, but I couldn't find anyone who would sell just the back half of a horse costume."

"Shall we close in prayer?" I asked.

"I can't believe it, Bible study canceled so we can celebrate the devil's holiday."

"Oh, Gerhard."

"G, come on over anyhow," Scotty said. "We'll have a prayer vigil for their souls."

Gerhard winked, and I once again sympathized with poor Petey.

"She kissed you?" Dirk asked. We were watching the World Series.

"That's right," I said.

"And you're not sure?"

"I've been kissed by other girls," I said.

Scotty and Dirk both looked at me.

"I mean a little 'Thank you' kiss on the cheek," I said. "That doesn't mean anything."

"Okay, let's recap," Scotty said, reaching for the popcorn. "She asked you to go to a football game, before which she made you dinner, during which she bared her soul to you, and after which she fussed over your hot chocolate?"

"She didn't actually make me dinner. She heated up dinner."

"Which she made a few days before. She made you dinner. Then she asks you to go with her to an old friend's wedding. She makes you close your eyes and leads you around by the hand, then asks you to dance, then buys you ice cream and asks what your ideal wedding would be like. And then she kisses you on the cheek. And you're not sure if she likes you?"

"I'm pretty sure," I said.

"So what's the hang-up?"

I sighed. "I just want to be positive. I'd rather wait a little too long than be wrong."

"What if Mark 2.0 comes along?"

"Well, the way I figure it, if she's really into me, he's not going to sweep her away. And if she's not into me, then I don't want to start anything."

"You know, Rosie, you're the epitome of cautious."

I turned to Dirk for help.

"There's nothing wrong with biding your time," he said. "Just know, there are other players on the course, and they're going to attack the easy pins."

"Erica being 'easy pins'?"

Dirk nodded.

"So now I'm in danger of making too many pars when the guys behind me on the course are knocking down flags and making birdies."

"Maybe not yet, but the last thing you want is to play 13 and 15 too carefully and have to make up strokes on 17 and 18."

"So what do I do?"

Dirk leaned forward. "Women want to be pursued, Josh. They'll pursue you a little, hook you, and then wait for you to follow. If you don't, they'll cut bait."

"Wait," Scotty said. "A non-golf metaphor?"

"Shocking, isn't it?" Dirk grabbed the popcorn bowl. "I dated a girl in high school—Jenny Walker. For the first few weeks, she was relentless."

Scotty held up a hand. "If this is a 'before the blood' story, go easy on the details."

Dirk smiled. "To make a long story short, she chased me around the proverbial playground. She even hinted about marriage."

"And?" I asked.

"And, I was seventeen and enjoying having the chase. I was nowhere near ready to commit to one girl. When I didn't bite, she cast her line elsewhere."

I nodded. "And you think that'll happen to me?"

"I think if you drag this out too long, maybe. But that doesn't mean you should go ask her out tonight, either."

I sighed. "I liked your golf metaphors better."

"You're the only one," Scotty muttered.

Our attention turned to the game for a while. Dodgers pitching squelched a Red Sox rally, and Dirk went to get us another round of cream sodas.

"How's your survey coming?" he asked.

"My survey?"

"Scotty told me you're taking the temperature of a lot of folks about church."

I nodded. "I want to know if I'm out in left field, or if I have some legitimate concerns—ones shared by other people too."

"What's the verdict?"

"Mixed," I said. "But more people have agreed with me than not," I said.

"So what's next?"

"Well, I work up my courage and talk to Teasdale about talking with him and the elders."

"Alone?"

"I'm going to rope Scotty into being my second."

Dirk nodded, then the Dodgers' slugger hit a homer, and our thoughts drifted back to baseball. Sort of. Mine also lingered on Erica and whether I was dawdling to the point of her cutting bait or if I was just taking it slow and enjoying the ride.

Like with my survey about church, the verdict was mixed here too.

Chapter 43

"Come, my lover, let us go to the countryside . . ." Song of Solomon 7:11

Every year, Morgan Bible Church has a Harvest Hayride at Dave's farm. Sometimes the hayride is incorporated as part of our Missions Festival. Sometimes it's a diversion from Halloween. And sometimes it's just an event, period. Like this year.

Friday after work, I headed out to Dave's place to help him prepare for half a hundred or more hayriders, pyros, and cocoa drinkers. It had become a tradition when I was a teenager and Dave was my primary employer, and after a two-year, college-induced hiatus, I saw no reason for the tradition to cease. So I arrived at five-thirty and spent an hour helping whittle elderberry branches into roasting sticks, build a fire, and arrange hay bales in the loft of his barn. I updated him on things with Erica, and he briefed me on how the harvest was looking. It was a yearly struggle, wondering if he'd reap enough to last through the winter. This year, he said, he would be set.

By six-thirty, Curtis Teasdale and his gang had arrived lugging more guitar cords and amps than U2's roadies. While they conducted a sound check that shook hay out of bales and scared cows milkless, Dave and I began brewing coffee and heating hot chocolate and apple cider.

The format for the night was simple. The event started at seven, worship and testimonies in the barn around seven-fifteen. Hayrides departed, starting at eight, every half hour or so until the festivities died down or Dave got sick of driving his tractor around the back forty.

Back in the old days, when we sang hymns and songs I knew and for just a few minutes each, I often spent about half an hour in the barn. That left me plenty of time to sear a hot dog before the first hayride departed.

But this year, I doubted the songs would be singable anyhow, and would probably be interlaced with long, tearful testimonies. And testimonies confused me. People tended to ramble and use Christian terms and buzz words in the wrong context, and half the time I wondered, based on what they had said, if they were really saved or not. The other half of the time, when they were coherent and their testimonies substantive, I came away wondering if I was by comparison. So I found it more enjoyable to hang out around the fire with Scotty burning food.

Once Dave and I had everything set in the shed, I camped out by the newly-lit fire. It was a cool evening, and I was bundled up in two T-shirts and a hoodie and long underwear under my jeans. I was comfortable.

Another thing I had learned over time was pacing. It didn't do any good to eat four hot dogs in the first hour and be sick all night. I had one, washed down with a cup of cider, while people trickled in. Scotty showed up at seven-thirty, grabbed a hot dog, and sat down beside me. The World Series had concluded Wednesday, so we weren't missing any action.

"Think she'll come?" Scotty asked.

"Yeah. If she doesn't have to work."

"Want me to beat it if she does?"

"No. I'm not like that."

"We can pinky swear and make a blood pact, Opie, but every guy is like that."

"I'm not."

"Okay."

I was just about to get up and get hot dog number two when she arrived. She wore jeans, a maroon sweater, and matching knit gloves and scarf. Her hair was loose and seemed to float as she walked. Scotty began to hum "Pretty Woman" and I elbowed him discreetly before anyone heard.

Erica waved with her fingers before heading into the shed/hot dog stand. "You still need proof, man?" Scotty said. "She digs you, dude."

"I'd feel better if you had, say, a girlfriend to prove you know what you're talking about."

"I could have plenty," Scotty said. "I just don't want them."

Erica came and stood beside me, a marshmallow on an elderberry branch in her right hand. "Hey, guys."

"Hey." The juvenile side of me wanted to pull her scarf. I did not.

"Hey," Scotty said.

"I haven't seen you in a while," she said, over my head at him.

"Yeah, I've been around."

She nodded. "How you been?" This was aimed at me.

"Not bad. Yourself?"

"Okay. Busy week." She lifted her marshmallow to inspect it, then lowered it back toward the flames. "But that is over with, finally."

The band in the barn cranked up again, playing "Better is One Day." I got out of the chair. "Mallow?" I asked Scotty. He nodded and I went into the shed to grab a handful of sugar puffs. When I returned, Erica was sitting in my chair, legs crossed, licking the last marshmallow residue off her thumb. She smiled coyly.

I returned something of a flirtatious eye-leveling and tossed two of the mallows to Scotty. I skewered the other two and, with another playful leer at Erica, toasted from a standing position. If I was getting even a passing grade in Signals 101, things were progressing nicely.

Dave brought around the wagon and announced that the first ride would be departing in five minutes. I looked down toward Scotty and Erica. "You guys going?"

"I'm not huge on hayrides, dude," Scotty said. "I'm a little past the thrill of bumping along on a hayrack at five miles an hour."

"I think it sounds like fun," Erica said.

"Of course you do, Iola."

"Iola?"

"From the Hardy Boys," he said. "Joe's good-natured girlfriend."

"I thought Callie was the good-natured one," I said.

"Callie was spunky," Scotty said.

"I thought Callie was frail."

"Dude, it's been like twelve years and I really don't care."

I looked at Erica, who was holding back a giggle.

"We're going, aren't we?" Scotty asked.

Erica smiled triumphantly (and yet good-naturedly—perhaps even spunkily) and got up, returning her elderberry branch to the stick bucket. Scotty sighed and got out of his chair, and the three of us moseyed over toward the empty wagon.

"Are they still singing that song?" Scotty asked as we climbed up into the hay. "It's now been two days."

The wagon—an old holdover from the days of a regular square baler when the wagon didn't need walls to catch errant bales—had temporary sidewalls and a high back rack, and bales had been arranged on both sides and along the back for seating. With the chorus of "Better is One Day" looping in the background, we found seats at the back of the wagon.

As usual, the first ride was full of happy harvesters. It lasted for about twenty minutes, going down along the lane leading to Dave's back fields. He drove through several of the fields, along the railroad tracks, and occasionally onto the road that would lead back to his front drive. There were a couple dozen of us, including Mike and Cora, and we talked about everything from the Huskers to the harvest (the actual crop harvest, not the spiritual soul harvest) to holiday plans.

Over the years, a pattern had emerged. The first ride was full of families and was usually quite tame. Either the second or third ride was filled with worshipers from the barn, depending on how long things ran in the loft, how long they needed to warm up by the fire, and how hungry they were after singing. The third ride was filled with kids, often unsupervised, and often partaking in wrestling matches in the hay. The trouble arose when the worshipers and wrestlers converged. One group wanted to sing some more and the other wanted to goof off and find any way to annoy the singers. Kids will be kids.

We got back just as things were letting out in the barn, and there was a mad rush on hot dogs and marshmallows, elderberry branches, and seats around the fire. We waited our turn in line, standing to roast our second round—at least for Scotty and me—of hot dogs.

"Who's Nebraska play tomorrow?" Scotty asked as we skewed our hot dogs.

"Michigan State," Erica and I answered in unison.

"What about LSU?" Erica asked.

"Troy, Ole Miss, I don't know."

"Some fan you are."

"Hi, Erica," I looked to see a boy, eleven or twelve maybe, waving at her.

She waved back, just the fingers moving, like she had waved at me. "Hey, Dustin."

"Is that little Dustin Reed?" I asked.

Erica nodded.

"Man, he's grown up."

"Still, a little young for you, isn't he?" Scotty asked.

"Shut up," she said, jabbing his shoulder.

Dang. She hit other guys too.

"My parents had his parents over last Sunday," she explained. "He had nobody else to talk to, so I made us some hot chocolate and chatted with him while I did my homework."

Hot chocolate? With a tweener? Was nothing sacred?

"That's awkward," Scotty said. "They make you go play G.I. Joes and Barbies in your room too?"

"Thankfully, no."

I happened to glance over my shoulder, where Dustin and several other boys had formed a semicircle. They were facing our way, and Dustin pointed.

"Don't look now," I said, "but I think he's telling his posse about the two of you."

"What?" she asked.

"What's that line," Scotty asked, "'the U.S.S. *Erica* leaves a large wake'?"

We both looked at him. "Are you quoting *Runaway Bride*?" Erica asked.

"Maybe."

"Don't you have to give up your man card now or something?"

"Hey, I'm not the one leading on twelve-year-old boys," he said.

"Okay, seriously, I made him one cup of hot chocolate and asked like three questions about school. Guys." She shook her head. "I'm going to find a seat." The second hayride had departed, opening seats up around the fire. I was about to follow her when I saw Gia approaching, cradling a Styrofoam cup in her hands, and wearing what could only be described as an afghan. Maybe a poncho.

"Don't *you* look now," I said to Scotty, "but here comes trouble."

Gia came around the fire and stopped directly in front of us.

"Man, all you need is a mustache and a sombrero and you'd look like the Folgers guy," Scotty said.

"I thought that was Colombian," I said. "Folgers has mountains."

He shrugged.

"Can I talk to you?" Gia asked through a sigh. She was looking at Scotty.

"Yeah."

"Privately."

He looked at me, then at her. "Okay. We need a referee, Kid Chocolate?"

"What? Who?"

"He was a Cuban boxer back in the day."

"How could you possibly know that?"

Scotty shrugged.

"No, we do not need a referee. Will you please come on?"

With a nod, he followed her off into the darkness. Curious as I was, I turned my attention to Erica. She was seated on a wooden bench, an empty space beside her. I took my hot dog on a stick and joined her. The bench was angled so that I could glance at her while still sort of looking at the fire. The combination of shadows and flickers played upon her face, hair, and curvaceous figure, and I did my best to admire her sinlessly.

Just as my dog was perfectly singed, Scotty and Gia returned. She disappeared into the crowd and Scotty headed for the shed. Checking if Erica needed anything, I stuffed my dog into a bun and followed him. "What was that about?" I asked.

"Peacemaking," he answered as he poured himself some cider. "I guess we're friends now."

"Friends?"

"At least non-enemies. Frenemies?"

"How's that supposed to work?"

"Well, we both agreed if we do everything in our power to avoid one another at all times, it should work."

"Really?"

He nodded. "She thought it was best for all parties involved. One too many arguments in Sunday school and Bible study. Bad testimony, she says."

"So does that mean she's out?"

He blew on the top of his cider and took a sip. "Yeah, for the time being. She asked me to tell you."

"This isn't going to help our age demographic," I said.

"No. Sorry, dude."

I shrugged.

He nodded toward the fire. "So . . . any progress?"

I glanced over my shoulder where Erica was talking with Cora. I thought of her waving at me, then of her waving quite similarly at a twelve-year-old. With whom she had also shared hot chocolate.

"Maybe," I said.

Scotty nodded. "I'm going to get out of here."

"What?"

"I'm bored. Besides, I don't want to be your third wheel."

"You don't have to go."

"I know."

I shrugged. "Watch some football tomorrow?"

"Yeah. Come over whenever."

I nodded and got myself some cider. Erica found me as I was exiting the shed. "Where's Scotty going?"

"Home."

"How come?"

I shrugged. Did a shrug count as a lie?

"So Mom's making French dips for the game tomorrow."

"Sounds good."

"Want to come over?"

I nodded. "Sure," I said, just as Scotty disappeared around the corner of the barn. On a very small scale, I felt like Peter as the rooster crowed. I dismissed such nonsensical comparisons.

"Unless you and Scotty have plans or something," Erica said.

"Scotty's indifferent to Husker football. I'd rather watch it with true fans."

Cock-a-doodle-doo.

"Okay," Erica said with a little head flip.

"Your mom won't mind?" I asked.

"No, of course not."

"Okay."

A group of people re-gathered for more singing, and soon the barn was rocking. At least we were able to find seats around the fire again. After a chorus of "Breathe" died out, I got up to get a couple of mallows. I impaled them both on a stick and decided to perfectly toast one for Erica.

I told her my plan as I sat back down.

"Make sure it's golden brown."

"Of course."

I had to dodge teenagers dropping hot dogs and burning their marshmallows to a crisp, and the distraction of Dustin Reed (presumably — Erica wasn't able to ID the guilty party) sneaking up behind Erica and flicking her scarf. But I managed to singe my pair of marshmallows to a golden brown, as requested. I tipped the stick to Erica, and she plucked one off. I removed mine and returned the stick to the fire, burning off the excess. I sat back and was about to enjoy the perfect mallow when Erica's scarf flew into my hand, its tassels draping over the marshmallow.

I jerked my head around, but not fast enough to spot the culprit. I turned to Erica, who sighed as she picked marshmallow cream out of her scarf. And I picked yarn out of my marshmallow. Our hands both got messy, and we got up to get some water to wash them off.

"Tell me, Josh, did you have a way-older crush that you bugged when you were twelve?"

"Can't say as that I did. Never been a fan of cougars."

"You're calling me a cougar?"

"Comparatively."

"Well I'm glad you're finding this so humorous." She sighed. "I'm going to get some cocoa. Want some?"

"I'm good."

She disappeared into the shed and I listened to Teasdale and Company's grunge version of "The Stand." I contemplated what my roll was in telling Dustin—assuming it was Dustin—to knock it off. I wasn't the boyfriend, and even if I was, he was twelve. Where were the little brat's parents? Taking a stand elsewhere?

I nodded at Cora and Tim (separately) and turned back to the shed as Erica returned. I was in time to see a little urchin dart around behind her and slap her on the butt. She jumped a half-step forward, sloshing cocoa but managing to keep it in the cup. She was steaming as much as the cocoa by the time she reached me.

"I see scarf-flicking has become passé," I said.

"I'm pretty sure that was the second one too," she said. "That or the hot chocolate line is very competitive."

"Want to tattle on their mothers?"

"I'm not a tattletale, Josh."

"This is practically sexual harassment."

"No, I know sexual harassment."

"Right. Sorry."

I looked away, then checked to make sure another butt-slapper wasn't zooming in as she took a sip of the cocoa.

"You want to take a walk?" I asked.

"Huh?"

"Get away from little brats?"

Erica studied me with her beautiful brown eyes. "Walk to where?"

"Just down the lane a little ways," I said. "We have time before the next ride."

She thought for a second. "Okay."

We slipped around the shed, past the tractor and wagon, and started down the gravel lane leading to the rest of Dave's property. I made several glances behind us to make sure we weren't being followed. Unless these kids were good at being sneaky — and twelve-year-olds generally aren't — we were in the clear.

"You can stop watching my butt," Erica said.

"I was — I . . ."

"I know what you were doing," she said. "That's what I meant. I think we're in the clear."

I nodded and exhaled. "I thought you thought I was pervert."

"Just paying you back for that 'story to tell our kids' comment last week."

I made a face. Erica sipped more hot chocolate. I could smell the cocoa, along with her perfume, along with Dave's cows. Two out of three wasn't bad.

Behind us, the tractor revved. "Should we get back?" Erica asked.

"If you want," I answered. "But ride three is usually full of kids. Twelve-year-old kids, often."

"Okay, but you know what happens if the tractor beam illuminates us strolling down the path?"

"Rumors?"

"Like you wouldn't believe."

"We can cut through the corn," I said.

"Cut through the corn?"

I nodded.

"To where?"

I shrugged. "Wherever."

She looked at me good and hard. I tried not to blink.

"What if we get lost?" she finally asked.

"We won't."

"You're awfully confident."

I was sure trying to be, wondering if this might be the magical moment. Cool, crisp air. A beautiful girl under the stars. An adventure, of sorts. It had possibilities.

Erica took another sip, then formed a crooked smile. And then she offered me her gloved hand. When I hesitated, she wiggled her fingers. I didn't hesitate any longer, grabbing her hand and letting her pull me into the corn.

Some signals can't be missed.

Chapter 44

"To the elders among you, I appeal . . ." I Peter 5:1

cassiemay1014: so what happened?!?!?!

softspeakingstickcarrier: We got lost.

cassiemay1014: you got lost

cassiemay1014: in the corn

softspeakingstickcarrier: Uh-huh

cassiemay1014: then what

softspeakingstickcarrier: Not much. We followed the sound of the tractor until we realized it was leading us further from the farm. So we concentrated on walking straight until we came to the road. From there we just walked back to Dave's.

cassiemay1014: didnt people wonder why you came up the front driveway

softspeakingstickcarrier: Presumably.

cassiemay1014: ☺

There was a pause and I flashed back to Friday night at Dave's. Even if we had gotten lost and my male ego had taken a hit, I had loved every minute with Erica. She had not rescinded her offer to watch football the following day, and as of Sunday, there were no obvious rumors floating around.

cassiemay1014: did she keep holding your hand

softspeakingstickcarrier: No.

cassiemay1014: ☹

softspeakingstickcarrier: She let go as soon as we were in the corn.

softspeakingstickcarrier: But she did bounce a corn cob off my head when I told her we were lost.

cassiemay1014: so thats something i guess

398

softspeakingstickcarrier: And again when I told her we were following the tractor further away from the farm.

cassiemay1014: thats really something

cassiemay1014: if corn cob chucking is any sort of sign

cassiemay1014: i mean if id have had a corn cob i might have chucked it at tyler harte

softspeakingstickcarrier: Your secret's safe with me.

cassiemay1014: it had better be

softspeakingstickcarrier: So how's it going in AZ?

cassiemay1014: good

cassiemay1014: still busy

cassiemay1014: but back to you

cassiemay1014: what else is going on with erica

softspeakingstickcarrier: Not a whole lot

cassiemay1014: not what scotty tells me ☺

softspeakingstickcarrier: Oh?

softspeakingstickcarrier: And what is Scotty telling you?

cassiemay1014: that youve dumped him for erica

Dumping was a little strong. Yes, I had bailed on him Saturday to watch football with Erica (Nebraska had survived a nail-biter against Michigan State, winning on a late field goal, and I had been joined by the entire Chamberlain family in screaming until I was hoarse) but he said it was no biggie, telling me he was going to have to get used to it. I typed as much to Cassie.

cassiemay1014: so shes inviting you to watch football with her and her folks...

cassiemay1014: thats another good sign

softspeakingstickcarrier: Plus there's the wedding.

cassiemay1014: wedding

cassiemay1014: waht wedding

cassiemay1014: im ean what

cassiemay1014: i mean

cassiemay1014: sigh

cassiemay1014: very excited

cassiemay1014: what wedding

I briefed her on the invite to Tara's wedding, the craziness with gifts on the way, our blindfolded sightseeing tours afterwards, and dancing with Erica at the reception. Cassie clapped (or so she told me) as I regaled her.

cassiemay1014: this is very promising

softspeakingstickcarrier: Yeah...

cassiemay1014: you think otherwise

softspeakingstickcarrier: No

softspeakingstickcarrier: Not really

softspeakingstickcarrier: I just worry

cassiemay1014: well dont

cassiemay1014: worry is bad for you

softspeakingstickcarrier: I know

cassiemay1014: ulcers

softspeakingstickcarrier: I know

cassiemay1014: youll stop sleeping

softspeakingstickcarrier: I know

cassiemay1014: and eating

cassiemay1014: besides i dont think you have anything to worry about

softspeakingstickcarrier: (Sighs)

softspeakingstickcarrier: I know. Thanks, Cass.

cassiemay1014: welcome

softspeakingstickcarrier: So is it nuts by you today too?

cassiemay1014: today

softspeakingstickcarrier: Halloween.

cassiemay1014: oh

cassiemay1014: right

cassiemay1014: oh my goodness

cassiemay1014: its insane

cassiemay1014: people are coming to class in costume and hanging spiderwebs across hallways and i think theyre having a seance in the basement

cassiemay1014: they are crazy

softspeakingstickcarrier: Speaking of holidays...

softspeakingstickcarrier: Any chance on Thanksgiving?

cassiemay1014: no

cassiemay1014: ☹

cassiemay1014: and now youve gone and depressed me

softspeakingstickcarrier: Sorry. Didn't mean to.

cassiemay1014: christmas for sure

cassiemay1014: if I have to walk

cassiemay1014: or drop out

softspeakingstickcarrier: Scotty and I could come get you.

cassiemay1014: no!

cassiemay1014: wait

cassiemay1014: for thxgiving or christmas

cassiemay1014: i refuse to abbreviate christmas

softspeakingstickcarrier: I'm surprised you left it uncapitalized

cassiemay1014: its okay

cassiemay1014: its just im

cassiemay1014: ☺

cassiemay1014: and it doesnt matter

cassiemay1014: you two are not coming to get me

cassiemay1014: understood?

softspeakingstickcarrier: Understood.

cassiemay1014: so what are u doing 4 thxgiving

softspeakingstickcarrier: Mom and Dad's, probably.

softspeakingstickcarrier: Although the drive is a killer

cassiemay1014: and you want to drive to az

softspeakingstickcarrier: Arizona has scenery. Kansas doesn't.

cassiemay1014: (looking at clock) You have Bible study tonight

cassiemay1014: i capped Bible

softspeakingstickcarrier: I see.

softspeakingstickcarrier: No. Canceled for Halloween.

cassiemay1014: what???

softspeakingstickcarrier: Not my choice. Just everybody else's.

softspeakingstickcarrier: Except Scotty's.

softspeakingstickcarrier: And Gerhard's.

cassiemay1014: ugh

cassiemay1014: people

softspeakingstickcarrier: I know.

cassiemay1014: so...

```
cassiemay1014: (looking at clock again) i should really
do homework
    cassiemay1014: and have to work tonight
    cassiemay1014: should be an adventure
    softspeakingstickcarrier:  Yeah...Scotty  and  I  are
hanging out.
    cassiemay1014: have fun
    softspeakingstickcarrier: I will
    cassiemay1014: say hi
    softspeakingstickcarrier: I will
    cassiemay1014: later then
    softspeakingstickcarrier: Later.
```

I closed our little chat window, then glanced at my own clock. I still had time before I was supposed to be at Scotty's, so I fired off an e-mail to my parents and then killed some virtual baddies.

October became November. The weather actually warmed a touch. Nebraska's run to the Big Ten Championship Game rolled along with a couple of comfortable wins. Erica missed church, and we didn't see each other for way too long.

I didn't miss church. I even went extra. I had finished my survey, and Monday the fifth of November, I called Pastor Teasdale and asked if I could possibly meet with him and the elders to discuss some concerns I had. My knees knocked the entire time.

On Thursday evening, before the regularly scheduled elder meeting, Scotty and I met with Curtis Teasdale, Greg de Boer, Larry Iverson, and Dale Ten Pas. (Charles O'Reilly wasn't able to make it early.) I had spent the last three days going over what I wanted to say, how I wanted to say it, and if it was the right thing to say. I talked to Dave, Mom and Dad, Dirk, Cassie briefly via the internet, and Scotty, and concluded that this was what was best.

We met in Teasdale's office. He offered coffee. We were all polite, but I got the feeling this group wondered what I had in store. I hadn't told Teasdale much on the phone, just that it had to do with directional issues.

"Josh, what's on your mind?" Teasdale asked once we all had our coffee, tea, or water.

With my silent partner on my left, I took a deep breath and began. I prefaced my comments by explaining how, in case anyone didn't know, I was the son of the previous pastor. I said I knew it was very possible that his dismissal was influencing my thoughts. I felt being transparent was the way to go, and wanted them to know that if I came across as jaded and biased, I was aware of it.

I had their attention, and I laid more groundwork. "I want to be clear that I don't think this church is doing anything that is blatantly opposed to Scripture. I believe that our beliefs and values and intentions are accurate." I swallowed, which wasn't easy, what with my being without even a speck of saliva. "I also realize that there are a lot of different preferences when it comes to style and method, and that just because something is contrary to my preference, it doesn't make it wrong. However, I think we have to be careful before we just sweep things under the 'different strokes for different folks' rug."

"What kind of things?" Larry asked. I sensed by the look on his face that, of everyone, he was taking my comments the worst. And I hadn't really said anything yet.

"I've identified three major categories," I said. "The first is the music. Again, I get there are different preferences in style. But it seems to me we have tipped the scale way to one side, and I don't believe it's the side that the majority of people in this church would prefer."

"Do you know that?" Larry asked.

"As a matter of fact, yes. Well, at least sort of. I've spoken to a lot of different people, some on the record, some off, who agree with my position."

"And what exactly is your position?" Dale asked. He was taking notes of our conversation on a yellow legal pad. I was officially in the church's records. Gulp.

"I think a lot of the songs we sing are very difficult to sing for a lay person like myself with no musical training. It also seems that they lean toward the fluffy side."

"Fluffy?" Teasdale asked.

"Yes, sir," I said. I had determined to be Mr. Polite, especially since much of what I had to say could easily come across as a personal attack. "There just doesn't seem to be a lot to many of the songs. The message is often vague or very simple, and seems to lack a lot of the doctrine and theology prevalent in many hymns."

"There are some pretty abstract hymns," Greg said.

"Yes, sir, there are. And there are some very meaty 'praise choruses.' But in both cases, those seem to be the exception rather than the rule." I again attempted to swallow. "Furthermore, a lot of the songs seem to be recounting someone's experience."

"What's wrong with that?" Larry asked.

"Nothing. If a person has an experience and they want to share it via song, they certainly have that right. But in church, I don't get much out of singing a song about someone else's experience—especially one I haven't had. I'd rather sing about things that are true for all of us—Christ's death on the cross, the hope of eternal life, etcetera."

Greg raised his hand. "You said you aren't getting much out of the songs." He shook his head. "But church isn't supposed to be about what you get. It's about what you can give to God."

"Respectfully, I'd have to disagree."

Larry startled, as if I'd slapped him in the face.

"We are supposed to give our worship to God," I said. "But don't we also come together to get fed and nurtured? It's a give and get, isn't it? By coming and getting in that sense, we also worship. Plus, I feel like we can give much better if the songs are musically accessible to everyone and have sound doctrine."

Greg pursed his lips. No one else answered.

"You said three main categories?" Teasdale said.

"Yes, sir. The second would be that we seem to be chasing experience. The Sunday where we didn't sing because our amps didn't work. Can't we sing without instruments? Or the interpretive dancing, the whistling, the barefoot service, and seeking to be undignified. It seems like we're trying to generate something."

"We're simply seeking to create an environment where people can experience God," Teasdale said.

"'God is spirit,'" Larry said. "'And his worshipers must worship in spirit and in truth.'"

"Yes," I said. "But it often feels — not just to me — like we're putting the emphasis on having the experience. Shouldn't our focus be on obeying and worshiping God as He has commanded, and letting the experience come? If we seek experience, I think we're in grave danger of getting an experience, but not one that has God in it."

My only response was some thoughtful looks. And a stern frown from Larry Iverson.

"And I also don't see how any of those things create any more of an environment for worship than not having them would," I added. "It just seems like stuff to me."

The thoughtful looks took on a trace of glare. I glanced at Scotty for strength. Or at least a non-glaring face.

"Thirdly," I said, "it seems we're drifting toward the culture. I know that Paul was 'all things to all men' and that what worked in 1950 may not work in the twenty-first century. But I also think there are certain standards we should uphold, and if the culture doesn't like it, so be it."

"Do you have examples?" Teasdale asked.

"I do. I think we've become very casual. The worship team leading the service wears ripped jeans and tattered clothes and no shoes. Making music with web apps. The style of the music in general. The jazzing up hymns and translating them into modern language — I know there's nothing in the Bible that tells us we have to wear suits to church or sing in the king's English, but . . . I don't know. It just doesn't sit right, and I can't explain exactly why. But somewhere between the being 'all things to all men' and watering down the message of the gospel there's a line, and I think it's getting very blurred by our footprints — our in the general sense, not just this church."

"If we don't adapt for the culture, we run the risk of losing them," Larry said.

"But at what point do we gain the culture but lose what it is we're trying to gain them for?" I looked around the room. "Jesus didn't make His message appealing to the masses. He told them the truth—told them what they needed to hear, often bluntly and offensively. And if it caused them to fall away, He let them fall, because He wasn't looking to gain a following. He was looking to save souls."

"You said earlier that you didn't think we were opposed to Scripture," Larry said. "Doesn't that indicate we haven't compromised?"

"On a large scale, yes. But I see a number of smaller issues, and I'm afraid, like I said, that the line is getting blurred."

"So what would you propose?" Greg asked.

I sighed. "I don't have that answer. I think things were pretty good the way they were, but I also understand that you can become too attached to tradition and 'the way things have always been' and that sometimes there's a need for a change. What specifically those changes are, I don't know. And I hate to be the guy who points out faults without any solutions, but I think these are things we should consider and discuss." I shrugged. "Maybe they already have been—maybe you've already debated everything I've talked about. But I haven't heard of it if that's the case. I know there are certain things that need to be discussed and dealt with privately. But I think a little more transparency would be good, especially when it comes to these type of changes. You have to admit, things have been shaken up quite a bit in the last few months."

Everyone took a deep breath. My coffee hadn't been touched, and I had a sip now just to moisten my mouth. It was cold and bitter.

"Is there anything else on your mind?" Teasdale asked.

"No, not at present. And again, I don't want to be a rabble-rouser. But these things have weighed on my mind, to the point where I think they're more than just my preferences. Like I said, I can't exactly explain it, but . . . I think they're more than preferences."

He nodded.

"And I don't believe I'm alone. I have talked to other people, which I don't say as a blind threat or as some unnamed source. I have names I have permission to give to you, if you'd like. But this isn't some ultimatum from a derisive group. It's my thoughts. Others have merely echoed similar ones, and I checked with them to make sure I wasn't out in left field. At worst, I think I'm playing a deep shortstop."

Teasdale nodded again. He did not smile at what I thought was a rather clever line.

"Josh, I appreciate your candor," he said. "I appreciate your courage. These things can be difficult to hear, and difficult to say. And I don't know you that well, but I take from your words tonight that your heart is indeed in the right place."

It was my turn to nod.

"You've certainly given us some things to talk about and discuss this evening and going forward," he continued. "And we will discuss them."

"I appreciate that. And thank you for your time."

We stood and shook hands. Only Larry seemed grudging about it.

I thanked them again, then Scotty and I struck out into the night air. It was cool, but not as cool as it could be in November, and we walked to his house to watch some Big 12 football.

"You did good, man," Scotty said.

"My hands are still shaking," I said, my entire body feeling limp. I also felt as if a weight had flown off my shoulders. "I kind of rambled, and I forgot about ten things I wanted to say."

"I think you gave them plenty of food for thought."

"You think anything will come of it?"

Scotty shrugged. "You did what you could," he said. "Now the ball's in their court."

Chapter 45

"He says to the snow, 'Fall on the earth,'" Job 37:6

The following Sunday I went to church with a new attitude, determined to give Pastor Teasdale and the church elders the benefit of the doubt in light of our conversation. I also went in a shirt and tie, figuring after my little lecture on ripped jeans, I'd better look sharp.

I also went hoping to see Erica. It had been two weeks, and while absence made my heart grow fonder, growing fonder made the absence seem longer. I sat with Scotty and Dirk, middle back on the right, and saw her on the other side of the sanctuary. She wore a pink sweater with a purple and white argyle pattern on the front, over top of a white blouse. It was all I could see without staring. Scotty even caught me once during one of the songs, and sent a subtle elbow to my ribs.

Speaking of the songs, they were all worship choruses, somewhat fluffy and hard to sing. But it had been four days, so I wasn't expecting the return of the organ and all six stanzas of "Jesus Only." I did notice, however, that the slacks—not blue jeans—of the worship team were immaculately tailored.

Greg de Boer was the first person to find me in the hall as I was getting coffee. The warm November had cooled, and they were even talking snow for the afternoon—actual snow.

"Hello, Josh."

"Mr. de Boer."

He offered his hand. "I just wanted to personally thank you for taking the time to care," he said. "A lot of young people don't, and would just stop coming or drift off into the spiritual ether instead of seeking to have their opinion heard."

"Well, sir, I felt it was important. Not caring isn't an option."

He nodded. "I also wanted to let you know that we talked about the things you brought up, and we're going to continue talking about them in the future. It's a very complex dynamic, as I'm sure you know, but I want you to know that we're not sweeping your concerns under the rug." He leaned a little closer. "And it's not official yet, but I believe we're also going to conduct a survey of our own. See what folks are thinking and feeling. Perhaps we didn't have quite the feel of the congregation's pulse that we thought we did."

"That sounds good," I said (although it didn't bring Mom and Dad back to Morgan). "And I appreciate your listening to me and not discounting me."

He nodded, pumped my hand again, and drifted off. I finished filling my coffee and turned into Dave. We chatted for a few minutes, and I told him about my feat on Thursday night. He said I'd done the right thing, and we both agreed that though there was plenty I disagreed with the church about, the core values and truths were intact. And while the other stuff mattered too, the core was what ultimately mattered. If it was damaged, there was trouble. If not, everything else could be worked out. I just hoped it would be.

I headed to Room 104. We had wrapped up Revelation a few weeks ago, and Petey was now teaching a short series on stewardship—financial and otherwise. I mostly went for Erica. She was waiting when I arrived, in her normal seat, one down from Scotty, leaving room for me between them.

"Don't you look spiffy," she said, grabbing the end of my tie and flicking it lightly back toward my shirt.

"You too. I'm a big fan of argyles."

She deftly lifted a pant leg to reveal black socks with thin pink and white argyles.

"Very nice," I said, for just a moment picturing the ankles beneath the socks. For just a moment.

Erica leaned forward, at the same time lowering her pant leg. It was, after all, Sunday school. "Doing anything today?" she asked.

"Not that I know of."

"Want to come over later? Watch a movie or something?"

"Sure."

"I've got a pile of homework I really should get to this afternoon," she said. "I'll call you when I see the light at the end of the tunnel."

"Okay."

Class started and Petey began lecturing about our role in preserving the environment or something. I knew to tithe, not abuse bunnies, and avoid idling an SUV in the driveway—I figured that made me a pretty good steward.

After class, Erica promised again to call me, I exchanged looks with Scotty, and then we headed to our respective homes. He and Dirk had winter-proofing to do in the attic, something about an overdue project. I told him I would have offered to help, but I just didn't know when Erica might call. He said it had been nice knowing me.

I watched the Raiders and the Chiefs while I ate a Lean Pocket and some pretzels. With no professional sports teams in the state, Nebraskans are forced to find loyalties elsewhere. A lot of people, especially in the southeast part of the state, become Chiefs fans somewhere along the line. I am not among them, not having found any NFL loyalties. But I did sort of monitor the Chiefs.

Today was not a good day for Kansas City, as Oakland stormed into Arrowhead Stadium and opened up a 21-3 halftime lead. I spent some time watching the Vikings pound the Bears (Minnesota is another Nebraskan favorite) but lost interest in that too. So I hit the computer and emailed the folks, and then resumed my battle to free the world from virtual terrorists.

The snow started around the time the Chiefs attempted to forge a comeback. It was raining in Kansas City, but a hundred and fifty miles north, it was all snow. The weathermen had predicted up to an inch in spots, a dusting for most people. But after ten minutes, the lawn was glazed white, and I closed down my video game to check the forecast online.

The low pressure front was tracking north, apparently, and a line from Grand Island to Des Moines could now expect three to five inches of snow. And it was only mid-November!

I turned my attention back to the Chiefs, whose rally was interrupted by a local weather alert—they were predicting up to six inches in Omaha. In Kansas City, the rain was coming down sideways, and the Chiefs fell just short, 27-24. I felt disappointed, and determined I might be a very casual fan after all.

Chicago had not staged a comeback against Minnesota, and Fox had switched me over to the end of the Saints-Eagles game. Since it was thrilling, I watched. It was sunny in Philadelphia (they say it always is), and the Eagles won on a last-second field goal as my phone rang.

"Hello?"

"Forget a movie, want to go sledding?"

"Crazy, huh?"

"So, I'm putting the finishing touches on a paper," Erica said. "Then I just have one teeny-tiny little project. Say, five o'clock?"

"Sure."

"Do you like tacos?"

"Yeah."

"Okay. We'll have tacos. How do you feel about *Last Ounce of Courage*? Mom and Dad watched it the other night and said it was good."

I shrugged to myself. As long as I was watching it with her, what did I care? "Sure, that'll be fine. Need me to bring anything?"

"Nope. Got it covered."

"Okay. I'll see you at five."

"Drive carefully."

Her concern warmed my heart. "I will."

For the next hour and a quarter, I monitored a Patriots-Chargers tilt from warm, sunny San Diego while considering the night's possibilities. Getting lost had somewhat sullied the magic of a walk through the cornfield, and Erica and I had not discussed our "relationship" during football the following Saturday. So our status was still technically nebulous.

At quarter to five, I brushed my teeth, freshened my deodorant, and headed for the door. I was wearing a Husker hoodie, and figured it would keep me warm enough. I was wrong. I was shivering by the time I dusted a solid two inches of snow off the windshields of my Escort.

I was reminded of the huge snowstorm that had hit southeastern Nebraska in October of 1997. A foot of snow fell in Lincoln, and as much as 23 inches in Clay Center a couple counties west of us. Trees, still full of leaves, had snapped — trees, not branches — and the power had been out in some places for weeks. I had no memory of it, but those who did said it had been crippling. We weren't quite to that point, I didn't think.

The streets weren't in bad shape, still being too warm for much accumulation. But that was quickly changing as the snow continued to fall, and the roads were slushy enough that I took it slow. Nick Chamberlain was just putting away his shovel when I arrived a minute after five.

"Season's greetings," he called out to me from the garage.

"Can you believe this?"

"I hear they might get a foot down by the border," he said.

"Good place for it."

"And to think, it was raining in Kansas City this noon. Have you figured out how to make a living in this world, Josh?"

Was this the scene where the father made sure the boy was good enough for his daughter?

"Um, no, sir."

"Be a weatherman. You'll never have to worry about losing your job due to gross incompetence."

"Yes, sir."

"Here, come on in the back way." He brushed a few flakes off his coat and led me in through the garage. Then he dusted off his hair, which reminded me that my own had been subject to the elements for a while. I hoped it didn't look too ridiculous.

"Hon, we've got fifteen minutes," Amanda called as she came down the stairs. "Hello, Josh," she said, adjusting an earring.

"I just wanted to clear the driveway," Nick replied.

"I didn't know it was—Goodness, it's coming down out there." She turned from the window to Nick. "I put a sweater on the bed for you."

"Josh, if you decide to get married, remember this," Nick said. "It's the last decision you'll ever make."

"It was your decision to wait until five o'clock to shovel the driveway," she said, then smiled my way. "How are the roads?"

"Not bad. Getting worse."

"Terrific," Nick said.

"Maybe we should call and cancel."

"We've got four-wheel drive," Nick said. "And I didn't just catch pneumonia shoveling for nothing," he added as he started up the stairs.

Amanda rolled her eyes. "Erica will be right down," she said to me. "She's finishing a paper, I think."

I nodded.

"You want something to drink?"

"No, I'm good, thanks."

Amanda headed for the refrigerator and retrieved a pitcher of purified water.

"Where are you guys off to tonight?" I asked. I was excited that Erica and I would be alone and hopeful that that excitement was purely motivated. It was so hard to tell sometimes, inside even a redeemed male's mind.

"Carl and Tonya Peterson's," Amanda said as she poured water into a clear glass. "You know them?"

I nodded. Petey's parents.

Amanda returned the pitcher to the refrigerator, took a drink, then spent a few minutes looking through some papers on the counter. I waited patiently, and excitedly, remembering how good Erica had looked the last time I had waited for her to come down the stairs. My heart rate increased as I heard footfalls on the stairs, but they belonged to Nick.

"Not jeans, honey," Amanda said.

"We're not meeting with heads of state," he said.

"And you didn't comb your hair."

"I thought we were late."

"I'd rather be late than sloppy. Can you go change your pants and run a comb over your balding scalp?"

"Which pants should I wear? I'm getting too old to make all these trips up and down the stairs."

Amanda sighed. "I'll show you. Josh, will you excuse us?"

I nodded and smiled, and spent a few minutes after they had gone upstairs thinking about what kind of in-laws they might be. They were hospitable, funny, wealthy enough to buy me sweet Christmas presents. I had always worried that the girl of my dreams would be the daughter of a chain-smoking, vulture-necked hag and a pot-bellied drunk who argued with the TV. Nick and Amanda were a refreshing alleviation of that fear.

I heard daintier footfalls on the stairs, and this time they were Erica's. Same pink argyle sweater over a white blouse, now with dark blue jeans and pristinely white socks. Her sleeves were pushed up, and her hair was in a bouncy, schoolgirl-writing-a-paper ponytail, with a fringe tucked behind her ear and a few strands loose around her rosy cheeks.

"Hey," she said. "Sorry about that. Work wasn't submitting."

"No problem," I said.

"Um, tacos," she said, spinning and going to the refrigerator. "What do you like in 'em?"

"Doesn't matter," I said. "The basics."

I watched her for a minute as she pulled things out of the refrigerator. She then slid — purposefully — across the hardwood kitchen floor, and it hit me that she was making me dinner. Actually making it, not just heating it up. I allowed myself to dream for a few moments about Erica the potential wife. Making me supper on snowy Sunday nights, sliding across the floor in her socks because she was still a girl at heart, smiling at me demurely after we ate . . .

I cut the fantasy off. "Do you want some help?" I asked.

"Sure. How are you with a knife?"

"Petrified."

"Really?"

"Really. I am deathly afraid of knives."

"How do you make anything?"

"I can live with butter knives," I said. "Anything else and I get the heebie-jeebies."

"So this—" She whipped an inch-thick chef's knife—practically a machete—out of the kitchen drawer. " —would scare you?"

"More than somewhat."

She grinned and slipped it back into its sheath. "Think you can brown hamburger?"

"Wooden spoons I can handle."

She handed me a Tupperware of ground beef and pointed me toward the cookware hanging from a rack over the island in the kitchen. While I browned the beef, she used a much smaller knife to dice tomatoes and olives and mushrooms. I had never had mushrooms on tacos, but why not?

Nick—properly dressed and with hair combed—and Amanda came downstairs and popped into the kitchen to say goodbye.

"Drive carefully," Erica warned. I remembered that Zach had died in a car accident, and wondered how it must worry her each time a loved one took to the roads, especially in inclement weather. I decided to take her mind off things.

"So what was this paper on?"

"Um . . ."

"Do you know?"

"Yes, I know. Sociology. Racial impact of various socioeconomic factors."

"I sure miss school."

She stared out at the snow for a moment.

"Erica?"

She looked back at me. "Sorry. Let's not talk about school."

"Okay. Watch the game yesterday?"

"Only the first half. Had to work."

"Bummer."

"I hear it wasn't that exciting."

"Not really." Nebraska's defense had intercepted three Illinois passes in the first half, staking them to a 17-3 lead. The defense had continued to dominate, and the Huskers had won 20-3. The week before, the Huskers had held Purdue to two field goals in a 27-6 win. The Blackshirt defense was rounding into form, and I said as much to Erica.

"Who's next week again?" she asked.

"Minnesota."

She frowned. "We always used to get a bye week before Thanksgiving."

"We also used to play Oklahoma."

Erica came over to check on my hamburger. I looked up at her and smiled to myself. Was this grand or what?

"Speaking of Oklahoma," she said, going back to her vegetables. "You going to see your parents for Thanksgiving?"

"Yeah, probably. How about you? Going anywhere?"

"Mom's parents in Norfolk. Probably. Then we always watch the game Friday with Dad's folks." She stopped. "Is it a morning kick?"

I nodded.

"I have to work Friday night."

"Another bummer."

"Yeah," she said, grabbing a hunk of cheddar from the refrigerator and a cheese grater. "Sharp okay?"

"I prefer it."

Our light chatter continued while we prepared all the taco ingredients, and then Erica "fried" the soft shells with butter on a flat skillet. We took our meal into the dining room. Other than the kitchen, all the lights in the house were off, and with the snow still falling softly outside, I again thought how perfect things were. A quiet dinner with the girl of my dreams — who could ask for anything more?

We were both quite hungry and ate quickly and quietly, looking at one another from across the table. The tacos were excellent, and even though common sense told me Erica had done little to influence the taste of the food, I couldn't help thinking how great it would be to have a beautiful wife who could also make gourmet meals. (Or tacos.) Weren't those qualities supposed to be mutually exclusive?

"When was the last time you went sledding?" Erica asked.

I looked up. "Sledding?"

"You know, down a hill on a cheap piece of plastic."

"Let's see . . . About fifteen years ago."

"Really?"

"They had sledding parties at VB," I answered. "Brother-sister floor events, technically. Organized flirting."

"And you didn't go?"

"Are you saying I'm a flirt?" I asked, trying to flirt without flirting as I asked the question. I wasn't even sure how to flirt.

"I'm saying it sounds like fun."

"Sledding or organized flirting."

"Sledding," she replied.

I nodded and took a bite of my taco. Because I wanted the relationship to go somewhere, I chewed and swallowed before speaking. "Yeah, it's right up there with taking a walk in a cornfield."

She sent me a side-of-the-eye look and took a bite of her taco. She too swallowed. "We used to go sledding out at Pioneers Park," she said, swallowing again. "And there was this one hill in our old neighborhood that led down to a little duck pond that froze over in winter. We used to go there all the time, Zach and me." She grinned, and it turned into a laugh.

"What?"

"He nearly broke his neck once, trying to snowboard on one of those cheap red sleds."

"I can see that."

She wrinkled her nose. "How? You never met him."

"I mean, see myself doing that."

"Would you have been trying to impress your sister's best friend at the time?"

"Is she cute?"

"Yes, she was cute."

"Then yes, but I would have been cool about it."

"You mean you would have thought you were cool, and then would have almost broken your neck."

"Right."

"You are like Zach."

I didn't know what to say to that, so I continued on my taco.

"Wow," Erica said, leaning ahead to look out the window. "It's really coming down again."

"I heard as much as six inches," I said, before realizing I was trying to take her mind off the bad weather.

"I wonder . . ."

"You wonder what," I said.

"There aren't any good hills around here, are there?"

"You're serious about sledding, aren't you?"

"Don't you think that sounds like fun?"

"Do you have a sled?"

"Party pooper."

"Yes, it sounds like fun."

We finished eating, loaded up the dishes, put away the extra food, and headed into the living room—since there were no good sledding hills around. Erica let me load the DVD while she stood by the window, watching the snowflakes.

"You ready?" I asked.

"Come take a look at this."

I walked over and stood beside her, and she slid open the sliding glass door. The snow was flying, and everything was blanketed in white.

"There are so many of them," she said. "It's so beautiful."

"Yeah. It'd be even more beautiful if we were coming up on Christmas, not Thanksgiving."

"We should have a snowball fight."

"No thanks. I've seen you throw corncobs."

"It's been a long time since I've had a really good snowball fight."

"Longer than sledding?"

"About a draw," she said, wrapping her arms around herself. "Sometimes I miss being a kid."

"Yeah, me too."

"And I miss Zach. I don't know why—it just comes out of nowhere sometimes. Thinking of him standing on that stupid sled . . ." Her voice trailed off, and it took me a few seconds to realize she was fighting off tears. Because it seemed like the thing to do, I put my hand on her back and rubbed gently.

"I'm sorry," she said.

"Don't be."

I rubbed a little more and then removed my hand.

Erica sniffed and wiped her cheeks. "Start the movie?"

"Sure."

We took one last look at the falling snow and then she shut the door. Very cleverly, I made sure I was the first one on the couch so I could see exactly how closely she chose to sit. I was starting to have romantic notions. All we were missing was the crackling fire.

Erica undid her ponytail, shook out her tresses, and because my heart wasn't racing yet, ran her fingers through the back of her hair a few times. Then, either completely carelessly or with deft calm and cool, she plopped onto the couch a good foot to my left. She tucked her left foot up under her right thigh and turned her head. "Roll 'em."

I sat casually with my hands on my legs, palms down. I still wanted to let her make the first move, in case I had misread all the signals and somehow she wasn't having romantic notions. And, because I was something of a coward, in case she didn't reciprocate. As much as I wanted to know that she shared my feelings, my second preference was to go on not knowing but hoping and thinking she liked me as opposed to finding out she didn't. I told myself I could let this play out forever. In truth, I could hardly concentrate on the movie because I kept glancing at her with the corner of my eye, hoping to see her beautiful, delicate little hand reaching over for mine.

We paused the movie halfway through. (It was not a blockbuster—but it did have some compelling moments. And it was clean.) Erica got up to make popcorn and I got up to inspect the snowfall. It was still coming down, and I guessed another two inches had topped the two that had fallen during the afternoon. Early November, I kept reminding myself. This was nuts.

Erica returned with a bowl of popcorn and set it between us on the couch. This eliminated imminent snuggling (as if it were a possibility) but also brought up the hands-meet-over-the-popcorn-bowl prospect. It was all so junior highish, only I hadn't had a girl to reach for popcorn simultaneously with in junior high. I sighed to myself as I pressed play. A greasy, buttery handhold wasn't what I'd had in mind anyhow.

Then the power went out.

Chapter 46

". . . a time is coming when I will no longer use this kind of language but will tell you plainly . . ." John 16:25

Every morning, all autumn long, I had started the day with prayer. Every day I had asked God to give me a sign. If Erica was the girl for me, I prayed that He would show me that, and show me when and how to "make my move." Alone with her, on a snowy evening, with the fireplace popping and crackling, and with candles flickering around the room, I gathered that the moment had arrived.

I had no idea why four inches of snow—even heavy snow—had caused a power outage (I later learned that a pickup had skidded off the road and into a utility pole). But looking out the window, it appeared to be widespread. Unable to finish the movie, we had lit a dozen candles and had done our best to heat up hot chocolate over the fireplace.

Erica had never looked more radiant. The firelight sparkled in her eyes and danced across her smooth cheeks. The candles around the room gave her dark hair a sense of depth and body. It was worthy of a shampoo and conditioner commercial. Her sweater hugged her body perfectly, as did her designer jeans, and I knew I had completely lost it when I found her socks cute. I didn't care.

The only thing missing was her typical smile, and I wondered if her thoughts weren't still on Zach. I tried to think of something to say, something to take her mind off her painful memories and concern for her parents and to segue toward the conversation that I was running in my head, over and over again. But nothing came to mind.

So we sat there by the fireplace, drinking hot chocolate and finishing the popcorn, not talking. Instead we watched the snowflakes out the window. I so badly wanted to reach my arm out, pull Erica toward me, and just hold her. But I thought that might be a bit too bold for a first move.

Erica tipped her cup up and drained her hot chocolate. "You finished?" she asked.

I nodded, and she looped her fingers through my mug and picked up the popcorn bowl with her other hand. She headed into the kitchen and I stood too. I paced to the window, working up my courage. That old Elvis song went through my head: "It's Now or Never."

I turned back as Erica glided back into the living room. I was once again struck by just how beautiful she was, even when she wasn't dressed up to sing in church or for a wedding. She was just naturally gorgeous, and it caused my heart to thunder in my chest.

So did my resolve that this was the time. It was one of those perfect, unscripted moments that can't be created—they just have to happen. And I didn't want to force anything, but I didn't want to let the moment slip by either. What if the power suddenly came back on or Nick and Amanda returned?

I took a few steps forward and met her in front of the fireplace. "There's something I want to tell you," I managed to say, relieved that my voice didn't betray my nervousness.

"I have something I need to tell you too," she said, tucking the hair on one side of her face behind her ear. "But you go first."

"Okay." I took a deep breath. "This is probably going to come out babbled, but just bear with me." I took another breath and wondered if she knew what was coming. If so, her eyes didn't give it away. Oh, those eyes.

"Erica, from the day I first saw you at the spring game, I've been crazy about you. You're the most beautiful girl I've ever seen, and the beauty goes far beyond your looks. *You* are beautiful—everything about you. Your sensitivity and your fun-loving demeanor and your spiritual conscientiousness and your sense of adventure and the way you spit out food because you haven't prayed and wrap candles in the backseat of the car, and your spontaneity and—I could go on and on. And the more I've gotten to know you, the more I've fallen for you. These last few months have been magical for me. And at the risk of ruining what has become a wonderful friendship, I have to know if I've been misreading signals, or if, like me, you're interested in being more than just friends."

As I spoke, a smile had slowly played over Erica's face, from bel air to sheepish to beatific. When I was finished, she reached for my hands, and the sensation of her gentle touch was incredible.

"I am interested," she answered at length. "Very interested."

My heart nearly exploded with joy.

But I heard it in her tone before she said it, and instead my heart plummeted.

"However, I don't think it would be a good idea."

I nodded, trying to stay poised as my world collapsed.

"I felt the chemistry too, Josh," she said. "From day one. But I didn't pay much attention to it, and I was gone and then Haiti came up . . . and then Mark . . . And then you were there to pick up the pieces — and I mean that in a good way. I needed a friend at that time, and you were that friend. And the chemistry was there again, and I'm feeling the same things you are."

"But . . ."

"But, I'm not going to be around much longer."

Fear welled up in me. "Is something . . . Are you sick?"

"No," she said with a soft smile. "I'm moving. To Los Angeles. I'm starting school at Biola University next semester."

I immediately thought of what they always said about how long-distance relationships never worked. I was determined to prove everybody wrong.

"I'm going to be a missionary, Josh. A nurse. I've been thinking about it a lot lately, and praying about it. Fighting it, maybe a little. But I'm convinced it's what God wants me to do, and it's what I want too."

I nodded.

"I know that doesn't exclude a boyfriend, but unless God is calling you down that same path, I don't think it would be wise to start a relationship now. Especially across the continent."

We were still holding hands, and I didn't want to let go. But being a man, I did. Slowly.

"I understand," I said.

But I didn't. Why would God allow us to the threshold of bliss, only to dash it at the last second? I knew I couldn't blame God, but I had to blame somebody.

"I'm sorry," Erica said, reaching for my hands again. "I truly am. But I can't give up what God has called me to, and I can't ask you to commit to something God hasn't called you to."

I nodded. "It's all right," I said.

But it wasn't all right. My rollercoaster of a summer had reached the peak, the highest point in the whole amusement park, and then had come off the track, plummeting down to the ground, cars kinking and snapping apart, people flying everywhere. How could that ever be all right?

She dropped my hands and reached to wipe tears from her eyes. What did I say now? "Let's still be friends"? "We'll always have the Haymarket"? "Maybe you can be one of those back-office, works-in-the-States missionaries"? No, nothing I could say seemed right.

So I hugged her instead. She hugged back, and it was a tight, warm hug. But my first step in recovery was to try my hardest not to enjoy it.

"I suppose I should probably go," I said when we pulled apart.

"Would you stay a little while?" she asked. "Either until the power comes on or Mom and Dad get back?"

"Sure," I said, my pride swelling at the thought that Erica wanted me there, in a protective role, a comforting role. I dismissed the feeling, though, because now she was just a friend, not the girl I could put my arm around and assure everything would be all right.

We sat down on the couch, a few feet apart, her turned sideways, sitting cross-legged. We talked about school, why Biola, her plans, life as a missionary nurse. It sounded like dangerous work, and I almost volunteered to go along and serve as bodyguard. But I wasn't exactly Clint Eastwood, and I didn't want to look pathetic.

After thirty minutes, the power came back on. I looked at Erica, who was picking at the hem on her jeans. "Power's on," I said.

"Yeah."

We both slowly stood and walked toward the back door, where I had left my shoes. Erica walked with me to the edge of the garage, where she stood with her arms across her chest, hands on her elbows.

"If you ever need a friend," I said, "I'm still here."

"Thank you," Erica said. Then she leaned forward and kissed me on the cheek, with the snow fluttering down and onto our shoulders. I wished the brief moment would never end.

But it did end, and we said goodbye. Then I trudged through several inches of new snow to my car, and proceeded to brush it off, all alone in the cold.

How's that for a metaphor?

Chapter 47

"I will explain to you the mystery of the woman . . ." Revelation 17:7

Sydney embraced me in a tattooed hug when I told her what had happened. Our shifts on Monday both ended at four, and she offered me a shoulder to cry on and an ear to confide in. I did need someone to talk to, but determined my lifelong best friend was better than a slightly crazed coworker with more hairstyles than Hillary Clinton. So I called up Scotty and we met for dinner at the Morgan Family Restaurant.

His hat was backwards, his sleeves long, his legs still in shorts. It was fifty degrees outside, and the snow was melting as fast as it had fallen. On and off afternoon drizzle had helped — helped melt the snow and helped me get into a depressed mood as I recounted the previous night again, this time to Scotty.

"I know this sounds cold, dude, but you'll get over it," he said, wolfing down some fries. The weather had not, at least, diminished his appetite.

"You're right," I said. "That is cold."

"It's like anything in life," he said, reaching for more fries. "You eventually get over it. Even my mom . . . It still hurts, but not as bad as it used to."

I sighed and sat back. "I know, I know. I just don't know how I'm supposed to move on and find somebody else. Yeah, there are plenty of fish in the sea, but after you catch 'the one' and it jumps off the hook, how can you be happy with some guppy?"

"Okay, can we please quit the metaphors?" Scotty asked. "You don't even fish."

"Erica was my dream girl," I said. "Any girl I meet, I'm always going to think, 'she's nice, but Erica was better.' That doesn't make for much of a relationship."

Scotty had more fries and a huge bite of his burger before answering. And a slurp of soda. "First of all, I would still argue that Brookline girl was just as hot as Erica, and secondly, you were in love with Erica. You're bound to think she's untouchable. Give it time, and you'll realize she was just another cute chick."

"Maybe so, but it wasn't just looks," I said. "She was . . . perfect. She's a solid Christian, she can cook, she's hospitable, she can sing, she's a Husker through and through, she can—"

Scotty put his hand up. "Dude. Not to be cold again, but do you really think that in all this world, there aren't any other girls as good-looking as Erica that can sing, cook, banter with you, and know the words to 'There is No Place Like Nebraska' that can make you happy?"

"Maybe one or two, but what are the odds I get them?"

Scotty buried himself in his burger for a minute, and I worked at my chicken strips. A grown man of twenty years eating chicken strips, but what did I care? I was sulking.

"You know, I've never really bought that 'one soul mate for everybody' business," Scotty said.

"No?"

"No," he said, reaching for more fries. "Just think, if one person marries the wrong person, it's a domino effect that screws up the world for everyone."

"Or if one person doesn't marry the right person. Or date them."

"Exactly."

I sighed for the four thousandth time that day. "So basically you're saying 'there's other fish in the sea.'"

"I'm saying, this stinks, dude. And we should go back to my place, put on our sweats, let our hair hang in our face, and eat ice cream all night. But, I don't think you're destined to be a lonely bachelor all your life. Eventually, you'll find there is a girl for you."

I nodded.

"And if not . . ." he said, pausing to take another mammoth bite of his burger. He did not continue the pause to finish chewing. "You can live with me and we'll be like Walter Matthau and Jack Lemmon."

"Great. I go from a life with Erica to a life with a shriveled old coot in Minnesota in the span of one day."

"I thought they were in Canada."

"Thanks, Scotty."

"Sure thing."

I dipped my last chicken strip.

"So, you want to come over, hang out, drown your sorrows in a case of cream soda?"

Sigh four thousand and one. "No, not tonight. I need one night alone, moping, having pity on myself."

He nodded. "Fair enough, dude."

"Tomorrow night," I said. "Tomorrow night we'll move on."

I had been home ten minutes, and was in the process of deciding whether I should sit in the dark with the TV on or sit in the dark with the TV off, when the phone rang. I thought about letting it go, but decided to be a man.

"Hello?"

"Josh."

It was Cassie. I took a deep breath and tried to put on a brave front.

"Scotty just called me and told me."

"Word travels fast."

"I'm so sorry, Josh."

"Thanks. Me too."

"You want to talk about it?"

I didn't, but I did anyhow, giving her the blow-by-blow. When I was finished, she was quiet.

"Cass?"

"I'm going to cry."

"That makes two of us."

"I wish I could be there to give you a hug."

"So do I."

"Why Biola?"

"She says they have a great nursing program, something about integrating nursing with being a missionary."

"When?"

"Next semester."

"I'm so sorry, Josh. What can I do?"

"Don't let my problems get you down."

"What?"

"I mean it. You're in beautiful Arizona, where the sky is probably blue and the temperature is in the 90s."

"Eighty-six."

"And you're killing your classes and on your way to debunking *The Da Vinci Code*."

She laughed through tears.

"And Scotty is right, I will get over this in time. So don't let my depression spread to you."

"Okay, I'll try. I really am sorry. I feel . . . I feel like I encouraged you when I shouldn't have."

"No, you were all right. She did have feelings for me. She was just overruled by a Higher Power."

"You aren't bitter at God, are you?"

"No. Not really. I'm just confused as to why He led us on. And I know that's not it, but it feels like it. I'm just an emotional mess right now."

"You really need a hug."

"I do."

"I'll pray for you, Josh."

"Thanks."

"A lot. Every hour. I'll set a 'Josh time.'"

"That'd be great."

"I'm sorry, but I do have to get going. Work."

"Go. Thanks for calling, Cassie."

"I really am sorry. I'll hug you twice at Christmas. Scotty only gets one."

"I can't wait."

"I love you, Josh."

"I love you too, Cass."

I hung up the phone and sat in the dark for another minute, thinking about what great friends I had. Somehow, I found the ability to pray, thanking God that Cassie was doing well at Arizona State and asking Him to keep her from going in the tank. Cassie was the type who would take the breakup worse than I did.

I was about to get up when the doorbell rang. It couldn't be Scotty, because he knew I wanted to be alone. It couldn't be Sydney because, well, it could be Sydney, but I doubted it. And it couldn't be anyone else, because there wasn't anyone else. Curiosity trumping depression, I got up and opened the door.

It was Erica.

"Hi," I said, likely visibly taken aback. Had she changed her mind?!?! Was she spurning missionary nursing so we could be a couple? Would she forever be abiding outside the will of God if so?

"Hi," she said back with that smile I loved so much. She was dressed in a lavender blouse, black slacks, her coat open with a scarf dangling to her waist.

"Um, you want to come in?" I asked.

"You forget to pay your power bill?"

"I just got home," I said. It was sort of true.

She nodded as I reached for a light switch.

Erica took a deep breath. "I felt I owed you an explanation," she said. My heart fell again as my tiny little hope that she had indeed come to tell me she had reconsidered died. *Better your hope than disease-ridden children in Africa*, a Still Small Voice whispered in my ear.

"Do you want to sit down?" I asked, motioning toward the living room. She nodded again and sat. I sat beside her, leaving an appropriate amount of space.

"You don't have to explain," I said. "I understand, and it's okay."

I was getting good at lying.

"No, I do," she said. "And I've been working this up all day, and I may babble a little myself, but bear with me."

I smiled and nodded.

"Like I said last night, Josh, we had great chemistry from day one. Especially over the last few months. And I really wanted this to work between us, and that was part of the reason I didn't tell you what I was thinking. I've been considering being a missionary nurse for a long time, but this fall, it's been like a burden on my shoulders. I've really wrestled with it, wrestled with where to go to college — I mean, there are other Christian colleges that offer nursing degrees that aren't in California. And in fairness, I should have told you what I was thinking, so you would have known. But I wasn't sure, and I didn't want to blow things with you, and I was afraid if I told you, you would have tried to convince me otherwise, and I was afraid I wouldn't have been able to resist if you had."

I was moved by how strong she apparently felt for me. Moved and more depressed. But I sensed it was my turn to speak.

"I wouldn't have," I said. "Tried to talk you out of it, I mean."

"Not overtly, at least."

"Yeah."

"And . . . I don't know, Josh. This is the hardest decision I've ever had to make, but I truly am convinced in my heart of hearts that this is what God wants for me — what He wants me to pursue right now. And I think it's best if it's a solitary pursuit."

I nodded again. "I understand."

"All that to say," she said, placing her hand on mine, "that I'm sorry if I led you on. I should have told you and trusted you, but . . . part of me didn't want to let go, either." She shook her head. "I intended to tell you a few weeks ago, but backed out, and then yesterday, but it took me all night to work up to it . . . I kept putting it off because I just didn't want things to end."

"Me either."

"I'm sorry."

"It's okay," I said. "You have nothing to be sorry about. I wouldn't have traded our times together over the last couple of months for anything."

"Me either."

Erica smiled, and then leaned over and hugged me. I allowed myself to enjoy it guilt free, since it would probably be the last. In those two seconds while her cheek was pressed against mine, while her hair hung on my neck, while her hands pressed against my back, a hundred thoughts flashed through my head. From our first interaction at the spring game to her promise of postcards on vacations and missions trips to her flouncing around the pool in her red bikini, and from our day in Lincoln at the wedding that culminated with Erica kissing me on the cheek on her front stoop to getting lost in Dave's cornfields to how beautiful she had looked last night just before bursting my bubble. I sighed as we separated, and forced a brave smile onto my face.

"I should be going," she said.

I nodded and walked her toward the door. "Thanks for coming tonight."

"I thought I needed to clarify things."

"I'm glad you did."

She paused in the doorway for just a second, and our eyes locked one more time. "Goodbye, Josh."

"Goodbye, Erica."

With a tight-lipped smile, she turned to leave, and I closed the door on Erica Chamberlain.

Chapter 48

Wednesday night our group was down to the core regulars. Bobby and Adeline, who had attended the previous few weeks, were absent, and Gia no longer was a part of the study. That left Scotty, Damon, Amy, Gerhard, and myself. And Sydney. I had invited her on the spur of the moment, on a total whim — or a prodding by the Holy Spirit. She had told me five minutes before my shift ended on Wednesday that she would be coming, and I gave her directions to Scotty's house. She had been the first to arrive.

We looked at the final chapter of Titus, examining beautiful language describing how God *"saved us, not because of righteous things we had done, but because of his mercy"* and that it was by *"washing of rebirth and renewal by the Holy Spirit whom he poured out on us generously through Jesus Christ our Savior so that, having been justified by his grace, we might become heirs having the hope of eternal life."* Sydney had lots of questions, and we did our best to answer them.

Then we moved on to Paul's exhortation *"to stress these things, so that those who have trusted in God may be careful to devote themselves to doing what is good."* But the real fun started when we addressed the passage about avoiding *"foolish controversies and genealogies and arguments and quarrels about the law, because these are unprofitable and useless."*

"Does that include Halloween?" Amy asked.

"Maybe."

"What about Halloween?" Sydney asked.

"These guys think it's evil," Amy replied.

"It is," Scotty said.

Amy rolled her eyes.

433

"Are we getting into a foolish controversy over what constitutes a foolish controversy?" Damon asked.

"So what about that *'quarreling about the law'* part?" Amy asked. "Does that mean when you guys busted me for a speeding ticket, you were out of line?"

"No, you were out of line," Gerhard said with the gentleness of an old man. "For speeding."

"I was going five miles over," she said with a huff.

"Which is five miles more than what the law allows."

"Everybody was going five over. Most of them more."

"The law doesn't say to do what everybody else does."

"What about keeping up with the flow of traffic?"

"You must have better eyes than me," I said.

Amy turned my way. "How's that?"

"I can't see the fine print on the speed limit sign."

She rolled her eyes again.

"How is this not quarreling over the law?" Sydney asked.

"This isn't talking about debating whether a law is right or not or whether we should obey it or not," I said. "The entire passage is talking about how we are to be obedient because Christ has saved us by His grace and mercy. It's not adherence to the law that saves us, but that's what tripped up so many people of that day—and this day—thinking they needed strict obedience to it. Which led to quarreling."

"Yeah, but don't we have freedom in Christ?" Amy said.

"Yeah."

"So isn't it more saying that we should stop haggling over little things like speeding and Halloween and focus instead on the list in verses one and two?"

I nodded. "But what does verse one say? *'Remind the people to be subject to rulers and authorities.'* That includes speed limit signs."

"So how are we not quarreling?"

"When you shut up," Scotty said.

Amy stuck out her tongue.

I guided us to Paul's final remarks and parlayed his *"Grace be with you all"* into a closing, thanking everyone for participating in the study and

434

saying that I hoped they'd all want to renew the study come the new year. Damon said it would depend on his rec basketball schedule. Amy and Gerhard both sounded positive, and I knew I could count on Scotty.

Sydney hung around and was the last to leave. "Thanks for the invite, Josh."

"You're welcome. Think you might come back next year?"

"Maybe. I'll think about it." She smiled. "I'll see you tomorrow."

I nodded back, said goodbye, and closed the door behind her. Then I headed up to the living room to join Scotty. "What'd you think?" I asked him.

"Of what?"

"Tonight's study. The study in general. Sydney."

He looked at me funny. I'd thrown him a curveball on purpose, just to see if he'd swing. I wasn't sure, but I thought I had noticed a few glances between him and Sydney. Maybe it was nothing, or maybe he — like me my first time around her — had been checking out her tats. But I thought I had detected a smirk tugging at his mouth, and a slight upturn of her chin.

"Study was good," Scotty answered, tossing me a cream soda. "It's been good all year, and she seems nice," he said with a shrug.

My hunch was confirmed. Sydney was many things, but no one would describe her as "nice." Especially Scotty, who should have come up with some nickname for her. I'd have to grill her tomorrow, see if she thought Scotty was "nice" too.

We sat down and watched TV, a rerun of *NCIS* on cable. Dirk joined us and, at commercials, expressed his sympathies over Erica. I had been feeling all right the night before, and with a study to prepare, had passed on chilling with Scotty and drowning my sorrows in cream soda. So it was the first time I had seen Dirk since the "breakup."

"Thanks," I said. "I'll get over it, I guess."

"Breakups are like losing a major on the seventy-second hole," he said.

"Oh boy," Scotty mumbled.

"You put all that work and effort in, practice, train, and then play three rounds of good golf to get in contention, play well enough to win on Sunday, but then things don't go your way. And you're left there, walking off the green, thinking about how long you'll have to wait for another major — all the practice, all the training — and then have to put together three and a half good rounds to get back in contention on the back nine, just to be in another situation where you could win or could lose."

"Is this supposed to be encouraging?" Scotty asked.

"Yes. Because at the time it seems daunting, tons of guys have lost majors and come back to win later. Look at Phil all those years. Or McIlroy blowing the Masters and then running away with the U.S. Open two months later."

"So keep my chin up, there are other fish in the sea, dust myself off and try again."

"More or less. But also learn what you can from this loss."

I mulled for a moment as a black and white still of Mark Harmon, gun drawn, appeared on the screen. "When it comes to choosing between me and God, any girl worth having will choose God," I said.

Dirk shrugged.

We watched the next segment without talking. When it was over, I turned to Dirk and Scotty again. "One thing that's been bugging me about this," I said. "Maybe you guys can help."

Dirk nodded.

"Shoot," Scotty said.

"Well, all along I've been praying that God would show me what to do about Erica. And everything seemed to point to a relationship, all my advice from everyone, all the inclinations in my gut, right up to that snowy evening by the fireplace when I popped the miniature question."

"So what gives?" Dirk said.

"Exactly." I shrugged. "Why would God lead me along if He wasn't going to hook us up?"

"Why did God lead Abraham up a mountain with Isaac?"

"You think this was a test?"

"I think it's possible. Or maybe God was trying to teach you something, work in your heart somehow."

"Hmm."

"Is that a thinking 'hmm' or an I need to think 'hmm'?"

"A little of each," I answered.

"Or maybe you misread the signals," he said.

"I was afraid of that, but she confirmed that she was into me too."

"I don't mean her signals. I mean, maybe you misread what you thought God was doing in your life."

"Possible," I said. "I have no idea what else He's doing in my life, and I don't mean that disrespectfully."

"Often times you don't see it until afterward," Dirk said. "At least in my life."

"Mine too," Scotty said.

"Sometimes life is sort of like golf," Dirk said.

"Sometimes?" Scotty asked.

"Your tee shot goes into a bunker, and you're mad because there goes your chance to reach the green in two. But maybe if you'd tried to reach the green in two, you'd have buried yourself in a greenside bunker, or blocked the ball into the pond or something. By being forced to lay up, you might actually find yourself in a better position to make birdie."

"A blessing in disguise?" I said.

"Something like that."

"If that's the case," I said, "it's a world-class disguise."

Thursday was a beautiful morning. The sun was out, the temps were up, and what was left of the snow was melting quickly. Looking at piles of dirty snow and patches of still green grass, I marveled at how weird this autumn in Nebraska had been. Then I marveled at how amazing the seasons and weather in general were.

I put my hands in my pockets and strolled leisurely toward Nebraska Novelties. I sucked in several lungfuls of crisp, fresh air. It was mind-cleansing.

Six months ago, I had come home from college with no direction in life, a stagnant walk with God, and smitten with a girl I barely knew. In other words, a midlife crisis. Now, I still had no direction in life and was still smitten with a girl I knew all too well and couldn't have. But my relationship with God had changed. Perhaps I was climbing out of crisis mode.

The change, and thus the climb, was subtle—no groundbreaking reformation or transformation. I still was frustrated with a lot of things at Morgan Bible and was worried that despite my talk with the elders and their promises, not much would change. There was still much I didn't understand about the Christian life, and there was still a lot of darkness in my heart. But I sensed that the light was spreading.

There were a number of factors that contributed to the change. Good advice and good talks with family and friends. Experiencing those frustrating things at Morgan Bible to help me understand what was truly important and where my focus and heart needed to be. Of all things, a pool party and subsequent sermon. And our Bible study.

Despite our potpourri of attendees and the crazy discussions and rabbit trails, it had been invaluable. Through the study, I had gained a greater appreciation for the love that prompted God to send Jesus into a sinful world, and that prompted a sinless Son to become a Savior. Love like that refused to be ignored and, while I still battled with selfishness and spiritual apathy and with uncertainty on how exactly to express my grateful response, the desire in my heart to serve God was growing. A flickering match had caught the kindling.

Being a teacher forced me to dig deeper into the Word than my typical surface reading. Slowing down caused me to see things I normally didn't see and to gain insights that had just hung there, like fruit waiting to be plucked from a tree. The result was a greater desire to dig even deeper, to explore passages I'd never explored and analyze verses I had always glossed over. I was hungry, and the more I ate, the hungrier I got. With real food, that would lead to obesity. But I didn't think there was anything wrong with being spiritually fat.

I'd had numerous talks with Scotty and Cassie, pouring out my soul to them. In return, I'd been a sounding board and a prayer partner for Cassie. I had to believe my being there for her had been as important in her life as her being there for me had been in mine. And as for Scotty, while everything always seemed perfectly fine with him, I had no doubt that if he ever was in crisis mode (either over the girl he finally felt like pursuing or because he was missing too many cuts on the PGA Tour) I'd be there for him too.

And I couldn't forget Sydney. All my talks with her about Erica and love and even sex had opened a door that had led to her coming to Bible Study. Maybe that's all it would ever be, a one-time appearance. Or maybe she'd come back, be drawn by the Holy Spirit, and put her faith in Christ. At any rate, it was something.

Turning onto Main Street, I exhaled deeply and let my eyes wander over the white snow, green grass, brown trees, and blue sky. Ahead was historic downtown, with its red brick buildings basking in the bright morning sun. It was just the backdrop of my small town, but it was still a beautiful canvas. Usually I took God's creation for granted. Today, I found myself thanking Him for the simple beauty of an autumn morning.

It hit me in that moment that God had been pursuing me. While I was bitter and lazy and apathetic and more worried about Morgan Bible's music ministry and winning the heart of a certain brunette than living "*a holy life in Christ Jesus*," God was trying to draw me to Him. It dawned on me that He was trying to get me to pursue Him instead of direction, Him instead of the right method of worship, Him instead of Erica.

I stopped for a moment, realizing how far I had yet to come. As was so often the case, just when I thought I was making some progress, I saw how far off perfection was. But with a smile, I started walking again. If God had cared enough to pursue me when I was lost, and to pursue me when I was spiritually lethargic, how much more likely was He to keep pursuing me now that I was no longer playing hard to get?

Yes, God had always been pursuing me. He had always loved me — always would. And maybe He had allowed some of the things that had played out in my life this past summer to happen in order to get my attention.

And now, finally, He had it.

Like I said, this is a love story.

But it's not all about me.

Epilogue

"Then all the people went away to eat and drink, to send portions
of food and to celebrate with great joy . . ." Nehemiah 8:12

Sixty-nine million people felt free to move about the country, and the lines at the Southwest Airlines check-in counter had been terrible. The terminal at Eppley Airfield had been crowded and loud, and I was pretty sure the airplane was actually shrinking.

It was hot because we were still idling on the tarmac and because the sun was blistering in through the window and because a hundred people were flailing about as they removed coats, stowed bags, found and switched seats, and otherwise scurried about. I pushed up the sleeves on my sweatshirt and leaned my head back against my seat.

A pretty brunette passed by, luggage in tow, and I thought about Erica. It had been a good week and a half, all things considered, since she and I "broke up." Oddly enough, I felt a sense of contentment and peace. I still felt a warm rush over my body when I thought of her, and still felt a pain in my gut and tingling in my fingertips when I realized I was never going to be with her. But, I was okay. Or at least, on the road to okay. I trusted that it was God's will for her to be a missionary and for me not to be a missionary's husband. I also trusted that He was working in my life, and I just had to be patient enough to wait for His timing and be obedient to whatever call I received. I know that sounds like a Sunday school answer, but then again, there's a reason they're Sunday school answers.

Finally, everyone was seated and we pulled away from the gate. We ran up the meter taxiing around the runway forever, and I wondered if I couldn't have sooner driven. But finally we were airborne, soaring over the Missouri River, then banking right over Iowa, then right again. It was making me dizzy, so I sat back and reflected on the summer and fall.

It had been crazy, but also a lot of fun. Just like with the *Lord of the Rings* trilogy, it hadn't had the ending I wanted, but it had still been a good ride. And it wasn't the ending, I reminded myself as the perky stewardess asked what I wanted to drink. Cranberry juice, I told her. Peanuts? Yes. It wasn't the ending. I still had, barring a crash landing, the majority of my life ahead of me.

I made the peanuts last as long as possible, and sipped my cranberry juice slowly. I was sure I could get a refill, but then I ran the risk of a full bladder on a crowded airplane. No thanks.

The sun was still in my eyes, so I closed them and thought of Mom and Dad. Dirk and Scotty had offered that I could spend Thanksgiving with them, but it just wouldn't be the same. For one thing, I had serious doubts as to whether either of them could cook a turkey. That was the sort of thing that just required a mother or grandmother's loving attention.

But it wasn't just the turkey, or the stuffing or the sweet potatoes or the canned cranberry sauce (the one thing I was sure that Dirk and Scotty could properly prepare) that made Thanksgiving. It was pumpkin pie and cherry pie during a movie Thursday night. It was leftover turkey sandwiches during football on Friday and Saturday. It was the smells of my parents' home, even if it wasn't the same home I had always smelled. It was wearing a sweater because it felt right to wear a sweater on Thanksgiving. Most of all, it was just being there, being comfortable, being cozy with my family all weekend. It was a part of growing up that I wasn't ready to leave behind just yet.

I felt a small jolt, and I realized the pilot had decreased power. We were already descending. I still had half an inch of cranberry juice!

I drank it and felt my stomach tighten. I had never acted on a whim before, except for that time when the snow was falling and the lights went out and I took it as a sign to tell the girl of my dreams how I felt about her.

I had debated what to do all weekend, run things past Scotty, and checked with Mom and Dad to get their opinion. The weekend lingered into Monday, when I had also sought Sydney's opinion. She gave me the final encouragement I needed, and Monday night I had called Southwest and finagled my way into a reasonably priced seat on the 2:20 flight out of

Omaha. And so here I was, on the day before Thanksgiving, with a whimsical knot in my stomach and no more cranberry juice to moisten my suddenly dry mouth.

I thought again of Thanksgiving with the folks, of filling my plate high with food, of having another slice of pie even though my stomach was about to explode, of telling and listening to old stories about my grandparents, and laughing as if they were new stories. The thoughts warmed my heart, and confirmed that my choice had been the right one.

We banked sharply, and I looked across another single guy seated next to me. While the view from the air was always unique, there wasn't much to see over Nebraska or Kansas (except a failed attempt to spot Morgan). But as we descended, I found myself mesmerized by the view, and watched the scenery for a few minutes, until my ears started to pop and the pitching and rolling caused my already volatile stomach to flop. I leaned back again, closed my eyes, and prayed. I asked God for wisdom and for the faith to trust that He wasn't just leading me around.

I felt the rush of the engines, a surge of air from the little fan above me, and then a thud-THUD as the wheels touched down onto the pavement. Airport scenery raced past at a hundred miles an hour as the airplane's brakes squealed.

We slowed and turned off the runway, and the pilot's voice broke over the intercom with a squawk. "Ladies and gentlemen, on behalf of Southwest Airlines, welcome to Phoenix, Arizona."

Acknowledgements

"I have not stopped giving thanks for you . . ." Ephesians 1:16

Sierra, thank you for your love and patience. I could never undertake a career as a writer without your support. Thanks for listening to my myriad ideas and giving much-needed insight.

Mom and Dad, thank you for showing me the way. Admittedly, I sometimes miss the mark, but it's not for lack of guidance. Thanks for looking over my manuscript and providing suggestions throughout the process.

Mark and Tiffani, thank you for proofing and editing. Thanks for serving as sounding boards, for your recommendations on content and style, and for your friendship.

Caleb and Gabe, thank you for praying for me and my book. Thanks also for being my pals.

To my grandparents, thank you for leaving a legacy of love and faith. Thanks for always offering me a home away from home and for memories I will cherish for a lifetime.

Mark and Bonnie, thank you for your prayers and encouragement. Thanks for your godly influence and constant help and care.

Aaron, Hank, John, Matt, Paul, and Pete, thank you for serving as iron that sharpens iron. Thanks for your biblical knowledge and acumen, for allowing me to bounce ideas and concepts off of you, and for bouncing others back off of me.

Cliff and Dave, thank you for the years of tutelage, both in class and out. Thanks for helping me form a well-rounded (I hope) and biblical worldview.

To my extended family, thank you for encouraging me and praying for me. Thanks for the serious talks and the multitude of laughs.

To my church family, past and present, thank you for your support. Thanks for praying for me and encouraging me long before I had any aspirations as an author.

To everyone who in some way, shape, or form inspired this novel, thank you for being you. Thanks for whatever role you've played in my life, from your friendship to your advice and teaching to your quirks that found their way into the DNA of one or more of my characters. Thanks especially for the laughs. I hope any humorous anecdotes in my novel that are rooted in reality will bring a smile to your face. I'm laughing with you, not at you (mostly).

To my readers, thank you for taking the journey with me. Thanks for reading, commenting, and encouraging. You give me your money and your time, and I hope the investment is worthwhile.

Finally, Lord Jesus, thank you for writing the ultimate love story. Thanks for saving my life and defeating my death. Whatever writing talent I have is a gift from you, and I hope it reflects the Son well.

Discussion Questions

". . . as reminders to stimulate you to wholesome thinking." II Peter 3:1

Whether you read *God, Girls, Golf & the Gridiron (Not Always in That Order) . . . A Love Story* by yourself, as part of a book club, or along with some friends, the following questions can help you reflect on some of the issues faced by characters in the novel. They're by no means exhaustive or authoritative; rather, they exist solely in an effort to stimulate you, the reader, to wholesome thinking.

CAUTION: The following questions may reveal spoilers. If you haven't finished the novel, be forewarned that reading these questions may give away plot elements.

1. Do you believe in love at first sight? What kind of love is it?

2. How much should the message of the gospel or the method of delivering that message be adapted in order to appeal to culture? Is there a danger in winning over the culture but no longer having a worthwhile gospel message for them?

3. Is it important to "dress nice" for church? How nice? Should some basic standards be adhered to, or does it not really matter as long as the heart of the worshipper is right?

4. Is the style of music sung in church important? Are certain songs better for congregational singing than others? If so, what makes a "good" worship song?

5. Read II Samuel 6:12-23. Should a lack of dignity be something we pursue, or something we are willing to experience if authentic worship of God and obedience to God result in it? Whose definition of dignity is important?

6. What advice would you give, or what advice have you been given, about knowing if "the time is right" to initiate a romantic relationship? Is it best to take it slow and let the relationship develop, or should a person "strike while the iron is hot"?

7. Would you support sending money to a third-world country so Christians there could purchase electric musical instruments for their worship service? Why or why not? Would other factors come into play?

8. How much of the responsibility for men to remain pure is on women to dress modestly? What does an appropriate standard of modesty look like and where does that standard come from? Where is the line between appropriate or inappropriate attire for women?

9. Read Psalm 119:9-16. How can a person remain pure? How does that look in day-to-day life?

10. How do the concepts of man's free will and God's predestination come together? Are they mutually exclusive?

11. Have you ever had trouble reading "signals" of the opposite sex (be it a friend, someone you were dating or wanted to date, or a spouse)? Why do you think that is? How have you improved at discerning those signals?

12. How well do you think Josh ultimately handled his concerns with the direction of his church? Was going to the elders the right move? Did he respectfully disagree in love, as his dad suggested?

13. How important is experience or emotion in church? Should having an experience be the focus when attending church? Are positive emotions a sign of good worship?

14. How do you think Josh and Erica handled their feelings for each other? What could they have done better? What do you think of their ultimate decision not to pursue a relationship?

15. Has God ever worked in your life in such a way that He gave you a "blessing in disguise"? What was that like? Did realizing the blessing at the end help in dealing with the struggle experienced during the "disguise" period?

16. Do you see evidence of God pursuing you? In what ways? Are you pursuing Him? How so?